The Summer of 1974

Book 1 of the Gavrielle Series

Yael Politis

The Summer of 1974
Book 1 of the Gavrielle Series
Copyright 2019 Yael Politis
All Rights Reserved

Cover photo by Nochi Politis
Cover design by Tatiana Vila

February, 2019

The Summer of 1974

Part 1

Gavrielle Rozmann

Prologue

Jerusalem, British Mandate Palestine
Sunday, February 22, 1948

Ilana Rozmann kept her hands in her coat pockets as she tagged along behind her parents, on their way to lunch. The pockets were deep, allowing her to lovingly caress her swelling belly. *Am I far enough along?* She wondered. *Is it too late for them to try and force me to get an abortion? I have to tell them sometime. Maybe I should do it today. They wouldn't dare make a scene in the fancy-shmancy dining room of their precious Eden Hotel.*

She was astonished, hurt, and relieved that her mother hadn't noticed yet. To be fair, in the cold weather it was easy for Ilana to keep herself covered in loose garments. But still. *How pathetic is that? You've only got one kid. Can't you pay more attention than that?* In baggy beige trousers, sweatshirt, and raincoat, Ilana rambled along behind them, happily aware that she didn't look like she belonged with them.

Tall and thin, her father, Viktor Rozmann, was an imposing and unapproachable man. His dark gray three-piece suit was expensive. A fedora hid much of his bald, bullet-shaped head. Ilana's mother, Nella, was delicate, pretty, with softly curling blonde hair and great legs. She was also expensively clothed – tailored red raincoat over a white silk blouse and black skirt. Her high-heeled shoes and the umbrella tucked under her arm were also red. The Rozmanns were an obviously prosperous couple, living in a mostly poor city in a mostly poor soon-to-be-country, during a time of great turmoil. They strode regally down the street.

2

Just look at the two of them. Forget about touching each other – they don't even speak. Not unless it's absolutely necessary. Lou and I will never be like that.

Ilana followed as they turned down Ben Yehuda Street, which was lined with the stalls of a street market. Just seventeen years old, Ilana knew she was pretty like her mother, but hoped the resemblance ended there. Ilana loved her mother, but did not approve of her.

If asked how she felt about her father, Ilana wouldn't have known how to respond. He taught mathematics at the Hebrew University, but Nella's impressive wardrobe was paid for by the wines and liquors he imported. He always said his meetings with British officers – most of which took place far from the offices of the Mandate authorities – were strictly business, arranging import licenses. But both Nella and Ilana were aware of the rumors. The Jewish underground accused him of being a traitor, spying on his countrymen and reporting them to the British for smuggling arms and refugees into the country. In exchange, they said, the Brits helped Viktor get rich.

Nella made an effort to believe her husband, but not because she loved him. It would have felt dishonorable to despise the man who'd saved her life. Perched in his fancy motor car – and lost – he'd come roaring into the tiny Polish town where Nella's family lived, slammed on the brakes, and leapt out of the car. He bowed slightly at the waist before asking Nella how to get the hell out of there. He ended up staying a week, stubborn in his efforts to lure her back to Germany to marry him. Only a few years later he'd declared they had to leave. That nasty little corporal with the funny mustache hadn't yet seized power, but Viktor assured his young wife that he would. And that he would do exactly what he'd said he would in *Mein Kampf*.

3

"But why to Palestine?" Nella wailed. "Why can't we go to America? We're better off staying in Germany than going to some horrible desert in the Middle East."

Viktor patiently explained that he didn't have any connections he could bribe for visas to the United States. Then he lost his temper and ordered her to pack, which she did, throwing things into cases, resentful and angry. From that and other decisions Viktor had made over the years, Nella had learned to trust his instincts. No matter what people said about him, he was a smart man. It was almost as if he could smell whatever was coming.

Viktor stopped abruptly and Ilana almost collided with him. "I have a meeting to go to," he said to his wife, tapping his watch. "In that apartment building right down there." He pointed. "It won't take but a few minutes. You two wander around, see what kind of rubbish they're selling today."

Nella nodded, her expression blank.

Ilana watched silently as her father entered the building of weathered Jerusalem limestone. So people call him a rat, so what? What do they know? And, if they really thought that was true, someone from the Irgun would have grabbed him off the street by now. Ilana had chosen to remain oblivious, neither defending nor condemning him. He made enough money that the kids at school whispered the dirty secrets behind her back, never daring to shout them to her face. Anyway, that was the last thing on her mind now.

She closed her eyes and tilted her face up to the soothing winter sun. *Seven weeks. In just seven weeks I'll have a little baby to take care of.* That's what they'd told her at the clinic that morning. *I hope it's a little baby girl. It has to be a girl.* Then she cringed, imagining telling her parents – and not only that she

4

was pregnant. When they started grilling her about the father, she'd have to admit that she didn't even know his last name, or have any way to get in touch with him.

My mother will probably drag me into the ladies room, to shout all the things she can't say in front of him. "How could you be so stupid?" she'll say. "It's bad enough that I –" No, she'll catch herself, won't really say, "It's bad enough that I had to go and ruin my life." But she is going to say something like, "I was a yokel, an ignorant village girl. But you? You're modern, educated. You know better."

Ilana would feel like an idiot, having to admit that she didn't know where the father was or how to contact him. It was always Lou who found his way to her, when he could. Which wasn't often. She'd been dismayed by her own stupidity – finding out she was pregnant and realizing she had no idea how to contact the father. Even so, she had no regrets. *I love Lou and he loves me. He'll come back as soon as he can. After all, these are not normal times, with the British planning to leave and all those millions of Arabs waiting to pounce.*

Nella turned to her daughter. "I'm going to see what kind of scarves that man over there is selling."

Ilana nodded in response and pretended to be interested in the store window behind her. The growl of an approaching British armored car broke into her thoughts. She turned to watch it crawl down the street, followed by three British army trucks. They passed her in a cloud of fumes and she turned her face back up to the sun.

Then the world changed. She would never remember hearing the blast, or feeling herself propelled through the plate glass window. The men who found her in the shop, unconscious and covered in blood and shards of glass, considered it a miracle that she still had a pulse. The shop next door had been totally demolished, and the front walls of the entire block of buildings had collapsed into mountains of rubble. The air was thick with clouds of dust and smoke. Her rescuers didn't wait for a stretcher. They grabbed her ankles and underarms and carried her back toward King George Street, in the hope that ambulances would soon begin arriving. They left her there and ran back down Ben Yehuda to search for more survivors. Half an hour passed before Ilana was transported by car to Bikur Holim hospital. A woman doctor was examining her when she briefly opened her eyes and said, "I'm pregnant."

"Yes, I know." The doctor smoothed her hair. "I just heard the heartbeat. You've been badly hurt, but your baby is still alive. You're safe now, where we can take care of you, get you strong enough to keep it that way." The nurse lulled Ilana back into unconsciousness.

Doctors came from other hospitals to study her case. "This young woman had such serious injuries that no one believed she would survive – and yet it seems she is going to carry a healthy baby to term." She was in pain and sedated most of the time, but occasionally woke for long enough to exchange a few words with the nurses. She insisted she was carrying a baby girl.

"Her name is Gavrielle," Ilana whispered. "She's my guardian angel. She's keeping me alive."

Neither of Ilana's parents came looking for her. Weeks after the bombing, a woman with a clipboard informed her that her father's body had been pulled from the rubble and identified. But the name Nella Rozmann did not appear on any of the casualty lists.

"So why hasn't she come to see me?"

"Maybe she hasn't been able to find anyone who knew where they'd taken you. You can't imagine the chaos on Ben Yehuda that day. Three trucks packed with explosives. Close to sixty dead, two hundred wounded. The whole street was a pile of rubble. The rescue teams were busy digging out survivors, not making lists."

"But I've been here for a long time, haven't I?"

"Yes you have, honey." The nurse started to tell her a story about someone who'd suffered from amnesia and hadn't been reunited with his family for months after a bombing. But Ilana had already drifted away.

Days later the beeping machine connected to her flat-lined. The baby wasn't due for another three weeks, but a doctor held his stethoscope to her belly and ordered, "Get her into an operating room. Now!" Only after the caesarean birth of what was indeed a baby girl did he pronounce Ilana dead.

"Poor little girl." The nurse rocked the baby. "Poor little Gavrielle. You would have loved your *ima*. She was a real sweet girl and you were all she cared about."

The nurse called the police and asked them to report this birth and death to whoever was in charge of identifying and reuniting victims of the bombing at the street market. The hospital staff kept tiny Gavrielle as long as they could, but all the wards were appallingly overcrowded, as were the city's orphanages. So Gavrielle was taken to the only place that had room for her – a small orphanage run by Catholic nuns.

Gavrielle

**Campus of the Technion, slopes of Mount
Carmel
Haifa, Israel
Sunday, July 30, 1967**

It was the woman's haircut that caught Gavrielle's
attention – cropped short into a feathery brown cap, *à
la* Mia Farrow. It emphasized her striking cheekbones
and large brown eyes. She stood just inside the
entrance to the cafeteria, scanning the tables, obviously
looking for someone.

"After you graduate, I'm hoping you'll choose to join
us," Jesse was saying.

Gavrielle refocused her attention on him, unsure
she had understood him correctly. He was soft-spoken
and hard to hear over the clatter of dishes and loud
voices. He was wearing his green uniform, three bars
on each shoulder. *He must have an army staff meeting
to go to,* she thought, since guest lecturers from the
military didn't normally teach in uniform. She had both
hands around her Styrofoam cup of coffee, but
somehow managed to slop some of it on the white
Formica tabletop.

"Oh! Sorry. What a klutz." She accepted the paper
napkins he held out and soaked up the brown liquid.
"You don't have to bother trying to recruit me. I'm an
atudait," she said, referring to the program that
allowed students to defer their army service until they
got their degree – with the Israel Defense Forces (IDF)
heavily subsidizing their tuition – and then use their
skills and knowledge in service of the IDF.

"I know. I've got a file on you." He raised his
eyebrows and leaned forward, teasing. Then he

8

retreated, serious again. "I wasn't trying to convince you to join the army in general. I meant I want you in my unit. We're part of the research department, specialize in technology. Intelligence Branch gets first pick of the Technion's students and we like to get you involved early, during your studies. If you're interested, I could steer you toward the type of research projects that would be relevant for us."

Gavrielle took a sip of coffee while she wondered if there was any non-professional reason for this offer. There were so few women studying at the Technion that she'd gotten used to an extraordinary – and unwelcome – amount of male attention. She glanced over at him. Tall, thin, sandy curls, green eyes. He was an attractive man. *Just not my type*, she thought regretfully. The problem was, she didn't seem to have a type. She'd never had a boyfriend. Never felt drawn to any guy that way.

But she was thrilled at the prospect of working with Jesse. He'd taught one of her classes and come in as a guest speaker in others. She'd had only a few brief conversations with him, after class and when their paths crossed on campus, but somehow felt comfortable with him. He was approachable – did not need to maintain distance in order to command respect. He was brilliant, engaging, and good-natured. The type of commanding officer she could only hope for. One she could trust and admire, without being afraid of him. The only thing she would fear was not being like him. Worthy of him. She looked into his face. No, there was no ulterior motive. Jesse wasn't like that.

"So, are you to blame for all the psychological tests they've been giving me?" she asked.

He smiled and nodded.

"They decided I'm not crazy? Or maybe you're looking for crazy."

"You're just exactly the right amount of crazy." He held his thumb and forefinger in an O, before pushing his chair back and standing. "You don't have to decide now. I just wanted you to know that the offer is on the table. We're aware of your situation at home ... with your grandmother and all ... But unless you want to reconsider and ask for an exemption from service – which you would get, by the way – you're eventually going to have to work out a solution."

"I don't want an exemption," Gavrielle said hurriedly and a bit too loudly, as if afraid he was about to whip one out of his shirt pocket.

"Okay, then –"

"Gavrielle? Are you Gavrielle Rozmann!?" The woman from the doorway was standing at Gavrielle's side. "I apologize." The woman looked at Jesse. "I'm sorry to break in on you ..."

He held up both palms and backed away. "I was just leaving. I'll talk to you tomorrow, Gav."

Gavrielle clumsily got to her feet and turned to face the thirty-something woman she had noticed earlier. She wore a simple black and white print shirtwaist dress, no make-up, and a silver filigree necklace around her neck. *Elegant simplicity*, Gavrielle thought, aware of her own faded jeans and T-shirt.

"Yes, I'm Gavrielle."

"I knew it had to be you. Lord, you look exactly like your mother."

"You knew my mother?" Gavrielle whispered the question and the woman moved forward as if to embrace her.

Gavrielle took a hesitant step back. Her voice was hoarse when she asked, "Who are you?"

"I'm sorry. You must think I'm some kind of lunatic. Can we sit?"

10

The woman pulled her chair closer to Gavrielle's and reached for her hand. Gavrielle did not pull it away and the woman held it in both of hers.

"You're the image of Ilana. The absolute image. Same blonde curls. Same pretty smile." She grew teary-eyed. "I guess I'm still acting like a crazy lady. Sorry." She took her hands away and sat up straight. "My name's Tonia. Tonia Amrani."

Gavrielle's eyes grew wide. "You're Tonia? Tonia Shulman?"

"Yes, yes. That was my maiden name."

"My grandmother used to talk about you all the time. You're the one from the kibbutz. The one who came to stay with them?"

"Yes. Just for a short while. A long time ago, back when I was in high school. Ilana and I were in the same class at the Hebrew Gymnasia. Your grandmother and mother were wonderful to me. Just wonderful. But then the war came ... I never graduated."

Her eyes bright, Gavrielle hesitated but couldn't help asking, "Do you know who my father was? Did my mother tell you anything about him?"

Tonia smiled sadly and put her hand back on Gavrielle's. "No. I'm sorry. I didn't know that was a mystery. I lost touch with your family during the war, when Jerusalem was under siege. Then my mother and I moved to Tel Aviv and I never saw Ilana or your grandmother again. I went to your house several times, but it was always empty. And then I went to live in America for a few years."

Gavrielle looked into Tonia's face and said softly, "My grandmother always says you were like family. Because your family came from the same village in Poland as ours. And no one else from there survived the Nazis."

"Yes, that's right. When I saw your grandmother yesterday, it was like finding a long-lost relative."

11

"Where did you see her? She hardly ever leaves the house."

"Amos – my husband – was wounded in June. In the war. I took him for his physical therapy and your grandmother was there, in the same corridor, waiting to get her new prosthesis. Actually, it was Yaffa I recognized first, despite her gray hair. She worked for your grandmother way back when your mother and I were young. It was so sad for me to see Nella Rozmann in a wheelchair. Until yesterday, whenever I dredged up memories of her she was always dancing."

Students began migrating toward the door of the cafeteria, and Tonia asked Gavrielle if she had to go to class.

Gavrielle shook her head and asked, "So why did you come here looking for me?"

"Your grandmother told me what happened – about the bomb that killed your grandfather and destroyed her leg. Nineteen years ago ..." Tonia paused, staring blankly over Gavrielle's shoulder. "It seems a lot longer than that. Another world." She jerked her head as if shaking off unwelcome thoughts and looked back at Gavrielle. "She told me how brave Ilana was, how she managed to hold onto life long enough to bring you into this world." Tonia paused again. "And how you ended up in an orphanage for a while – until Nella recovered enough to come looking for you. So I know that since then the two of you have been living by yourselves, in your old house in Rehavia ..." Tonia held Gavrielle's gaze for a long moment and touched her hand again, raising her voice slightly when she spoke. "I told her that was nonsense. No way should you be living like that. Amos and I have a big house in Old Katamon and you and your grandmother are going to come live with us."

Gavrielle shook her head in disbelief. "That's crazy."

"No, it's not. When I needed help, your Grandmother Nella gave it to me. I won't have her alone all day in that big old house. And Yaffa is getting old. She probably keeps working out of a sense of loyalty, but she won't be able to manage that forever. And I won't have Ilana's daughter trying to manage on her own. How are you going to finish your degree, having to take care of her all by yourself? Even if she's able to get around better with her new leg, it's still not a good situation for either of you. And you haven't even begun your army service. So coming to live with us is not crazy at all. It makes perfect sense."

Gavrielle's expression was blank and her head moved slightly from side to side. Where did she come from, this fairy godmother? Jesse says I've got to find a solution for Nanna Nella and, poof, this lady pops up? Okay, it's weird, but who cares? She seems okay. Stop sitting there like a lump of clay. Say yes. Say yes before she changes her mind. But wait, no, it really is crazy. Go live with a bunch of strangers? What if I don't like them? Shut up, who gives a crap? Like, don't like, who cares? She's right. I have to get my degree, start my military service. She closed her eyes for a few seconds, imagining what it might be like to walk out of the house in the morning, young and free, without a boulder in the pit of her stomach.

"I already have Linor," Tonia continued. "She's a lovely woman who comes every afternoon to help with the twins. They're six. A boy and a girl. We also have a nine-year old girl and an eight-year old boy. Linor might be glad to have more hours and start in the morning, but if not we can get someone else. And if you're like Nella and worried about the money, so rent out the house in Rehavia and use some of that to pay for Linor's extra hours. Cooking for seven isn't much different than cooking for five, so you see, you won't be

13

any trouble to me. And you'll be able go off to your studies in the morning without worrying – what if she falls, what if she has a stroke?"

Gavrielle glanced up, her face still blank. *So you're a mind-reader too?*

Tonia went on. "Nella will never be alone. And she can help the twins with their reading, work puzzles with them, tell them stories about Poland. Before Hitler, of course," Tonia was quick to add.

Tonia pushed her chair back. "Once you've had time to think about it, you'll see that it does make sense – and not just because of the practical side of things. I'm not here out of pity for your grandmother, or trying to rack up *mitzvot*. I'm much too selfish for that. I *love* her. I want her around to talk to. And I know I'll come to love you. Your mother was a wonderful person. You and Nella are part of my family. And even if you turn out to be unbearable," Tonia said with a smile, "students and soldier girls are hardly ever at home."

Gavrielle sat speechless. The lost little girl part of her wanted to grab Tonia's hand and beg, "Now. Take me home with you now!"

"I'm going to let you get back to your studies," Tonia said as she got to her feet. "I've already made plans with your grandmother – the two of you are coming to spend the Sabbath with us. As far as we're concerned, you can move in next week."

Friday, August 4, 1967
Rozmann home
Rehavia, Jerusalem

"We should take your wheelchair," Gavrielle said.

Her grandmother was wearing her new prosthesis and moving slowly about. One hand always lightly touched the doorframe, chair, sofa, shelf — whatever was nearest. Just in case.

"I mean, you've never been without it for a whole day. So I'd take it, even though you're doing so well."

Nella scowled for a moment and then shrugged. "I suppose. Tonia said Amos drives a pickup truck, so he ought to have room for it. Hand me my canes, please." Nella took them from Gavrielle and held them so they didn't quite touch the tile floor, using them only as backup while she navigated the hallway toward her bedroom. "You sure you didn't forget to pack Yaffa's cookies?" she called back over her shoulder.

"Yes, Nanna, I'm sure."

"Tonia always loved those cookies."

"You might as well have a seat until he gets here," Gavrielle said softly as she followed her grandmother into her bedroom.

Nella obeyed, staring at Gavrielle for a moment before reaching for her hand. "I know it's hard for you, the idea of moving in with people you don't know. Don't forget, they're all strangers to me too. Except for Tonia."

"You never met Amos?"

Nella shook her head. "Mm-mm. I got a look at him once, but from a distance. Good-looking fellow."

"What do you know about him?"

"Yemenite boy. Religious. Belonged to the underground. That's all I know."

"Irgun or Lehi?"

"Irgun."

15

"Were Tonia and my mom best friends?"

"No. They got along all right, but they'd never even met before Tonia got accepted at the Gymnasia and started sleeping over here a few nights a week. Saved her having to travel back to the kibbutz. The roads weren't safe back then. Arab gangs all over them."

"But they got to be best friends." Gavrielle pressed.

"Not really. They were different. It was funny ... the principal at the Gymnasia introduced Tonia to their class as the brave pioneer girl, went on and on about how she was building the homeland with all her hard work on the kibbutz. You should have seen those hands of hers." Nella's palm went to her cheek and she shook her head. "Lord, good Lord, the cuts and scrapes and bruises. Hardly any fingernails left at all. And all her sweaters had holes in them. All two of them. Made kids like Ilana feel like spoiled brats. I don't mean on purpose. It wasn't anything Tonia said or did. Just that her life was so much harder than theirs. But the funny thing is – all that brave pioneer girl cared about was getting the hell away from that kibbutz – and from Palestine – as fast as she could. When it came down to it, it was my girl who was the real patriot."

"I think he's here," Gavrielle said and hurried to the living room to pull the curtain back.

A tall, thin, ridiculously good-looking, caramel-colored man got out of a dirty old truck and came up the walk, limping noticeably. *Okay*, Gavrielle thought, amazed at the way she caught her breath. *Now I know what my type is. That. A younger him.* He stopped abruptly when Gavrielle pulled the door open.

"Wow. You do look just like your mother." He mounted the porch steps. "Hi, I'm Amos."

She barely managed to say her own name and hold out her hand, but Amos ignored it and bent to kiss the air next to each cheek. He wore no aftershave, but carried the clean scent of soap.

"You knew my mother?" she asked.

"No. I mean, we never met. But I used to hang around outside the Gymnasia, waiting for Tonia, and I'd see them together. She was very pretty. Like you. Vivacious. Always made me smile, the way she'd throw her head back and laugh. Especially compared to Tonia. Back then my dear wife was all somber and serious – thought people like me and her father were about to bring on a second Holocaust. But Ilana ... Tonia said she was an eternal optimist."

Gavrielle pursed her lips in a sad smile and Amos touched her arm. "Listen, before we go in, I just want to say ... I figure you gotta be wondering how I feel about this whole thing. So don't. I grew up in a big family, in a small house. I think a bed with no one to sleep in it or an empty chair at the table is a shameful waste."

Gavrielle looked into his eyes and murmured a soft thank you before turning to lead him into the house. He made a fuss over Nella, quoting all the wonderful things Tonia had said about her over the years.

"So," Nella said, "I finally get to meet the boy who promised to take Tonia to the movies and then ditched her."

"She told you about that?" He grinned. "That was a long time ago and absolutely unavoidable. For the sake of the homeland. But, even so, I beg your forgiveness." He bowed at the waist.

"I suppose you did all right by her after that," Nella said. "Except for doing your best to get yourself killed. You and I will make a great team. Two good legs between us."

Amos grinned again. "You ladies ready to go? You'll have to squeeze in together up front."

Only while helping Amos load the wheelchair into the back of the truck did Gavrielle notice that his left hand was missing two fingers. "Is that from the war?"

she asked.

"Yeah. Grenade."

"Where?"

"Besides my hand – my back and leg."

"I meant, where did it happen?"

"Ammunition Hill."

"Oh." Ammunition Hill, on the outskirts of Jerusalem, had been one of the bloodiest battles of the Six Day War. Gavrielle could think of nothing to say, so turned to go get their bags.

Amos turned up a broad, tree-lined street and parked in front of a home of thick Jerusalem stone. Its black shutters and grillwork made it even more imposing, as did the low wall of stone that surrounded it. Amos opened the gate and bent at the waist, extending his arm to welcome them up the front walk, before returning to the truck for the wheelchair and their suitcases. Gavrielle kept a tight hold on her grandmother's arm.

"They certainly have done well for themselves," Nella murmured. "Not much of a garden though." She sniffed at the sparse front yard, which was barren, except for a huge tree and a few red geraniums by the door.

Gavrielle smiled broadly, but refrained from reminding Nella how neglected their yard in Rehavia was. When Gavrielle was younger she'd attempted to contend with the weeds, but for the past years had settled for paying a neighbor boy to come over and mow them.

"You're here." Tonia pulled the front door open. "Come in, come in."

They stepped hesitantly into the front hall, where the floor was inlaid with colorful mosaic tiles, and then followed Tonia into the living room. The ceiling was

18

high, the walls newly whitewashed, and the windows bare of curtains, making the good-sized room seem even larger. The furnishings were simple. Two couches – one seating two and the other three – end tables, mosaic coffee table, two armchairs, a rocking chair, and two straight-back chairs standing in corners. All the upholstery was the same – stripes of various shades of blue, brown, and yellow. A number of frames leaned against the far wall, apparently waiting to be hung. The coffee table was laden with cakes, cookies, and fruit.

Before Gavrielle had time to sit down, the six-year-old twins – Nurit and her brother Coby – raced down the stairs and each grabbed one of her hands, dragging her into the spacious kitchen. A large wooden table dominated the room, but a folding table stood next to it, to accommodate a half-finished jigsaw puzzle of the Roman aqueduct in Caesarea.

"Oh, I love to work puzzles," Gavrielle said, which wasn't a lie. "Can I help too?"

As they sorted the pieces, the children bombarded her with questions. "Are you really going to be a soldier? With a gun? Where did you live before? Why did you bring that chair with big wheels? Do you like chocolate cake? Do you have a boyfriend? How old are you? Do you like to play Monopoly?"

"Do I get to ask any questions?" Gavrielle said.

"You just did." Nurit giggled. "You just *asked* a question."

"Yes, I did. Now I'm going to ask another one. I've heard that twins can read each other's minds. Is that true?"

For the next half hour they enjoyed making up ridiculous things that each claimed the other was thinking. Then nine-year-old Sarit came in the back door. She stared at Gavrielle for a long moment before saying, "Hello, I'm Sarit," and plodding through the room. She glared over her shoulder at the twins saying,

19

"I get the shower first, but you guys better start getting ready."

Nurit decided it was time to take Gavrielle up to her room. There she explained – at great length – where everything was and mentioned several times that it was she who had changed the sheets on the bed. Loud footsteps clomped up the stairs and a curly head appeared in the doorway – "Hello, I'm Seffie" – and disappeared. Then Tonia looked in and asked Gavrielle if she needed to shower.

"No, I'm fine." Gavrielle was already wearing her "good clothes," a simple, short-sleeved shift of dark royal blue with white embroidery around its V-neck. On her feet were silver, low-heeled pumps – an enormous concession to Nella. When not in her black army-type lace-up shoes, Gavrielle seldom wore anything but flip-flops or sneakers.

"I feel like I abandoned my grandmother down there. Is everything all right?"

"Everything's fine," Tonia answered and turned to her daughter. "You have to let Gavrielle get settled in. You can bring her suitcase in here, if you want. *Abba* left it at the top of the stairs."

Soon Tonia called them to Friday dinner. Standing at the head of the table, Amos waited for each of his four children to come, in turn, to stand by his side and receive a whispered blessing. Then he looked around the table for a moment before saying, "Tonight we are especially thankful for being reunited with Nella and Gavrielle. They have always been family to your mother. Now we have the privilege of welcoming them into our house and hope they will choose to make it their home." He closed his eyes as he murmured, "Blessed are You, Lord our God, King of the Universe, who has granted us life, sustained us, and enabled us to reach this occasion."

"Amen," the children mumbled back and Amos poured wine for the Kiddush.

After the meal Gavrielle went upstairs to read the twins a story, then came back down and helped her grandmother get ready for bed. Nella whispered a stream of arguments, determined to convince Gavrielle that this would be good for both of them, but she needn't have bothered. Gavrielle was already looking forward to her freedom.

Freedom to – among other things – try to find out something about her father. She'd never believed her grandmother when she claimed not to know anything. *Alright, yeah, I'll buy that my mother kept the guy she was seeing a secret – especially after she started having sex with him. That's not something a 17-year-old girl would go around advertising. Especially back then. But after she found out she was pregnant? And she was what, six or seven months gone when that bomb went off. You never noticed that, Nanna? Give me a break. But now I'll have a chance to see if you've been hiding anything in your room. One way or another I'm going to get it out of you. Maybe when I was little you thought you were protecting me from something, but I'm grown up now. What could have been so bad about him anyway?*

Gavrielle thought she could count on Tonia to help convince Nella to finally tell the truth. *She has to realize how awful it is. I walk down the street and every man who goes by, I wonder if maybe that's him.*

Later Gavrielle joined Amos and Tonia in the living room. Amos poured them all a small glass of arak and they raised their glasses. "To family." He drained his glass and said goodnight, leaving Gavrielle alone with Tonia.

21

"Do you have everything you need?" Tonia asked.

"Yes. Nurit took good care of me. I ... I don't need any time to think about what you said. It would be good to live here. For my grandmother and for me."

"I'm so glad." Tonia rose to plant a kiss on the top of Gavrielle's head and then sat back down.

"I don't know how great it'll be for you." Gavrielle couldn't seem to stop blinking as she watched Tonia's face. "I've never been in a family. It's always been just me and Nanna Nella. I don't know how to be a big sister."

Tonia visibly relaxed in her chair. "You'll figure it out. You have your mother's genes. She was an only child with a distant father, so I pretty much expected to feel like some kind of Cinderella in their house. But Ilana made me feel welcome. She was my great protector at school." She sipped from her glass and then leaned forward and smiled. "There's something I'm dying to show you, but first I must tell you about the first time I saw your grandmother."

Tonia held out the bottle of arak and poured some into Gavrielle's glass and her own. Then she leaned back and stared at the ceiling. "It was in the middle of the coldest, clammiest, rainiest Jerusalem winter and I'd spent weeks, day after day, freezing, walking up and down the streets of your neighborhood, searching for the Rozmann family. For my mother's long-lost childhood friend from Poland. I thought maybe she could help me get accepted at the Gymnasia. You should have seen me patrolling those streets, covering every house, like a soldier on a mission.

"And then one day this cloud parked itself over me and it was like someone unzipped it – buckets of rain came pouring down on me. I was so cold and tired and completely soaked to the bone. So discouraged. I sank down on the curb and just sat there like a big soggy lump, getting wetter and colder, mud all over my feet and legs, but I didn't care. I sat there crying my heart out. Lost. Hopeless. Truly despondent. Yes, I had a family back in the kibbutz. A wonderful family." She paused to drink. "But I wanted ..." She didn't complete that thought.

"And then I looked up and could hardly believe my eyes. A vision was walking up the street. A princess. A movie star. I mean, Grace Kelly, eat your heart out. She was holding a gold umbrella, but none of those raindrops would have splashed on her. They wouldn't have dared. Nella Rozmann was a sight to behold. Golden hair and perfect make-up. Her coat and shoes and umbrella all *matched*!" She turned to look at Gavrielle with a slightly tipsy giggle. "If you think people in this country dress like slobs now, you should have seen them back then. But Nella Rozmann. Your grandma was one classy lady."

"Wouldn't a kibbutznikit like you have thought her awfully bourgeoisie?"

"Absolutely. Of course. Horribly bourgeoisie. But that's exactly what I wanted to be! I hated the kibbutz. I wanted to be like *her*." Tonia laughed again. "Then this magical lady stops and bends down to ask me what's wrong. And *she* turns out to be the one I'm looking for. She takes me into her house – a real house, solid walls of Jerusalem stone, no tent or rickety hut – and Yaffa does her best to clean me up and wraps me in towels and blankets. And the smells in that kitchen. My God. Meat. Real meat. And Yaffa's cookies. All I wanted. Of course I was too embarrassed to eat as much as I really wanted, but I stuffed myself plenty."

Gavrielle tried to imagine her nanna as a young woman. It wasn't that difficult. Nella still took good care of herself.

Tonia leaned forward to set her glass on the coffee table and stood. "Now I can show it to you. Then I'll let

23

you get some sleep. You must be exhausted."

"No, I'm fine." Gavrielle leaned back and closed her eyes, but she wasn't tired. For the first time in years she didn't feel tired.

She remembered sitting in a coffee shop, eavesdropping on the women at the next table. One was telling the other about the marriage counselor she and her husband were seeing. "She tried to explain to the big bump-on-a-log how a wife feels, having to juggle so many things, trying to hold everything together. How exhausting that is – like having to hold a glass of water up high, over your head, all the time. No matter how tired your arm gets, you can never put it down. All day, every day you're holding that glass. But in a good marriage, when the wife just can't do it any longer, when she's about to let that glass drop and break ... she knows she can count on her husband to step in, just in the nick of time, and take over."

Gavrielle felt her arm and back relax as she let go of her imaginary glass of water, getting used to the idea that she wasn't going to be alone any more. She would have backup. She could hear Tonia rummaging around in their bedroom and exchanging a few words with Amos. She soon returned, triumphantly bearing a pale pink box with a shiny red bow.

"This," Tonia said, her voice strained with emotion. "This I found on my bed one evening when I came back to your nanna's house." She carefully slipped the lid off and folded back the tissue paper. "I wore it only once – on my wedding day. To tell you the truth, I didn't really want to wear it then, I was so scared some idiot would spill wine or food on it."

She held up a white dress of silk, lace, and beads and hugged it to her body. "It was the most beautiful dress I'd ever seen. You have to realize – I'd never owned a single thing that wasn't a hand-me-down. And utilitarian. So imagine receiving a present like this!"

Gavrielle picked up the crumpled-looking lid and turned it over to study the red bow. "You still have the box it came in? From, like, over twenty years ago?"

"Yes." Tonia smiled, shaking her head. "And don't ask me why I saved it. Of course I saved it. I would have been thrilled just to get a *box* like that, even if it was empty. Do you think I was used to getting gifts, much less with red bows on them? The once or twice my mother gave me something, she wrapped it in brown paper that she had drawn a few flowers on. With my greasy crayons."

Tonia stood silent for a moment, remembering, then brightened. "She's going to come visit on Sunday, to see Nella. My mother, I mean. Her name's Leah. She lives with my sister on her kibbutz. My mother and Nella never even saw each other back then. Not once. My mother was always saying Nella should come visit the kibbutz, and Nella was always inviting them to dinner in Jerusalem. Half an hour of winding road was all that separated them, but neither of them ever made the trip. And then by the time my mother and I were evacuated from Kfar Etzion with the rest of the women and children, you guys were gone. Your house was empty. But I broke in. I confess. Climbed in a window to get this." She nodded at the dress, grinning.

Tonia returned the dress to the box and carefully folded the tissue paper over it. "And do you know whose idea it was to buy this for me? Who picked it out? Your mother. So I want you to have it." She held it out to Gavrielle.

"Oh no, I couldn't take it. You've kept it all these years. It was your wedding dress. One of your daughters will want it."

"It wouldn't mean anything to them. And how many things do you own that your mother's hands touched? Please take it." She placed the box in Gavrielle's hands, picked up her glass of arak, and sat back down. "I didn't know it, but I've been saving it all these years just for you. I bet it fits you. Maybe you can wear it the next time you go out with that nice young man you were in the cafeteria with."

"Jesse isn't my boyfriend. He's an officer who wants me to serve in his unit after I finish my degree."

"You're an *atudait*?"

"Yes."

"What are you studying?"

"Computer Science and Electronic Engineering."

Tonia looked puzzled. "I thought he was in the infantry."

"Intelligence Branch also wears green uniforms." Gavrielle couldn't hide the pride she felt for being wanted by that unit.

"Aha," Tonia said and tipped her glass toward Gavrielle. "Our own little genius. But you can't be that smart if you think soldier girls never get involved with their commanding officers."

"He's not my type."

"Ha! Now I *know* you're stupid. That one is every girl's type."

Gavrielle shrugged. "Not mine."

"So who is?"

Your husband, Gavrielle thought, but shrugged. "I don't know. But not Jesse." She quickly changed the subject, asking if Tonia had a job.

"Part time," Tonia said. "Three mornings a week I do some English-Hebrew translating and editing for a small publisher. And I volunteer once a week at Yad Vashem." She referred to the complex of Israel's Holocaust memorial, museum, and archives. "I transcribe the testimonies of survivors who speak English, Hebrew, or Yiddish."

"How do you know Yiddish?"

26

Tonia smiled and shook her head. "I didn't realize that I did. I mean, my parents spoke Yiddish between them, and the aunt and uncle we lived with before we moved to the kibbutz spoke Yiddish, but I never used it. Then one year I started taking a class in Yiddish at the university and was amazed that I understood everything. All this passive knowledge, I guess."

"So you like going to school?"

Tonia shrugged. "Yes, I suppose I do. This year I've registered for a class in Arabic." She stood up and patted Gavrielle's shoulder. "I guess it's past my bedtime."

"Yeah, mine too." Gavrielle got to her feet.

Tonia gave her a hug. "You know, with you here ... it's like I can feel Ilana up there, smiling that big wide smile of hers, so relieved and happy that we found each other. That you and Nella have a new home. I just hope I don't let her down."

Saturday Night, August 5, 1967
Amrani home, Old Katamon, Jerusalem

After Amos performed the Havdalah ceremony that marked the end of the Sabbath and beginning of a new week, Tonia pulled Gavrielle aside.

"Would it be alright if I came along when Amos takes you home?" she asked. "I ... I'd like to see the house again. My old room. Before you start packing things up."

"Sure." Gavrielle spoke hesitantly. "But isn't it full of sad memories for you?"

Tonia let out slow sigh, but managed a smile. "That was a time of chaos. For me the inner turmoil was almost worse than the war – trying not to fall in love with Amos, planning to leave my family, defying a man like my father. I can't describe how much I loved and respected him. He was so ... alive. So sure about what he was doing. A bulldozer. That's what he was. A human bulldozer. When they told me he was dead, buried in a mountain of rubble, I couldn't believe he hadn't come crawling out. I thought he was invincible." Tonia sighed again. "But I guess our brains protect us. Now I only remember the good things."

Fathers are so important, Gavrielle thought, briefly wallowing in self-pity. Then she reminded herself that she would soon have an opportunity to start searching for her own father. Maybe even tonight.

She asked Tonia, "Do you think ... would it be alright if my grandmother stayed here tonight? I mean, your mother is coming to visit you tomorrow and I'm sure Nanna Nella will want to see her. And it would give me a chance to start packing. If she needs more clothing or anything, I could send it back with you and Amos tonight."

"Sure." Tonia shrugged. "That's no problem. Actually that solves a problem. That way neither of us will have to ride in the back of the truck on the way to your house."

Tonia paused to stare at the Rozmann house. Its large blocks of pinkish Jerusalem stone bore streaks of black mold, the front door and shutters needed a coat of paint, and the small yard was overgrown with weeds. When she opened the wrought-iron gate to the front walk she gasped. "I remember that squeak!" She turned to put a hand on her husband.

From the front hall Tonia went straight to her old room and slowly opened the door. "It's exactly the same."

"Yaffa's been using it," Gavrielle said. "Sometimes she needs to sleep over. But she hasn't changed anything."

Tonia sat on the bed and then slipped her shoes off and stretched out. "I thought this was the most heavenly mattress that ever existed. Like sleeping on a cloud. And my precious reading lamp!" She raised a hand to touch it. "All that's missing is the smell of frying onions. Or baking cookies."

Then she suddenly sat up. "Oh Lord. Yaffa! What have I been thinking? She's worked for you forever. You can't just let her go. Do you think she'd want to come to our house in the mornings, instead of me giving Linor more hours?"

"I'll ask her. That would be nice for Nanna. And she could make her cookies for you all the time. Do you want to go upstairs?"

Tonia shook her head as she put her shoes back on. "I can't remember ever going up there. My nostalgia is for this room and the kitchen. I never cared much for the living room. Too fancy. Kind of furniture you're scared to sit on."

They walked back to the kitchen.

"Where'd Amos go?" Gavrielle asked.

"Probably outside to have a cigarette."

"Should I make coffee or tea?" Gavrielle asked, just as the back door opened and Amos came in.

"No thanks," he said. "We have to get home. Sarit is a responsible nine-year-old, but she's still a nine-year-old."

Tonia shook her head. "I don't think we have to worry. Mrs. Rozmann is there, in full possession of all her faculties. You know..." Tonia turned to Gavrielle. "As long as we're here with the truck, you could send some of your belongings home with us. Do you want to take any of the furniture?"

"I'll go upstairs and have a look."

Gavrielle came back downstairs empty-handed, then went past Tonia's room to her grandmother's and brought a few things out to the living room. "I'm pretty sure she'll want these things."

"I guess we'll have to wait and see who you rent the house to, before you can figure out what to leave here and what to put in storage," Amos said. "Do you want me to help you with that?"

"With putting the furniture in storage?"

"No. I mean, sure I'll help you with that. But I meant with finding renters."

For a moment Gavrielle feared she might start to cry. She hadn't realized how daunting that task had loomed before her – having to deal with a rental contract. It hadn't occurred to her that anyone would help.

She managed to smile when she said, "That would be great."

"Amos knows everyone in the city," Tonia said. "He'll get you a family that'll pay their bills on time and take care of things."

"And pay the rent under the table," Amos added.

Tonia and Amos drove off with a rocking chair, an old mantel clock, and a floor lamp in the back of the truck.

Gavrielle went inside, closed the front door, and slumped against it. She tried to remember when she'd ever had the house to herself. She must have been home on some Saturday or Sunday when Yaffa had taken Nella somewhere. But that wouldn't count anyway – wouldn't have allowed Gavrielle run of the house, as she had now, without having to worry about them coming through the door any minute. She smiled slyly. *At last, I can poke around wherever I want, for as long as I want.*

She checked that both doors were locked, before making a cup of tea that she took to her grandmother's room. Sitting on the bed, she surveyed the nightstands, wardrobe, bureau, dressing table, and tiny built in closet. *Where oh where would you hide a secret, Nanna?*

She was prepared to be disappointed, knowing she was unlikely to find any concrete evidence hidden in this room – no picture, diary, old schoolbook filled with Ilana's doodling, or jewelry engraved with names or initials. Why would Nella keep something like that? But if by some miracle there *was* anything to be found, Gavrielle was determined to find it. She didn't care if it took all night and all the next day. Short of slitting open the pillows and mattress, she intended to tear this room apart.

The tiny closet was first. There wasn't much in it – just a rod from which Nella's dresses and robes hung. On the floor were her winter slippers and an extra pair of shoes. They looked so sad and lonely. Nella always got teary-eyed when she reminisced about the row upon row of different colored high heels she'd once

31

owned, but since the bombing her cloddy shoes had to be custom-made. Gavrielle picked them up and shook them, not actually expecting anything to fall out. *Maybe now, with her new leg, she'll be able to wear nice shoes again.*

She went through all the hanging garments, searching the pockets. On the shelf above the rod were four enormous hat boxes. They contained stacks of hats – most with floppy wide brims but also fedoras, cloches, berets, pillboxes with and without tiny veils, and fancy going-out hats embellished with velvet, lace, and piles of flowers. Gavrielle paused to try on most of them, hamming in the mirror, imagining young Nella getting all dressed up to go out dancing. She felt no shame for invading her grandmother's privacy. *If you ever answered a single question about anything that mattered, I wouldn't have to do this.*

When she stepped back onto the chair to return the boxes, she found her treasure trove. On the shelf, pushed far back into the corner, was a simple shoebox. It contained a stack of letters tied with a ribbon, a few envelopes filled with photographs, and a few dozen newspaper clippings. She flipped through the photographs first, but had seen them all before. There was only one of her mother, and Gavrielle had spent more hours than she cared to remember staring at it.

Then she untied the ribbon around the letters. Most of the yellowing envelopes were from Poland. There were a few Rosh Hashana and birthday cards. Even two Valentines from Viktor. But there was one more, attempting to lurk unnoticed in the center of the pile. It had the crinkly look of paper that had gotten soaking wet and dried out. The blue ink had run and smeared, but the first letters of the name on the front – Miss Ila – were legible. She turned it over but there was no return address. Nor were there any postal markings. A short strip of yellowed tape still clung to the point of the flap. Gavrielle took a deep breath and wiped her hands on her trousers before carefully removing the single folded page and smoothing it on the bed.

Dearest Ilana,

I hung around your street for as long as I could, hoping to catch you on your way in or out. Then I gave up and knocked on the door. Maybe you're relieved no one was home, but I hope not.

I did get up enough "chutzpah" to ask your neighbors about you. They said everyone expects the war to hit Jerusalem the hardest, so your family went to look for an apartment in Tel Aviv.

So there's no way I'm going to find you before I leave, but I have to go. I got a telegram saying my dad is real sick, so day after tomorrow I'm flying back to Chicago.

Your neighbors said your parents haven't sold your house or anything, so I'll just leave this in the letter box and sooner or later you ought to get it.

I'm not so great with words and don't know how to tell you how wonderful it was, the last time we were together. For so long my world has been nothing but filth and death. You brought back sunshine, warmth and caring. I bless the day we met.

I'm afraid you might be feeling like I took advantage of you and then ran off, but that's not true. I pray we will be together again soon. You say you can't imagine a future for us together, but I can. You know there are lots of Jews in America. And neither my Italian mother, nor my Irish father managed to make a good Catholic of me. We can find a way of our own.

If you want to hear from me again, write to me at the address below. If you don't, I will understand

33

that you prefer for me to remain a memory.

I am anxiously waiting to hear from you and can easily send you a ticket to Chicago. I will be praying every day that you and your parents are safe and well.

With love,
Lou

Gavrielle reread the letter several times, the tears she wiped away quickly turning to anger. Much of the writing had been smeared by the water damage, but only Lou's address at the bottom was blurred beyond legibility. *You did that, Nanna! I know you did. Yeah, sure, it got rained on, sitting in the mailbox, but you dripped a lot more water on that part, made sure no one could read his address. I'll never forgive you for that. Never, ever.*

She rose and paced through the house, finally pausing to wonder why Nella hadn't simply burned the letter. She could think of no answer to that and began pacing again, now pondering the chances of finding a man named Lou in Chicago. *How many people live in Chicago? There must be hundreds of thousands. Maybe millions. Can I even assume he still lives there? Hell no. It's hopeless. But wait, stop. At least it's a place to start. A clue. You want to be an intelligence officer, so think like one. What would an American – a Gentile no less – have been doing in Palestine in 1947?* Gavrielle had always suspected her father was a British soldier or diplomat and that was why Nella lied. *You didn't want your daughter accused of being a rat collaborator. Not with all the rumors about your rat husband.* Gavrielle continued searching her grandmother's bedroom, but made no other discoveries and fell into bed a few hours before her alarm went off.

34

She quickly dressed and caught her busses to Tel Aviv and Haifa, where she went directly to the tiny office the Technion had allotted to Jesse. He made her a cup of coffee while she told him why that woman in the cafeteria had come looking for her.

"So, abracadabra, my domestic problem has been solved and I can start working on your projects with the other students."

"Wow." Jesse came around his desk to give her the first of what would be many quick brotherly hugs. Then he held her at arm's length, smiling broadly. "Wow. That is great. Some story. Really unbelievable. I hope it all works out. Do they have a phone?"

"What?"

"The family – that Tonia and her husband – do they have a telephone?"

"Yes. Why?"

He lifted the receiver of the phone on his desk and held it out. "Don't you want to call, talk to your grandmother? See how she's feeling after her first night in a strange house, without you?"

"No. She's fine. She adores Tonia." Gavrielle literally backed away from the receiver, as if it might bite her. She didn't dare speak with her grandmother while she was still furious enough to strangle her.

"So, come to the lab. There's something I want to show you about the new transponder they sent us."

She hesitated for a moment, part of her wanting to tell Jesse about the letter from Lou in Chicago. But no, she wasn't ready to talk about that yet. *Anyway, what's he going to do, send the Mossad out looking for him? And no matter how nice Jesse is, no matter how much he acts like we've been best buddies forever, he barely knows me. He wouldn't want to be bothered with my problems.*

"Sure. Why? Is there something wrong with it?" She followed him down the corridor, admiring his graceful

35

stride and wishing she had a brother. Only then did it occur to her. *Chicago Lou probably has a family. I might have half-brothers and sisters.*

The tattered packaging of the transponder still lay on the table, but someone had already begun dismantling it. Gavrielle couldn't help laughing.

"What's so funny?" Jesse asked.

"It just reminds me ... back when I was in high school I read this newspaper article – about an American lady who'd gotten a patent for this revolutionary new home security system. She'd stuck a camera behind the peephole in a door and it displayed whatever was outside the door on a monitor. You know, so you could see who was out there. It even broadcasted sound along with the picture.

"I thought that was so cool and I just had to have one. It took me forever to figure out how to order one and badger my grandmother into letting me spend the money. Then I had to drag her to the bank with me to get a cashier's check. When the notice from the post office finally came, I was so excited, I ran all the way there and home. And then my grandmother comes into the kitchen, wanting a look at this wonderful gadget I just had to have, but its guts are already hanging out all over the table. You know, I just had to see how it worked."

Jesse's grin had grown wider as she spoke. He laughed, shaking his head. "I did the exact same thing. Read that same article. Had a cartoon of a big eye outside the door?"

"Yes, that's it. That's the one." She nodded happily.

"Like minds," he said. "But I was already in the army, so I could have a procurement clerk get it for me. You're going to *love* this job. The Intelligence Branch is always a first adopter for every new walkie-talkie and remote-controlled gadget that comes on the market.

We constantly demonstrate our unwavering faith in the American system of private enterprise – and equally great faith in our ability to improve upon whatever they do."

From then on, "play with toys," was Gavrielle's response when asked what she intended to do in the army. But it was spoken with great pride. She would have been useless on the front line, in combat. What she could do was help make sure there was no front line. She was going to become a guardian angel, harnessing the super powers of electronic waves and using them to fend off evil-doers. She wanted that job and intended to do it well. She basked in the warmth of Jesse's smile, feeling appreciated. She wouldn't be a poor little orphan girl any more. She was going to be an officer in the IDF. She was going to be someone who mattered. And someone who could figure out how to find her father.

Later that week Amos took Gavrielle to get the last of their belongings and they were officially moved in with the Amrani family. Since leaving her old home Nella hadn't gone back, and she did not seem to miss it. Apparently the bustle of the Amranis' comings and goings agreed with her, and Yaffa had happily accepted the job of looking after her in the mornings.

So Gavrielle had spent another three nights in their old house, alone, packing all evening after work, until she was exhausted. Each night before she fell asleep she stared at the ceiling in the dark, unsettled. She frowned, noting that the house felt scarier without Nanna Nella in it. *Like what, she was going to get up and fend off a burglar with her wooden leg?*

It was August and the nights were hot, but Gavrielle found herself shivering under the covers. It would be terrible to go to bed like that every night, listening to the lonesome sounds in the dark. She lay awake, thinking about the blood relations she might have somewhere in America. *What if I have a sister?*

When her alarm went off, she rose in an entirely different mood, eager to greet another sunny day. She had never felt so young and capable. *Now my real life begins. Tonia and Jesse have changed everything.* She was no longer a pathetic lone student, lost in the crowd. And she could look forward to a future of doing good.

She continued to avoid her grandmother, staying late nights in the lab and library, asking to crash on any free bed she found in the Technion's student housing. The summer session was nearly over, but she would be taking no days off. There was always something to do on one of Jesse's projects. When Friday arrived, there was no plausible excuse for not going home, but Tonia's mother Leah was there, a welcome distraction, and Gavrielle managed to behave as she always did with her grandmother.

That became the pattern of Gavrielle's life for the following weeks – studying long into the night and going home only for the Sabbath. Until the afternoon that Jesse came into the lab where she was working. He cleared away some of the clutter of wires and tiny electronic components, and placed an important-looking white envelope in front of her. She pulled a thick white card out of it and opened her eyes wide.

"You're getting married? And here I thought you were secretly in love with me."

"Hah. You think I don't know how far out of my league you are?" He joked and leaned forward, both palms on the desk and his face close to hers. "No excuses, Gav, you have to come," he said, his deep voice never seeming to belong with his shy smile. "I can't wait for you to meet Shana."

Gavrielle's bottom teeth bit into her top lip as she ran her finger over the fancy lettering, wondering how

38

such things came to be. Tonia and Amos were the only couple she'd ever had the chance to observe close-up and they were no less a mystery to her. Gavrielle often paused to stare at the young people she studied with, watching them being drawn to one another by some invisible force. *What is it about them? Why should those two be together? Why don't I ever feel anything like that?*

She leaned back and tilted her head to one side, as she asked, "I know it's none of my business – but what made you decide to marry Shana? I mean why her? Out of all the women you've ever known, why her?"

As soon as she'd spoken she flushed, afraid he might think she'd been serious about thinking he was in love with her. But nothing like that showed on his face.

He stared at her for a moment before saying, "Come on, get up. Let's go for a walk. You're wasting a beautiful September day in here."

She followed him outside, afraid she'd gone too far, even for an officer as informal as Jesse. He stopped under a tree, stared out at the gentle white waves on the Mediterranean, and then sank down onto the grass, patting the ground next to him.

She sat and he turned to look her in the face. "What you asked before – nobody knows that, Gav. Not really. It's not something you decide. I don't think we make rational decisions about most of the important things we do in life. We just do them, because something inside pushes us to. Haven't you ever met some guy and felt ... like this one is different? Not better looking or smarter. Just ... like something about him makes you want to be in the same room with him all the time? To touch him all the time? I don't mean sex. Just the feel of his skin against yours is comforting?"

She shook her head and shrugged. "Have you seen me hanging around with anyone, acting like that?"

39

"No. But one of these days someone *will* make you feel like that. And, as long as he doesn't do anything to ruin it, he'll be the one. With all the guys you've got chasing after you –"

"For an intelligence officer you're not very observant." After interrupting him she looked around, as if to make sure no one was listening, and then cupped her hands around her mouth as she mock whispered, "They stopped chasing a long time ago."

"Think that might have anything to do with the way you look at every guy who tries to start with you? Like he's a cockroach, but you're too merciful to actually squash the pathetic bastard?"

"I do that?" She sat straighter.

"Yes, you do."

"That can't be true. You wouldn't have wanted me on your team if I was that nasty."

"I'm not talking about work. You're fantastic to work with. Helpful, co-operative, honest, always ready to admit when you're wrong – well, that hasn't actually happened yet, but I know you'll admit it, if you ever are wrong. You just wait patiently for the rest of us to catch up and figure out why you're right.

"When it comes time for me to write your evaluation, I'm going to have to make up something to say about 'room for improvement.'" He paused, grinning as he watched her squirm. "God, look at you. You really have to learn how to take a compliment. When that special guy comes along, he's going think you expect him to tell you how beautiful and all-around wonderful you are. When he does, it will go a lot better if you don't look like you're about to puke."

She pulled a handful of clover and pelted him with it, then turned a serious gaze on him. "I ... I don't know how to have relationships like other people do. Not just with guys. I've never really had a friend. Not until you.

And I suppose it's inappropriate for me to think of you as a friend, since you're going to be my commanding officer."

"That's not true. I am your friend. But you need a lot more of them. I've noticed you never eat lunch with the other students. Always keep to yourself. That's a bad habit, but I'm sure one you can break."

"I don't know how to talk to them, except about the projects we're working on."

"You're talking to me."

She shrugged. "I don't know. It's different with you. I don't know why – what makes me feel comfortable with you."

"Start hanging out with them. Eventually you'll get to feel comfortable with some other people. And I've got to ask you, Gav. How come you haven't been going home? Is everything all right?"

"Yeah, everything's fine. The Amranis are great." She paused and looked out at the sea before blurting out, "I'm just scared of murdering my grandmother."

Then she told him about the letter. She knew it by heart and he asked her to repeat it several times.

"So, he's American, not Jewish, and was in Palestine right before the War of Independence started." He thought for a while and then said, mostly to himself, "Yes, that makes sense."

"What makes sense?"

"What did he say – filth and death? Sounds like a soldier to me. He could have been one of those *Machal* guys."

She knew she'd heard that term before, but her face remained blank.

"You know, the foreign volunteers. Allied soldiers who got mustered out of the western armies after the war was over. They stayed in Europe and then came here – volunteered to help us. Like Mickey Marcus."

41

"That's the guy they made that movie about – *Cast a Giant Shadow*?"

"Yep. Kirk Douglas."

"Do you think you could find out about them? Like maybe there's a list of names somewhere?"

"I'll try," he said. "But don't get your hopes up. Those were chaotic times. The bookkeeping wasn't so hot." Then he sniffed his nose before saying, "Listen, you've got to start going home like a normal person. Somehow your Tonia got my phone number and left a message with the secretary – complained that I was working you too hard."

Gavrielle flushed. "Oh, I'm sorry."

"Don't worry, I didn't rat you out. I called her back and apologized, said I'd try to be more sensitive to your family situation. But from now on you have to go home. At least twice a week, besides Shabbat." He got to his feet and held out his hand to help her up. "And you're coming to the wedding. In a dress. That's an order." He turned to walk away.

"Yessir." She called to his back. "What *are* you going to write in my evaluation? About room for improvement?"

"What do you think?" He said over his shoulder. "Interpersonal skills."

In truth, it wasn't only because of her grandmother that Gavrielle hadn't been going home. Being part of a family was more demanding than she'd imagined. She feigned interest when Tonia went on about how they were beginning to rebuild her old kibbutz, Kfar Etzion, which the IDF had taken back in the Six Day War. And when informed that the twins had a birthday coming up, Gavrielle smiled, but was actually irritated that she would have to waste time shopping for presents. How was she supposed to know what to get for them?

42

She knew she should have more interaction with her new "siblings." The twins were easy but Sarit and Seffie basically ignored her existence. That was more than fine with her, except for making her feel painfully inadequate. Then she discovered an easy approach – help them with their homework and explain how various household devices work. That certainly seemed to please Tonia.

Every time she went home Gavrielle thought, *Do it today. Now. You have to confront Nanna about that letter sometime. Sooner better than later.* She couldn't have said why, but she kept putting it off.

In early October Jesse asked her to take another walk with him. "I'm sorry. I haven't found any information that will help you find your father." He led her to the same patch of grass and sat, leaning against the tree. "I did find one guy who'd been in the British army. after World War II was over, he came here to volunteer. I could arrange for you to talk with him if you want. He said he would guess there were something like 3,000 foreign volunteers and most of them were Jewish. He has no memory of anyone named Lou. And no idea how many of them might have been killed, like Mickey Marcus. But that is a possibility you have to consider. I mean, it's not likely, since he said in the letter he was leaving the country, but he could have come back. Or he might have had a heart attack or whatever, back in Chicago."

"Yeah, I know he could be dead. People die. Did you ask this guy how many Americans there were?"

"He would guess two hundred. Three at the most."

"That's not so many. I mean if I could find a few of those Americans, it's not impossible that one of them might remember him. You'd think someone would have kept a list."

"Well, actually, no, you wouldn't. See, by joining up to serve in a foreign army, they were breaking the law in their own country. Even the ones who were planning to stay and live in Israel wanted to be able to go home and visit their families without getting arrested. Back then *nobody* wanted to leave a paper trail."

"Oh."

"But you're right, a few hundred people isn't that many. Except that finding other Americans isn't all that likely to help you. I mean, it's not like they served together by nationality. Whatever they'd been doing in the American army, they'd have been doing the same kind of thing here. So it would help if you knew what he did. What kind of unit he might have joined up with. Anyone else who was in the same unit would probably remember him. I mean an American, especially a non-Jew, ought to stand out in their memory. So don't give up hope. Have a talk with your grandmother."

"Yeah. Okay. Thanks, Jesse." This time she was first on her feet, offering her hand to him.

Back in the lab, Gavrielle took out her date-book to check when the Jewish holidays began this year and issued a silent groan when she saw that the following Wednesday was Erev Rosh Hashana. The two-day holiday ended just as the Sabbath began, meaning she would be home for four straight days. *God, why did you have to give the Jews so damn many holidays? But I suppose there's no better time to have my little talk with Nanna. After all, Rosh Hashana and Yom Kippur are all about settling accounts, aren't they?*

She'd always dreaded holidays – noisy families gathered around tables piled with far too much food, either laughing too loudly or arguing too much. Neighbors always felt compelled to invite strays like Gavrielle and Nella. Even with her new substitute family, Gavrielle still wasn't looking forward to Rosh Hashana. All those meals to be prepared, dishes to be

44

washed. And since the Amranis were observant, much of the food had to be prepared ahead of time. *If I was a good daughter, I'd go home early to help. Lord, are they also going to expect me to spend most of the day in the synagogue with them?*

She did arrive home a day early and helped Tonia with grocery shopping, laundry, and ironing. Then she volunteered to bake a batch of Yaffa's cookies. As she was taking the last sheet out of the oven, she felt a tap on her shoulder.

"Feel like coming outside with me?" Tonia asked.

"Sure, just let me get these last ones on the plates to cool."

Tonia led her up the street and sat on a wooden bench under a streetlight. She fished a pack of cigarettes out of her pocket, put one in her mouth, and offered one to Gavrielle, who shook her head.

"I didn't know you smoked."

"I don't." Tonia struck a match, lit the cigarette, and inhaled deeply. "But these holidays do us all in. I don't know why this disgusting thing provides any relief." She held the cigarette out and contemplated it. "But it does." She took another long drag. "Just don't tell Amos. So, how are you holding up to the stresses of family life?"

"Pretty well, I think. It's certainly a change from what I'm used to. Some ways good and some ways not so much, but mostly good."

"I can guess the bad. All the commotion. Not enough time to yourself. Suddenly having to accommodate other people's needs."

Gavrielle smiled and nodded.

"Anything that's fixable?"

Gavrielle took a deep breath. "Nothing about you guys. But I ... I've been wanting to ask you to help me with my grandmother."

Tonia's face took on a panicked look and Gavrielle put a hand on her forearm. "Nothing's wrong with her. Don't worry. At least not as long as I refrain from hitting her over the head with something."

"What on earth?"

Gavrielle told her about the letter from Chicago Lou and the conversation she'd had with Jesse. When she finished, Tonia lit another cigarette and sat smoking while she thought.

"Well," Tonia said at last, "I understand the urge to bash her head in, but please don't. Not in my house, anyway." She tossed the cigarette butt down and leaned forward to step on it. Then she took Gavrielle's hand. "But seriously ... of course I understand why you're angry. But don't be. Try to put yourself in her place for a minute."

"What, just because she's disabled I'm not allowed to get mad at her?"

"You're smarter than that. Think about her life." Tonia paused for a long moment. "Thanks to the Nazis, her husband and daughter were the only family she had. And then one nice sunny winter day the three of them are walking down the street and boom! Nella wakes up in a hospital minus a leg, her husband is dead, and no one can tell her if her daughter is alive. One explosive flash and her life is gone. Some time later she finds out that her daughter also passed away, after giving birth to a little girl in some other hospital. Only no one can find the record of which orphanage or foster home took the baby."

Gavrielle had never heard that part of the story and turned to Tonia, horrified. "How could that happen? A hospital loses a baby?"

"Didn't Nella ever tell you any of this?"

"She never tells me anything. Same stories over and over again, but never anything important. Just that my

46

mother was also injured, but lived long enough for them to save me. 'The past is the past,' she always says. Tells me to leave it alone."

Tonia shrugged and sighed. "I can only assume that Ilana was found at some distance from Nella and wasn't carrying her ID card. Or if she was, it was destroyed in the blast. They ended up in different hospitals and Nella was stuck wherever she was for I don't know how long. And when she finally got released and went home, what did she find? A letter from some stupid man – a Catholic, no less – who'd been trying to steal her daughter away to Chicago. And if that man somehow found out there was a baby, what was to stop him from coming to claim her? Men being what they are, he probably wouldn't have done that, but I get why she lied to you. As soon as you learned how to write, you probably would have sent him a letter. Kids do things like that and she couldn't risk it. What court was going to take a little girl from her father and give her to her crippled grandmother? And once she'd lied to you when you were little ... Oh, what a tangled web we weave ..."

Gavrielle put her elbows on her knees and her face in her hands. They sat in silence for a long while, before she said, "I guess I'm pretty dumb. I never thought of it from her point of view."

"Most of us are like that," Tonia sighed. "We don't see our elders as actual people. Their lives were nothing but a backdrop for the main event – our own grand entrance into the world."

"But none of that matters now. I'm nineteen years old."

"No, it doesn't matter any more. And since you already know she's been lying to you all these years, she has nothing more to lose by telling you whatever she does know. Just try to be kind. You don't want to become alienated from the one blood relative you do

47

have. Tell her you found the letter while packing and were really angry with her, but now that you've had time to think about it, you understand why she acted as she did. And don't do that until you really have gotten over your anger. You can't be mad at her for being terrified of losing you. And now she's an old woman, dependent on other people. She loves you. I'm sure you can find compassion in your heart."

"Thank you, Tonia." Gavrielle stood up.

"And remember what a miracle it was, her finding you in that orphanage. She spent months searching. On crutches."

"How come you knew all this?"

"I didn't. Yaffa told me last week. If Nella wasn't so stubborn, you could have been raised by a bunch of Catholic nuns."

"Can I ask you to be in the room with us when I talk to her?"

"Sure. That's a good idea. We all behave better when there's   a   witness."

On Sabbath afternoon Gavrielle finally confronted her grandmother. The children were occupied upstairs and Nella was alone in the living room, leafing through an old Life magazine that Tonia had saved from November 1963, after the assassination of President Kennedy.

Gavrielle set a wooden tray of refreshments on the coffee table – nuts, dried fruit, Yaffa's cookies, and mint iced tea. Then she stood next to her grandmother, kissed the top of her head, and removed an envelope from the pocket of her apron. She silently placed it on Nella's lap and took the chair next to hers.

"I found it while I was packing," Gavrielle said. "You had a lot of pretty hats up in that closet."

48

Nella turned the envelope over, her hand shaking. She said nothing, but began silently weeping. Gavrielle reached over to give her a handkerchief and put a hand on her knee, waiting a few minutes before speaking. "When I first found it I was furious with you, but I'm over that now. Just please don't lie to me anymore. I want you to tell me every single thing you know about the man who wrote that letter." Surprisingly calm, Gavrielle stood and poured iced tea for both of them.

Nella dried her eyes, drank a little, and set the glass on the tray. "I really don't know anything. Except there was this one day. Ilana came home and couldn't stop talking about some American soldier she'd met." She kept her head down, studying her hands.

"He'd been there when they liberated one of the camps in Germany – that one where General Eisenhower rounded up all the local townspeople and forced them to walk through it, so they could see the wonders their Thousand-Year Reich had done. Later, he saw one of the camps for Jewish refugees. He said it wasn't like a prison, they could go out whenever they wanted to. But none of them had anywhere to go. So they were still looking at the world through a wire fence. He thought it was the most shameful thing he'd ever seen. So he came here." She lifted her chin, so her gaze held Gavrielle's. "She only talked about him that one day. And she never even told me she was in trouble, so of course she never said he was the one. But after – when I found out about you – I guessed it must have been him. And then I found this letter. That's all I know. I swear."

"You never saw him?"

Nella shook her head.

"What about the address that was at the bottom of the letter?" Gavrielle's eyes narrowed. "Did you copy it anywhere?"

Nella shook her head.

49

"But you must remember something. The name of the street ..."

"No. I'm sorry." She clutched the handkerchief and began weeping again.

"Nanna, please, stop crying. That doesn't help anything. I know you feel bad, but now I need you to think really hard. Try to remember any detail she might have mentioned about that American soldier – who he fought with or where he worked. Did he wear a uniform? Did he remind her of anyone else? Did he carry a weapon?"

Tonia slipped quietly into the room and sat across from them.

Nella sat shaking her head. "She never mentioned him again. Just that one day. Probably after that they ... you know, for the first time, so she was keeping it all a big secret." Nella looked up, her eyes pleading. "I swear I would tell you if I knew anything. Now that you're all grown up."

"He was a mechanic," a familiar voice said from the arched entryway. They all looked up, surprised to see Yaffa standing there. "I didn't mean to be snooping," she said. "You left your good specs in my purse," she said to Nella. "So here they are." She removed the glasses from her pocket and took a few steps to set them on the coffee table. "The back door was open, so I let myself in. Thought I'd say hello, hearing you all having a chat in here."

Gavrielle was on her feet and steered Yaffa to an armchair. "Sit, sit. I want to ask you so many things. Can I get you some coffee?"

The tiny gray-haired woman looked like a child in the chair, her feet barely touching the floor. She shook her head. "But some of that cold tea would sit right. Hot out there, once you get out of the shade."

Gavrielle pulled her chair closer to Yaffa. "So my mother told you about the man she was seeing?"

"Man? I don't know that he was all that much older than her. She didn't have a lot to say about him, but I remember that he was a mechanic because she liked to complain about him always having grease under his fingernails."

"What kind of a mechanic?" Tonia asked.

Yaffa let out a puff of air and frowned as she thought for a minute. Then she raised her eyebrows. "Yes, I remember. Boats. Engines on boats. He heard how the Haganah was bringing Jews over here in those old tubs you had to pray would make it out of the harbor, much less across the whole Mediterranean. After he saw that refugee camp he went down to Marseilles. He found the people running those boats and asked if he could give a hand. Made the trip to Haifa with them a few times. That was how he met Ilana. In Tel Aviv. In a store or something. That's all I remember. I did get a glimpse of him once, but just from the back."

"You saw him?'"

She shrugged. "I think it must have been him, 'less Ilana was smooching with more than one boy. I only saw him from the back and just for a second. Tall skinny thing. Hair the color of yours," she said to Gavrielle. "Curly like yours."

"You mean like my mother's."

"Yes." Yaffa opened her eyes wider. "Now I remember her saying that. That they could have passed for brother and sister."

"Was he wearing a uniform?"

"No. Regular clothes. Sorry I can't tell you more."

"You're an angel from heaven," Gavrielle said. "At last I know something that might help me find him."

"Curly hair?" Yaffa frowned. "Lots of people got that."

51

"No," Gavrielle smiled. "Not his curly hair. That he was a mechanic. I might be able to figure out who he worked with and they might remember his last name."

"Oh. I didn't know that was so important." Yaffa frowned again. "So I think ... when he was still in the American army he worked on tanks and jeeps and that like. But when he heard the Jews needed people what could fix boats, he said 'an engine is an engine.' He could fix any kind of engine. Said when he got back to America he wanted to work on airplane engines. On the biggest airplanes he could find."

Gavrielle continued to question her, hoping to jog more memories, but no other useful information was forthcoming. Obviously tired, Yaffa rose to go home. Then she turned back. "He did give her one present. A teddy bear. You know, the one Nella keeps on her dresser. Guess it was some kind a joke between them."

Gavrielle paled and looked at her grandmother.

"I didn't know it was from him," Nella whispered. "I had no idea. She said she won it at a Purim party at school. I kept it because it was hers. She'd taken to sleeping with it."

Yaffa left and soon afterward Gavrielle went out for a walk. At first she was teary-eyed, but then quickened her step, smiling at the sky and wishing she could sing at the top of her lungs. Even if she never found him, at least she knew he was a good man. Her father was a good man. She'd already known from the letter that he'd loved her mother, had not abandoned her. And now she knew that he was not a smuggler, nor an arms dealer, nor a Brit trying to get information out of a naïve young girl. He was a brave man with a generous heart. With integrity. Courage. She couldn't wait to get back to work tomorrow and tell Jesse all about it.

Then she frowned, calculating. She wouldn't finish her degree and mandatory military service until May of

1974. Five years and nine months away. Only then would she be free to search for him. *Never mind, that doesn't matter. I'll just keep asking about the Machal volunteers and if I get any real information, the IDF will just have to give me a few weeks off. Just, please God, don't let him die the day before I find out where he is.*

Tuesday, October 2, 1973
Intelligence Branch, Research Department, one
of many technical units,
Glilot Junction, North of Tel Aviv

Gavrielle had earned her degree with honors, excelled at both basic and officers training, and owed just seven months more service to the IDF. She'd always planned on making her career in the military, but lately suffered from nagging doubts. Knowing a little too much had become exhausting. Her security clearance wasn't high enough for her to know what was really going on, but she overheard enough to be constantly reminded of how vulnerable they were – unlike the people who lounged around coffee shops in Tel Aviv, blissfully ignorant. Trying to be a guardian angel had come to feel like a heavy burden.

It was after 10 pm when Jesse stuck his head in the door, giving her a welcome excuse to remove her headphones and the high-pitched electronic screeches they emitted. She tilted her head to one side, waiting to hear what he needed her to do and was taken aback by how pale he looked.

"Working late again," he said. "What a surprise."

"Hello to you too."

Recent weeks had been a special hell of wondering what was going on. Should they believe their eyes and ears – the aerial photos and radar pulse signals that showed the build up of Syrian and Egyptian troops, tanks, artillery, and aircraft along Israel's borders. Or should they accept "The Concept," which was adhered to by most of the intelligence community?

The Concept insisted that: "Egypt will never start another war with us until the Soviets give them long-range bombers and Scud missiles that enable them to target Tel Aviv, *and* the Arab states manage to unite in

54

a coalition against us. Until those two things happen, not a chance that they will attack us. Never. No way." This despite some top-secret source, referred to only as "The Angel," who had warned the Mossad that Egypt and Syria would launch a concerted attack against Israel on Yom Kippur. Just four days away. King Hussein of Jordan had given them the same warning.

The believers in The Concept had other explanations for all the activity along the borders. Both Syria and Egypt were conducting routine annual exercises. The Syrian deployment was also defensive. Since September – when Israel had downed twelve Syrian MiGs – Hafez al-Assad had been jittery, afraid Israel was planning an attack. And Assad was under intense pressure to retaliate for those twelve aircraft. He had to do something. Perhaps he'd try to shoot down an Israeli jet. The Concept dismissed the warnings Israel had received as disinformation. If you wanted to destroy Israel's economy, all you had to do was goad them into needlessly calling up their reserves every once in a while.

Jesse stood silent in the doorway.

"How are you?" Gavrielle asked softly. "Anything intelligent going around Intelligence Branch today?"

He reached for the top of the door frame and leaned in, stretching his back. "Same arguments over and over." He bent to touch his toes, straightened, and changed the subject. "Listen, Gav, you've managed to dodge two offers for promotion, but you know you can't keep doing that."

"Nag, nag, nag. Why don't you go away and leave me alone? I'm where I belong, where I'm good at what I do. I'm not like those guys in 848. They see patterns and dots to connect. All I see is things that work, and things that don't."

"I didn't recruit you because I needed another technician."

"Haven't you heard that saying – about people rising to the level of their incompetence? No thanks."

"Your test scores don't agree with you. Haven't you heard that other saying – about people in large organizations being like sharks? Keep moving or die. Anyway, there are plenty of other jobs besides being an analyst."

She shrugged. "I'd rather go on playing with all these nifty gadgets for gathering raw intelligence."

"The guys in 848 aren't any smarter than you."

"People are smart in different ways. Have confidence about different things. I know I don't read minds. For instance, I wouldn't have a clue if the Mossad's big secret source was doubling or not. Are you allowed to tell me anything about him?"

He thought for a moment. "Not really. You shouldn't even know he exists. Neither should I, for that matter. And I have no clue about who he is. All I know is that he started as a walk-in."

"And that makes you more suspicious than if we'd recruited him?"

Jesse paused to think again. "I don't have the impression that he was ever caught in the wrong bed or in desperate financial straits. If a guy's in trouble and we manage to get our claws into him – that's a story I get. But a guy with no secrets or money problems suddenly decides to betray his country?" He shrugged.

"Is he the same guy who warned us about the attack last May – the one that never happened?"

"Guess so."

Gavrielle leaned back in her chair, every muscle tense and something churning in her gut. How can anyone, no matter how much experience they have, be so damn sure what the truth is? Give me my radar pulses. They say what they say.

"There's at least one big gun who still isn't buying The Concept," Jesse continued. "Hofi up in Northern Command. He believes the warnings and keeps reminding everyone that there's no Suez Canal between Syria and the Golan. Keeps trying to convince everyone that Assad is a worse immediate danger than Egypt."

Gavrielle forced herself to swallow the bitter taste of fear. "Let's talk about something else."

"Okay. No one cares what we think anyway. You interested in my job?"

"God no. The last thing I want to do is boss people around."

"Then gently guide and direct them." He took a step and rested a hip on her desk. "You don't see what a rut you've dug yourself into. Working in the same place for years, no friends, never go out with anyone."

"I went out with that guy you fixed me up with."

"And ditched him after half an hour."

"Come on, Jesse, bug off. I've made my peace — accepted the way I am. So other people think I'm weird. That's their problem."

"No one thinks you're weird."

"Please." She put her chin down and gave him her schoolteacher look, over the reading glasses she now needed. "Anyway, I've made some spiritual progress. I do believe there's a man for me. The poor bastard is out there somewhere."

"So you're waiting for him to fall through the roof?"

She laughed. "Pretty much. Things happen when they're supposed to, not when we will them too."

"Shit." He threw his head back. "Now she's going all New Age on me."

Gavrielle made a face.

"You're not getting any younger, you know." He mimicked his version of a nosy old woman. "Twenty-five." He shook his head. "Tick-tock, tick-tock."

She made another face. "When he comes along, I'll know. Until then I don't intend to test-drive a bunch of lemons."

"Wow. I mean, WOW. Now I do think you're weird. Saving yourself for Mr. Right, are you?"

"You're the only friend I have, and that's working all right for me. So if a girl can have just one friend in her life, who says she can't have just one man in her bed?"

Using both hands he scratched his head through his unruly curls and then shook himself like a dog. "Well, it was nice talking about something important for a change, but I've got another pointless meeting to go to."

"Now?"

"Haven't you heard? War's a-comin'. Or not."

After he left, Gavrielle worked a bit longer and then rose to stretch. She shoved her desk toward the door, making room to set up the cot and mattress she kept leaning against the wall. She pulled her crumpled sheets from the bottom desk door and her gray woolen blanket from the top of the bookshelves, doing a strikingly un-military job of spreading them out. She was sitting cross-legged on the cot, reading *The Day of the Jackal* in English, when Jesse returned an hour later. He looked shaken.

"What's wrong?" she asked and leaned over to put her open book facedown on the floor. "What happened?"

"Nothing, nothing." He waved a hand. "It's just ... I don't know." He closed the door behind him and slumped down on the cot, next to her. "These guys around here seem so cocky. So damn sure of themselves ... I keep trying to convince myself they know what they're doing. They see more intel than I do."

He put his elbows on his knees, his head drooping between them. Gavrielle was unsettled. During the six

58

years they'd been working together, she'd never seen him like this. Jesse was always steady, the definition of an even keel. Despondency wasn't part of his repertoire. Suddenly he shook it off and sat with his back ramrod straight.

"Listen, I have to go up to the Hermon tomorrow, check on something. And I'm going to stay for a few days, including Yom Kippur. Figure I might as well let one of the religious guys go home and pray for us."

"Send me," Gavrielle said. "You should be with Shana. I don't care if I'm home for Yom Kippur or not."

"Thanks, but no. She'll be next door at her parents all day, and I get enough of them as is. Anyway, I need you to do something else for me. I've got one of Shabtai Brill's toy airplanes – you know, with the remote control. It's all ready to go, loaded with one of the cameras you rigged to take a picture every ten seconds. I want you to take it to a guy I know, works in the pit." Jesse referred to the underground command bunker, beneath the compound of IDF headquarters in Tel Aviv. "It's on my desk, together with authorization to get you in. Go first thing in the morning."

"Does this guy know I'm bringing it?"

"No. And he won't be happy to see you. But I need you to do your best to convince him."

"Convince him to do what?"

"Get it down to the Sinai. To someone on the canal. There are instructions in the box – how to send it to fly over those huge walls of sand, take some pictures, and come back."

"I thought they shut down Brill's program."

"They did. Would rather wait for the air force to finish developing a real drone."

"I never understood why they didn't keep him going, at least for the meanwhile. Didn't his toy planes fly over Egypt and come back with really good photographs?"

59

"Yep. I have no idea why. Probably because the bigger a bureaucracy gets, the dumber it gets. Maybe there are budget rules, like they couldn't have budget items both here and in the air force for the same thing. Something stupid like that. You know what Brill's budget was? For three planes and extra engines and joy sticks? Eight hundred and fifty dollars. Bought off the shelf at some store in Manhattan."

"That doesn't count the cameras, though," Gavrielle pointed out.

Jesse burst out laughing. "No, that doesn't count the cameras." He shook his head. "What the hell, Gav. I don't know what the Air Force is spending on their drone program, but it must be in the millions. Everything they do is in the millions. And they haven't produced a damn thing yet."

"So-o-o-o ... how unhappy is this guy going to be?"

"Why do you think I'm not going? To you, he'll at least be polite. I've already had this argument with him. A few times. He'll brush you off, make some disparaging remark about my ridiculous toy. All you can do is repeat Brill's arguments – why being a toy is exactly what's so great about it. It weighs almost nothing. Costs almost nothing. It presents a tiny target that flies under the radar and doesn't set off a shit-load of SAMs. And when none of that works, just say, 'Look, Bud, this toy is right here on your desk and I don't see any drones lying around.' Ask him what he's got to lose."

"All right." She sighed. "I'll try. Use all my impressive interpersonal skills."

She expected him to get up and leave, but he didn't. He took a few deep breaths and allowed himself to gently slump against her. She twisted around and stood to put her hands on his shoulders, telling him to lie down. He did.

"I'll go get you a glass of water."

"No." He grasped her hand. "Just give me a minute. I'm all right." He stretched his legs out and closed his eyes. "Some guy told me other details about what Brill said. Dots he connected. Among all the other millions of Egyptian army vehicles heading for the canal, we tracked three hundred trucks of ammunition." He rested his forearm over his eyes.

"So?"

"So who uses three hundred truckloads of live ammunition in an exercise?"

"Oh." She sat back down beside him on the cot.

"And there's something else, but I'm going to let you try to connect those dots on your own. The Syrians moved their precious Sukhoi fighter jets down to our border."

"And? So?"

"That's for you to figure out." He moved his arm to look at her, then closed his eyes again. "Think of it as a riddle. You like those."

"Okay, okay."

She sat in silence, watching him. Then the cot creaked in protest as she stretched out beside him, her head on his shoulder and her arm across his chest. He bore the faint scent of aftershave, dust, and khaki. The scent of Jesse.

We shouldn't do this. Risk ruining our friendship. But, God, I'm so sick of being alone and afraid. I need this – another beating heart close to mine. Let me steal an hour with him. Just one hour. His skin is so warm. Is it so selfish? I don't know. He needs it too. Needs to escape to some other place for a while. Is it really so terrible?

She gently stroked his cheek. "It's okay, Jesse. Everything's going to be okay. Take a few deep breaths."

After a while he turned on his side and looked into her face, his eyes questioning.

"Yes," she said and moved closer to him, astonished at how easy it was for her to do this forbidden thing. How natural it felt. Not because she had suddenly fallen in love with him. Precisely because she hadn't. This moment had nothing to do with the rest of their lives.

"It's okay. You don't have to worry." She stroked his cheek again and smiled. "I'll still respect you in the morning."

"I'm not Mr. Right."

"Right now you are."

"But you're a virgin."

She pulled back to look him in the face. "Yeah. Ridiculous, isn't it? And unkind of you to hold it against me."

"Ach, Gav, be serious. I swore this would never happen." But he made no move to leave.

"You talk too much," she said.

Four days from now we might be ash and dust. Just shut up and keep your arms around me for a while. Please.

He put his hand on her cheek, saying, "You're so beautiful," before kissing her. Then he ran his finger down her cheek and neck, and unbuttoned her shirt. She sat up and pulled it off and then unbuttoned his, trying to ignore the annoying squeaks of the cot. He kissed and caressed and further undressed her – and himself – and then pulled her under him and touched her.

"God, you're wet." He groaned. After more kissing and caressing he said, "You have to raise your legs, Gav." He arranged them around him. "Like this."

Then he entered her, asking if he was hurting her.

"No. Yes. A little. Stop talking." She kissed him hard and then grasped his buttocks, wishing they could stay like that forever.

Afterwards, despite the dull pain between her legs, it was bliss to lie in his arms, running their hands over one another. On the verge of falling asleep, Gavrielle forced herself to sit up.

"Jesse." She shook him. "You have to get out of here. God, the door isn't even locked." She struggled into her clothes.

He pulled her back down on the cot and mumbled, "So, go lock the door. But let me stay. I think I'll be able to sleep here."

"What's the matter with you? Tomorrow morning you can't unlock my office door and go strolling out."

"Ach, I know, I know." He slowly sat up, shook his head, and began pulling his pants on.

"Don't worry." She held his face to kiss his forehead. "This will never happen again. Shana will never know. No one will ever know. That's the advantage of fooling around with a girl who doesn't have any friends. Who's she going to tell?"

"Was it so bad you don't even want to talk about it?"

She turned flippant. "Ah. Time for me to evaluate you?" She shook her head. "Idiot. I can't think of any room for improvement." Then she leaned toward him to put her hands over his ears and turn his face toward hers. "Seriously, I'd guess it was the best first time anyone ever had and I'm glad it was with you. I know you care about me. I trust you. I love you. But I'm not in love with you."

"I know."

"So you know nothing needs to change between us. This will be a lovely memory that I'll relive every night before I fall asleep."

"You're not going to end up feeling bad?"

"No. I can't explain why, but I don't feel like we did anything wrong. Maybe I'm stupid and don't realize how guilty you must be feeling. But for me ... you saved me from being scared and helpless for a while, wrapped me up in a nice safe bubble. Why don't we agree to never talk about it again? Forget it ever happened. Except in the private corners of our minds."

Gavrielle cleaned herself up as best she could and early the next morning wadded the blood-stained sheet into her backpack. When she went to Jesse's office to get the toy plane she was surprised to find him behind his desk. "Oh, hi, sorry for barging in. I didn't know you were here. Thought you must have gone home last night."

"I was about to come wake you. I didn't want to leave to go up north without giving you this." He opened his desk drawer and handed her an envelope.

"What is it?"

"A message. Shana left it on the answering machine last night. While I was out of my office. It's really for you."

Gavrielle unfolded the paper that was in the envelope and stared at it. A name was printed on it, in English, along with a ten-digit number. "So? What is it?"

"One of the guys I asked about the *Machal* volunteers finally called me back at home last night. Shana said he didn't know any Lou or remember any American from Chicago, but he'd heard that one of the American volunteers has started compiling a list. That's his name and phone number. The first three digits are the area code. Somewhere in Florida." He smiled broadly at her.

"Oh my God. This is wonderful. Thank you so much, Jesse. Thank you so, so much. I didn't know you were still making calls, after all these years."

"Didn't want to get your hopes up for nothing," he said, obviously pleased.

"You are the best. The best, the best, the best." She picked up the box containing the airplane.

"I hope something comes of it."

"You never told me the name of the guy I'm supposed to give this to." She nodded at the box.

"Colonel Beni Shaul. It's on the envelope in there, which contains a note to him. Go fix your hair and put some lipstick on. You're his type." Jesse stood, surveyed his desk, and picked up the duffel behind it. "See you next week." He turned and walked out.

Gavrielle went back to her office and stared at the paper. Jesse had carefully printed "DAVID SHAYNE 863-337-6938." She tore two pages out of a spiral notebook and copied the name and number on both of them, checking them twice. *That's all I need, to finally get my hands on something like this and then lose it.* She put one copy in her desk drawer and punched holes in another and filed it in one of the binders on the shelf. The original she folded and put in the belly pack she wore when traveling. Then she did as told, trying to make herself presentable before catching the bus to Tel Aviv.

It let her off near the gate to the Kirya – the compound of IDF headquarters – and she quickly passed through the checkpoint and found the dark gray, trapezoid-shaped, one-story structure that bore the logo of the Operations Division. The IDF's central command post was deep in the ground beneath it. She entered and kept her fingers on the handrail as she descended the steep stairs.

She entered the narrow corridor on the level she was looking for. The ceiling was low, with fluorescent light fixtures and thick bundles of wires and cables running along the top of either side. All the doors were closed and she opened the one with the right number on it, entering a small octagonal space. Cramped offices opened out of each side, each holding one or more desks.

"Where can I find Colonel Beni Shaul?" she asked the soldier in the office closest to her. "My name's Rozmann and I have something to deliver to him."

"Wait here," he said and rose to go into one of the other offices. "He'll call you. You can wait here." He nodded at the other desk in his office, which was unoccupied.

Phones rang and monitors beeped, but it was not the frantic flurry of activity she had expected. While waiting for Colonel Shaul to become available, she surveyed the grim faces that passed by, and eavesdropped on unsettling whispers. Soon her name was shouted and she went into the Colonel's office, saluted, and handed Jesse's note to him.

Colonel Shaul tossed it on the desk. "Doesn't the guy ever give up?"

"Not when he's right," Gavrielle said.

He leaned back, looking amused. "Alright, Gavrielle Rozmann, Jesse's Girl Wonder. Sit down." He extended his arm toward a wooden folding chair. "Convince me."

As expected, her arguments were to no avail and he dismissively shoved the box aside.

"I'll leave it here," Gavrielle said. "In case you reconsider. Thank you for your time, sir." She saluted again and turned to leave.

"Wait. Hey, listen, I know you're not a secretary, but you know how to type don't you? Use the damn telex? Operate a radio?"

She nodded in response to all those things.

"Translate into English?"

She nodded.

66

"Okay, that's it." He picked up his phone. "What's Jesse's number?"

"He's not there. He went up to the Hermon and won't be back until Sunday."

"Then you can call him on Sunday. From here. We're short-handed and I'm hijacking you."

"Yessir. Do you need me to stay now?"

"I don't know. Wait." He rose to stick his head into the central hub between the offices and shouted to another officer. "When is Karni going for that surgery?"

"They put it off," the man answered. "Not until Sunday morning."

He returned to Gavrielle. "Okay, you've got tomorrow and Thursday at Glilot. Finish up anything you're in the middle of. Come back here Sunday morning. Early. Catch the first bus." He hurriedly wrote out an entrance authorization and handed it to her.

"I don't mind working on Yom Kippur, if you need me."

"Sunday morning. And don't be late." He walked away.

Gavrielle caught the bus back to Glilot. She had just entered her office when the phone rang.

"So, what did he say?" Jesse asked.

"What you said he would."

"Yeah, I figured."

Always careful about what she said on the phone, she continued. "It wouldn't have made any difference, Jesse. You know that. Your toy could have worked better than anyone else's and it wouldn't make any difference. The whole place is plastered with pictures of everything, everywhere. More pictures of the same wouldn't change the way the same eyes look at them. So how are you? Everything okay?"

"Yeah. Fine. I always forget how nice and cool it is up here on top of the world. Air you can actually

67

breathe, not like down there. And you can't beat the view – turn to the west and there's Haifa. Turn to the east and, wow, look at those minarets – that's Damascus."

"Enjoy. At least your friend was nice about ignoring me. Up until he commandeered me. I'm supposed to go back there Sunday morning, replace someone who will be gone on medical leave. He didn't say for how long. Is that going to be a problem?"

"What's he want you for?"

"Someone he calls his gadget guy is the one with the medical problem. So I guess I'm going to be his gadget girl. He seems to be stumped by anything more complicated than the phone."

"Yeah, he's a connect-the-dots kind of guy. Definitely not a how-things-work guy. So, yeah, that's fine with me. It'll be interesting for you, seeing what goes on there."

"I guess."

"Listen, Gav ... what day is it, Wednesday?"

"Yeah. Still Wednesday."

"So take one of the million vacation days you've got coming. You wouldn't be working on Friday anyway, so don't come in tomorrow either."

"Why not? With you gone –"

"At this point, there's nothing especially productive either of us can do. We're as useless as everyone else, sitting around waiting to see what happens. There are plenty of eyes and ears where they need to be. And if you're going back to that place, you'd better get all the rest you can now. Seriously, I mean it. It isn't a suggestion."

"All right. I'm not arguing. I do feel pretty useless. Is everything really all right up there? Normal?"

"Yeah. Very normal. You go home now. On your way, stop for coffee somewhere. Sit at a sidewalk cafe and enjoy normal. Enjoy the time with your family. Call that guy in Florida."

"Yessir. Hey, I forgot to tell you – I figured it out. Your riddle. On my way back on the bus ... You know, about those toys that start with 's'."

"Okay, let's hear it."

"Ever since ... you know, the last time we got in a fight with those kids and broke all their toys, before they even got to start using them ... so since then, they've kept those toys as far away from us as they can. They even built special toy boxes, really strong boxes, to keep them in." She referred to the bomb-proof hangars the Syrians had built for their Sukhoi fighter jets, after watching Israel destroy their aircraft squadrons on the runways in '67.

"Yes, so?"

"So now all of a sudden they decided to move them all the way down to our border and leave them sitting outside? They're not scared of us trying to smash them. And they wouldn't leave those kinds of toys outside for practice either."

"See, there you go – dot-dot-dot."

"Yeah, how clever of me, all you have to do is shove it in my face and I get it. I would never have thought of that on my own."

"Yes, you would. Once you got in the habit of asking yourself the right questions about *everything* your enemies do."

"So that leaves us with answer number 3?" she said tonelessly. "In three days there's going to be a really big game. A game we aren't preparing ourselves for?"

"Yes, I do believe so. But don't worry. We'll break their bones. They'll never know what hit 'em." He paused and his voice was strained and somber when he said, "Gav ..."

"I know, Jesse, I know. You take care. I'll see you next week."

When Gavrielle got home she quickly put the bloodstained bed sheet and her other laundry into the washing machine and turned it on. She found Tonia in the back yard, weeding her herb garden. "Gavrielle Rozmann, how nice to see you in the light of day. Is the world coming to an end or something?"

"Everything's fine. They just want me to stop accumulating so many vacation days," Gavrielle said and then stepped into the row next to Tonia to help.

"It's nice," Gavrielle said. "Digging in the dirt. Relaxing." Thank God Jesse sent me home. I'm so sick of thinking about double agents and sneak attacks. Que será, será.

"Yes, it is." Tonia agreed. "Never thought I'd say that, after all the hours I spent working on the kibbutz and hating every minute of it. I guess mostly because there the work was never over. By the time you finished watering or weeding the last row of trees, it was time to start over with the first. This little garden is more my speed. I just wish Amos would quit griping every time I plant anything we can't eat for dinner."

Tonia soon declared the job done. She removed her gloves and tossed them into her pail of garden implements. "Amos and I might catch whatever's showing at the Smadar tonight. Feel like coming?"

"You don't know what's on?"

Tonia held the screen door open for Gavrielle. "We're not allowed to. Neither of us. We just decide if we feel like going out – and if we do, we watch whatever Chechick's got."

"Who's Chechick?"

"You know, Arie Chechick. The owner. Owner, ticket seller, usher and projectionist."

"Oh, him. That crazy guy who's always rolling soda bottles down the aisles?"

"Don't be such a grump. He's a lovely man."

70

"If you say so. So why aren't you allowed to know what's on?"

"If we found out ahead of time, we'd never see anything. Amos would only agree to go to movies with Chuck Norris or Charles Bronson, and for me it's romantic comedies and musicals." Tonia filled the kettle with water. "This way we are both forced to broaden our horizons. I have to admit, some of those action movies are fun. And don't tell anyone, but I've heard Mr. Amrani humming tunes from *My Fair Lady*."

Gavrielle grinned as she got the lemonade out of the refrigerator and poured two glasses.

"Listen, Jesse found something out about the *Machal* volunteers," she said and told Tonia about the man in Florida.

"And you're only now telling me this! That's wonderful. So what are you going to do, write him a letter?"

"I don't have his address. Just the phone number."

"Oh, well then, come on. Let's call him right now."

Gavrielle screwed up her face. "Isn't Golda always complaining that she can't understand a word anyone says on an international call? That she has to get on an airplane if she wants to have a conversation with anyone?"

"So you'll just have to shout and keep asking him to repeat things. Ask him for his address. You ought to be able to get that much out of him, even over a bad connection."

"I suppose."

Tonia drank her lemonade and set the glass on the table with an emphatic thud. "But don't tell him why you're asking – that you think one of those guys might be your father."

"Why not?"

"You think he'll want to be responsible for getting a

71

paternity suit slapped on one of his old friends? Not the way men stick together – especially with their army buddies. Like there's some kind of sacred bond between them." She turned back to the stovetop. "I'm going to have a cup of tea. Want one?"

"No thanks." Gavrielle thought while Tonia brewed her tea. "So I'll say I'm a journalist, writing an article about them for *Maariv*."

"That's a good idea." Tonia patted her arm. "People always like publicity about the good things they've done. Let's try right now."

Gavrielle dialed the number several times, but no one picked up. She tried a few times the next morning, but still no answer. *I'll have to try again after Yom Kippur.*

Saturday, October 6, 1973

Friday afternoon Gavrielle accompanied the Amranis to the synagogue, for the *Kol Nidre* service. Sarit stood at her side, running her finger across the lines of the *Siddur,* to help Gavrielle follow. But Gavrielle was distracted. Not by worries about the war that might break out the next day, but by the best opportunity she'd had to study Amos Amrani. She couldn't stop staring at him through the latticework partition that separated the women's section from the men's. She couldn't have articulated what she found so fascinating about him. He was a building contractor – or maybe more like a glorified fix-it-upper. Gavrielle wasn't sure what he did, but did know he was just a regular guy who went to work and came home. He had an awful lot of friends, but so what? But fascinated she was. So on Erev Yom Kippur she watched him swaying in prayer and wondered if it was all tradition and habit, or if he actually believed in all this religious nonsense. *If we pray hard enough and follow all the rules, will God spare us? Yeah, right, ask Europe's Jews about that. But Amos is such a smart man. Sees the world for what it is. Nothing delusional about him. So what motivates him to wrap himself in a prayer shawl?*

After the service the whole family went for a walk together. Afterwards Gavrielle and her grandmother sat in the living room with Tonia and Amos, all of them reading the newspapers. Gavrielle went to bed early.

At 6:00 am the phone broke the peaceful silence, its deafening jangle echoing off the kitchen walls. Gavrielle woke instantly and hurried downstairs in her nightshirt. Filled with dread, she snatched the receiver off its hook.

"Gav." Jesse's voice was calm. "There's no reason to get hysterical, but they're starting to call up some of the

73

reserves. I don't know how many – some kind of compromise number worked out between Dayan and Dado. So you're going to see military vehicles in the streets, going around to synagogues with lists of names. They say it's just a precaution."

"Should I go back to where I was yesterday?"

"Yes, but you don't have to be all frantic about getting there. Are you fasting?"

"Yeah. I mean, everyone else here is."

"Well don't. I guarantee you the Chief Rabbi will be granting a matter of life and death dispensation to military personnel. So at least start drinking water. The last thing you want to be today is dehydrated."

"Okay. That stuff doesn't matter to me anyway. Were you officially notified about the call-up or did you just overhear something?"

"It was official. There's no way to keep jeeps in the streets on Yom Kippur a secret. So, yes, you can tell your family. But if this call didn't wake them up, let them sleep. If there's reason to worry, they'll know."

"You're staying up there?"

"Yes."

"Are you hearing much activity?"

"Yes."

Gavrielle sensed movement behind her and turned to see Amos standing in the doorway, bare-chested and barefooted, wearing only his jeans.

"Okay," Gavrielle said to Jesse. "I'll go out and hitch a ride."

"Listen, I've got to go," Jesse said abruptly and a metallic click cut them off.

Gavrielle replaced the receiver and turned to face Amos.

"How bad?" he asked.

"All I know is that they're starting to call up some of the reserves. As a precaution. I've got to get to Tel Aviv

74

—"

"I'll take you."

"Oh, no, I didn't mean, I wasn't asking ... There's no need. Soldiers are driving around delivering emergency call-up orders. I won't have any trouble thumbing a lift."

Amos shook his head. "My unit musters in Tel Aviv. Even if they don't want me, they'll want my truck. Go get dressed."

From the stairs she could hear him dialing the phone. When she came back down in uniform Amos was also in his, making another phone call. "An hour or so," he said and hung up. Then he opened the refrigerator, took out two bottles of water, and slipped them into his backpack.

"Do you want something to eat?" he asked and she shook her head.

Gavrielle again sensed movement behind her and turned to see Tonia staring at them.

"You haven't even been called," Tonia said to Amos and took a few steps to reach for his hand.

He kissed her forehead. "Don't start. I'm just a medic."

"That's what you said the last time."

"And here I am, aren't I? Stop looking like that. I'm a really old geezer this time. No one's sending me into battle." He put his arms around her. "I'll call you as soon as I know anything. Stop wasting energy imagining every horrible thing that could possibly happen." He pulled back and kissed her forehead again. "Come on, Gavrielle. We should get going."

"You realize we have a whole army?" Tonia continued an old argument, but her voice was weak. She knew there was no point. "Lots of young men who don't have four children."

"I'll probably be home for breakfast with them tomorrow. Let's get going," he repeated to Gavrielle.

75

He went out the back door and Gavrielle hurried to keep up with him. He stopped to pick up anyone who stuck his hand out and by the time they started down the highway to Tel Aviv eight men were crowded in the bed of the truck.

"So, are you going to give me your learned opinion of what's going on?" he asked Gavrielle.

Gavrielle hesitated only a moment. "There will be a war. Sometime today both Egypt and Syria are going to attack."

"Based on?"

She told him about the Syrians moving their Sukhoi aircraft and the trucks of ammunition the Egyptians had sent to the Suez Canal.

He let out a deep sigh. "That's no exercise." He turned to glance at Gavrielle. "What exactly do you do, anyway?"

"Nothing exciting. I'm in a small unit you've never heard of that develops monitoring technology. We design and modify some of it ourselves, but also keep track of what other countries are putting out. And we work with IAI and other companies that produce electronic equipment, make sure they understand exactly what we need." She looked over at him, her voice apologetic. "I'm small potatoes – don't get briefed on anything top secret. But I hear the rumors and see the pins on the maps."

He nodded. It took Gavrielle a few moments to get up the nerve to ask a question of her own. "Where do you go on Wednesday nights? Some kind of philosophy class?"

He looked back at her and smiled. "Not exactly. We're just a group of guys – five or six of us. We ... we get together and ... and ..."

"Like a study group?" She prompted.

"Not really. I mean, not like studying anything

specific. We used to do reserve duty together, sat around talking every evening. Most of the guys are like me – totally uneducated. I never finished elementary school. But one of them has degrees in philosophy and religious studies. It started with us razzing him one night. You know, making fun of the big philosopher, our mad professor. But after he started answering our idiotic questions we shut up and listened. Somehow he got us discussing all kinds of things – that always seemed to end up coming back to the same question – why is it so damn hard for human beings to behave themselves?"

Gavrielle shrugged. "Because they're weak and stupid."

He smiled. "Anyway, since we got to be old geezers who don't get called for reserve duty every year, a few of us who live in Jerusalem decided to keep getting together."

Gavrielle frowned for a moment. "So is that still what you talk about?"

Amos hesitated before answering. "Well, yeah, basically. Lately what we've been discussing is ... How can a man try to get to be the kind of person he wants to be. On the inside. Every religion talks about it. Every philosophy. But it's not something you can be taught. Not like a light bulb goes on and you say, 'Okay I get it,' and that's that. It's a constant struggle – for everyone. You have to work on yourself all the time. The Mad Professor gives us something to read every week, but that's just to give us something to think about." He took his eyes off the road to glance at Gavrielle. "The thing is, you know you've got zero chance of ever actually becoming a virtuous being. The most you can hope for is some better behavior ... and moments of clarity every now and then."

Gavrielle turned and stared at this man who was full of surprises. Then, embarrassed, she lowered her eyes to his dark caramel-colored hand on the gear shift. After a long while she said, "Thank you for telling me that. I know I'm way too nosy."

"That's your job, isn't it? Sticking your nose in? You should come with me some time. After all this is over."

He switched on the radio, but there was no broadcast. Neither of them spoke again until they neared Tel Aviv and Amos asked, "Where do I drop you?"

"The Kirya."

Before she got out of the truck Amos made a fist and mock punched her upper arm. "Try not to screw up too much," he said.

"You try not to kill some poor guy who gets stuck with you instead of a doctor."

"See you." He handed her a bottle of water.

"See you." She climbed out and watched until his taillights disappeared.

There were a few other vehicles on the streets but the city was still quiet. Gavrielle didn't enter the base immediately, but wandered up the street, trying to do as Jesse had said – relish the last moments of normalcy. Peacefulness. She longed for a cup of coffee, but of course everything was closed. After walking for close to an hour, trying to prepare herself for what was to come, she went back to the Kirya and descended into the end of normal.

She set her backpack next to the desk she had used on Wednesday, went to the tiny kitchen corner to make a cup of instant coffee, and on her way back peeked into Colonel Shaul's office. It was empty. At 9:30 he appeared.

"You're here. Good. You work with people at IAI, don't you?"

"Yes."

"You know any of their home phone numbers?"

"Yes. A few."

"Good. We need one of their business jets to take someone to Europe. Today."

"Where in Europe?"

"Wherever there's a connection to Washington."

"Who's the passenger?"

"Dinitz." He referred to Israel's ambassador to the United States. "He's here sitting *shiva* for his father, but we need him back in Washington. Not just for consultations. We need him to deliver a shopping list. You have to make sure the people at IAI know how urgent it is."

Gavrielle's IAI contacts had nothing to do with business jets, but would know how to get in touch with people who did. It took a long hour on the phone, apologizing and explaining to startled people why she was disturbing them on Yom Kippur, then waiting for them to bicycle or, if necessary, drive to the homes of other people who had disconnected their phones. Finally, someone called back to inform her that Dinitz was scheduled for a late afternoon flight to Rome, in time to make a connecting flight to DC. She reported that to Colonel Shaul and spent the next lonely hours translating the sheaf of documents he handed her, from Hebrew to English and vice versa.

Later Colonel Shaul came in and placed a sandwich on her desk. "Eat," he said and rifled through the documents she had already translated. He apparently found the one he wanted and perused it for a moment. "I see why Jesse thinks he's lucky to have you around," he said and turned to go out.

"I'm not finished with that yet," Gavrielle said to his back. "I haven't checked the spelling."

"It's ready enough. Get the rest of them this unready, as fast as you can."

Later he came back in with a sense of urgency. He reached up to the old RCA console radio on one of the shelves and switched it on. A siren began wailing from its speaker, rising and falling. Only then did Gavrielle notice the actual siren outside, weakly resonating in the stairwell. A voice said: "You are listening to the Army Radio of the Israel Defense Forces. The IDF spokesman has announced that today at around 2 pm Egyptian and Syrian forces launched an attack in Sinai and the Golan Heights. Our forces are acting against the aggressors. Our correspondents have reported that due to the activity of Syrian aircraft on the Golan Heights, sirens have been heard throughout the country. These are real sirens."

"Already," she whispered. "The Angel said it would be at 6 in the evening."

Colonel Shaul looked as ill as she felt. He wordlessly strode out of office, and she didn't see him again for hours.

Suddenly desperate for daylight and fresh air, Gavrielle raced up the stairs, gasping for breath by the time she reached the top. The world was still there. Everything looked the same. But the siren started wailing again, sounding even more sinister in the sunlight than it had underground. The few people in the streets were shouting to one another.

She braced her back against a wall, breathing deeply, remembering Jesse's voice. "When you're under a lot of pressure you have to force yourself to block it all out. There's nothing else in the world, nothing matters. Nothing but the job in front of you. The one you've been assigned. No matter how insignificant it may seem, you work on it as if it's the most important thing you've ever done. You do that one job. And then the next one. And then the next one. Your mind is clear of everything else. Other people get paid to worry. You get

80

paid to track radar pulses or whatever it is you're doing. That's all you think about. As if the whole country depends on your getting it right. Because you never know when it might."

She went back down the stairs and visited the ladies room to splash water on her face, before returning to her office. There she arranged the papers on her desk in order of urgency, drank a glass of water, and went back to work. Later Colonel Shaul moved her to another office and sat her in front of a monitor. Listening to shrill electronic beeps was usually her least favorite part of her job, but today she was grateful for the headphones. Nothing did a better job of blocking out the rest of the world. Hours later she felt a hand on her shoulder. She removed the headphones and looked up, surprised to find the desks on either side of her unoccupied.

Colonel Shaul stood at her side, red-eyed. "Outpost 104 ..." His voice was barely audible as he mumbled the code name for the listening post on Mount Hermon, where Jesse was.

"What?" Gavrielle was paralyzed for a moment, before she stood and grabbed his shoulders. "What? What about it?"

"It's gone." He looked like a lost child.

She stared at him as if he'd lost his mind. "Stop acting stupid. Tell me what happened."

"Everything's gone to shit. We've lost communication with the Hermon. And in the Sinai ... the Egyptians ... they walked right past the Bar Lev line. Those Sagger missiles the Russians gave them ... they're incinerating our tanks. Dozens of them. They generate so much heat, the hydraulic fluid in the tanks bursts into flames when they hit. Nobody is getting out alive."

"What about Outpost 104? What have you heard about the Hermon?"

He shook his head and began weeping. She took the few steps to the door, shut it, and returned to stand in front of him. "You've got to get it together," she said softly, her voice kind, even when she asked, "Do I need to slap you?"

He quickly regained his composure. "No, no. I'm alright."

She handed him the bottle of water from her desk, but he put up a hand.

"Drink," she ordered and he obeyed. "Now take a few deep breaths."

"Okay. I'm okay." He couldn't meet her eyes.

"I'm no one to judge you," Gavrielle said quietly. "We all panic. When the sirens went off, I had to run outside to get some air. Thought I was going to pass out. Please, tell me what you know about 104."

He pulled himself up to stand taller. "It started at two o'clock. Heavy artillery fire. An hour or so later Syrian helicopters landed commandos south of the lower ski lift. As far as we can guess, there was also infantry that came in by foot, over from the Syrian Hermon. We took a lot of casualties, but no one knows how many. No names. It was chaos. Right now we're guessing that anyone who survived the initial breach is holed up in the bunker, waiting for us to counterattack."

"Okay. So, that's where Jesse is." Her mind raced frantically. "That outpost has all kinds of tunnels underneath it. Plenty of places for them to hide until we take it back," she said, mostly to herself. Then she looked up at Beni Shaul. "Listen, until this is all over, I don't want to hear anything else about him. Not unless it's that he's out and safe. As far as I'm concerned, that's what he is. Safe. And you stop underestimating our guys in the Sinai. They'll find a way to deal with the Saggers. They always think of something." She gave his

82

arm a light squeeze and went back to pull the door open.

"Thank you for the information, Colonel Shaul." She saluted him.

I wonder if this is what a moment of clarity feels like, Gavrielle thought, as she turned back to her desk to glue herself to her monitor. People with responsibility sometimes make bad decisions. And then other people die. Lots of people. When she no longer felt able to concentrate she found an empty cot and took a short nap. When she awoke, Colonel Shaul assigned her to communications security – monitoring internal IDF communications for possible security breaches. While doing so, she heard a report that ten Israeli soldiers had escaped from Outpost 104 and reached Israeli tanks. Jesse's name was not on the list, but she put that out of her mind. Too many of the people around her were dissolving into puddles of anxiety. She was determined not to be another one.

The news from both fronts constantly worsened. Someone in another office began shouting and heaving books against the wall. Many of Gavrielle's colleagues sat with their heads in their hands. She blocked them all out and lost track of time. She continued to take occasional ten minute catnaps, but mostly stayed at her desk. Then, on her way back from the ladies room, she heard someone mention what day of the week it was – Tuesday. She blinked. *Have I really been down here for three days?* She looked around. The faces she saw were desperate. Depressed. Terrified. There was a loud crash – a radar console being smashed against the wall by another distraught officer. Something terrible must be happening. She went to Colonel Shaul's office. He was at his desk marking-up a read-out. Calm and composed.

"What happened?" she asked and he studied her, as if weighing how much he should say. "I want to know,"

83

she said. "Tell me."

He motioned for her to close the door and sit down. "Rumor has it that a short while ago Dayan asked for – and received – permission to have nuclear weapons readied for launch."

"Oh God."

"He also had a bit of a break-down – muttering about the Third Temple falling. Went on about preparing for a last stand, fighting to the last bullet, how we have to arm the civilian population with antitank weapons. Anyone capable of holding a rifle must be mobilized at once. The enemy will soon be in the streets of Haifa and Tel Aviv, but there can be no surrender. I guess he was in really bad shape. His performance was a disaster and, unfortunately, everyone down here seems to have heard about it."

She sat in silence, her face blank. Shut your stupid mouth up. I don't want to hear this.

"Another officer on the floor beneath us also broke down. Literally collapsed on the floor, like he was having some kind of conniption. Some of the men saw it. That's why everyone out there looks the way they do. But, listen," he said, leaning forward, earnest. "It's bad. I won't say it's not. For the past 72 hours we've lost every battle, taken hundreds of casualties, and I've lost count of how many of our tanks and planes they've destroyed. But it's not doomsday yet. Not by a long shot. I see things starting to turn around. You were right about our tank commanders – they've figured out a way to deal with the creepy-crawlies."

"The what?"

"That's what they call the Egyptian grunts with Saggers. They're everywhere. Bury themselves in the sand, waiting for a tank to get close enough. Then they stand up in their beige camouflage, like they just materialized out of nowhere. Like a bunch of lizards

84

with lethal weapons. But they still have to direct the missile with a joy stick. So now, before the tanks move forward, they call for a massive concentration of artillery fire in front of them. Then they zigzag back and forth, shooting into the ground around them and kicking up all kinds of dust. That way the Egyptians can't see *us* through all that sand. The tank commander takes out the creepy-crawly and pushes forward. So that advice you gave me – repeat it to yourself and don't let the panicked expressions and brawling out there get you down."

"Yessir."

"I mean it. Things have quieted down a bit. At the moment I think the fighting in here is fiercer than on either front. And we're loading those nuclear warheads onto Jericho missiles and F-4 aircraft right out in the open, making sure Kissinger will see them and tell the Kremlin, who will tell Assad and Sadat."

"Yessir." She stood and saluted.

"Bad as it is, we're pulling ourselves together. No bullshit."

She rushed to the bathroom and vomited. Not from fear for her own safety. She wasn't thinking about that. Or about Jesse. Or Amos. She was newly sickened by the magnitude of the responsibility people had to take upon themselves. *Nuclear weapons. God.*

A new stack of documents had appeared on her desk, with a note telling her to retrieve the hard data from them and put it into a useful format. She finished that task and took the resulting tables to Colonel Shaul.

"I would like permission to go home, sir. I need to shower and change."

"And sleep. Take as long as you need."

Amos wasn't home – at least his truck wasn't parked anywhere on the street. Gavrielle went through the back door into the kitchen. It was empty. The radio was on, the volume low.

"It's me," she called out loudly, not wanting Tonia to hear her moving about and come rushing out, bitterly disappointed that it wasn't Amos. Gavrielle walked down the short hall to their bedroom and saw that the door was closed. Tonia must be sleeping.

Then she peeked into her grandmother's room and found Nella snoring softly on her bed. She climbed the stairs and heard the children's voices. All four were in the twins' room, playing Monopoly on the floor. They had the light on, since all the windows in the house had been covered with thick black paper, as per the orders of the Home Guard.

"Hi guys."

"Were you at the war?" Coby asked.

"No. I was in Tel Aviv, doing things to help the soldiers who are at the war. That's why I have to go back as soon as I've gotten a little sleep."

"Okay. We'll be quiet," Nurit said and then proceeded to bombard her with questions.

"Stop bothering her," Sarit ordered.

"You never bother me." Gavrielle stroked the little girl's hair. "But I really have to get some sleep."

She fled from the room, stood under the hot shower for a long while, and collapsed in bed. When she woke it was eerily dark. She opened her window but there were no streetlights and ghostly cars glided slowly by, their headlights off. She lay in bed for a long while. Now she could hear the children's voices coming from downstairs and the radio was louder. She shivered, imagining enemy tanks in the streets. *That's not going to happen.* She forced herself up and pulled on a clean, but wrinkled, uniform. She rolled her dirty clothes up, tentatively sniffed them and issued a loud "pee-yew." Too embarrassed to put them in the hamper, she tucked them under her arm to take downstairs.

From the stairs she could already smell the Yemenite soup simmering on the stovetop. She made a detour to shove her clothes into the washing machine and then found Tonia and Nella at the kitchen table. Gavrielle bent to kiss her grandmother and Tonia rose to give her a lengthy embrace, fretting that she'd hardly said goodbye.

"Sit," she ordered Gavrielle and set a bowl of the thick soup in front of her.

"How are you, Nanna?" Gavrielle asked her grandmother, patting her hand.

"I'm fine. Getting to spend a lot of time with the children. They're so bored without school, they'll even play cards and work puzzles with an old lady."

"Sorry if I'm slurping," Gavrielle said. "I didn't realize how starving I am. Has Amos been home?"

Tonia shook her head. "Some guy called. Said Amos couldn't get to a phone, but asked him to tell me he was all right."

"What are they saying on the news?" Gavrielle asked.

A loud male voice boomed outside. "Hey lady ... on the third floor. Turn off the lights."

"The Home Guard," Tonia said, as she sat and rested her chin on one fist. "They drive around all evening, shouting like that, enforcing the black-out. Golda was on TV the first night. I don't remember much of what she said. It was all vague. The Arabs attacked and we are pushing them back. They've stopped showing the regular evening news. There's just one army guy, giving a summary of what happened that day. The radio seems to spend most of its time telling us what to do. I don't pay much attention to any of it. But I leave it on, in case there's an air raid and the siren in the neighborhood fails to sound. So how are you?"

"Okay. Tired." Gavrielle raised her head from the soup to look into Tonia's eyes. "Everything's going to be all right. They caught us off-guard, but we're starting to turn it around. It's good that you don't listen to the news all the time. Try not to worry. We're going to be okay." Gavrielle believed what she said – regarding the country as a whole – but knew those words offered little comfort to Tonia. No one could make any promises about the safety of any particular soldier.

"All of the men are gone ... A lot of the shops are closed." Tonia noticed Gavrielle's empty bowl and stood to refill it. Then she smiled. "The radio is announcing all the babies that are born. So all the new fathers who aren't near a phone will know."

Gavrielle smiled back. "That's nice. I would never have thought of that."

"Oh, there was one big announcement," Tonia said. "Nixon is finally going to start airlifting equipment to us. Replace what we've lost."

"Yes, I know. It will take a bit longer to get organized, but El Al planes are already delivering some of it."

"This is a good country," Nella mumbled to no one in particular. "We are safe here. We take care of each other."

Four days later Gavrielle came home again. She showered and was in the kitchen with Tonia when Amos pushed the screen door open with a loud bang.

"Oh my God, Amos." Tonia threw her arms around him.

He picked her up and spun her around, saying, "I told you so. Told you they'd send me home." Then he patted Gavrielle on the shoulder and went to the bottom of the stairs. "Any bratty kids up there?" They all charged down shouting, "*Abba, Abba.*"

"Are you home for good?" Tonia asked from behind him.

"Yes. Well, you know, that can always change, but as of now, it's for good. They've got no use for me. Just for my truck."

"Where have you been?"

"Sharm el Sheikh."

"In the Sinai?" Tonia paled.

"Don't worry, the most dangerous thing about it was the flight down. They loaded us into this decrepit old Dakota, looked like it was going to fall apart during take-off."

"What do you want to do first – eat or shower?" Tonia asked.

"Shower. But I'm starving."

Amos showered, ate, and answered an onslaught of his children's questions. Then Tonia took the children upstairs to get ready for bed, and Amos went outside for a cigarette. Gavrielle followed him.

"What was it really like?" she asked.

He placed his back flat against the wall and closed his eyes for a moment. "They scared the shit out of us when we got down to Sharm. Assembled us, passed out weapons, and pretty much informed us that we had 48 hours to live. That was how long before they expected 5,000 Egyptian soldiers to come marching down the coastal road. They thought there was a slight chance they might cut inland by Abu Rudeis, try to outflank our forces that way, but that they were more likely to try to make it all the way down to Sharm and take the airfield, thinking that could force us to pull out of Sinai.

"Then they gave out ammunition. Twenty rounds each, and there were 120 of us, so you do the math. We'd each have to kill two Egyptians with every bullet, and there'd still be some of them leftover. There was also a mounted Browning with a thousand rounds and some grenades and mortars, but still. The next day some of the religious guys got out of their foxholes, started looking around for debris they could use to

89

build a Succah. This one officer, real idiot, gets on them, yelling about how he's going to have them court-martialed. 'Well, you'd better hurry up about it, jerk-off,' they said, 'since by this time tomorrow we're all going to be dead.'"

Gavrielle grinned and then asked, "So what, the Egyptians turned off at Abu Rudeis?"

"I don't know. Maybe. All I know is that they never showed up at Sharm. There was one dogfight – our two Phantoms took out some MiGs. And they bombed the airfield. Took out the whole command post." He hung his head. "That was horrible. Thirty-two dead, two of them girls. That's why I'm here. They sent me back on the plane, escorting some of the wounded who couldn't be moved before today."

"Didn't you have any anti-aircraft missiles?"

"Yeah. Hawks. But apparently the Egyptians had radar-detecting bombs. That's what one of the guys said, anyway. You know more about those things than I do. He said the minute we heard them coming and switched our radar on, those bombs just followed the radar laser down to the command post."

"Shit." She remained silent for a minute. "I don't remember hearing that the runways down there were out."

"They aren't. The planes that went after the runways came in too low, so the bombs hit before they had time to go live. They never exploded, just fell and made a bunch of potholes that we fixed right away. But the water pipes are gone."

"What'd you do for food?"

"Truck came around, but all they had to give us was eggs. Trays and trays of eggs." He shook his head. "The Egyptians shot some of their FROG missiles at us. There's nothing you can do – just stand there and watch the bright yellow streak across the sky, coming right at you. Hit pretty close to us. Massive explosion. I don't know how to describe it." He dropped his cigarette butt and squashed it out. "You gotta go back soon?"

"Tomorrow morning. But tonight I intend to get a full night's sleep." She rose to go in.

"Gavrielle."

"What?"

"It's nice having you around. You're good to talk to."

"So are you ... and I couldn't help thinking before – when I woke up – what it would have been like now – if it was still just me and my grandmother. It's so different, coming home to a house that a whole family lives in."

She turned again and stopped again. "Can I ask you a question?"

"No promises. Let's hear the question." He lit another cigarette.

She flushed. "Is it true you were in the Irgun?" she asked timidly.

"You get right to the point." He grinned. "It's always the quiet ones."

"I know it's none of my business. But were you?"

"So I'm told." He put his head back and blew a short string of smoke rings.

"Did you believe the rumors about my grandfather?"

"About passing information to the British, turning in other Jews?"

Gavrielle nodded.

Amos shrugged. "I heard them and Tonia had me ask around, but I never saw any proof. I couldn't even find anyone in the Irgun who'd ever met him. A few Haganah guys I asked said the same. So I can't see where he'd have gotten any information to sell to the Brits."

"But you can't say for sure."

"Well, there is one really strong piece of evidence in

91

his favor. We never grabbed him to interrogate him. Get other names. If anyone seriously believed those rumors, that's what we would've done. Anyway, why get yourself all stressed over that? You're just starting your life. Focus on the present. Leave all the dwelling on ancient history to us old fogies."

Sunday, October 21, 1973

When Gavrielle returned to the pit after spending Shabbat at home, Colonel Shaul called her into his office, where he thanked her for all her work and told her he was releasing her back to her unit at Glilot.

She felt a tinge of anger – *Would it have killed you to tell me that on Friday and save me shlepping back here?* But she quelled it. What was one more bus ride? Anyway, she couldn't say she was surprised. A ceasefire was being negotiated and things had been quiet. In the pit anyway. Outside, the public was increasingly enraged, as the lists of casualties were published and more soldiers told their stories. In the corridors of power, politicians and generals pointed their fingers at one another.

"Thank you, sir," she said and saluted. Annoyed by the formality of his tone, she gave it back in kind. "It was my privilege to serve." She turned on her heel, quickly retrieved her backpack, and climbed back up to the fresh air.

Back in Glilot, she walked down the corridor to her old office. There she found an unfamiliar officer sitting behind the second desk that had been squeezed next to hers. She pulled herself to attention and saluted.

He returned the salute but then waved his hand, as if dismissing that formality. "You must be Rozmann. I'm the temporary CO. Giora Levi."

"Good to meet you, sir."

The office had been cramped enough. Now she had to turn sideways to squeeze between the wall and the side of her desk.

"Sorry for the intrusion. I didn't know how long Shaul was going to keep you," Giora Levi said. "And I didn't want to take over Braverman's office."

Gavrielle blinked. Jesse Braverman. She'd rarely used his family name.

93

She spent the next morning at her desk, headphones on, monitoring signals and struggling to ignore the constant ringing of Giora Levi's phone. Then something made her push the earphones aside and eavesdrop. He said little as he listened to the voice at the other end of the line and hung up, looking ashen.

The effort to control his voice and facial expression was obvious as he turned to Gavrielle. "Our forces have recaptured Outpost 104. They discovered a large grave, where the Syrians buried our casualties. Jesse was one of them."

"They're sure? No doubt?"

"They're sure."

Gavrielle sat frozen and said nothing. All this time she'd tried to pretend there was a sliver of hope – he could have been hiding or taken prisoner – but she'd known he was dead. After a long silence she carefully set the headphones on the desk, stood, and left the room. She walked down the corridor to the storage closet, took three flattened cartons back to Jesse's office, quickly assembled them, and began packing. She opened one drawer after another, setting aside all property of the IDF. She did not pause to study the personal items before shoving them into the boxes. She became vaguely aware of Giora Levi standing hesitantly in the doorway, but ignored him, relieved when that hovering presence retreated. She plucked the three personal photographs off the walls, placed them face down, on top of everything else, and taped the cartons closed. Then she went to the secretary's office and asked her to have them delivered to Shana Braverman.

"Your office is ready for you, sir," Gavrielle said to Giora Levi and then turned to go get a cup of coffee.

By the time she returned, the second desk had disappeared from her office. She closed the door and sat staring at the wall in silence. Then there was a quick

94

rap and one of her colleagues stuck his head in, to inform her that the ceasefire had been signed.

Gavrielle didn't attend Jesse's funeral. Nor did she pay his wife a condolence call. To do so would have acknowledged the fact that she would never again hear his voice, nor see that smile of his.

January 1974

Gavrielle did not dislike Giora Levi. She was indifferent to him – followed his orders but otherwise ignored him. She had grown weary of saluting and endless meetings. And far more weary of the dismal reality she had to accept – she was doomed to be a lousy guardian angel. There would always be people she failed to protect. They would die. The longer she stayed in the army, the more responsibility she would get. More people would die as a result of the mistakes she made.

She spent hours in her silent office, staring at the wall, knowing she needed a change. *But what? How?* This was all she had ever prepared herself to do. Last month, in a moment of weakness, she had signed on for another year. Now she cursed herself. *No, grow up. That wasn't a moment of weakness. It was your one moment of strength, of sanity. Do doctors stop practicing medicine just because they can't save every life? Alright, so you miss Jesse terribly, but quitting the army isn't going to change that. He'd be terribly disappointed in you. You're behaving like a five-year-old.* But she couldn't stop the argument from playing over and over in her mind. No matter which way she thought she'd decided, it brought her no peace.

She did have one plan for escaping this dilemma – worry about something else for a while. The way the IDF prides itself on being sensitive to family issues, I'm sure they'd give me time off to go look for my father. All I have to do is ask. But if I'm serious about that, I should go to America. Go talk to the guy in Florida in person. Even if he doesn't have anyone named Lou on his list, I could ask him how he goes about finding these people. But I'd be all alone. And I might find my father and wish I hadn't. He'll probably be appalled to learn of my existence. Not to mention his wife.

So she always pushed the idea aside, and then felt diminished for doing so. How many times had she heard Tonia say to her kids, "I'll never be upset with you because you tried something and failed. But if you don't even try? You'd better not let me find out about that." *Why am I such a coward?*

After a few days of non-stop, bone-chilling rain, the sun came out and Gavrielle decided it was time to pay Jesse a visit. She got the location of his grave from the secretary and took the bus to the Yarkon cemetery. She'd always thought placing flowers on a grave was a ridiculous custom – a racket started by the flower growers – but she sighed and bought a ridiculously fancy bouquet from a vendor outside the cemetery.

A woman was standing near what Gavrielle thought must be Jesse's grave and when she turned around, Gavrielle saw it was Shana. Gavrielle approached her slowly and held out a hand.

"My name is Gavrielle. I worked –"

Shana ignored the hand and embraced Gavrielle, crushing the flowers. "I know who you are. Jesse talked about you all the time. I remember you from our wedding."

Shana took a step back and Gavrielle said, "I'm sorry I didn't come to the funeral. Or the *shiva*. I ... I couldn't ... I ..." Gavrielle burst into loud sobs. "I'm sorry. I'm sorry." She took a tissue from her pocket.

"Shh." Shana rubbed Gavrielle's back and then took the flowers and placed them on the grave.

When Shana stood back up, her coat came open and Gavrielle grew still, staring at her swollen belly. "I didn't know," Gavrielle said.

"Jesse didn't tell you?"

"No. I was thinking about that on the bus ride here – how he knew everything about me and I hardly knew

97

anything about him. Sort of like it must be with a therapist. I sometimes wondered if you ever suspected that he and I ... I mean we worked together for so long ... But Jesse wasn't like that."

"I know he wasn't," Shana said. "I never suspected that. He thought of you like a little sister. Spent a lot of time worrying about you."

"So I guess you know everything about me too?"

"I suppose so." Shana took a few steps off the grass, onto the gravel pathway. Gavrielle followed and Shana turned back to face her. "You hadn't cried for him until now."

"How do you know that?"

"It took me a long time too. I didn't want to go to the funeral either. My parents had to drag me. It's like, if you don't see the grave, he isn't really gone."

"But he is gone." Gavrielle's voice broke and the two women fell back into one another's embrace, crying.

When they regained their composure, Shana asked, "Why don't you come home with me?"

While she'd been weeping, Gavrielle's thoughts had raced ahead. I promise, Jesse, whatever she needs, however I can help, I'll be a friend to Shana. She'll never be alone. I'll babysit, help with the grocery shopping, anything I can. I promise. I won't let you down.

"My sisters are coming over soon," Shana said. "I'm sure they'd love to meet you. And my parents live right next door."

Stupid. Could you be any more pathetic, thinking she needs anything from you? She has a family. A real family. She's not asking you to come home with her because she's lonely. She's asking out of pity for you – the poor little orphan girl.

"No. Thanks. I'd love to meet them, but I have to get back to work."

"You've been awfully quiet lately," Amos said to Gavrielle one Wednesday evening after dinner. "Feel like coming with me tonight?"

"To your meeting with the Mad Professor?" She shook her head. "No thanks. I wouldn't know what to say about the kind of stuff you guys talk about."

"You don't have to say anything. You can just listen."

"No thanks. You're all guys. And you all know each other. It would be weird for me to come."

"No, it wouldn't. We're always saying we could use a feminine perspective."

"You should go," Tonia said. "It's not very cold out tonight. If nothing else, it'll be a nice walk."

Gavrielle thought for a long moment, not relishing another evening alone in her room. So why not? "Okay. I'll come. As long as I don't have to talk."

"Good. Come on, let's go."

"Don't you have to call and tell him I'm coming?"

"They don't have a phone. Anyway, he doesn't need advance notice in order to set out another chair."

Neither she nor Amos had much to say on the way, other than to admire the enormous moon.

Lior – the Mad Professor – looked nothing like the scruffy Einstein she had imagined. He was a slim thirty-something with a crew-cut, wearing jeans and a sweatshirt. Gavrielle and Amos were last to arrive and he quickly introduced her.

"Make yourself comfortable, Gavrielle," Lior said, extending his arm toward the armchair he had vacated and pulling a straight back chair into the circle for himself. The guys each nudged their chairs aside to make room and then said their name and welcomed her.

"Lately we've been discussing the general dilemma of how a man who wants to think of himself as moral should behave in an immoral world." Lior turned to face her. "Would you like to ask anything?"

She nodded shyly, surprised at herself. "Do you have a definition of 'moral' that you all agree upon?"

He shook his head. "I'm sure we could come fairly close, if we tried to formulate one, but that's not the point. Each of us must try to clear all the common wisdom rubbish out of our minds and define for *ourselves* what is moral and what is not. What kind of man – or woman – we want to be. For the purpose of discussion, let's assume you've already achieved your own inner vision of what is good and what is bad, but you find yourself living in an environment that behaves according to an entirely different set of values."

Gavrielle nodded, looking around the circle at the men. Two of them wore yarmulkes, like Amos. The other three did not.

Lior followed her gaze and said, "None of us feel the need to choose between religious belief and reason. The two are not incompatible. But that is a topic we can leave to another evening."

He looked away and she was grateful that he no longer paid any special attention to her. The group continued its discussion from the previous week. She tried to concentrate, but her mind constantly wandered. Later she remembered only a few sentences. "Truth doesn't change because we find it inconvenient … We can't stop searching for truth simply because we know we will never find it … Look at all the wonderful things the search for truth has given to mankind."

"So," Amos said after the meeting broke up and they parted ways with the others. "That wasn't so bad, was it?"

"No. It was interesting. I'd like to come again, if they don't mind. If only for that killer cheesecake his wife served." She grinned. "But I did find it difficult to follow. I don't know why, but it was hard for me to focus."

"You've got a lot on your mind and it's all new. Plus your brain's probably preoccupied with trying to put the rest of us into boxes. Okay, so that guy's a lefty and the way that one likes to talk, he must be a teacher. But you'll get used to us."

"Does Tonia ever come?"

"Nope." He stopped to light a cigarette. "That's a rule. Not 'No Women.' Just 'No Wives.'"

She nodded. "So you can speak freely, without risking an argument at home?"

"I suppose so."

"And you feel you can speak freely in front of me?"

"Why not?" He shrugged. "You haven't nagged me about anything yet."

She was surprised to find herself looking forward to Wednesday evenings.

April 1974

Gavrielle's unit was part of a renewed effort to improve the security of Israel's northern border. So far that security consisted of a fence topped with barbed wire and what was called in Hebrew the *tishtush* – a wide strip of dusty ground that ran parallel to the fence, but far enough from it so that no one but Superman could have leapt over both without leaving tracks. Several times each day a vehicle dragged a large rolling brush over the dust, making it easy for the next patrol to spot any new footprints. Knowing how long ago the *tishtush* had last been brushed, they knew how far away they had to set up a perimeter in order to capture the infiltrators. It was a simple system and surprisingly effective, but the IDF always wanted more and better.

So they were trying to enhance the quality of CCTV transmissions and analysis and also looking into ground surveillance radar systems. But Giora Levi had decided they must first acquire hands-on experience with even the most basic equipment. He took Gavrielle and three of her colleagues up to the Lebanese border, where they each had to install one of four cameras, while competing with one another to find the best way to disguise them and hide and protect the cables.

Once the system was set-up, they were to evaluate it from the point of view of the operator – a policy that had originally been instituted by Jesse. "Getting the device to do what you want it to is the easy part," he'd always said. "It's the human beings who are unpredictable. It's not just how the thing works – it's how it will be *used*." So Gavrielle and the others had spent two nights working shifts at the monitors, learning what it was like to stare at a totally boring screen for four or six hours.

"So," Giora Levi asked at their next meeting, "what brilliant ideas have you come up with for keeping them alert, or at least awake?"

"How about a big old lion popping up and roaring on the screen?" one of the guys had suggested with a smart-alecky grin.

"You tell me how about that," Giora said, unamused. "The most obvious solution is to make them prove they're awake by pressing a certain letter on their keyboard at a set interval. But try to think of something less boring."

"How about we flash them a trivia question every 15 minutes and let the computer keep track of how many they get right?" another colleague suggested. "Winner for the night gets a six-pack."

Gavrielle smiled. "That's creative thinking. But ..." She paused to calculate. "That's close to 3000 questions a month. Are you volunteering to write them?"

"And that sort of thing would be too much of a distraction," Giora said. "I can imagine some operators spending the night searching through encyclopedias and dictionaries, while the entire membership of the PLO strolls across their screen. But that is the kind of thinking we want."

It was obvious that all the operators should be together in one room, so they could converse, cover for each other's bathroom breaks, and notice if anyone fell asleep. But the small base they were at consisted almost entirely of tents. Its single wooden structure that could house the computers consisted of a long corridor lined by two rows of tiny offices. So on the night of April 11 Gavrielle was spending her third night alone in one of those tiny offices, staring at her screen.

There weren't any squawks from the radio. It was the sound of people running down the corridor, shouting, that woke her up. She lifted her head from her crossed forearms and turned in her chair, groggy, wondering where she was. The voices grew louder, frantic. At once she understood. She had fallen asleep on duty and something terrible had happened. She turned to scowl at her monitor, but there was no gaping hole in the fence. Nothing seemed to have changed. A brief feeling of relief washed over her. *It's all right. Nothing happened that I missed, and no one knows I fell asleep.* She strained to understand what the voices outside were yelling and caught a few words. "Infiltrators ... Border Police ... Trackers."

She bent over, head between her knees, and vomited on the floor. She sat up and was wiping her mouth with a tissue when Giora Levi burst through the door. He barked a loud but incoherent order.

"Where are they?" she asked.

"Trackers think they're heading for Route 89." His voice regained some control. "Get northern command on the radio. See what they know." He turned and hurried down the corridor.

"Route 89?" She stared at the spot where he had been standing. That was much farther east. Nowhere near their sector. *It really isn't my fault. It couldn't possibly be my fault.*

Not that it mattered. Her initial, brief sense of relief had dissipated. What difference did it make, where they'd crossed the border? She'd still fallen asleep on duty. It *could* have been in her sector. *I am irresponsible. Not to be trusted.* Feeling ill, she used a sheet of yesterday's newspaper to clean up most of her vomit and chucked it out the window, which she left open in hopes of dispelling the smell. Then she went outside to pour a bottle of water over her head and wash out her mouth.

She was in no hurry to contact northern command, sure that they had more urgent things to do than keep Giora Levi in the loop. She did eventually speak to them and was told there was a situation in the small town of Kiryat Shmona, but no details were available. The impatient voice hurriedly gave Gavrielle the radio frequency over which updates would be broadcast. Gavrielle passed it on to Giora and the others and then there seemed to be nothing for her to do. They all sat watching their monitors, listening to the radio, making and receiving phone calls, trying to look busy. But they knew they were useless. It was afternoon before they learned what had happened.

No one could say how the terrorists had managed to cross the border undetected, only that they'd done it early in the morning, with the foggy, rainy weather on their side. They walked the long distance to Kiryat Shmona and broke into a school to hide. The assumption was that they'd planned to remain there until the children arrived and take them hostage. But it was Passover vacation and no one came.

So they changed plans and entered a nearby residential building, shot the first people they came upon, and continued to the building next door, where they decided to work their way up from floor to floor, kicking in doors and shooting everyone they found. It seemed to go on forever, until the IDF and police finally began shooting and one of their bullets set off the explosives the terrorists were carrying, killing them.

The attack took the lives of sixteen civilians – half of them children – and two soldiers. It was a shocking disaster for the IDF – the first time terrorists had entered a town, the first time they'd gotten so far from the border, and the first time they'd killed indiscriminately. They'd made no attempt to take hostages, and seemed to have had no plan for their own escape.

For the next two days Gavrielle barely spoke – only as was necessary to do her job. Finally she went to Giora's office. He appeared relieved when she asked for some time off. On her way to the Amranis' she bought all the newspapers that were still carrying reports of the attack. She said a polite hello to Tonia, made a cup of coffee, and took it up to her room. She stayed there for hours, reading the reports over and over, the radio on at low volume. One of the photographs haunted her – a close-up of the stunned face of nine-year-old Iris Chitrit. The little girl had been in her living room when the door was kicked in and two men began firing at Iris and her mother, older sister, and two little brothers. When the man nearest her paused to change the clip in his weapon, Iris grabbed her five-year-old brother by the hand and ran to one of the bedrooms. But he broke away from her and turned to run back, crying for his mommy.

When the shooting finally stopped, Iris opened the bedroom door and had to step over the blood-soaked bodies of both her brothers. In the living room her mother and sister were still barely alive, lying in pools of blood. Iris knelt over her mother, who with great effort managed to whisper, "Get away from here. Go hide," before she died.

Who fires an automatic weapon at a five-year-old? What kind of human being is capable of such a thing? Gavrielle wiped her eyes and blew her nose. Thank God Iris's father had already gone to work. At least she still has him. How could we have let something like this happen? Trackers picked up their trail, but they still made it all the way into that apartment building. We're supposed to be better than that. We have to be better than that. How can people live in a country where any minute some maniac with a machine gun might burst through the door?

Gavrielle put the newspaper down and turned on her side, curled up. She'd never felt this despondent, not even when eleven of Israel's Olympic athletes had been murdered in Munich – and the games had gone on as if nothing happened.

Somebody really screwed up. If it was me, I'd want to kill myself. How could you go on living, with the image of that little girl in your head? Iris got up that morning, so happy there was no school that day, maybe fighting with her little brothers, maybe helping them get dressed. And then a monster came and they were all gone. What's worse – never having a family, like me – or having one slaughtered before your eyes? How do college students in America and Europe demonstrate in support of the PLO? How do they convince themselves that they are different from the Nazis, killing every Jew they can get in their sights, even little children?

Gavrielle conducted long imaginary conversations with Jesse. If he'd still been alive, she would have confessed to him about falling asleep on duty – how she deserved to be kicked out of the army. How she *wanted* to be kicked out of the army, have the decision made for her. She knew what he would have done – thrown her in the brig for ten days and come to visit her for every one of those days. She could hear his voice.

"Gav, you're really good at your job and I need you back. You think I never fell asleep on guard duty? If they threw out everyone who did, we'd have an army of zero. Learn your lesson and get over it already. You're a grown up now. You're always going to have responsibilities. So in the military, the decisions you have to make are sometimes matters of life and death. So what? Every day you are alive is a matter of life and death. You could get distracted while driving and kill someone. A mother takes her eye off her child for one second and he runs into the street. I hope nothing like that ever happens to you, but you are going to make a lot of mistakes in your life. You can't fall apart every time you do."

107

She finally dragged herself out of bed and went back to work, happy to remain in Glilot, far away from the border.

On May 15 – a little more than a month since the attack in Kiryat Shmona – there was another massacre. The newest "worst attack we've ever had." This time it was in the northern border town of Maalot. The terrorists again chose a school as their target. They'd entered it at night – expecting to find it empty – but it wasn't. More than a hundred high-school kids on a class trip had received permission to sleep there. When the army went in, guns blazing, the terrorists began shooting the hostages. Throwing grenades at them. Twenty-five of them died. Sixty or seventy were wounded. A photograph taken in the aftermath of that attack would win awards – a soldier carrying his badly wounded younger sister out of the school.

Gavrielle's initial response was to work sixteen-hour days. When her colleagues gathered in the kitchen to gossip, she couldn't help giving them dirty looks. *Why do you people waste so much time – drinking coffee, nibbling biscuits, chatting about nonsense? The PLO isn't on a break. Ahmad Jibril doesn't take vacations. We can't let this keep happening. No more children are going to die.*

Then one morning she found herself at her desk, feeling empty, drained. Indifferent. *I can't do this anymore.* She rose and went to Giora Levi's office. "Tomorrow would have been my last day in the army," she said. "You know I already signed – committed myself to another year – but is it too late for me to change my mind? To ask to be discharged?"

He stared at her for a long moment. "Is there trouble at home?"

She shook her head.

"No special problems with your grandmother?"

108

"No, she's fine."

"You know," he said softly, "there is counseling available. Many of us struggle after these kinds of events –"

"No thank you, sir," she said stiffly.

"Sit down, Rozmann. Please." He stretched back in his chair, fingers laced at the back of his neck, and then leaned forward. "Don't ask for a discharge. You might change your mind again and once you've left, it can be more difficult than you'd think to get back in. Ask for an extended leave. Say it's because of your grandmother. I know you're not a liar, but think of it as doing them a favor – making it easy for them to check off the right box on the form. They need a reason that is stated clearly in the regulations – like 'special family circumstances.'"

She studied his desktop.

"Nobody's going to make a home visit," he said.

"What if I say I want time off to go to America, to try and find my father? That's almost true. I might decide to do that."

He looked up in surprise. "Your file says your father is unknown."

"I know. He is. But Jesse helped me figure out that he might have been a *Machal* volunteer who left the country without knowing my mother was pregnant. And my mother never told my grandmother his name. But I found a letter he wrote to my mother and that gave me something to go on. Then right before the war Jesse found out about some guy in Florida who's making a list of all the *Machal* guys."

Giora raised his eyebrows. "Well, if that doesn't qualify as 'special family circumstances' nothing does. I'll get the papers for you to fill out."

How did Tonia do what she did – just up and go to Grand Rapids, Michigan? Start a business? Buy a

109

home? Gavrielle still wasn't sure she had the nerve to actually get on a plane to New York. It was so far away. So expensive. She didn't know a soul. She didn't even know how the phones there worked.

She needed time to think about it and wished there was someplace she could go to be alone. Clear her head. Away from the radio. Just for a week or two. It wouldn't have to be far. Maybe Greece? But for her entire life she'd been hearing the same refrain from Nella – all of Europe is nothing but one gigantic graveyard. So Gavrielle began thinking about the Sinai. She'd been there twice since the war, once for work and once for a "roughing it" weekend with the Amranis. *It's beautiful there. Those pristine beaches and the stars at night. Clean air. A clean kind of silence. But maybe that's too much silence, even for me.*

Then one afternoon she was flipping through one of Tonia's magazines and paused at a magnificent photo-spread of Rome. It accompanied an interview with an Italian Jew who had returned home after the war.

"How could you go back there?" the Israeli reporter asked.

"Italy was different."

"Different! They were allies of Hitler!"

"Mussolini may have been a murderous bastard, but Italy never gave up its Jews. Maybe they caved in to Hitler and passed some anti-Jewish laws, but relative to every other place in Europe, we were safe. The Italians even set up camps for Jews, but the opposite of the Nazis. The Italian camps were for *protecting* Jews. There was food and medicine. No torture or killing. The Italian Jews only got deported to Nazi camps after Germany invaded. But even then the Italians gave them a hard time. The SS handed the Italian police the lists of Jews they'd found in the synagogues, with addresses and everything. Ordered them to round them all up, like the cursed French police had. But for once the Italians' reputation for bungling incompetence was a good thing. They went back to the Nazis scratching their heads, claiming they hadn't been able to find anyone.

"But no one knows about any of that. Everyone's heard of Anne Frank so they think the Dutch were all scurrying around building secret annexes for Jews. But you know what percentage of Dutch Jews went up in smoke? Some books say seventy-five, but I say it was even higher. Ninety-four. Ninety-four percent. And the Italians? Some say twenty, but I say less. Fifteen. They saved eighty-five percent. This is my home. These are my neighbors. Why should I leave?"

Two weeks later Gavrielle boarded an El Al flight to Rome. The next day she would begin five mornings of classes at an Italian language school she had found. She'd remain through the next weekend and then get on a flight back to Tel Aviv and from there to Sharm el Sheikh. She planned to stay down in the Sinai for as long as it took to get her head straight.

Part 2

Charlie Freeman

West Bloomfield Township, Michigan
Tuesday, June 4, 1974

The drive home from Ann Arbor passed quickly. The windows were rolled down and Charlie slapped the outside of the door – WXYZ was playing a marathon of Smokey Robinson's greatest hits. He turned off West Maple Road onto the Valentis' driveway and followed its curve around the old farmhouse. As always, he sat in the car for a long moment, taking in the view of their three acres of land – the peaceful, beautiful place he had called home for the last seven years. The shaded streets of white bread land were hardly more than half an hour's drive from his old neighborhood in Detroit, and Charlie didn't really understand how a black boy like him could feel as comfortable as he did in this new universe.

But he did. He never lowered his gaze when he passed all those white faces on the street. Never felt unentitled. He didn't get the best grades in his class because he needed to prove something to the white boys. He didn't care what they thought of him. His successes were all for himself, Charlie Freeman. He was going to do well. It wouldn't be many years before he'd have a home and car that he'd paid for. And maybe some day, decades ahead, Charlene and Reeves Valenti would need him just as much as he needed them. Then they would feel like a real family.

He got out and lifted his last two suitcases out of the trunk. He had brought the bulk of his belongings home on his last trip, and told Charlene and Reeves not to bother coming to Ann Arbor for the graduation ceremony. He wasn't even sure he was going to attend it. He neglected to mention that he wasn't quite eligible for his degree yet, still owing a paper on Bernini to one of his professors.

114

"Oh, hi," Charlene said when he entered the kitchen. "You sure made good time." She was seated at the table, a bunch of papers spread in front of her. "How many times you get stopped for speeding?"

"Ha ha." Charlie's grandmother was at the counter chopping onions and he hurried over to give her a warm embrace. "Hey, Grandma Julie. Charlene workin' you to the bone as usual, I see."

"Wouldn't have to, you ever pitched in." Grandma Julie slapped his shoulder with a grumpy smile.

He turned to lightly pat Charlene's head. "So white girl, what's all this stuff?" He picked up a brochure for the Galleria Borghese. "You guys takin' another trip to Rome?"

"No." She craned her neck to look up at him. "But you are. If you want. Seems about time."

"What you talkin' about?" he asked, eyebrows raised.

"Remember when you decided not to tag along on our honeymoon?" Her face split into a wide grin.

"Yeah, how I gonna forget the dumbest dumb ass idea you ever had?"

"Well, I may be dumb, but I set aside the money my dad gave us for your ticket. And now that we all know you're destined to be a world class architect and urban planner, I think you should use it, get your skinny butt over to the Eternal City, home of the greatest-ever artists and architects. Before you meet a girl and do something stupid like get married."

"I heard that," Reeves said, as he clumped up the basement stairs. He set his toolbox on the table, punched Charlie's arm, and took a beer from the refrigerator.

"How come I ain't never heard about this ticket money before?" Charlie asked.

"I wasn't sure we could afford to give it to you. You know how tight money has been. But since I got my job

115

driving the Bookmobile, and Rick hired me to oversee his fitness club, we're doing okay. Once Reeves gets the wiring in the apartment over the garage fixed so we can rent it out again, we might even be able to start saving."

"I can take a hint," Reeves said and picked up his toolbox. "I'm going to need a hand over there in about an hour."

"Dirty work?" Charlie asked.

"Nah, just handing me things and turning switches on and off. You don't need to bother changing."

"Okay, I'll come over," Charlie said as he seated himself at the table and started looking through all the papers. "Where you get all this stuff?"

"Turns out there's an Italian cultural center over in Clinton Township. It's mostly just a place to have weddings and parties, but I met a woman who'd just come back from Italy and she gave me all this information. She told me about this new school that just opened, for teaching Italian as a second language. Immersion they call it. Throw you right in. No one speaks anything but Italian. You can sign up to go for one week, two – as many as you want. I think that kind of course would be great for someone like you."

"What the heck do I need to learn Italian for?"

"You don't. But you'll be there all on your own. Don't you think it'd be a good idea to have a class to go to every morning? It's only three hours and it's not like you have to worry about a grade or anything. Whatever you learn, you learn. But you'd meet other young people from all over the world. Make friends to hang out with. I mean, there's only so many hours a day you can wander around looking at buildings, no matter how beautiful they are."

He pursed his lips and stared at her. Charlene never ceased to amaze him, the way she treated him like family. Reeves did too, but it was Charlene who had all the ideas that her husband gladly went along with. Charlie couldn't help but wonder how much of that would change when they had kids of their own. He never asked but always wondered what was taking them so long. They'd been married for seven years.

"You hungry?" his grandmother asked.

"I can eat." She set a plate of rice, beans, and greens in front of him.

"Anyway, think about it," Charlene said, gathering up her papers. "We've been wondering what to give you for graduation. The cost of two weeks tuition at that school is about as much as we were thinking of spending. So you'd have that and your airfare. You'd have to cover your day-to-day expenses out of your own money. Oh ..." she looked at the folded newspaper she had just picked up and handed it to him. "Looky here. I forgot to show you. You got your picture in the Free Press. Some reporter started out writing an article about that Horizons program you were in at Cranbrook, but pretty much the whole article ended up being about you. Even has a picture of you with your big smile."

He ran his eyes over it and cringed, wondering who back in Detroit might have seen this paean to his miraculous journey, from inner city to suburbia. *Don't sweat it, no one in Detroit even remembers you exist.* He tossed it back on the table. "Ain't they got nothin' better to write about?" He hated being "that colored boy who is doing so well." He craved recognition as much as anyone else, but was determined to gain it for the things *he* had done, not for the things someone with his shade of skin had done.

"Oh." She brightened. "And here's this." She pushed another pile of material toward him. "Stuff I asked U of M to send me about their Urban Planning program. It is *so* perfect for you. But it seems strange that you haven't gotten anything from them about registering for classes. Shouldn't you have gotten a catalogue by now?"

He shrugged and hunkered down over his plate. *Probably shoulda, if I'd really registered to go there.* A year ago he had made up his mind – he was going to return to Cranbrook for graduate school. But he'd never found the courage to tell Charlene. *Damn fool. I shoulda written her a letter while I was back in Ann Arbor. Wouldna had to look her in the face.*

The next morning Charlie woke with a plan. He'd grown excited about the prospect of seeing Rome – and wasn't it some kind of sign that he was writing a paper on Bernini? What better place to do it than Rome, sitting in the Piazza Navona, sipping wine or espresso, contemplating the master's works. Two weeks sounded like a good length of time. Get there on a Thursday, have Friday, Saturday, and Sunday to explore alone. Start school on Monday for two weeks. Leave to come home on Friday, after the last morning at school.

He would leave a letter for Charlene on his bed, explaining why he had no interest in studying Urban Planning. Why he wanted to keep as far away as he could from anything political. He wasn't going to be the next Martin Luther King or Stokely Carmichael. *Why would I? They already did all the work. Opened all the doors. Job of my generation is to walk through them doors. Take advantage of the opportunities. That's the best way to honor Dr. King. I guess leaving a letter is pretty chicken, but that will give her two whole weeks to get over it. And, more important, two whole weeks with no way to talk to me.*

A week later he boarded a plane for Rome. But booking the flight and registering at the Italian language school had turned out to be a lot easier than composing a letter to Charlene. He never did get around to it.

Part 3

Rome

Monday, June 17, 1974

After three days of exploring the city alone, Charlie Freeman arrived early for his first day of class – three hours of Italian lessons, Monday through Friday mornings, at a school not far from Piazza Navona. It was a three-story building of small classrooms, with a modest cafeteria in the basement for the budget-minded. A friendly little man in Groucho Marx glasses and mustache gave Charlie a brief test to confirm his description of himself – "Ignoramus American, don't know a single word of any foreign language" – and directed him to room 3B on the top floor.

On his way up Charlie peeked into the classrooms. They were all the same, clean and unadorned. Blackboard and small table for the teacher in the front, lots of windows, and eight to ten chairs with desk arms. In room 3B he found an earlier bird occupying one of the chair desks. A girl – or woman he should say, since she looked older than Charlie's twenty-two years – was sitting there reading. He paused in the doorway for a better look before deciding whether to take the seat next to her. So far she hadn't raised her eyes from her book. Not a glance. *Like you don't notice a whole human body suddenly darkening the doorway? You too snooty to say good morning?* When she did lift her chin it was to frown and bite her top lip as she stared at a fixed point on the wall, apparently reflecting on something she'd read. Then her hand flew to her chest as her head jerked toward him.

"Oh. Sorry. You startled me," she said. "Good morning."

Gavrielle Rozmann hadn't actually been reading, but staring at the book thinking. Stupid, stupid, stupid – why did I think taking a class sounded like such a good idea? Now I either have to figure out how to make small talk or have everyone in the class referring to me as "that weird girl." No, worse, "that weird Israeli girl."

"Hi," he responded and removed his backpack. Okay, she ain't snotty, just really into that book. Or really frettin' and sweatin' on something.

He couldn't decide how attractive she was. Girl's got a Barbra Streisand thing going, only in a pretty way. But she sure ain't got no Barbra Streisand wardrobe or sense of style. Gavrielle was wearing khaki shorts, a black T-shirt with a white stripe running diagonally across its front, scuffed up hiking shoes, and no make-up. Her hair was pulled back as if for a pony tail, but clamped in a long barrette that ran vertically up the back of her head. Wispy blonde curls had escaped and surrounded her thin face, softening it. Not bad, he decided. Sure, I'd notice her on the street. Something interesting 'bout that face.

"My name's Charlie." He walked over and offered his hand.

"Gavrielle," she said and took it. *Yes, he is American.*

She'd liked every American she'd ever met back home in Jerusalem, though one did have to make allowances for ridiculous plaid Bermuda shorts and excessive use of mayonnaise and ketchup. But how could you dislike people who were so exuberant? So trusting. Their teeth so straight and white. Ask them anything and they answer. What a wonderful luxury this generation of Americans is blessed with, being able to go through life without losing their naiveté. She stared up at Charlie, the first African-American she'd ever met. *It must be different for them – they have it tough. But he sure looks like a nice, easy-going guy. Look at that smile.*

Gavrielle had arrived in Rome the day before and spent the late afternoon and evening wandering, looking at beautiful buildings. It had felt lonely, as she'd known it would, which is why she had signed up for this class. Maybe it had been a good idea. This black guy in cut-off jeans and white T-shirt had managed to spark her curiosity. *Wasn't the Mad Professor always saying that a person needs someone else to think with – and sometimes it's helpful if the other person is a stranger?* That thought immediately felt ridiculous. *What are you, delusional? This place is brimming with sweet young things with hair that moves. He's going to pick one of them for his summer romance. Why would he want to spend five minutes sitting around listening to your stupid problems?*

"You look a little lonely," he said.

"Not any more." No, no, no. I shouldn't have said that. Why do I always forget the way guys take things? Their internal one-track interpreter that translates every sentence and gesture to the same thing – see, she wants me. He must think I'm pathetic.

He took the seat next to her and rummaged through his pack to retrieve a notebook and pen. Then he glanced at her book, thinking that might be something they could talk about, but the words on the cover were in some strange alphabet. *Persian maybe? They got blonds in Persia?*

"What language is that?" He nodded at her book.

She paused before replying. "Hebrew."

Everything about her – the way her body stiffened, her blank expression, even the way she managed to say that one word – seemed to Charlie to be all "in your face." *What bug got up her butt?* But he decided to ignore the attitude.

"Hebrew. So that means you're from Israel?"

"Yes."

"What?" He stared at her. "What's with the look? Like you're fixin' to punch me in the face for calling you a kike or something?"

She tilted her head to one side and raised her shoulder, the way small children do when they say, "I dunno." What she said was, "Kike? No. That's out. These days it's Nazi, Fascist, oppresser, baby killer."

He consciously put on his most boyish grin – yes, he knew he was a charmer. People told him so all the time. "Charming and disarming," Charlene always said.

"You know," he said, "on the whole, it's us *shvartzes* get called the names. Not the other way around."

When Gavrielle allowed her face break into a genuine smile Charlie thought she was pretty. Sort of beautiful even, if you liked faces with character. Charlie did. But her reticence did not escape him. *Okay, this chick ain't flirting. Ain't in the market for no fling. Least she don't know it yet. But that's okay. Don't seem like hangin' with her for a while would be a waste of time. Find out something 'bout Israel. I can do friend.*

Other students started straggling in and they acknowledged one another with nods. There were three college-age girls – the type Charlie always thought ought to be named Wendy, though he'd never actually met a girl named Wendy. They had varying shades of very long, very straight hair and all wore expensive outdoorsy clothes. They came in separately – didn't seem to know each other – and each gave Charlie the same series of furtive glances. *Sorry girls, but I don't care to be on the unofficial part of your resume – the "Oh, yes, I went out with a black guy for a while" part. Bet I could nail any one of you – but I'd probably die of boredom in the process.*

There were also two high school girls, obviously friends, one gray-haired woman, one guy who looked Korean or Japanese, and a blonde guy who looked like the twin of Illya Kuryakin in *The Man from U.N.C.L.E.* The bell rang and the teacher bustled in, radiating energy and enthusiasm.

"*Buongiorno,*" she said. "*Sono Francesca.*" She

123

pointed to her chest and then stood in front of Charlie, pointing at him. "*E tu?*"

"Hey, I know that one," he said. "*E tu, Brute?*"

Francesca frantically waved her forefinger back and forth, saying, "*No, no, no. Inglese non è legale.*"

"All right, all right. How do you Eye-talians say 'all right'?"

"Va bene."

"*Va bene. Va bene.*" Charlie imitated her.

"*Sono Francesca,*" she repeated, pointing at herself again. Then she added, "*Sono di Roma,*" as she pointed at the floor. "*E tu?*" She pointed at Charlie again.

"*Sono Charlie. Sono di America.*" Francesca clapped her hands in applause and repeated the exercise with four other students.

"*Molto bene. Molto, molto bene.*" Francesca beamed enthusiastically.

When Francesca started asking questions involving their *mamma* and *papà* Charlie grew visibly uncomfortable, all but cringing every time he had to say, "*mio papà,*" or "*mio mamma.*"

He doesn't like that at all, Gavrielle thought. *Wonder why.* She began hoping that when the bell rang for the break he would suggest they go get a cappuccino. But then she glanced at the American girls with their shiny hair. *You can forget that. Those girls all have legs up to their necks.*

But when the bell rang he leaned over. "Hey, Gay-vrielle, you feel like gettin' some of their *molto bene* coffee?"

"Sure. But it's Gah-vrielle. Short a."

"Okay. Gah-vrielle."

They squeezed in at the counter to get their coffee, maneuvered through the noisy crowd, and shoved aside the dirty cups on one of the little round tables. "So where in America are you from?" she asked.

"Michigan."

He might as well have said, "Mars," the way her mouth fell open. "What?" he asked. "Somethin' wrong with Michigan?"

"No. Of course not. It's just ..." She paused to sip her coffee. "I know someone who lived there for a while. In Grand Rapids."

"Yeah? Nice town, Grand Rapids. My uh ... foster grandfather lives there."

So that's why he doesn't like saying "mio mamma" and "mio *papà*." He's like me, doesn't have real parents. "Are you a student?" she asked.

"Just graduated from U of M. You?"

She shook her head. "I'm way past that. I got a degree from the Technion in Haifa and then went into the army."

"Oh yeah, that's right. I read about that. How you got women warriors over there. You drive a tank or something?"

"No," she smiled. "They don't take women into combat units any more."

"How come?"

She thought for a moment. "The question is more why they used to. When there was no choice, they took everyone. Teen-aged boys and old men just off the boats from Europe got rifles shoved into their hands and sent onto a battlefield. Before the state, young girls and women did everything. But now ... it's a matter of ... how do you say, allocating resources?"

"Yeah, that's how we say. Don't that piss you off?"

"No. Not at all. If I were in charge, I'd decide the same thing. It costs a fortune to train a soldier for combat, and the women are going to have children. You won't be able to call them up for reserve duty at a moment's notice."

"I thought it was all about equality."

"No." She shook her head again. "It was never that.

125

The IDF isn't a social science project. It's for keeping us alive. You spend the little money you have training the people who will do each job the best and for the longest time."

"So what's your job?"

"I work in intelligence."

"No kidding? A lady James Bond?"

She smiled and shook her head. "No, nothing like that. Military Intelligence. My unit helps develop new methods of gathering information about our enemies. And I can't tell you any more than that."

The bell summoned them to return to class.

"Have lunch with me," Charlie said as they rose. "So we can talk some more."

"Thanks. That'd be great."

"Later I was thinking of going to the Vatican, see Saint Peter's. You up for that?" They started moving up the stairs.

"The Basilica?" she shouted to be heard above the crowd. "Yeah, sure. I'd love to."

That was the first place she'd gone yesterday, right after she arrived in Rome and dropped her backpack off at the hostel. She'd been overwhelmed by its beauty, hypnotized by the sunlight filtering down from the tiny windows up in the dome. When a choir began singing Mass she took a seat and remained to the end, almost wishing she were Catholic. She was more than happy to go back there. *Especially with this guy. He really is nice.*

Nice girl, Charlie thought. But I still ain't gettin' that vibe. I guess friends it is.

They didn't get a chance to speak much until they were out on the sidewalk at the end of class. It was a beautiful day and they both dug through their backpacks for sunglasses and baseball caps. Gavrielle also retrieved her guidebook. She felt tiny standing next to Charlie. He casually took her elbow between thumb and forefinger and started walking in the general direction of the Vatican.

"Tell me when you're ready," he said, "and we'll stop to eat. Or get something to drink."

"I'm not really hungry. Are you?"

"No. Where do you live in Israel?" he asked.

"Jerusalem."

"Really? Man, we don't even think of that like it's a real place. I mean not any more. Just in the Bible."

"I know. Christian tourists always freak out that Bethlehem and Nazareth have sewers and traffic lights and all that. Why'd you come to Italy?"

"Charlene and Reeves – they're like my foster parents or guardians or whatever. Only since I'm over eighteen, I guess they aren't officially anything – just the people I live with. Anyway, they bought me the ticket. Paid for the school. I was glad to get away from home for the summer."

Then he elaborated more about his relationship with the Valentis. It was the first time he'd told anyone about his home situation. The principal at Cranbrook Schools must have had a talk with the all-white 10th grade class before Charlie showed up for his first day there. None of his classmates had asked him any questions. When Charlene and Reeves invited the whole class over for one of their barbecues, no one registered any surprise that Charlie had a white "family." And he'd never invited anyone from U of M to go home with him. When asked where he was from he responded, "Detroit." He'd never known what to call the Valentis. "My parents" would have been ridiculous – they were only seven years older than he was. So he solved the problem by avoiding any mention of them. But explaining how he came to live with them to this friendly stranger had been surprisingly easy. And this particular stranger really surprised him with the matter-of-fact tone of her next question.

"Are they black?"

"Nope. Don't come much whiter than them."

"Do they live in Detroit?"

"Nope. Out in a suburb."

"So your school was mostly white?"

"Real mostly. Like 98% mostly."

"Was that hard?"

He looked puzzled when he finally answered, "No. I don't know why it wasn't, but it wasn't."

"What's funny?" she asked, noting the way he was smiling to himself.

"Americans don't ask questions like that. Not straight out. They find a sneakier way. Like, 'Where are Charlene's folks from?'"

"I guess Israelis are famous for being blunt. Do you mind my nosy questions?"

He shook his head. "The opposite. But then you gotta let me ask some." He stopped and glanced into the coffee shop they were passing. "This place look okay to you? If we're getting into nosy, I need some refreshment."

After they had ordered coffee and tiramisu to share, Gavrielle asked, "How come you know the word 'shvartze'?"

He grinned. "Lots of Jews out where Charlene and Reeves moved to. White flight out of Detroit after the riots. You know, in the summer of '67?"

She nodded. "Yes, I know about that. We'd been busy having a war earlier that summer, but I do remember hearing about it on the radio. And there were pictures in the newspapers – a lot of smoke. Looked worse than our war."

"Didn't they show it on TV?"

"We didn't get TV until '68. The riots weren't just in Detroit, were they?"

128

"Nah. Cities all over were burning."

"So Charlene and Reeves – they're Jewish?"

"Nooooo. But most of the colored ladies my gramma made friends with out there work for Jewish people. You know, cleaning their houses."

Gavrielle laughed. "So those ladies learned Yiddish and taught your grandmother?"

"Just the good words." He scowled and switched to a high-pitched voice, meant to sound like a crabby grandmother. "*Nu, nu, nu,* Charlie Freeman, y'all get your *no-goodnik* lazy bones out there, *shlep* them groceries into the kitchen, and don't be trackin' no *drek* onto my clean floor."

Gavrielle laughed again and then hesitated before saying, "Please, don't answer if this is too nosy ... but what happened to your parents?"

"It's okay. I don't mind. My father –" He stopped to look at her. "When I was nine my father was beaten to death by some officers of the Detroit Police Department."

"My God, why?"

"They didn't like the way he was walking down the street." Charlie looked as if he regretted choosing to answer the question, but went on. "He was sick, going to Cunningham's to get some medicine, and I guess they thought he was drunk. And beating on black men – that's just what they did back then. Carried these bats they called 'nigger sticks.' I don't suppose they meant to kill him, but they did."

"So what happened to them?"

"Nothing. There were two witnesses who'd been hiding in the alley where it happened, but they weren't about to testify against the po-lice. My mom married this other guy, but then she got run over by a car and I was stuck with him – until after the riots started. Then my wonderful stepfather found a way to evaporate and I ended up soon to be homeless."

129

"Oh my God, Charlie, that's terrible." Gavrielle reached over to take his hand.

"Yeah. It is. But it was a long time ago. Anyway, Charlene turned up to save the day. But let's leave that story for some other time. I got another reason for coming to Rome." He changed the subject and his tone of voice. "I still owe one of my professors a paper on Bernini, so I'm going to see everything Bernini."

Her face was blank.

"Don't tell me you've never heard of Gian Lorenzo Bernini?"

She shrugged. "Michelangelo and Leonardo Da Vinci. That's about it."

"Girl, you are so coming to the Galleria Borghese with me. They've got both of his best sculptures. I'll get us tickets for someday this week. You ready to get out of here?" He slurped the last of his coffee and left money on the table. "I'll save the questions I got for you for later, when we got a couple of beers on the table."

"Or a bottle of wine? No 'when in Rome' for you Americans?" Gavrielle grinned, opening her guide book to look at the map.

"Nah. We stay crude and uncultured wherever we go."

They walked on, their attention focused on the city, Charlie noting different architectural elements and styles, Gavrielle pointing at every faucet from which a constant stream of water ran into the street. Coming from a country where they were constantly admonished that "every drop counts," she couldn't get used to that.

When they reached the Piazza Navona, Charlie led her to the *Fontana dei Quattro Fiumi* – Fountain of the Four Rivers – and said, "That's a Bernini," as he released an involuntary sigh.

"What's wrong?"

"Much as you gotta love the art ..." He sighed again

and surveyed the buildings around the piazza. "You gotta hate the scumbags who commissioned it. Those popes and cardinals were such a fat-ass gang of crooks. When Bernini was working on this one ..." He nodded at the fountain. "The people who lived around here were practically starving. All but had a riot. 'We don't need obelisks and fountains! We need bread!' And the Villa Borghese, where the gallery is, all its enormous gardens, and all the art in it, you'll see what I mean — all that belonged to one guy. And you know what that guy did for his money? Nothing. He wanted something, all he had to do was think up a new tax."

"Are you going to educate me about this fountain?" she asked, hoping he would.

He turned back to stare at it. "Nah. Not yet. First you gotta walk all the way around Bernini's *David* with me, see it from all sides. I don't believe in saving the best for last. The best ought to be first, so you see it with nice fresh baby eyes, before you're all arted out and feel like taking a hammer to the next sculpture you're asked to look at. So, first things first. I will educate you about Bernini, how good old Gian Lorenzo started a whole new style. All it takes is one look at Michelangelo's *David* and then at Bernini's *David* and you get it. A whole different way of looking at what a block of marble can be made to express. But for now, how about *you* start educating *me*? About Gavrielle ... What's your last name?"

"Rozmann."

"About Gavrielle Rozmann and what she came to Rome to get away from."

"Who says I'm running away from something?"

"Takes one to know one. Aren't you?"

"Sort of, I guess." Gavrielle stared at the fountain for a long while and then asked, "What are the four rivers?"

"Danube, Nile, Ganges, and Rio de la Plata," he recited in a flat voice, followed by another silence.

131

"Okay, we can talk about something else. I just thought ... You seem like a girl who might need someone to talk to."

"I do, actually," she said, to her surprise, but turned to survey their surroundings. "I bet it's beautiful here at night. They probably have everything all lit up."

"Yeah, they do. You know, Gavrielle is a really pretty name."

She looked embarrassed. "My mom chose it. After the archangel Gavrielle."

"Oh yeah, good old Gabriel – Michael, Gabriel, Raphael and ... somebody else. I remember one of our professors saying that Gabriel was originally female and her name was Gavrielle. Then some pope decided that all the archangels had to be male. Don't remember why. So do Jews still think that angel is a girl called Gavrielle?"

"Jews think all angels are both male and female. Or neither." She shrugged and smiled. "We never make our minds up about anything. Why ruin a perfectly good topic to argue about?"

He smiled and asked, "How long are you going to be here?"

"Six more days."

"You got a long list of things you gotta see?"

"Not really. I didn't make any plans. Thought I'd just look at my guidebook every night, pick one thing to see the next day."

"I got a list. But I'll still be here for five more days after you leave. How about this – as long as you're here, every day I let you pick something off my list and we go together?"

That sounded wonderful to Gavrielle but she paused, a bit confused by her own reaction. *I didn't come here to make friends and I'll never see this guy again, so why would I want to spend the whole week with him?* But she did. There was something Jesse-like about Charlie. Comforting. Nothing threatening or challenging. And sitting around by herself was no longer something she felt like doing. *My mind has blanked out on me anyway, and I'll have all the time I want for that later, in Sinai.*

"I'd like that a lot," she finally answered. "But I ..."

"It's okay. I know you ain't looking for no romance. You got that written all over you. But I'm going to do this anyway." He took her hand in his. "Just friendly like. That okay with you?"

She nodded, but he was so much taller that the hand-holding quickly became awkward and he let go.

"How 'bout we leave the Basilica for tomorrow?" he said. "Walk our feet off tonight and then get a great meal. I'll even go for a bottle of wine. How's that sound?"

"Perfecto."

At the Trevi Fountain she allowed herself to lean against him, wishing she were falling in love. This city would be such a great place for that to happen. Like in that movie – *Three Coins in the Fountain.* Charlie gave her a quick hug at each of other fountains they passed, but they were also Jesse-like. Warm and reassuring, without any urgency – which was exactly what she needed and far better than a half-baked romance. Since Jesse had died she'd had no one to talk to, and a temporary friend was better than none.

They finally chose a restaurant and ordered. The waiter brought the wine right away and Charlie squirmed his way through the tasting ritual. Then he reached beneath his chair for his backpack, pulled out a large-size paperback book, flipped through it, and placed it open on the table. He studied the photograph on the page for a moment before turning it around and nudging it toward her.

"Okay," he said, "looking at a picture of a sculpture

is like looking at a picture of a person – nothing like seeing the real thing. But we aren't going to be in Florence for me to show you Michelangelo's *David*, so a picture is going to have to do. That's it." He thumped his forefinger on the page. "They built a whole museum, just for it."

She pulled the book to her and studied the image. "David as in David and Goliath, right?"

"Yeah." Charlie couldn't help rolling his eyes. "See," he said, "that's Renaissance style – the way everyone sculpted before Bernini came along. They liked nudes, especially men, and the way he's standing, all his weight on one leg, that's real typical for that period. It's called *contrapposto*. See how it puts his hips and shoulders at opposing angles? That was their idea of a dynamic figure."

"Okay. So?"

"So you tell me, what do you think he's doing?"

"Not a whole lot. Just standing there. Thinking. Probably wondering how the heck he's going to get out of fighting the humungous *goy* in all the armor."

"So you think this is before the fight?"

She shrugged. "How would I know?"

"That's what the experts say. They say it's after he volunteered to fight Goliath, but before they started going at it. They say you can tell by all the tension in his brow and neck and the way the veins in his hand stick out."

"What do you say?"

"I say any non-snooty-art-expert person looking at this sculpture is going to be way too distracted by his boy parts to notice any of that stuff."

She blushed and put her fist in front of her mouth.

"Come on. You can't tell me that ain't the first thing that got your attention – his one-eyed third leg staring you right in the face. And anatomically incorrect, I

134

might add."

She grew redder and drank some wine.

"I mean," he continued, "give me a break. Nice Jewish boy, future king of Israel – he ain't circumcised? Mm mm. That ain't right." He slid the book back, opened a different page, and returned it to her.

"Now that's Bernini's David. I don't have to ask you what this guy's doing. None of that calm Renaissance composure, like he's posing for a photo opportunity. Look at the face on this David." He tapped his finger on it. "You *know* what he's looking at. You can just about see old Goliath standing across from him, about to get it, pow, right in the kisser.

"See, Bernini drops you into the story, at the most dramatic moment, right before David gives it to Goliath. Michelangelo portrayed tension? I'll give you tension. Maybe it doesn't show in that picture, but you'll see what I mean. The muscles in those legs are so tight, almost hurts to look at them. You're waiting for him to get on with it, let loose with that sling. That marble is *alive*."

"It is beautiful." She ran her finger over the photograph. "Amazing. I'm so glad I'm going to have you with me at that gallery. You make it so interesting. You must have had great teachers." She closed the book and pushed it back to him.

"Can't argue with that," he said as he returned the book to his pack. "I had the best teachers. Went to the best school. I mean high school, not college. U of M was okay, but high school is where I learned to love art."

The waiter served their food and they ate hungrily, idly chatting about the other students in their class and how wonderful their teacher Francesca was. When the waiter cleared their plates away Charlie asked for another bottle of wine. And then they talked – until the waiters started flicking the lights on and off – and then they found a bench where they could sit and talk some

135

more. He finished his story, telling her more about his childhood and moving to Detroit and going on one of the Freedom Rides with his mother, and the riots, and how he had come to live with Charlene and Reeves. Then he said it was her turn.

She spoke in hesitant spurts until the words began to pour out – the bomb that killed her mother, growing up with no one but her grandmother, and looking forward to finding a substitute family in the IDF. She spoke at length about her wonderful CO and friend, Jesse, leaving him alive in Charlie's mind for now. It would take her a few more days to speak those words.

"You remind me of him," she said. "The way I'm falling in friend with you."

She cried silent tears while telling him about the terror attacks and falling asleep on duty and the slaughter of nine-year old Iris Chitrit's family. The sun was peeking over the tops of buildings when Gavrielle told Charlie that she no longer felt she belonged in the army. No longer felt she belonged anywhere.

Then she stood and said, "Let's go. We should try to get a little bit of sleep before school. I'm exhausted." She went over to the nearby faucet and splashed water on her face.

Charlie remained seated on the bench. "I swear, there's something different about the way the sun shines in this city," he said. "Like it knows it's shining on the most beautiful things in the world. I mean, the most beautiful things *people* ever made. You know, beautiful dead things. No human ever made anything holds a candle to a tree or a butterfly. I mean, Michelangelo's *David* is amazing and Bernini's is a whole lot better – but what the heck, God made a real-life *David*, who besides being beautiful, could run around shooting slingshots and playing harps. Still, I think there's something divine about folks doing their

136

best to make the physical world as beautiful as they can. Even if all they've got to work with are inanimate objects."

"Amen," Gavrielle said and held out her hand to him, to tug him to his feet.

"Of course," Charlie continued as they started walking, "folks who can make music, now that's a whole different story. They give God a run for His money. Come as close as a person can get to making something brand new and alive. The sound of the waves lapping on the sand and the wind in the trees – yeah, that stuff's cool – but I'll take Mozart and Marvin Gaye on my eight track any day."

Outside the hostel she touched his face before turning to go in. "See you tomorrow. I'm really glad you're here."

"Me too. See you tomorrow."

Every day after class they did their homework in the coffee shop up the street from the school and then began roaming the city. They didn't sleep more than four hours a night and never felt tired. They enjoyed their classes, knowing they'd quickly become Francesca's pets. Well, Charlie had, and some of it rubbed off on Gavrielle. She couldn't remember ever feeling so relaxed – waking up each morning with a wide smile on her face. No responsibilities. Another day to do whatever she wanted. She had never tried to flirt with anyone before, let alone in a foreign language, but she often said she wanted to take a table by herself for a while, so she could practice her limited Italian on the waiters. Charlie sat nearby, making faces and laughing.

Then one day during the break Francesca approached Gavrielle and said something about "*un attacco terroristico in Israele*" the day before. Gavrielle rushed out in search of a newspaper. She found an article – in Italian – about the attack and pointed to it

137

as she asked the elderly man behind the counter of the newsstand to translate for her.

"*Quanti* ..." she paused to consult her dictionary. "*Morti. Quanti morti?*"

"You are speaking English, no? Three *terroristi* dead." He held up three fingers. "All the *terroristi*." He drew his forefinger across his throat. "One Israelean soldier dead. Three Israelean people dead."

In the first paragraph of the article she saw the name "Naharia" – a small city on Israel's northern border, by the Mediterranean.

"They came across the border from Lebanon?" she asked.

"No. They are coming from the water."

"*Sono venuto via mare?*" she asked, to be sure she'd understood him.

"*Sono venuti,*" he corrected her. "*Sì. In una barca di gomma.*" He pointed at a rubber eraser.

"*Barca, barca,*" she murmured. They had learned that word. "Boat? In a rubber boat? Like a Zodiac?"

"Sì. Bastardi. Diavoli."

"*Tutti i terroristiti* ..." She mimicked him, slitting her throat with her forefinger. "You're sure?"

"Assolutamente."

"Grazie."

Charlie was waiting for her and led her up the street to a bench. "So?"

"So why didn't you go back to class?"

"Let's see ... maybe because my new friend was all upset."

She opened her mouth to say something like "there's nothing you can do" and suddenly realized he *was* doing something. Just by standing there worrying about her, he was doing a very big something. "I ... I'm glad ... Thank you for being here."

Charlie shrugged, thinking, This chick got some

138

kind of weird idea of how friends behave.

She looked rather helpless and avoided his gaze. "I'm used to working things out for myself. For me ... people have usually felt more like a nuisance than a help."

"Hell is other people?" he said.

"I wouldn't go that far."

"It's a quote. From a play by Sartre. But he didn't mean it like it sounds, the way they translate it into English. What he meant was – most of what we think about ourselves comes from the way other people look at us. Or we think they do, anyway. A woman only thinks she's beautiful because men do. That's the hell we get from other people. Seeing ourselves reflected in their eyes."

"I didn't know you were so philosophical."

"Hey, even I can repeat something a teacher said. But, seriously, maybe it's sort of true for you. You can't stand for other folks to see you as all needy, so you just prefer they not see you at all."

She took a moment before nodding. "That's sort of true. All my life, the thing I've hated most is being the poor orphan girl. Or more to the point, other people knowing that's what I am. Wow, look how smart you are." She put her palm to his cheek. "Come on, let's go back to school. Me sitting here feeling like shit isn't doing anyone any good."

Charlie took Gavrielle to see the Basilica, the Galleria Borghese, and to a supper club where they saw a condensed version of *La Traviata*. He also walked her up the Aventine Hill, to hear the Benedictine Monks at the monastery of Sant' Anselmo singing vespers. There she sat mostly silent, mesmerized, but when someone walked past the rows of sparsely populated pews and handed her a small paper book, open to the score of what they were currently singing, she stared at it for a

139

moment, following the text, then looked up at Charlie. "Psalms," she said in obvious delight. "They're singing psalms in Latin." When it was over and the monks filed out in their black robes, two by two, she sighed and said, "The opera last night was beautiful, but this was even better. Thank you, Charlie. I never would have known about this. How did you?"

"I remembered one of my teachers talking about it." He beamed back at her.

The last church he took her to was Santa Maria Maggiore, where he pointed out Bernini's tomb. Then he told her to look up at the lavish ceiling, said to be gilded with gold brought back by Christopher Columbus and presented by Ferdinand and Isabella to the Spanish Pope.

She smiled a wry smile when Charlie mentioned that.

"Yeah, what?" he asked.

"History is such a matter of perspective, isn't it?" she said. "For you, I guess Ferdinand and Isabella are some kind of heroes – the ones who gave Columbus the money to go find America."

"I suppose. So what are they to you?"

"The people who signed the Alhambra Decree, expelling the Jews from Spain. Same year – 1492. And when you watched Errol Flynn play Robin Hood, waiting for Richard the Lionheart to come back, I bet you never gave any thought to what that good king had been doing while he was away – which was killing Jews and Muslims on his way to the Holy Land." She glanced at Charlie and poked his side. "Don't worry, those facts are true, but I'm not going all solemn on you. I loved that Robin Hood movie. But it is all a matter of point of view. In my country, too. I am aware."

"Well, it's good that you ain't going all solemn, 'cause the next place we're going to has another big dose of perspective for you. The Forum."

She frowned for a moment. "That's where the Arch of Titus is?"

"Yep. In honor of you guys getting your asses kicked. *'Judea Capta'* is what old Titus put on his coins that year."

"Well, actually, nowadays there's a whole new perspective on that." Gavrielle grinned. "It certainly is a celebration of our defeat, but it is also undeniable proof that *we were there*. The Arabs say all Jewish claims on Palestine are nothing but a hoax. The Jews never had anything to do with Palestine. It's all a big lie. So go tell that to the Romans. And they wouldn't have built a triumphal arch and minted coins if defeating us hadn't been a big deal. A really big deal. Meaning we were a formidable enemy, even for the strongest army in the world. So there."

They finally got around to taking a tour of La Sinagoga and the neighborhood that was still called The Ghetto. It was where, until 1870, all of Rome's Jews had been required to live behind enormous wooden gates that locked them in every night. But it was a beautiful afternoon and neither of them was in the mood to dwell on 2000 years of Jewish history. Charlie had his favorite meal at the kosher restaurant there. "That eggplant parmesan – man, that be to kill for," he declared.

The night before Gavrielle's flight back to Tel Aviv, Charlie said, "I think we need another 'two bottles of wine night' and she readily agreed.

After the first bottle had been served he said, "I got a real strong vibe from you – something's killing you. So what haven't you told me?"

She watched the passersby on the street and sighed before turning to meet his eyes and answer. "You go first. I need to get a little of this in me." She lifted her glass and said "*L'chaim.*"

"I've already spilled all my beans," Charlie said. "No secrets left. Well, except for this one thing – the reason I wanted to get away from Charlene for a while. But it's stupid. Real stupid. I know I'm a grown man and it's my decision to make, not hers, blah, blah, blah. I know all that. But still ..."

"What's the decision?"

"Well, it's like this. I know I can design good buildings. Beautiful buildings. I got that in me. So for graduate school I'm going back to Cranbrook. That's the fancy prep school Charlene got me into for high school. Their Academy of Art is the top rated graduate-only school for architecture, art, and design in the entire country and they've got a fantastic program."

"What's so great about it?"

"It's nothing like other schools. No classes, schedule, reading lists, exams. None of that crap. You get assigned a place in a studio and work on a project you choose. The teachers are there all the time – working on their own projects, right there with you in the studio. They even eat in the same dining hall. Looks more like you're working together than one teaching the other. I want to be there, working like that, more than I can tell you."

He stopped to drink and she waited for him to go on.

"It costs about a zillion dollars and they only offered me a partial scholarship so I'll have to take out a humungous loan, but I don't care. That's it. That's how I want to spend the next two years. Then I'll get an apprenticeship somewhere. Black graduate of Cranbrook? Shee-it. All the mucky-muck firms are gonna be fighting over this affirmative action baby. People will stand in line to pay me big bucks for designing their house or office. I know how white folks in places like West Bloomfield are. Every one of them is dying to have a nice tame black friend to invite to their cocktail parties. Someone like me, with enough of an edge on him to seem *really* black, but not enough to make anyone nervous."

"And the problem is?"

"Charlene ain't gonna go for it."

"Why would she object? Most parents would be thrilled."

"Charlene ain't most people and she ain't going to like it."

"Why?

"She thinks I'm going to do like she thinks I should – go back to U of M – to their new graduate program for Urban Design, so I can save Detroit or something. She's got no trouble making her own assumptions about how my life's supposed to go. Like parents who talk to their kids about *when* they go to college, not *if* they go. You know what I mean? So she just goes on talking about where I can live in Ann Arbor and stuff like that."

"Still, why would she object to Cranbrook if it's such a hot shot school?"

"She won't object. She'll just sit there looking sad, like I'm some sell-out money-grubber. Hell yes, I want to make money. Who doesn't? You got money, you got options. But it's not even like she does it on purpose, like she's trying to make me feel bad. She just can't help herself."

"All you can do is talk to her," Gavrielle shrugged. "And then go and do what you want to do. It is your life."

"Yeah, I know. So let's hear what's with you. You drunk enough yet?"

She took a deep breath and slowly let it out, staring at her hands while she said, "Jesse's dead. He was killed on the first day of the war."

143

She saw him stiffen and held up her hand. "Don't bother trying to think of something to say. There's nothing to say. I just needed to say it out loud. I never have before."

Charlie poured them both more wine and they sat through a long silence, both drinking. "That it?"

"No." She shook her head. "It's ... the reason I need more time to think ... why after this I'm going down to the Sinai for a while, instead of going home ... I ... I want to go look for my father. But then I don't want to go look for him."

"Your father? I thought you don't even know who he is."

"I don't. But I do know some things." She told him about the letter from Lou in Chicago and Jesse finding out about the man in Florida who was supposed to be making a list of *Machal* volunteers.

"Damn," Charlie said. "And here I been thinking you're real smart."

"What ..." She looked up, bewildered.

"That ain't no decision. Of course you're gonna go look for him. What are you, some kind of idiot, gonna sit around moaning and groaning till he drops dead? Then kick yourself for the rest of your own life? I mean, what's the big question here?"

"Even if I find him – and I have no idea what the chances of that are – but even if I do, who knows what that'll be like?"

"Ask me, anything's better than not knowing. Not even trying to find out. Going around wondering 'What if.' I mean, look, what can be?" He began counting off the possibilities. "You can't find him. So at least you'll know you tried. He's dead. But maybe he had kids and you find yourself some brothers or sisters. Or at least you can talk to folks that knew him, can tell you something about him. Or he's alive, but he's a jerk and

144

doesn't want anything to do with you. Okay, so you know you ain't been missing out on nothin'. Or he does want something to do with you, but you can't stand him. So, again, you know you ain't been missing out on nothin'. Or he's scared of his wife and she hates you. That's her problem. What else? I mean what could be? He's homeless? In jail? From outer space?"

She chewed on her top lip and didn't say anything.

"And, Gavrielle, you've got this-here American friend now. You can come stay with us for a while and I'll help you look."

"Oh no, I wasn't hinting about anything like that." She sat back in her chair, looking horrified. "Anyway, Florida is about a thousand miles from Michigan."

"Did you take a stupid pill today or what? Of course, you gonna come stay with us. We got a huge house. Sometimes people wander in there, never to be heard from again. And Charlene's always complaining 'bout me never bringing any friends home."

"I doubt I'm what she has in mind."

"And what do you care how far it is from Michigan to Florida? You ain't goin' to Florida. In America we have these things called telephones. I mean, ones that actually work. It's a miracle, you can hear what the person on the other end is saying. If Lou grew up in Chicago, better chances he lives near Michigan than near Florida. So you go have your little vacation in Sinai and by that time I'll be back home. You just send me a telegram, tell me when to come to the airport to get you. Tell the travel agent you want to go to Detroit Metro."

"I can't do that, Charlie."

"Sure you can. What's so great about this Sinai place anyway?"

"It's the most beautiful place. Black mountains that plunge down to the coast. Gorgeous empty beaches. A sea that changes from turquoise to blue to purple and

145

back. And the diving. You don't even have to dive with a tank. Get a snorkel and stick your head in the water, you see all these beautiful coral reefs with neon fish swimming around them."

They finished the second bottle of wine and Gavrielle looked sad as she said, "I'm so glad I met you. And so sorry that we probably won't ever see each other again."

"Not so fast," he said, frowning. After a long silence with a look of fierce concentration on his face, he slapped the tabletop. "I'm going to do it," he declared.

"Do what?"

"Come to Sinai, see them fish. Not right away. I've got another week of school. That'll be long enough to finish my Bernini paper. Long enough for you to get yourself settled into whatever you're going to do down there."

"I'll probably be working, Charlie. I'll need to make some money, and anyway I can't just sit on the beach all day."

"Didn't think so. Don't worry, I won't get in your way. Keep myself busy." Once he had said the idea out loud he radiated enthusiasm.

"What about your ticket?"

"I can work that out. There's some kind of charge for changes, but I've got enough travelers checks on me. And I've got plenty of time left before school starts." He stared at her dubious expression. "Don't look at me like I'm crazy. If I'm already all the way over here on this side of the world, I might as well make the most of it. Fly a few more hours and take advantage of this great Israeli guide I met in Rome." He held both hands out toward her.

"Really? Would you really come?"

"Shit, yeah. Ain't never seen no neon fish. And if you can take a day or two off, show me around Jerusalem, that would be a really big deal. Think you'd be able to do that?"

"Sure."

"Wow. Jerusalem! That's one city I never woulda thought I'd get anywhere near. This is the best idea I ever had."

"You just want to put off having to face Charlene for a while longer."

"That too." He grinned. "So it's settled. I'm coming to the Sinai. How long you gonna be down there?"

"I don't know. Probably a month or so."

"I can't stay no month, but I could do two weeks. And I'm inviting myself to Tonia and Amos's house for a day or two. See, that ain't such a hard thing for a person to do. Do you think they'll mind?"

"No. I'm sure they won't. But I don't know how you'll let me know when to come to the airport in Tel Aviv to get you."

"You don't gotta do that. I'll get down there by myself. Can't be that hard."

She looked doubtful. "I'll be in Sharm el Sheikh, all the way down south, at the very southern tip of the peninsula. Let's hear you say it. Sharm el Sheikh."

He did pretty well with the pronunciation, other than the guttural at the end, which came out a hard K. She made him repeat it a few times until she was confident anyone in Israel would understand where he wanted to go.

"You can either fly there from Tel Aviv or take a bus," she said. "I have to think about how you'll find me in Sharm, but don't worry, that won't be a problem. If you're imagining something like a city, forget it. Sharm is tiny."

"Okay, so how will I find you?"

She puckered her lips into a crooked kiss as she replayed a movie of Sharm in her mind. "I'll leave a message for you – at the ice cream shop in the strip of stores behind the gas station."

"What do you mean *the* gas station? Which gas station?"

She laughed. "I told you, Sharm is tiny. There's only one. Right next to where you get off the bus. If you fly, you'll land some miles north of Sharm and have to hitch a ride, but that's easy. Anyone going to Sharm will take you."

"You sure you're gonna be down there?"

"I'm sure."

"For a month?"

"Yeah."

"Still don't see how I'm gonna find you."

"I'll talk to the guy at the gas station and the people who work in the stores. Tell them to be on the look-out for you."

"How they spose to know who I am?"

She laughed and shook her head. "Believe me, Charlie, you'll sort of stand out." Then she reached for his hand. "Listen, I'll be really glad if you come, but I realize you probably won't. It's the kind of thing that sounds like a great idea at the time and then life gets in the way. So don't feel bad if you don't make it."

"Oh I'll make it. And then you're coming back to the old U. S. of A. with me."

Part 4

Sharm el Sheikh

Prologue

Tens of millions of years ago Africa and Asia separated, leaving two deep cracks between them. These crevices developed into long narrow waterways – the shallow Gulf of Suez on the west and the deeper Gulf of Aqaba on the east. This created the triangular land mass of the Sinai Peninsula. At the southern tip of the Sinai, a tiny promontory juts into the Red Sea, overlooking Sharm el Sheikh (the bay of the Sheikh) and commanding the entrance to the Gulf of Aqaba.

In the north of this mostly desolate peninsula, a large desert plateau slopes toward the Mediterranean. This coastal plain is where most of Sinai's scant population resides. In the south, gaunt mountain peaks of molten rock are sharply incised by canyon-like *wadis*. In the east, along the Gulf of Aqaba, these mountains all but plunge into the shimmering blue water, separated from it by a narrow coastline. No easy place for Moses and his flock to wander for 40 years.

The peninsula has been inhabited almost entirely by nomadic Bedouin, since the arrival of the Bani Sulaiman tribe in the 14th century. Despite vendettas and blood feuds, the various tribes managed, for the most part, to co-exist with one another. Smuggling was their main source of income and the transport of Turkish opium across tribal boundaries called for co-operation.

This beautiful but inhospitable land bridge between Africa and Asia, under continual Egyptian control from the First Egyptian Dynasty (3100 BCE) until the 20th century, was often the arena of conflict between Egypt and Mesopotamian powers. After the creation of the State of Israel in 1948 the expanses of Sinai served as an enormous buffer between the armies of Israel and Egypt and they fought four wars on its difficult terrain.

In 1956 Egyptian President Nasser nationalized the Suez Canal, provoking Israel, Britain, and France to occupy the peninsula, though they quickly withdrew and returned it to Egypt.

In 1967 Nasser closed the Gulf of Aqaba to Israeli shipping, built up Egypt's military presence in Sinai, and demanded the immediate departure of UN peacekeeping forces – thus precipitating Israel's pre-emptive air strike and the Six Day War. At the end of that war Sinai remained under Israeli control and Egypt initiated a long War of Attrition, which periodically escalated into full scale combat.

Prior to the Six Day War the population of south Sinai had consisted of twelve Greek monks residing at the Saint Catherine monastery (near the mountain many believe to be Biblical Mount Sinai) and about 10,000 Bedouin, who traversed the desert and mountain trails by foot, camel, donkey, and in rusty de-commissioned military vehicles, both American and Russian.

Following the Six Day War, that population doubled, as Israel established a military presence, as well as tiny civilian settlements along the eastern coast – at Nuweiba, Dahab, and finally at Sharm el Sheikh. Israelis fondly referred to the ragtag town as simply "Sharm," though the new road signs directed travelers to its official Hebrew name – Ophira. *"And they came to Ophir and fetched from thence gold, four hundred and twenty talents, and brought it to King Solomon," 1 Kings 9, 28.* Almost immediately after the war, the IDF established a naval base in Sharm and began building an air force base that would also service civilian flights. Six miles north of Sharm, along stunning Naama Bay, civilians threw together a makeshift holiday village, complete with a few fish restaurants and a dive club housed in an abandoned railroad car.

Entirely surrounded by hostile states, and now suddenly granted access to this paradise of stark beauty and year-round sunshine, Israelis began flocking south to enjoy temporary respite from the tension of everyday life in their embattled postage-stamp state. Crossing into the Sinai felt like taking a trip abroad – without the expense (then far beyond the means of most of them) of boarding an airplane. And Sinai's coral reefs are among the best in the world for snorkeling and diving.

The fourth war between Egypt and Israel began over six years later, on Yom Kippur in October, 1973. It was a disaster and in the summer of 1974 – when Gavrielle Rozmann was working in Sharm and hoping for Charlie Freeman to show up – the IDF was still digging its heels into Sinai. Most Israelis were skeptical about the ongoing peace talks and Moshe Dayan was widely quoted, "Better Sharm el Sheikh without peace, than peace without Sharm el Sheikh."

Sharm el Sheikh (Ophira)
Sunday, June 30, 1974

Gavrielle leaned on the sticky counter of Lazar's ice cream shop, chin propped on one fist, staring out the front window at the gas station that partially blocked her view of the bay. Today the water was a brilliant aquamarine that eased into deep blues and purples. Waves of heat shimmered up from the sand.

An enormous green-flecked fly made a kamikaze dive for her ear, bringing her back to reality. She batted it away and glanced at her watch, eager for her shift to end so she could take *To Kill a Mockingbird* and walk along the beach, in search of a patch of shade. She stretched, ran her fingers through her hair, and gathered it into a ponytail before continuing to scrub the countertop.

She'd stepped off the plane a few days ago and immediately fallen back in love with Sharm el Sheikh. Not everyone agreed with her. A lot of people couldn't wait to escape the long days of searing heat, the cold nights, and the lack of amenities. But she loved it. Life at the end of the world – Israel's Wild West – was so breathtakingly simple. All her necessities fit into a single backpack.

From the airport she'd hitched a ride into the tiny town and chosen to begin her search for a job at Lazar's. He offered her one on the spot and showed her the two tiny trailers he kept behind the shop – one for him and one that Gavrielle would have to share with his other employee, a busty, loud-mouthed girl named Mazal. As did all employers in Sharm, Lazar provided meals, as well as airfare to Tel Aviv every second weekend. Gavrielle had tossed her backpack into the trailer and begun her first shift.

Now she stopped scrubbing and frowned. What if Charlie does come here, but hates it? No, how could he?

It's so beautiful. Quiet. Elemental. Okay, it's hot. Really hot. But the heat is dry and the nights are cool and the stars – the stars are unbelievable. Even the air down here is different. Not just clean. There's a stillness to it. He said he'd come when he finished his paper ... But people on vacation say they're going to do all kinds of things they almost never do. Why would he come? What's he got to do in Israel, much less down here in the middle of nowhere? With some stupid Jewish girl who's not even sleeping with him? How many more days before I have to give up on him?

Gavrielle had known she would miss Charlie, but was surprised by how much. Not even the loss of Jesse had left her with this incredible sense of loneliness. *How can that be? I knew Jesse for seven years and Charlie for seven days. Of course, I never spent any large blocks of time with Jesse. We never did anything together but work. I never sat in a restaurant with him, sharing a bottle of wine. Never did anything normal at all, like go to a museum or listen to music. He never shared his problems with me, the way Charlie did. Boy, I'd give anything for one more day with Jesse. I'd get him to talk.*

Even if she never saw Charlie again, she knew he'd done something important for her – made her reconsider her indifference to having a social life. *I guess I'm not so self-sufficient after all. Maybe the torture of small talk is worth it, the cost of making some friends.*

She was unlikely to make any new friends in Sharm. Apart from blondes in bikinis (or the bottom half of one), who spent a day or two on the beach before moving on, there were not many women in Sharm. And Gavrielle didn't dare act friendly to any of the construction workers or soldiers. When they'd been drinking – which was pretty much every evening – they were a rough bunch. One moron had stood in the ice cream shop last night, staring at Mazal's truly enormous breasts and begging, "Just let me touch them. Please. Just one squeeze."

Gavrielle finished cleaning the counter, picked up the spray bottle and wash rag, and tackled the grime on the six pathetic-looking tables, all of which wobbled. She yelled toward the back room, where Lazar was. "You ought to close in the afternoons. There's no one wandering around in this heat." He shuffled in and shrugged, exhaling one of the woebegone sighs that invoked two thousand years of Jewish suffering.

"I got a chicken."

"What?" She turned to watch him hold up a soggy looking bag.

"A chicken. For dinner."

"It's Mazal's turn to cook."

Gavrielle went behind the counter and lit one of the gas burners. She had just put the kettle on for coffee when a familiar red and white El Camino pickup screeched to the curb. Last night Mazal had pointed out the owner of that truck, as he parked it and strode up the walk toward Simona's Milk Bar.

"That's Mike Heller — the new chief foreman for Hakama. Real big shot," Mazal had said. "That company gets just about all the military contracts around here. Bunch of crooks if you ask me. He used to be some big deal in the army or something. I don't know what. People say he got kicked out, but no one knows what for. Then he bummed around the world for a few years until he came back last year — to fight in the war."

"So I guess he can't be all bad," Gavrielle said, only half-listening.

"He's taken anyway," Mazal said, interpreting Gavrielle's comment as an expression of interest. "They say he's got a girlfriend. Swedish stewardess, no less.

Anyway, he drinks like a fish. And gambles." She put ominously drawn-out emphasis on "gambles." "Him and the other hotshots have these all-night poker games. You don't want to know how much they play for."

Today Mike Heller didn't pass by Lazar's on his way to Simona's. He came into the ice cream shop and stood in front of Gavrielle. Physically he was what Gavrielle had decided was her type – tall enough, wiry rather than muscle-bound, with dark curly hair, green eyes, coffee-with-a-lot-of-cream skin, and a slightly crooked mouth. But it didn't matter. A nice safe nerd with Heller's looks might have been appealing to her, but she'd never had a thing for bad boys. So she was unconcerned that she was wearing a stained T-shirt, khaki shorts the pockets of which hung a centimeter or two below the cuffs, and gray army socks rolled down over scuffed brown work shoes. Her hair needed shampooing and she couldn't remember the last time she had shaved her legs.

Still, she couldn't help recalling her Nanna Nella's favorite lecture. "You are pretty, dear," Nanna liked to say. "Not beautiful. Pretty. And it's not enough. You have no presence. No awareness of yourself. The way you just flop down, throw yourself around! And you're getting older. All the girls your age are married with families. That youthful glow won't last forever. You have to learn to take care of yourself. Cultivate yourself. Embellish yourself. That attitude you hide behind may serve you well in the military, but no man will find it becoming in his beloved."

Heller leaned closer, emanating a pleasant scent of perspiration and Brut aftershave. He didn't look like he wanted an ice cream cone. Gavrielle felt a bit intimidated and didn't appreciate it. *Who the hell does this jerk think he is?* She stuck her chin out and met his

156

gaze – and was pleased to see him blink.

"Can I help you?"

"My name's Mike Heller. I'm in charge of –"

"I know who you are."

"Are you interested in a job?"

"I have a job." She raised both hands, palms up, aware of Lazar's sigh behind her and his footsteps as he retreated out the back door.

"I can see that." Heller glanced around, looking amused. "I mean a better job."

The kettle whistled and Gavrielle turned to switch the gas off. "Coffee?" She raised her eyebrows as she took a mug from the rack for herself.

"Sure," he said. "Why not?"

"Milk and sugar?"

"Just sugar." He held up two fingers.

When she came around the counter, a mug of instant coffee in each hand, he bowed and extended an arm toward one of the tables, then stepped quickly to pull a chair out for her. He sat, placing his palms flat on the wobbly table, to steady it.

"What kind of job?" she asked as she scooted her chair closer to the table.

"At our company's camp. In the navy base." He jerked his head in the direction of the large military complex that stood atop the hill on the western side of the bay. "I need someone to help in the kitchen."

"Oh wow, yeah, that does sound *way* better than here," she said sarcastically and shook her head. "Anyway, I don't know how to cook. And have zero interest in learning."

"We have a cook. A professional. All you have to do is set the tables, serve the food, and then clear the tables. Either that or wash the dishes. We've already got a young kid – you can trade off who does what with him. That's between the two of you."

"Sounds fascinating. But no thanks."

157

"Don't you want to know how much we pay?"

"I'm more interested in where I'd be living."

"We'll find you a room up there."

"All to myself?" Gavrielle already hated sharing the tiny trailer with Mazal.

"Obviously."

The prospect of privacy was enticing. "How many gross, disgusting construction workers do you have working for you?"

A smile pulled briefly at the corners of his mouth and he looked away. "Around seventy."

She rolled her eyes to the ceiling. "Now that really is an attractive offer. Me and seventy horny men who get drunk every night. How enticing. You must think I'm a loony tune. Or else you are."

"You won't be the only woman in camp." He leaned forward. "Our electrician's wife lives down here with him. And there's a Yemenite woman, takes care of the office. She's single."

"How old are they?"

"I don't know. Sharona must be in her forties. Rachel too, I suppose."

Gavrielle stared at him, biting her bottom lip. Yesterday she had served ice cream to Rachel – the maybe-forty-something Yemenite woman – and then watched her roar away behind the wheel of the Hakama jeep. Rachel obviously enjoyed the kind of smug pride Gavrielle would have liked to feel, for venturing into this man's world and surviving, quite nicely thank you. *I could do that. I serve with all those men in the army, don't I?* But the guys in Sharm were different. In the army you were thrown together with people from all over the country, rich and poor, educated or not. But the Hakama employees were all rough working class. They all drank. And they all seemed to believe they *were* in the Wild West. Anything goes. Lazar's ice cream shop was adventure enough for Gavrielle.

Heller drank from his mug and set it down loudly. "Look, I give you my personal guarantee. You won't have any ... problems." He placed his right hand over his heart. "You can count on it. Anyone gets out of line, you come to me. The first time will damn sure be the last."

She raised her chin a little higher and continued to stare into his face. She had never seen eyes that green.

"You won't have to work many hours. I'd guess two a meal. Maybe less, if you're fast. In between meals, once you're done cleaning up, your time is your own."

"How much *do* you pay?"

"1700 liras a month."

That was more than Lazar was paying her. And a lot more free time to herself. And her own room. "I want 2000."

"I can't start you at more than 1700, but if you last past the first week, I'll raise it to 2000. Retroactive."

"You provide all my meals?"

He nodded impatiently, as if that was obvious.

"And airfare to Tel Aviv?"

"Of course. Every other weekend. That's standard everywhere down here."

She stared over his shoulder for a moment and then turned her gaze back on him. "In between meals ... during my free time ... can I use your jeep?"

He didn't smile, but still looked amused. "Where exactly do you plan on going?"

She shrugged. "Mostly just over to Naama Bay. Maybe Nabeq. I haven't been to Ras Muhammed yet."

"That shouldn't be a problem, as long as you square it with Rachel. If I know her, she not only won't mind, she'll want to go to Ras Muhammed with you."

"So when do you want to come back and get me?"

"Go get your things." He pushed his chair back and stood up.

159

"Now?" She looked up at him.

"Seventy gross, disgusting construction workers are going to want dinner tonight."

"I can't do that to Lazar. I only started working here a few days ago. I have to give him some kind of notice."

"Don't sweat it. The new face behind this counter never sticks it out for more than a week."

She raised her eyebrows, rose, and turned to walk toward the back door, saying, "Wait a minute," over her shoulder.

She found her employer hanging a dripping shirt over the line he had strung between the two trailers. "Lazar ..." she said.

"I know. I know. Enjoy your new job." He didn't sound angry, but his shoulders drooped even farther. "Come in for ice cream some time."

"Yeah, I'll be around." She lightly tapped his shoulder and stepped up into the flimsy little trailer, suddenly more than prepared for a new adventure.

She quickly shoved her wallet, flashlight, Swiss army knife, books, toiletries, and clothes into her pack. Then she stepped back into the shop and stopped short. It was empty. She stood staring at the chair Heller had vacated, until startled by two impatient honks. He was already behind the wheel of the El Camino, waving for her to hurry up.

"Toss that back there." He jerked his thumb toward the open bed of the truck. "I suppose you have a name," he said, as she got in.

"Gavrielle. Rozmann."

He backed up, shifted gears, and squealed away. *Big show-off*, she thought. *You're not really so sure of yourself.*

"You're an Israeli citizen?" he asked.

"Yes. What if I weren't?"

160

"We'd work it out." He kept his eyes straight ahead and said nothing else.

At the entrance to the navy base, the uniformed guard lowered the rope and waved them through with barely a glance.

"How do I get in and out of here on my own?" she asked.

"Go to the office and see Rachel. She'll fix you up with a card." He stopped by a group of unimpressive buildings, mostly of bare cinder block. Only the dining hall and office were of flimsy-looking wood. "This is it."

Heller got out, walked a dozen meters, and roared at the first man who happened into his line of sight. "Aviram! Why the hell isn't that room finished? I told you jerk-offs I was bringing her back with me."

"Don't worry," Aviram answered, his voice calm and soft. "Everything's fine." Smiling, he walked over to Gavrielle. "Hi, how are you doing?"

He seemed to expect her to recognize him. *Maybe I waited on him at Lazar's or something. But that can't be. This guy, I would remember.* True, to her the customers were an indistinguishable mass – same clothes, same smell, same jokes, same foul mouths – but this man should have been memorable. Forget about Heller being the physical type she could appreciate. Aviram she could worship. He had a mane of shiny brown hair, liquid eyes, and thick lashes. She had never met a man who radiated such warmth. Well, maybe except for Charlie.

"I'm good," she replied. "How are you?"

"Let me help you with that." Aviram reached into the bed of the truck for her pack. "I'll show you around while they finish up."

Heller gave her a stiff nod and marched off. Then he turned around and barked. "Remember, you have to come into the office before you can go off base. Fill in

161

some forms."

"Sure," Gavrielle shouted back as she followed Aviram.

"Boy, am I glad Heller talked you into coming," he said. "I've been doing your job for the last few days and ain't going to miss it."

"What's your regular job?"

"Welder. This right here is the dining room." He set her pack down, took a lone key from his pocket, and fit it into the padlock on the door. "There's a shackle on the inside too." He set her pack inside, pushed the door shut behind them, and slipped the padlock on the inside shackle. "When you're in here working alone, always keep the door locked," he said. "You'll open up for meals from in here."

"Have you worked here long?" she asked.

"Three years, off and on."

"What's that mean?"

"We work here for a while, then in Eilat for a while. Once in a while we get a job in Tel Aviv."

"Who's 'we'?"

"My partner and me. We always work as a team."

"Why do you move around so much?"

"Get tired of the same place." He shrugged. "And then Gurion – that's my partner – he never wants to be in the same place I do. I like working in Tel Aviv, even though it's less money. I got a wife and twin daughters, and I like being close to home. Gurion's got a wife too – and eight kids." He smiled. "He'd stay down here permanently if I'd agree. And I need the extra pay, so I don't always argue with him."

He spent a few minutes showing her where the plastic dishes and battered tin utensils were kept, explaining how she was to set each table before opening the door to let the animals in for feeding time.

162

"First time, you're going to be scared to take that lock off," he said with a grin. "They'll be out there pounding on the door and howling like a pack of starving wolves, but don't worry. These guys are alright. And Heller knows how to crack the whip, keep us in line." He opened the door to exit and said, "You might as well leave your pack in here for now."

They went outside and he replaced the padlock and handed her the key.

"Do you maybe have a key chain for it?" she asked. "So it won't be so easy to lose."

"Your wish is my command." He walked around, kicking at the sand, until he bent to retrieve a thick length of discarded twine. He threaded it through the hole in the key and tied a knot, leaving a loop large enough to slip onto her wrist or hang on a nail. He took out a pocketknife and cut off the straggling ends of twine before handing it to her. "There you go."

She shook her head, grinning, and then nodded at the large German Shepherd that was approaching them. "Whose dog is that?"

"Oh that's Azit. Don't belong to no one. Guy did some contracting down here, left her behind. But she gets plenty to eat. Everyone's always feeding her."

Gavrielle leaned down to pat Azit and scratch her head, pleased that the dog followed them when they walked away. Aviram pointed out the portable toilets and then led her to a structure of tall, corrugated tin walls. It had no roof – just four pipes running from one side to the other, shower heads extending from them at regular intervals.

"There's only one shower room?" she asked.

"Yeah. The women either use it during the day, while we're working, or have to wait until later in the evening, after us guys are done. There's a bolt inside, but first you pull this up." He demonstrated, raising the piece of wood nailed to the door. "That means there's a woman in there. And you gotta make sure all the peek holes are plugged up." He nodded at wads of toilet paper sticking out of the walls.

"That's for washing up?" She pointed at the aluminum trough next to the shower room. It was about ten feet long with a pipe running above the middle of it, faucets extending at regular intervals on either side.

"Yep. I bet your room's ready by now. Wait here while I go check."

She watched his back, noting his thick torso and short legs. Maybe he isn't so attractive when you aren't drowning in those eyes. But that's no reason not to ... No, forget it. Wild West or not, you can't do that in a place like this. Where the hell would we go anyway? Every time I go behind a sand dune to pee, I turn around and there's some Bedouin lying in the sand with a big grin on his face. No, forget it. This is most definitely not the time or place for another indiscretion.

She idly patted Azit's head and walked to the fence, to admire the view of the bay below. Her mind blotted out the ugly buildings; all she saw was the expanse of white sand and the sun glimmering over the sea. On the opposite side of the bay, a white cliff rose to a plateau, on which a row of stark white apartment buildings was nearing completion. Many of the units already housed families. This small community of permanent residents kept their distance from the soldiers, construction workers, and bedraggled tourists who composed most of the population. The transients were also happy to ignore "the civilians" and thus preserve their private vision of paradise, without the encumbrances and contingencies of ordinary life. To them Sharm was no place for mortgage payments and nursery schools.

She stared at "downtown" – the gas station (one pump for gasoline, one for diesel), bus station (two busses a day), a few shacks that housed a clinic (one nurse), post office (opened for an hour or two each morning by one of the shopkeepers), and police station (one cop). Farther back was the row of shops – tiny supermarket, restaurant, Lazar's Ice Cream Parlor, gift shop, and Simona's Milk Bar.

It suddenly occurred to Gavrielle that she had forgotten to tell Lazar about Charlie. She'd have to go do that tomorrow, after breakfast or lunch.

"Come on, girl," she said to Azit. "Let's go find Aviram."

That didn't prove hard to do – just walk toward the sound of men shouting at each other. Apparently her room was a newly-built, lopsided structure of unfinished cinder block, with a wooden frame for its still missing roof. Shirtless men on ladders were hoisting panels of asbestos into place and Aviram was on the ground, hollering for them to make sure it was airtight, no gaps between the walls and the roof.

"A little open space might not be so bad," Gavrielle said from behind him. "Seeing as there's no window."

He turned and shook his head. "You're going to hear a shit load of rats scurrying around up there over your head." He raised both hands in front of his chin, curled his fingers, and moved them in tiny clawing movements, while puckering his mouth into his version of a vicious rodent.

"Yuck."

"Don't ever leave your door open. You want to air the room out, you stand in the doorway while you're doing it. Even if you're just going over there to wash your face, make sure the door's closed tight. It's not just the rats. There's plenty of snakes around too. Vipers. Not to mention scorpions."

She watched them finish the roof and then carry a wicker chair and a stand of shelves inside. *What about a bed?* She hadn't seen them move one.

165

"All done," Aviram said with a bow. "Your castle awaits."

The other men had moved aside and stood watching her, exchanging comments under their breath. She forced an unfocused smile in their general direction and turned to press down on the handle of the door. It opened only halfway in, stopped by an iron-framed single bed. She stepped onto the sandy plywood floor, sat on the lumpy mattress, and shut the door. The enclosed space smelled sickeningly of wet cement and was completely dark. She waved her hand overhead and found a string to pull to turn on the single bulb she had noticed dangling from the ceiling. *Home sweet home.* She looked around glumly, wondering how long it would take the cement to dry. But she was determined not to complain, and composed her face before going back outside.

"You built the room around the bed, didn't you?" She looked at Aviram with a grin.

"Wouldna been able to get it in there the other way around." He shrugged. "But we had it all covered up with a sheet, so no cement got on it."

"So what, if you need the bed somewhere else, you'll just knock the wall down to get it out?"

He shrugged again.

"Do you think you could hammer some nails into the inside of the door?" she asked. "To hang stuff on?"

One of the other men removed the hammer from his belt and obliged. While he was pounding six nails into the door, Mike Heller emerged from the office and came to stand next to Aviram. When the hammering stopped and the man came out, Heller handed him the two pieces of a shackle. Then he turned to face Gavrielle and wordlessly handed her a padlock with a key taped to it.

166

"There's already a lock on the door," Gavrielle said, nodding at the shackle he was still holding.

"I know," Heller said gruffly. "This one is for inside."

"Oh. Yeah. Right."

"Make sure you put it on every night." He walked away.

"Hi, I'm Sharona," a female voice behind Gavrielle said. Gavrielle turned to a frazzled blonde woman and took her offered hand. "Hi. I'm Gavrielle. I guess you must be the electrician's wife."

"That's me." Sharona laid a hand on Gavrielle's forearm and said, "Come with me. We'll get you some bedding and towels."

Gabrielle was glad to see Azit still sticking with her.

Gavrielle moved the chair to the doorway of her room and sat on it reading her book, wondering how on earth she would sleep in there, even after the cement dried. At six that evening she set out to follow Aviram's instructions. There was no padlock on the door to the dining room; it was locked from the inside. She walked around back and knocked on the door to the kitchen. Hearing only a grunt, she knocked again.

"Open the damn door and come in already. You're late enough as it is."

She stepped inside and pulled the door shut behind her. "Actually, I'm exactly on time."

This is the professional cook? He must have forgotten his puffy white hat. She guessed him to be in his forties, though the long clumps of oily curls that hung from his head were entirely gray. He stood at a long stainless-steel table, chopping cucumbers with rat-tat-tat strokes of a large cleaver. The cigarette that hung from his lips was almost all ash and she stared in fascination, waiting for it to fall all over the food. He had also forgotten his shirt. Thick gray hair covered his chest and a fold of belly hung over his khaki shorts.

"What are you waiting for?" He finally looked up and tossed his cigarette, ash still miraculously clinging to it, onto the floor. "Aviram told you what to do, so go do it."

"My name is Gavrielle."

"Yeah, yeah. Fancy shmancy." He turned to take some tomatoes from the sink behind him and she diverted her eyes from the display of his butt crack.

"So I guess you're Mordecai the cook."

"I ain't Mimi the camp whore." He set to chopping the tomatoes.

Setting eighty places at ten tables didn't take long. She made sure the salt and pepper shakers were full, set out dispensers of olive oil and lemon juice, filled the napkin holders, and set ashtrays and plastic bowls for trash on each table. On a table at the back of the room stood a tall electric urn for hot water that she filled and switched on. Then she replenished the stacks of Styrofoam cups, filled two cups with plastic spoons, filled the sugar bowls, and made sure there was enough coffee, both Turkish and instant. When she finished and returned to the kitchen, Mordecai was filling plastic bowls with Israeli salad – finely chopped tomatoes, cucumbers, onion, and greens.

"Stick a spoon in each and put them out," he said. "And then the bread baskets. You know how to work that thing?" He nodded toward the bread-slicing machine.

"Yeah."

She finished doing as told, and then stood watching him. The inch of cigarette ash now dangled over the pot of soup he was stirring. That was going to be a hard image to erase before she ate anything prepared by this man.

As if on cue he threw the cigarette to the floor and said, "You might as well go sit down and eat. From now on I don't care what time you show up, long as you get everything done and open the door on time. Here's your soup." He ladled it into a bowl and set it on the metal table. "There's chicken and rice in the oven. Ain't nothing else for you to do until seven twenty-five when you put the soup on the tables. I'll have it on that cart there, ready to wheel out. At seven thirty on the button you take the lock off the door. Wait ten minutes before you roll out the chicken and rice. It'll be ready on the cart. One bowl of rice and platter of chicken for each table, but if they finish it and ask for more, you give it to them. All they want. Of the soup, too. You also eat as much as you want," he said.

"Okay. Thanks."

She took her soup to the dining room and shoved one of the place settings aside, suddenly aware of how hungry she was. The soup tasted surprisingly good. *Maybe Mordecai isn't so bad. Who was I expecting, Julia Child?* She went back for more soup and then helped herself to chicken and rice, both times forcing herself to smile and compliment the cook. His face took on a wary, puzzled expression, but he almost smiled back.

By seven-fifteen she could hear the first male voices outside and, as the volume rose, she began casting nervous glances at the door. It was shaking and rattling, but she also heard laughter. *Okay, they're just guys acting the way guys do when their mother isn't around. They aren't really going to break down the door and tear the place apart.* At seven twenty-five she wheeled the cart out, set a large metal tureen of soup on each table, then wheeled the cart back to the kitchen. She was considering telling Mordecai that she quit and he would have to do the serving, but then the back door opened. Mike Heller came in, hair still wet from the

169

shower, wearing jeans and a royal blue V-neck shirt.

He nodded to Mordecai and stiffly turned to Gavrielle, asking, "Everything all right here?"

She pursed her lips and nodded, following him into the dining room. He positioned himself ten feet from the door, arms crossed, and she all but melted into a pool of gratitude.

"Okay, go ahead. Open it."

She had been wondering how she was supposed to take the lock off and get out of the way, in time to avoid being bashed by the door and trampled in the stampede. As quietly as she could, she inserted and turned the key and slipped the padlock from the shackle. Heller waved her aside and stepped forward to pull the door open.

"Okay, jerk-offs, hold it." Heller's voice boomed at the mob of raucous men – loudly enough to startle Gavrielle as much as it did them. The silence was sudden and absolute. "This is Gavrielle. I'm sure you've all seen her around and know she's going to be working here." He lowered the volume, but went back to standing with arms crossed and a scowl on his face. "Unlike the lot of you, she's a civilized human being and is not going to get any crap from you. No looks. No remarks. You tired of working here, just try giving her some lip. You want to see if I can take you apart, try laying a hand on her." He glared in silence for a long moment. "Now let's see if you can walk through a door and sit down for dinner like normal human beings, instead of a bunch of animals."

Heller took his place at the "management" table at the back of the room and the men filed past Gavrielle, each giving her a furtive once over, but none daring to leave his eyes on her – except for Aviram, who winked. He was also damp from his shower, in jeans and black T-shirt.

Gavrielle returned to the kitchen and the initially low buzz of conversation gradually rose to normal volume. When she wheeled out the cart with the chicken and rice, the men lowered their voices a bit, though the novelty of her presence seemed to be wearing off quickly. They politely passed the empty soup tureens and stacks of plastic bowls to her and, if necessary, made room on the table for the serving dishes. She murmured her thanks and avoided making eye contact with any of them. When she reached Heller's table she pantomimed a long "Phew!" and mouthed, "Thank you."

Back in the kitchen, more to herself than to Mordecai, she said, "Well, that wasn't so bad. Thanks to Mr. Heller." Then she noticed a skinny, dark-skinned teen-aged boy and said, "Oh, hello."

He mumbled hello and turned back to the large tub he was filling with water.

"My name's Gavrielle," she said. "What's yours?"

"Shimon."

"Heller told me there's a young guy working here. I guess that must be you. He said we can trade off however we want – between washing dishes or serving in the dining room." She tilted her head a bit, trying to look into his downcast face.

"I only want to wash dishes," he mumbled. "If that's okay with you."

"Yeah, that's okay with me."

Mordecai grunted and pointed at the cart, which held more platters of chicken and bowls of rice. Gavrielle hurried out with it to offer seconds. The men continued to mind their manners and finally began rising in groups. They jostled one another around the table at the back, making cups of Turkish coffee to take outside. Keeping a safe distance, Gavrielle busied herself collecting scraps for Azit. As the first of the men took his coffee and headed for the door, he burst into a

171

deep tenor – "Hey, did you happen to see the most beautiful girl in the world ..."

Startled, Gavrielle looked up, but the singer never gave her a glance. She noticed Aviram vigorously shaking his head at Heller, who shrugged and let it go. One of the other men, who looked much too old to be working construction, shyly approached her, hat literally in hand, and said, "Thank you, miss."

"You're very welcome, sir." She flashed a quick smile and continued working, head down.

After that first brief serenade, the worker she always thought of as "The Singer" often burst into song when she came into sight, with his co-workers sometimes joining in for the chorus. Their favorite was the Mac Davis song: "She's a woman, she's a baby ... She's a witch, she's a lady." It always began as a solo, but the other guys never failed to join in for that song. They purred the beginning of the last line – "If she wants to be with me tonight" –but loudly shouted the last two words – "That's alright." Gavrielle opted to be a good sport, though she never went so far as to stop or turn to look at them as she passed by, shaking her head like a good-natured schoolteacher.

After her first night at work, serving that first dinner, she'd felt safe. Everything would be all right, as long as she kept her distance, never crossed the invisible line, never did or said anything that made her appear available. That illusion would soon be briefly shattered.

The next morning, after the usual shouting and laughing died down, and the roar of the men's vehicles faded away, Gavrielle stepped out of her room, remembering to pull the door shut behind her. The sky was a muted gray-blue that would soon reclaim its brilliance as the sun climbed higher. Behind her, the jagged black mountains plunged to the sand, and in front of her the grays, blues, and purples of the sea were mesmerizing. As usual, the early morning air shimmered in the gathering heat. She wore her khaki shorts, a navy blue T-shirt, and over it a striped men's dress shirt, unbuttoned and hanging almost to her knees.

She peeked around the corner and saw a lone man at the near end of the shaving trough, stripped to the waist. Even with his back to her she knew it was Mike Heller and paused for a moment to watch him. *He is one good-looking man, almost like Amos,* she thought and then ducked back to stay out of sight, waiting for him to finish. When he was gone, she went out and bent to the first faucet to wash her hands and splash water on her face. Having neglected to bring her towel, she used her sleeve to dry off and then took her toothbrush and paste out of her shirt pocket. After a lifetime of her grandmother's regimented fussiness, this simple action felt exhilarating.

That's why I love it here, she thought. It's so different from real life. You can do whatever the hell you want. Well, excluding anything to make the seventy disgusting, horny construction workers think you're a slut.

She often paused to remember the war that had raged over the Sinai just last year – the thousands of men who'd bled their lives into the sand, hundreds of tanks incinerated, the obliteration of the command center at Sharm's airport. But this morning Sharm had nothing to do with combat and killing. It was a paradise of peace. She might as well have been in Tahiti. Her anxieties were almost at bay.

Full of energy, she hurried into the kitchen and opened one of the doors of the wall refrigerator, looking for milk for her coffee. "Ach!" she shouted as she looked down in time to see a rat scamper over the toe of her work shoe. But not even that could spoil her mood. She watched it escape under the door of the room in which the produce and staples were kept. She looked over at Mordecai, but he stared back, daring her to complain.

No one sang any songs during breakfast. The men quickly finished eating and took their coffee outside. Gavrielle was alone in the dining room, clearing tables, when she suddenly felt the unwelcome warmth of a presence behind her. Someone's forearm pressed against her throat, pulling her against the man behind her, while his other hand groped her breasts. The incident lasted only a few seconds. Gavrielle instinctively thrust her elbows back, hard into his ribs, and blindly jabbed the fork she was holding into his thigh. He squealed and released her. She turned in time to get a look at him as he fled out the door. She hadn't screamed loudly enough for anyone to come running and she stood motionless, numb. Then she sank down onto the nearest chair and crossed her arms, hugging herself, trying to eradicate the imprint of that repulsive hand on her breasts. She couldn't hold her tears back, but they were silent.

Oh, boo-hoo. Stop being such a baby. So some scumbag groped your boobs, big deal. Did somebody die? Just get up and go back to work. No, no, no. You can't let him get away with this. Oh no? So what are you going to do? Go down to the police station and report it? Excuse me officer, I need to report a terrible crime. Some guy copped a feel.

It took her a while to get back to her feet. Still shaky, she cleared a few tables. *What am I going to do when he comes in and sits down for lunch, waiting for me to serve his table?* She shuddered – imagining him leering at her, winking – and sat down again. *I can't do this. Maybe Lazar will give me my job back. But the creep could come into the ice cream shop.* Then she got angry. *This isn't my problem. Heller gave me his big deal guarantee. Let him deal with it. Go to the office. Right now, before you chicken out.*

She got there just in time. Heller was getting into the El Camino.

He saw her and froze, arm resting on the open door. "What's wrong? What happened?"

She glanced nervously at the three men who stood nearby, waiting for Heller to drive them over to the building site at the new airbase, north of Naama Bay.

"Come into the office," he said and slammed the car door.

Gavrielle followed him, relieved to see that Rachel wasn't there. *This is going to sound so lame.* She felt herself beginning to shake again.

Heller closed the office door behind them and stood, waiting. "What? I can't do anything about it if you don't tell me." His voice was gruff, but she guessed that was to hide his embarrassment.

"You said ..."

"I know what I said. Did one of them do something to you?"

"It's not a big deal. Just ... I was clearing the tables ... I guess it's my fault. I forgot to lock the door ... somebody came up behind me ..."

"And? Did he put his hands on you?"

She nodded. Now there were tears in her eyes. *Why do I feel so humiliated? I didn't do anything.* "Yes," she whispered. "Like this." She moved behind him, her body not quite touching his, and held her own right forearm across his throat, her left hand in the air in front of his chest. Then she quickly stepped away. "Then I did like this." She demonstrated, thrusting her elbows back. "And I had a fork in my hand. I stuck him with it, so he probably has marks there." She put her fingers on her thigh. "After that he ran away."

"Did you see who it was?"

She nodded. "The Russian. With the gold front tooth and red hair."

"Sit down." He pointed at Rachel's chair and Gavrielle obeyed.

The rest of the men were either on their way to the airport or already there. Heller went to his desk, picked up the speaker to the Motorola radio, and ordered them all back to camp. Now.

Gavrielle and Heller sat through an unbearably long and awkward silence until the jeeps, pickups, and vans roared back into camp. When the men had gathered in the space between the office and the dining hall, Heller stood in the center of the half-circle they formed and glared at their curious stares.

"What did I say about Gavrielle?" he roared. "What in the hell made one of you think he was going to get away with putting his filthy hands on her? I want to know which one of you jerk-offs thought he was such a big man."

The men exchanged glances, but no one stepped forward.

"Gavrielle, come out here, please."

She turned white. Why was he doing this to her? She'd expected him to take care of it quietly, just fire the guy and be done with it. She reluctantly rose and stepped out onto the small wooden porch.

"Not man enough to admit it?" Heller looked around. Then he took a few steps and grabbed the red-haired Russian by the back of his neck and threw him to the ground. "You think I don't know it was you, you chicken-shit piece of crap?" Heller kicked the Russian in the side as he scrambled to get away, on all fours like a crab. Heller went after him and kicked him again, harder. "You think you can screw with me? Pull that kind of crap in my camp?" The Russian struggled, trying to get to his feet, and Heller kicked him again.

176

"Don't bother asking for the pay you've got coming, because that's gone."

"Listen Heller, I've got three kids —"

"You listen, cockroach. I don't give a shit if you have a zoo full of four-headed monkeys. I don't have time to waste on this kind of garbage. You've already cost me a morning. Now you've got five minutes to go get your crap and get the hell out of here. And I don't mean out of camp. If I see your face in Sharm again, your mother won't recognize you."

Heller turned his back on the Russian, who stood and retreated. The other men moved aside to let him pass.

"Five minutes," Heller called after him. "Unless you want me to come help you pack."

He turned to glare at the rest of them. The morning sun was already burning hot, but he kept them standing there, waiting to watch the Russian slink away. In less than five minutes he scurried past them, carrying a battered suitcase that looked like it was made of cardboard. When he was halfway to the gate he turned and raised an angry fist, middle finger raised.

Heller spat at the ground in his direction and then turned back to his work crew. "Was I unclear yesterday? Do I need to repeat myself for the rest of you?"

They all studied the ground.

"Do I?"

"I think we got it, boss," Aviram said.

Heller didn't wait for Gavrielle's muttered thanks. He barked orders and headed for the El Camino. Gavrielle slipped back into the office and waited to hear the last of them pile into their vehicles and disappear in a cloud of dust. After her stomach settled she returned to the dining room, where she found Aviram and Shimon clearing tables.

"You don't have to do that," she said. "I'm all right."

"You sure?" Aviram asked. "Heller told me to stay and help."

"Yes, I'm sure. Please. I'll feel better if you let me do my job."

The mindless routine was calming and after she finished clearing the tables and sweeping the floor she sat down for a rest. There was noise in the kitchen and she looked up to see Mordecai hesitantly approaching her with a cup of tea and saucer of cookies. He set them in front of her without saying a word.

Would you look at that, she thought as she nodded her thanks. Don't people always surprise you? I'll have to stop calling him Medusa in my mind.

She wasn't normally a tea-drinker, but it was surprisingly comforting. Even more unexpected was the way Heller's actions had affected her. The immense satisfaction she'd derived from his performance. By now she understood why he'd been so public – as a warning to the rest of them – and forgave him for the embarrassment it had caused her. What surprised her was the way each sickening thud of his boot had made her feel less helpless. Of course, it would have been better if *she* had been the one doing the kicking, but at least the kicking got done. She made a conscious decision to go back to feeling safe – but also to never again forget to put the padlock on that door.

She rose, dropped her empty teacup into Shimon's tub of dishwater, and marched to the office for the keys to the jeep, feeling almost as if nothing had happened. Except that now she had no time to go to Naama Bay. Rachel had agreed to let Gavrielle take the jeep every day, between breakfast and lunch, but today Gavrielle would only have time to make it to Lazar's and back. She had to leave a note for Charlie. Now she was really going to miss having a friend.

After dinner that night Gavrielle switched off the light in the dining room and put the padlock on the door. She turned to stare out at the water and the lights of a ship anchored in the bay. It didn't matter that she knew it was an old rusted-out tanker. With its lights twinkling in the dark, it evoked far away places, adventure, and romance. She jumped when Aviram spoke behind her.

"Me and Gurion and them two guys over there are going down to Simona's," he said, jerking his thumb toward his friends. "We'd be honored to have you join us."

He was all dressed up – tight jeans with metal studs down the side seams and a matching jeans jacket over a silky black and white striped shirt. He was taller than she remembered – a mystery that was solved when she lowered her eyes and noticed the thick heels on his pointy shoes. *Pimp shoes*, she couldn't help thinking.

"I don't know ..."

"Don't worry. It's okay," Aviram assured her. "You're allowed to talk to someone besides the dog. If it was just you and me going, that could get some guys all riled up, but it's not. And anyway we all made a pact."

"Pact? What kind of pact?"

"You're like our mascot. None of us starts with you. So don't bother trying to seduce me." He grinned. "You'd just be wasting your time. Come on, bring Azit if you want. Simona loves her." He paused a moment, giving her time to consider. "You gotta know there's nothing else to do around here at night. There's drinking at Simona's or drinking at the Tea House – or you can hang around here and watch your laundry dry," he said.

His touch startled her – the barest pressure of thumb and forefinger on her elbow – encouraging her to take a few steps and be introduced to Gurion, Nuri, and Benny. Gurion – a burly, gray-haired man who

179

looked much older than Aviram – was already holding the passenger door of the jeep open for her, visibly impatient. Gavrielle did her best not to stare at Nuri. He was badly scarred – a jagged lightening bolt ran diagonally across his face, from left temple to right ear lobe. He was painfully thin, his skin stretched taut over sharp features. *If I met this guy on a dark street, I'd run for my life.* She recognized Benny – he was the shy older one who had thanked her for serving their dinner.

She was reluctant to go with them, but took a deep breath and climbed in. Aviram got behind the wheel, and the other three piled in back. Simona's Milk Bar was last in the row of shops and opened onto a large patio. Downstairs they served mostly sundaes and milkshakes. Upstairs was the bar, where the serious drinkers congregated. Sephardic music blared and a few drunks were dancing on the sidewalk when they pulled up outside.

Nuri pulled out a chair for her at one of the tables downstairs. Seated, all four looked as gentlemanly as men with knives hanging from their belts, scary scars on their faces, and tattoos on their arms could. She was glad to have Aviram next to her and Gurion on the other side of him, far from her. There was something unsettling about Gurion, the way his eyes darted around, too often landing on her. He was already shouting to friends, telling a joke, demanding to be the center of attention. Beneath the bluster, Gavrielle sensed something vicious about him. She didn't understand how he and soft-spoken Aviram could be such good friends.

"Thank you all for inviting me to come with you." She looked around the table, clueless. What on earth could she possibly talk to these men about? She didn't know any jokes.

Nuri stood, saying, "I'll get the first round. What can I get for you, Gavrielle?" She would have loved a beer, but asked for a chocolate milkshake. He didn't bother asking the others and headed for the counter.

Gavrielle's mind wandered as the men talked about work, arguing over how many iron rods and of what weight were required for a certain amount of concrete. A popular song came over the loudspeaker and Gurion stood up and began dancing like a clumsy bear – eyes closed, arms raised high over his head, snapping his fingers. He stomped his way out to the patio. Then Benny nudged his chair over to hear what a man at the next table was saying. Aviram leaned closer to Gavrielle to ask, "So, what are you doing in Sharm?"

"Saving up some money."

"Doesn't a girl like you have a rich daddy?"

"I don't have any kind of daddy. That's what I'm saving for – to go to America and look for him."

Aviram looked as taken aback as she felt, hearing the words come out of her mouth so casually. She was relieved to see Nuri returning, carrying a tray with four glasses of whiskey and her milkshake. Benny claimed his glass along with Gurion's, which he took outside to him. Nuri sat opposite Gavrielle, downed half of his whiskey, and stared intently at her.

"I bet you know some good doctors," he finally ventured.

Gavrielle's expression was blank. Under the bright fluorescent lighting, there was something endearing and not at all scary about Nuri. Seeing how uncomfortable he was, Gavrielle wanted to be kind, but failed to comprehend what he wanted from her.

"I'm saving up," Nuri explained. "For an operation." He ran his forefinger over the scar. "Surprise my wife."

"Oh. You mean plastic surgeons. No, sorry, I don't know any of those kinds of doctors. But I'm sure your family doctor –"

"What's your father do?" Nuri interrupted and then emitted a loud, "Hey, ouch! What's with you?" when Aviram kicked him under the table.

"She just told me that she doesn't have a father, idiot."

"Gee, I'm sorry, Gavrielle. I didn't hear that. How about your mother? What's she do?"

Gavrielle almost snorted a laugh. *Oh dear, poor Nuri.* She didn't have the heart to tell the poor man her mother was dead.

"Leave it, Nuri," Aviram said.

"You leave it. You know the kind of people she must come from, with education and everything. They always know about that kind of stuff. Always recommending things to each other."

"When I go home for the weekend I could ask our family doctor," Gavrielle offered, astonished that a simple thing like finding a doctor seemed so difficult to this man.

"Would you really? That'd be great. I'd appreciate it, really. I don't mind paying, but I want someone good. The best. My wife, she's a real looker. Shouldn't have to go around with a mug like mine."

"How did it happen?" Gavrielle asked.

"Oh, you know, work accident. I'm banging on a length of pipe and this piece of something comes flying at me, out of nowhere, all jagged. Boom, right in the face. Doc said I was lucky I didn't lose the eye."

"I bet you thought he got it in a knife fight." Aviram grinned.

"Oh, no ..."

"Fight? Me? That's a good one." Nuri tipped his chair back on two legs. "Not hardly. Now Aviram, he got a gut full of knife once. Was in the hospital for two weeks, operation and everything. You'd never guess how." He looked at Gavrielle, waiting for her to ask.

182

She obliged. "How?"

"Being a big hero. See, last year some jerk is down here pushing grass. Comes into Simona's and there's this little Bedouin kid works for Simona, clears off the tables. The kid buys a pack of cigarettes he's supposed to take home to his father, but he forgets it, leaves it lying on one of the tables. Kid comes running back for it just as the pusher is picking it up. The kid's crying and everything, begging him to give them back, 'cause his old man's gonna beat the crap out of him. But the pusher just shoves him aside and starts walking off. So Aviram here, he can't do something simple, like just buy the kid another pack. Says it's the principle of the thing. Goes running after the jerk, punches him out real good, but ends up with four inches of blade in his belly. See, big hero. Army chopper took him to the hospital in Beer Sheva."

Gavrielle looked wide-eyed at Aviram. "Did that really happen?"

"Yeah," he said, staring at the table, one leg jiggling nervously beneath it. "Dumbest thing I ever did. All the way in that helicopter, all I could think was, 'That's it, I'm a dead man. My little girls are going to grow up without a daddy, just like I did, all because of a lousy pack of cigarettes.'" He took his packet from his jacket pocket and lit one.

"Who's coming upstairs?" Gurion came in from the patio and set his empty glass on the table.

"Get serious. That's no place for Gavrielle," Aviram said.

"That's okay," she said, quickly sucking the last of her milkshake through the straw before standing up. "It's time for me to go home. Thanks for bringing me."

"What do you mean, go home? We just got here," Aviram said.

"Past my bedtime. Thanks again." She nudged her chair aside and fished some coins out of her pocket, placing them on the table for the milkshake.

"Get that money off the table," Nuri said. "You're our guest. Long as you're in Sharm, your money is no good."

"All right. Okay. Thank you." Gavrielle nervously scraped the coins up and tried to manage a smile. Then she turned toward the door and fanned her fingers in a little wave. "Good night. Thanks again."

"Hold up. You think I'm going to let you walk?" Aviram stood and fished the keys from his pocket.

Gurion had started up the stairs but couldn't resist turning back for the last word. With a leer and raised eyebrows he admonished Aviram, "Don't take too long."

When the others had ascended out of sight, Gavrielle said, "Never mind driving me. I'd just as soon walk."

"Uh-uh." He shook his head. "It's late."

"It's not even ten o'clock."

"Well, maybe it's not so late, but it's dark out. You should've brought Azit if you wanted to walk back."

"Don't worry. I'll be fine. And I have to stop in at Lazar's for something."

"You sure?"

She nodded.

"Okay, have it your way. But how about sitting a while? Just a few more minutes." He pulled the chair out for her.

"All right. One condition – I get to hear something about your life."

"Not much to tell. Not much of a life."

"Where'd your family come from?"

"Iraq."

"Oh."

Gavrielle's Nanna Nella may have spent seven years being cared for in the home of a Yemenite Jew – but

184

that didn't stop her from clinging to her prejudices against the Sephardi Jews. "The Orientals" she called them. She'd always particularly singled out their Iraqi neighbors for ridicule, saying the Iraqi national costume must be striped flannel pajamas. But at least she'd never tried to stop Gavrielle from going over there to hear Grandpa Ezra tell about Baghdad – and to eat their huge, paper-thin Iraqi pitas, rolled up around delicious fillings. From Grandpa Ezra's stories, Gavrielle knew that the Iraqi Jews had not had an easy time.

"Was it ... Did you sneak out, over the border?" she asked.

"Nah. My mother was like the Jews in Germany. She was a loyal Iraqi, born in Iraq, her parents and grandparents born in Iraq, and she was staying put. No way was she going to scramble over rocks, sneaking out of her own country, like a goat. Then sometime or other they made it legal for Jews to leave – as long as they signed all their property over to the state. By that time we didn't have much property left, so she gave in and we registered to emigrate." His face and voice were calm, but under the table she could feel his leg jiggling again.

"What about your father?" She couldn't help asking, though she doubted the answer would be good.

Aviram sucked his front teeth and then lit a cigarette. "They arrested him in '48. For being a Zionist spy. That's really why my mother refused to leave. She was waiting for him to get out of jail."

"Oh." Gavrielle shook her head, not knowing what to say. "They didn't ..?"

"No, he wasn't one of the ones they hanged. They let him go, after about a year."

"Did you even know where he was all that time? That he had been arrested? Or did he just disappear?"

185

"We knew. I was with him the morning they took him. It was early Shabbat morning – we were on our way to *Shacharit* – and this Iraqi cop stopped us in the street, asked my father what time it was. When my father pulled up his cuff to look at his watch, the cop arrested him. The Iraqis had this genius theory – the Jews' watches weren't really watches. They were wireless radios for sending secret messages to the Zionists." He smiled as if telling a good joke, but the leg jiggled even harder and he held his lit cigarette between thumb and forefinger, tapping the filter on the tabletop.

"I'm sorry. I have a talent for asking the wrong questions."

"It's okay. Ask all the questions you want."

"So, what happened to your father after they let him go? I mean you said before – you know, how you were scared your little girls would grow up without a father, the way you did."

"They shot him, crossing the border. After my mother did whatever you had to do to get permission to leave, we were supposed to get evacuated in a truck. But they made you pay for the cost of your transport and my father was so pissed at the Iraqi government, he said no way was he going to give them his last few coins for the privilege of being exiled from his own country. He put us on the truck, but insisted that he could cross the border on foot, save that much of the cost. I remember my mom crying and begging, but he was stubborn. I mean, he was always a stubborn man, but after he got out of jail – there were things you just couldn't talk to him about. They never said who shot him – if it was smugglers or soldiers. We just got word that he was dead."

"I'm sorry."

He shrugged. "My mother remarried pretty quick, but her new husband didn't have any use for three

186

kids." He paused and obliterated the butt of his cigarette in the ashtray. "They sent us to different places. I got put in a kibbutz, but I never fit in there, with all those Ashkenazi kids. I ran away all the time and that got to be a habit," he glanced up, grinning and looking relieved to be finished talking about his parents. "I spent most of my army service either AWOL or in the brig for being AWOL. I'd take a broom and pretend like I was sweeping up the base – sweep, sweep, sweep." He held one fist above the other and made quick motions, as if using a broom. "I'd get all the way up to the gate and then pitch the broom and take off. They chased me around a lot – the MPs would be pounding on the front door while I went out the back window and over the fence. They finally gave up and kicked me out. Dishonorable discharge."

She studied him, perplexed, thinking this was the kind of story that was told either apologetically or with a swagger. But he offered neither, seeming to accept his own shortcomings as imperturbably as he did those of his friends. And she found herself disinclined to judge him. She couldn't help liking Aviram and it *was* easy to get lost in those eyes of his.

"Hey," he said. "Speaking of Iraqis, did you hear that they're getting into the space race?"

She studied his poker face suspiciously. This had to be the beginning of a joke. "Okay, I'll bite. What are they going to do?"

"They're working on this new program, to land a spaceship on the sun."

She smiled and shook her head. "Don't they know that it'll get all burned up?"

"Nah. They got that all figured out. They're going to go at night."

She hadn't heard it before and her laugh was genuine. *Nice going, Aviram. Perfect way to dispel the gloom.* It took her a few more minutes to convince him that she really did prefer to walk. While taking her leave she glimpsed Gurion standing on the bottom steps, watching them. She was both annoyed and relieved to see him there. *Why can't you just mind your own business? You big slob, standing there, giving us the evil eye. But good, see for yourself – here we were, right down here, just talking, all this time. So shut your fat mouth.*

She headed up the walk to Lazar's, glad to see it was him working behind the counter, and not Mazal. The shop was quiet, just a few young soldiers eating enormous sundaes at one of the tables.

"Fired you already?" Lazar asked gruffly.

"No, not yet. I just missed your winsome charm." She felt quite fond of the battered-looking man, now that he no longer held sway over her. "So, has anyone been in asking about me?"

"Five or six hundred guys, but no *shvartzes.*"

"African-Americans." She corrected him.

"None of them either."

"Don't kid around. Are you sure? It's important."

"I told you, no tall, skinny, African-American has been around."

"You've still got the note for him?"

"Right there under the bread thing."

"And you told Mazal?"

"Yes, I told Mazal."

She trudged uphill toward the base. A small stretch of the road where it curved was quite dark, convincing her that she should have brought Azit. But she was too distracted to bother being afraid. She suddenly felt as if she was somehow disintegrating, living inside someone else's skin. A high-functioning wreck.

Why am I wasting all this time, in Rome and now here? And planning on wasting a lot more time and money, searching for a man who is unlikely to

188

appreciate being found? What is wrong with me, working in a rat-infested kitchen, sleeping in an airless room that's probably full of scorpions? (She had asked Aviram to cut a short window across the top of the door and put screens over it, both inside and out. That had solved the fear of suffocation, but now served to conjure visions of swarms of baby snakes.)

I'm here to save up some money. Right. Making less than a fourth of what the IDF pays me. I need to stop acting like a moron and get back in uniform. Start working on my master's. Go for a promotion. Make something of myself. Jesse was right. The army is the best thing in my life. Who am I trying to kid? It's the only thing in my life. I'm twenty-seven years old, not some flaky teenager on a journey to find herself. Give me a break. Grow up.

For the next two evenings she sat talking with Aviram at Simona's, long enough to drink her milkshake, followed by a cup of mint tea. Then she walked home with Azit at her side. Gurion overhead some of their conversations – usually about Aviram's childhood – and started calling Gavrielle "the social worker." He didn't bother to hide his resentment, though Gavrielle couldn't decide which one of them he was jealous of.

Though often disturbing, Aviram's stories fascinated her. Many of his friends in Tel Aviv were full-fledged criminals and he was capable of saying, quite casually, things like, "Yeah, like this one time my girlfriend's brother asked if he could rob my wife."

"Your girlfriend?"

"Yeah."

"You have a girlfriend?"

"Yeah."

"Okay. So this girlfriend has a brother and he came to you, and asked your permission to rob your wife?"

"Yeah, that's what I just said. See, my wife manages this store and every night after they close, she's the one who takes the money to the bank. You know, puts it in the drop box. And this guy, he was in big trouble. Owed money to the wrong people."

"And so he asks if he can mug his friend's wife?"

"It's not like he hurt her or anything."

"You mean he did it? You told him it was alright?"

He shrugged. "I told him what time she closes up the store and which bank she goes to. Nothing happened to her. He came up behind her, said, 'Hand over the envelope,' and she handed it over. That's all."

"Was this a long time ago? When you were kids?"

He sniffed. "Mm mmm. Last year. Maybe the year before."

"So you cheat on your wife."

"Only a few thousand times." His voice was calm as he watched her face.

"You're serious, aren't you?"

"Maybe that's a little exaggerated, but yeah, I'm serious." He lit a cigarette and inhaled, looking amused. "Is that such a big surprise?"

"Yes, actually it is. You always sound like you worry so much about your family. I just figured you must be a really good husband."

"I am. She's never known. I wouldn't ... I mean if there were any chance of her finding out ... though I'm not so sure she'd care all that much. She's pretty busy with the kids and all. Tired all the time."

"Cheaters always get caught."

"The cheaters who want to get caught, get caught. Guys who want out of the marriage. I don't."

"Don't you feel bad about lying to her?"

He shifted in his chair. "You don't understand. You've never been married. You're still waiting to live happily ever after. That's not how life is. Aliza – that's

190

my wife's name – she's my second cousin. We been like this," he said, holding two fingers together, "ever since we were kids. Her family was a disaster too. Her parents were divorced, which was actually lucky because her father's a mean drunk. Real mean. But she's a lot stronger than me.

"Ever since she was about five, she went around telling everyone she was going to marry me when she grew up. I was going to be her Prince Charming. Then I grew up to be a big nothing. Zero. Kicked out of the army, no money, no job, no family, drinking too much, smoking too much dope. She saved me. She wasn't in love with me the way you think about, but she made me marry her and she saved me. Made a home. Made me stop drinking so much, got me pulled together. If I hadn't married her ... I don't know. But it wasn't any Hollywood love story. We were just two lost kids who didn't have anyone else, and decided to look out for each other. I'll always take care of her. I would never leave her. No matter what. She knows if she ever needs me, she picks up the phone, I'm on the next plane. But there's always another woman. Women like me. I like them. Where's the harm?"

Gavrielle settled into a routine and the days passed quickly. She still stopped at Lazar's every day to ask about Charlie, but she'd given up on him. Almost. This weekend she was entitled to plane fare to Tel Aviv, but she had no real desire to go home. Besides, what if Saturday was the day the Charlie finally decided to show up?

So she'd struck a deal with Heller – she'd forego the ticket, stay and work the next two weekends, and if a friend of hers turned up, Heller would give both of them tickets to Tel Aviv the weekend after that.

Working on the weekend would be easy. Only five or six men were staying and they'd be over at the air force base all day, only coming back for meals. Mordecai would have everything ready in the refrigerator. All she'd have to do was heat the food up and wash the dishes.

Monday after lunch she drove to Naama Bay. Every time she made that turn off the main road she had to pause to appreciate the sight of that enormous horseshoe of vivid blue water carved into the almost white sand. A newly constructed promenade skirted the edge of it, flanked by a few fish restaurants that looked as if they were made of nothing but palm fronds. How nice it would have been to sit on that promenade with Charlie, having a beer. Farther back were the Marina Sharm hotel – a cluster of yellow and white igloos that looked like Picasso had designed them – and the rusted out railroad car that housed the dive club.

She spent her break wading along the shore and lying in the sun. Then she looked at her watch and stood to face the water, doing her daily stretching exercises, ending with her arms high over her head and her face to the sun. When she turned to pick up her bag, she all but knocked him over.

"Charlie!" She caught her balance and threw her arms around his neck. She embraced him more tightly and for longer than was appropriate for their platonic relationship, finally leaning back and pulling his face down so she could kiss him on both cheeks. Then she stepped away. "Oh, Charlie, you really came. I'm so glad to see you. I can't believe you're here."

"Yeah, me neither." He looked over her shoulder, surveying the black mountains. "Tel Aviv was one heck of a culture shock, but this down here ... And that whole desert you drive through to get here ..." He turned his attention back to her. "So what's with the sun-worshipping routine? You get tired of bein' a Jew, change to some other weird thing?"

"No, still a nice Jewish girl." She smiled. "Just taking care of myself. How long did you stay in Tel Aviv?"

"Long enough to figure out this is one strange excuse for a country. Can't turn 'round without runnin' into a soldier. And I can't believe the way you people all drink out of the same glass."

"What?"

"Those guys in the kiosks, who by the way charge way too much for a glass of soda water. Soda water. Who the heck drinks soda water? Anyway, none a them guys ever heard of Dixie Cups. Just keep using the same glass for one customer after another."

She laughed but couldn't help feeling a bit defensive. "They have some kind of thingee under the counter, for washing the glass."

"Well, that must be one miracle machine. Takes about one half a second between customers."

"You don't seem to have fallen ill. So, did you try a falafel?"

"Yeah. Ain't bad. But that's another weird thing – the way you all eat your lunch while you're walkin' down the street. There's all these places selling food out of a window and ain't never no place to sit down."

"We have restaurants." Her brow furrowed as she idly wondered if there were rules for bad grammar. *Does a triple negative like 'ain't never no' result in a negative?*

With a quick shake of her head, she gave up. She'd have to give more thought to this puzzling "ain't" word some other time. "I ain't a coward" and "I ain't no coward" seemed to mean the same thing. She sighed, thinking English was an incredibly complicated language.

"And I didn't believe what you told me about the phones here, but, man, it's true. Ain't nobody got one. Course that's all right, since you got all these pay phones. But wait, I forgot – none of them work! How the hell can you run a whole country without telephones?"

"I didn't know you had someone you needed to call."

"I don't. But while I was standing out on the sidewalk like some kind of bum, with the goop from my falafel dripping all down the front of my shirt, I met these tourists who'd been walking all over, tryin' to find a shop that would let them use their phone. Only they couldn't find a shop that *had* a phone."

She sighed. "It costs a lot of money to get a phone put in. And you have to wait a long time."

"Like how long?"

She shrugged. "Two or three years."

"Three years. Three years! Are you people nuts? I don't get it – if you Jews can't run a phone company worth shit, how the heck do you keep winning wars?"

She grinned and asked, "Why? How long does it take to get a phone in America?"

"Two days. One day. I don't know. Ain't no two to three years."

"Well, what do you expect?" She spoke quickly and a bit too loudly. "So there aren't enough exchanges yet, so what? Stop being so hard on us. Israel's only been a country for ... mmm, twenty-six years. *I'm* older than that. That would be like, what, 1802 for you? I bet you Americans had plenty of problems in 1802. And you didn't start out after a third of your people had been annihilated, and then have another ten percent of your population killed in your war for independence, and then take in like a gazillion refugees – I mean like close to one refugee for every person already living here – and then get hit with one more war after another, one terror attack after another."

"Hey." He put a hand on her arm, his voice softening. "Take it easy. I was just givin' you a hard time."

She looked up and then rested her forehead against his chest. "I know. I know. Sorry. I've just been feeling like sort of a mess. Really missing having you to talk to."

Stepped aside, she stooped to pick up her bag. "I'd about given up on you. What took you so long?"

"Couldn't see leaving Italy without a couple of days in Florence and a couple in Venice."

She stood straight and looked into his eyes. "You know, having a friend like you, even for such a short time ... I don't know ... seems like it's changed something about me."

Apparently not in the mood to talk about anything serious, he said, "I guess you mean changed for the better, since you couldna got no worse."

"Ha ha." She tossed her flip-flops into the sand, and put a hand on his arm to steady herself while she wiggled her toes in place. "Tell me, Mr. Freeman, I've always wanted to ask you – is there any method to your manner of speech? I mean the way you switch back and forth, between perfect grammar and things like 'ain't got no.' Sometimes in the middle of a sentence. Is there any logic to it?"

"Don't know. Never thought on it. I suppose when I'm with black folks I speak black, and with white folks I speak white. And with white folks I feel comfortable with ... I guess whatever comes out."

"Come on, I'll show you where I work."

"You gotta go back right now?"

"No. I've got another half hour or so."

"So hold your horses, girl. I just got off a hot as hell, never-ending bus ride and you think I ain't goin' in that water?" He nodded toward the sea.

He handed her his wallet to put in her bag, kicked his sandals off, sent his baseball cap flying as he peeled off his T-shirt, and sloshed in, still wearing his cut-off

195

jeans. She dropped her bag, removed her wrap-around cover up, and waded in after him.

"Put your face in the water. Eyes open," she called to him. "It's salty, but it's worth it."

He obeyed and came up shouting something unintelligible. The only word she understood was "amazing."

He swam farther out and did a series of dives, each time staying under longer, and soon returned to shore. He shook himself and then shaded his eyes, taking a panoramic view of the black mountains, white sand, and blue sea. Then he turned to face Gavrielle and exuberantly declared Sharm to be the most beautiful place in the world.

"You got a towel I can use?"

She took it from her bag and handed it to him, along with her bottle of water. "What'd you do with your stuff?"

"Left it with your ice cream man." They started trudging through the sand toward the parking lot. "I gotta tell you, I ain't never felt like such a celebrity." He grinned. "My foot hardly hit the pavement off the bus 'fore this girl, woman, whatever – boobs out to here – comes running out, really trucking it across the parking lot, over to the bus station. 'Hallo, hallo,' she's calling. 'You must be Charlie.' After she's done giving me your message, this cop car pulls over and I'm thinkin', 'Oh shit, this place is just like Dearborn, Michigan,' but the officer's shouting, 'Hey, Charlie? Are you Charlie?' Then another lady comes out of another store. Same thing. Anyway, I got your message." He draped his arm around her shoulder for a moment.

"How else was I going to make sure you'd find me? So you hitched a ride here?"

"Nah, that cop gave me a lift. Nice guy. Let me off out there on the main road, where you turn in. But I didn't make it to the beach 'fore I got a guy comin' out of them yellow and white things, wantin' to know if I'm Charlie." He removed his arm from her shoulder and did a Charles Atlas pose. "You want my autograph?"

She smiled and nodded at the jeep. "That's us." She kept her expression blank, but was smugly certain he was going to be impressed.

"You got wheels? Jeep lady. Cool. No roof or doors — just like General Patton."

"Sharm's version of a company car." She looked over his shoulder and said, "Look at that yacht out there. And the fishing boat parked halfway to shore."

"Parked? Anchored, lady, anchored. What about them?"

"It's so strange. I noticed them the day I got here. First the yacht shows up and the next morning the fishing boat is there. Then they both disappear. Two days later, the same thing. Then they're gone again. And now there they are, back again. And the fishing boat's always too far out for someone to get off it and wade in."

"So what?"

"I don't get it. I've never seen anyone come ashore. Not a single person. Never seen anyone on the fishing boat period. Both boats appear and disappear — like magic."

"Ghosts." Charlie made his eyes wide and issued a long, low ooooohhhh. "Ghosts of the Barbary pirates." Then he shrugged and said, "Maybe they drop anchor out there 'cause it's a good diving spot. And you don't see them 'ccount of they're diving off the other side of the boat."

She shrugged. "I don't know. I've never heard anyone say that. The people from the dive club always go to Ras Muhammed or somewhere. They don't hang around here."

As they got in the jeep she said, "Listen, the place I work at is in the navy base and they aren't supposed to let you in without a pass. But I'm going to see if the guard doesn't just wave me through. If not, you'll have to wait outside while I go to the office and beg a card off them." Her mind was racing. "Do you want a job?"

"Wasn't planning on lookin' for one, but I never object to makin' a few bucks."

"How long are you going to be here?"

"How long are you?"

"I don't know. Before you almost knocked me over I was starting to think about leaving. But now you're here."

"So we'll just wait and see what we both feel like doing." He leaned back in his seat, enjoying the rush of air as she turned onto the main road.

A few minutes later, for no obvious reason, she slowed and pulled onto the shoulder. "Look, up there." She pointed ahead of them.

"What am I lookin' for?"

"That rock formation, over there. See it jutting up between those two hills? See if it reminds you of anything."

"Like what?"

She shrugged. "Guess."

"Reminds me of a bunch of rocks. Come on, give me a hint."

"A head. Of somebody famous. From the side and sort of behind."

He squinted at it for a while and then slapped the dashboard. "Damn! JFK! Looks just like JFK."

She nodded. "They call it Rosh Kennedy. Kennedy's head. Nobody did anything to it, you know, carved it or anything." She pulled back onto the road. "So, you've already been to Sharm, Naama Bay, and seen Rosh Kennedy. Now all you have to do is go diving at Ras

Muhammed and get drunk at Simona's Milk Bar, and you'll be an old timer. Have you ever worked construction?"

"Just road crews during the summer."

She thought for a moment. "Suppose they don't have an actual job, but you could work a couple of hours a day or something like that – for room and board."

"That be better than a job. Didn't come here to sweat nine hours a day. You ever been to that Ras Muhammed place? I heard some guys on the bus talkin' 'bout it, saying it's the best place there is to dive."

"No, I've never been, but everyone says it's gorgeous. You know how to dive?"

"Sure. You know how many sunken ships we got in the Great Lakes? They make great dive sites. Course you got to have a really good wet suit 'cause that water is *cold*. I sure am gonna do some diving down here in this bath water. With all them striped fish. Man, they are gorgeous."

"Those little striped fish are nothing compared to what people say you see around the corals. All kinds of colors. I guess some of them look like they're lit up with neon. There are bigger fish too," she said, grinning. "There's a place at Ras Muhammed called Shark Reef." She downshifted as they started up the hill to the base. "Okay, here goes."

They approached the gate and the guard indeed waved her through. She pulled up in front of the office and made a mental note – if she ever went back to the army she needed to recommend a review of gate security at all military bases.

"Wait here. The boss won't be around in the middle of the day, but I'll ask the secretary what she thinks."

Charlie saluted and settled back into his seat, long legs folded up to put his bare feet on the dashboard. Gavrielle skipped up the steps and rushed through the door, coming to an abrupt halt when she saw Mike Heller behind his desk, alone in the office.

"Oh, sorry for bursting in like that," she stammered. "I didn't expect you to be here."

He smiled. "So what, you busted in to steal the petty cash?"

For a moment she was dumbstruck and just stared at him. *He's never spoken to me like that before, in that tone, like he's teasing. And he's looking right at me. He's never done that before either.*

She felt so flustered that she was surprised to hear her voice sounding normal. "I didn't know there was any to steal. Thanks for telling me." Her heart stopped pounding and she regained her composure.

"Can I invite you to sit?" He nodded at the chair in front of his desk.

"Sure." She sat nervously on the edge of the seat. "I came in to ask Rachel when you might have a minute, when I could talk to you about something. Ask you for a favor."

"Okay." He leaned back and looked at his watch. "I've got five minutes. Ask."

"That friend of mine I told you about, that I thought might turn up ... Well, he just did and I, uh, was wondering if you might have a job for him. I mean, not really a job, but something he could do for however many hours a day you would expect him to work in exchange for room and board."

"I could probably think of something. Where's your boyfriend now?"

"Out in the jeep. But he's not my boyfriend. And he's American, if that's a problem."

"You brought him in without a pass?"

"The guard didn't ask to see one." She blinked.

"I thought you worked in intelligence." His tone was teasing again.

She was startled to hear he knew that, until she remembered the employment form she had filled in.

"Don't worry. I vetted him." She smiled and stood up. "Well, I apologize again for bursting in on you and I'll be grateful if you can work something out. And ... uh ... even if not, I'd like to invite him to stay for dinner here tonight, if that's alright with you."

"Sure. Put him at my table."

She took another step and stopped again. "Any chance of a pass for him? So we can go out and come back?"

He pulled a pad out of his desk drawer. "Tell him to come in, fill out the form."

She went out beaming. "He's there. Go on in and he'll give you a pass."

"Everything okay?" Gavrielle asked Charlie when he came back out.

"Yeah. Besides that form he asked me some weird questions, like what flights I took to Rome and from Rome to here."

"You're invited to sit at his table for dinner."

"Is that where you sit?"

"I don't sit anywhere. I eat before I let them in. You'll see." She grinned, certain that mealtime at the Hakama dining room would be *the* Israeli experience he would most often repeat when entertaining his friends at home.

Charlie's eyes widened when she showed him her room. "This is where you sleep? For real?"

She enjoyed his reaction, which made her feel less boring than she usually did. "They built it for me while I waited. But if you're going to stay here, he'll put you in one of those rooms over there behind the office. They're a bit more normal, you know, with windows and all, but you'd be sharing with two or three other guys."

He stepped outside and looked around. "Porta-potties? Seriously?"

She ignored that remark and showed him the shower and washing up trough. "Believe me, this part of it is great. I promise. You get up in the morning, the sun's just coming up, the air's still holding the night chill, and you stand out here, splashing water on your face. I love it."

"Like a cowpoke on the Ponderosa."

"Something like that. I've got to go start setting tables. You can wait here, but make sure you pull the door shut tight when you go out."

"Nah, I'd rather come help you."

"I don't need any help, but you can keep me company."

She sat him at an empty table with a cup of coffee and some cookies. When it was time to open the door, she led Charlie to the table at the back and waited another minute or two, intentionally provoking pounding and yelling. The men did not disappoint.

When she placed the tureen of soup on Aviram's table she noticed that he and some of the other men were still in their work clothes. That must mean they had to work overtime tonight.

Aviram jerked his thumb over his shoulder and asked, "Who's the *shvartze* sitting with Heller?"

"A very good friend of mine. He just got here and will be around for a few days." She quickly moved on to the next table.

Aviram swiveled in his chair to say to her back, "Hey, listen, we aren't going to Simona's tonight. Bunch of us gotta work, over at the air force base."

"Don't wear yourselves out."

She finished serving the soup. While Mordecai dished out the rest of the food, she stood in the doorway, watching. Charlie and Heller seemed to be hitting it off. It looked like Charlie was telling a joke and the men at the table did indeed burst into laughter.

Who would have guessed their English was that good?
She relaxed and went about doing her job, no longer
concerned that it might have been a bad idea to bring
Charlie here. Charlie helped her clear the tables and
when they finished, Gavrielle made two cups of tea.

"That Mike is a really good guy," Charlie said.
"There's an empty bed in one of the rooms and he said
he doesn't mind me using it. Said I don't have to work
or nothin' and can have my meals here too."

"You're kidding. Free room and board?" She
screwed up her face in disbelief. "You must tell really
good jokes if he liked you that much."

"Nah. That dude really likes *you*."

"Nonsense. We've barely spoken to one another,
and he's got some gorgeous Swedish girlfriend. But he
does seem like a good guy." She sighed and told Charlie
about the Russian worker who had groped her – and
what Heller had done about it.

"Damn. I'd like to get my hands on that guy. You
shouldn't be in a place like this by yourself."

"It's okay now. The rest of these guys are all right, so
long as I keep my distance. It's funny." She grinned. "If
I were in Tel Aviv, I could fool around with anyone I
wanted, sleep with a different guy every night, and no
one would bat an eye. But down here, in the wilds of
Sinai, I have to be super careful of my reputation."

"It's like a small town." He sipped his tea. "I been
thinkin' 'bout them boats. You know, the yacht and the
fishing boat. Are they even allowed to let people off
here? I mean, what about customs and passports and
all that?"

"Tourists who come in by sea are supposed to go
register at the police station."

He chuckled. "With that one cop? He's the whole
government 'round here?"

"Pretty much."

"This ain't paradise for you. It's paradise for smugglers."

"That's what I've been thinking," she said. "But I can't imagine what the heck they'd be smuggling. The first thing you think of is drugs, but who needs a boat to move drugs from Egypt to Israel or vice versa? Anyway, as far as I know, most of that traffic is north to south. They take the drugs out of Lebanon, down through Israel, and the Bedouin transport them over to Egypt. Unless maybe there are drugs coming here from somewhere in the Far East."

"That Naama Bay sure is beautiful." Charlie changed the subject. "I'm gonna rent some equipment from that dive club. Where the heck did that old railroad car come from?"

Gavrielle looked up in surprise. "Wow, that's a good question. I'm so used to it being there, I never wondered about that. Do you think it maybe could have fallen off a ship or something?"

"You're asking me?"

"Listen, some of the guys are working tonight, over at the air force base. They've done that twice before since I've been here, and both times I baked a cake and took it over to them."

He smiled and shrugged. "I like cake."

They walked down to the grocery store for cocoa powder and Charlie whisked sugar, eggs, and oil while she added the other ingredients.

"Never took you for the baking type," he said, after she slid the pan into the oven, turned the timer to thirty minutes, and led him back to the dining room.

"I'm not. It's an excuse to see what they're doing. That's another thing I wonder about – why they sometimes have to work at night. I mean, what's so urgent all of a sudden?"

"Man, it must be exhausting to be you, havin' to know everything. No wonder you're a spy lady."

"I just think it's interesting. Trying to fathom why people do the things they do. Let's see you figure it out."

"Okay. You said you been over there before, watching them work at night?"

"Yeah."

"Were they pouring concrete both times?"

She thought for a moment. "Yeah."

He opened his eyes wide and issued another creepy ghost Oooooooo. "Maybe your boyfriend Heller has a pile of bodies need burying."

"Foo to you too."

Then her face became serious and she studied his for a long moment. Outside the camp was quiet – the men who weren't working had gone to Simona's. Finally she asked, "You know why we got to be such good friends?"

"How 'bout 'cause we like each other?"

"Yeah, sure, that. But ... I mean, I know we appear to have absolutely nothing in common – white-black, Jewish-Christian, American-Israeli. But our lives are like mirrors of each other's."

"What's that supposed to mean?"

"Think about it. Neither of us have parents. And both of us were taken in by a family we have some kind of connection to, but we aren't actually related to them. And both those families took our grandmothers along with us. And neither of us have any blood relations, except for our grandmothers."

"Hmm. Never thought about that."

She sighed. "I don't know. Maybe the New Age flakes are right, you know, the way they say that people come into your life for a reason."

He shrugged, obviously less fascinated by this idea than she was. "Last conversation I had 'bout me having

205

no other blood relations was with Charlene. Know what she said? That I'd better get busy – settle down and make some new little people. They'll be my blood relations. Can't argue with that."

The oven timer rang, and Gavrielle started to push her chair back.

"Sit, sit. I'll get it," Charlie said.

"You know how to test to see if it's done?"

"Think they call me Mr. Betty Crocker for nothing?"

Gavrielle stopped the jeep and slid sideways to stand on the running board. "There. There they are, over there. See the lights? When they work over here at night, Nuri mounts projectors on one of the vehicles."

She put the jeep back in gear, turned off onto a gravel road, and parked a few dozen meters from the building site.

"You do realize this is a jeep, right?" Charlie said. "You can drive it right over there on top of them if you want."

"You do realize it's pitch dark and that's a boiling hot pot of coffee you're holding between your feet, don't you? Want it spilled all over you?"

Gavrielle got out and went around to the passenger side, relieved him of the sheet cake, and began trudging through the sand. He followed, carrying the pot of coffee and a paper bag containing Styrofoam cups, napkins, and a knife.

Whatever the eight shirtless, filthy men were building, it wasn't very large. They were standing in a knee-deep rectangular pit, about the size of a large bedroom. It was lined with weather-beaten wooden planks that the men were in the process of covering with a layer of sand. Judging by the nearby cement mixer and the pile of reinforcing bars that stood to one side, Gavrielle assumed they were getting ready to pour a big slab. Despite Nuri's projectors, Gavrielle was barely able to make out who was who. Nor could she understand what any of them were saying.

She approached the nearest silhouette and bent down, shouting, "Hey, hello, we brought something for you guys," to a man who turned out to be Benny. She handed the cake down to him. Nodding behind her, she shouted, "Just a sec, Charlie's coming with the knife and napkins." But by the time Charlie handed her the bag with those niceties, the other men had already gathered around Benny and were shoveling cake into their mouths with their unwashed hands. In what seemed no time at all, someone tossed the empty pan up onto the sand. Gavrielle grinned at Charlie, who seemed to have been struck speechless. Then The Singer began crooning Marvin Gaye's line – *I want to stop and thank you, baby* – and the others applauded.

As the brief serenade came to an end, Charlie set the coffee on a cinderblock, next to a stack of Styrofoam cups. He put thumb and forefinger to the sides of his mouth, gave a loud whistle, and pointed at it. Then something happened that Gavrielle would forever think of as magical.

The Singer's face split into a wide grin, as if he had been waiting for a cue. He pitched his voice high and began, *In the jungle, the mighty jungle, the lion sleeps tonight* ... The others immediately took up the underlying chant, *Wimoweh, wimoweh, wimoweh* ... and began stomping their feet and dancing, first hesitantly, then enthusiastically. One of them dropped to his knees facing Charlie and fell forward in worship, his torso moving up and down like an African villager in a Tarzan movie. Gavrielle glanced nervously at Charlie, wondering if this was offensive to him, but he was wearing his most charming smile and maneuvered between the protruding rods of iron to jump down into the pit with them.

The Singer was wonderful, yodeling and howling in an amazingly good imitation of the old hit record. Charlie and Aviram were suddenly standing in front of her, each holding up a hand, an invitation to join them. Her eyes grew wide, but Aviram mouthed, "Don't worry, it's all right." She looked up at the bright crescent moon before reaching for their hands and allowing herself to be guided down onto what she knew was the most unique dance floor she would ever grace.

"Watch me," Charlie said. "Dance a little African."

The singing continued and he began rolling his hips, his legs and shoulders almost stationary. *That's easy enough, like doing a hula hoop,* she thought, imitating him and then beginning to bend slightly to one side and then the other, lifting alternating legs as he did.

"Look behind you," she said, and he turned to see the men in two rows behind him, hilariously following his instructions as they continued singing.

She shook her head, truly sorry that no one was making a movie of this.

"Okay, now try this," Charlie said. "Stand on your toes and bend your knees. That's right. Now flap your knees together, in and out, in and out. Yeah, you got it, girl, you're a natural." Then he raised his arms over his head and threw himself into the rhythm, freestyle, sweat soon pouring down his face.

Gavrielle had always dreaded being expected to dance, but that night – in the dark, in the middle of the desert, surrounded by a crew of at least half-drunk roughnecks, protected only by two men she barely knew, without any instrumental music – for the first time in her life she thought, *the hell with what anyone thinks of me,* and really meant it. She forgot her inhibitions and moved with abandon.

Charlie and Aviram were careful to keep themselves between her and the other men, but she barely noticed.

After a while Charlie reached for both her hands and led her in some new moves. Then he let go of one hand and took Aviram's, so the three of them formed a circle. Not so long ago she might have expected an electric shock when Aviram took her hand, but now it was only comfortable. She couldn't have said how long they carried on; it felt both like forever and not nearly long enough.

It ended when the cement mixer growled on and then immediately off. The singing stopped abruptly, and they all froze. Mike Heller was silhouetted in front of one of the projectors.

"Sorry to interrupt the party," he said, actually sounding apologetic.

Gavrielle was momentarily hypnotized by the sight he presented, and then tried to shrink into the shadows, praying he hadn't seen her. Having cast Mike Heller in the role of her great protector, she felt as if she owed him impeccable virtue. And for some reason she suddenly cared what he thought of her. Was embarrassed for him to have seen her dancing like that.

Charlie stepped out of the pit, gave Gavrielle a hand, and they hurriedly gathered the kitchenware and fled. Her heart was thumping and she took a few deep breaths, waiting for her pulse to slow, so she could climb back into her own skin. She knew what it was to feel the rush of adrenaline in response to stressful, frightening situations – but like this, from something fun, exhilarating? That she'd never experienced before.

"Think he's pissed?" Charlie asked as they got into the jeep.

"He didn't sound mad. I just hope he didn't notice me there."

"Oh he noticed you all right," Charlie said. "He noticed you for a good long time before he turned on the big noise."

Her heart started thumping again. "You knew he was there and didn't say anything?"

"What was I gonna say? Anyway, that was a natural good time and those are sacred. You know, when nobody plans it. Just happens. It's some kind of mortal sin to interrupt one of those."

"That *was* a good time. I've never danced liked that before."

"No kidding." He rolled his eyes.

"How would you know?"

"Anyone known you for two and a half minutes knows that."

She looked away and turned the key. "You feel like stopping at Naama? Sit on the beach?"

"Surely do."

"Now you sound just like black people in the movies. 'Surely do. Indeed.'" She tried to imitate him.

"That's what I aim for."

When they were seated on the beach, he lay back and asked, "So, you coming back to West Bloomfield Township with me?"

"Maybe. I don't know. I mean part of me wants to, but how can I just show up at somebody's house?"

"Easy. I'm inviting you. Look, some fool offers you a hand, you grab it fast – don't give him no time to change his mind. You won't be imposing, but even if you were, so what? You gonna give up a chance to find your dad because you don't want to impose? Doesn't one of those things seem kind of more important than the other?"

She lay back. "Isn't that some moon?"

"Hey lady, I'm serious. If fate put us in that classroom together, this is what for. For me to help you find your father. Nice Jewish girl gonna argue with God? You come home with me, we'll make the phone call, and if we find out where he's at, I'll take you there. Up to a ten-hour drive. More than that, you're flying."

He sat up and threw a handful of sand. "You said having a friend like me somehow changed you, but it's not enough to learn how to treat someone like a friend. You have to let them be a friend back at you. That part – lettin' someone else help you – is probably hard for someone like you. You think it makes you all needy and pathetic. You gotta figure out that a two-way street ain't so scary. That it's actually the greatest thing you can hope for. And you gotta get over this thing with your father, one way or the other. You'll either find him or you won't. But not trying ain't no option."

She sat up. "Okay. I guess that's a winning argument. I'm coming."

"First you gotta show me Jerusalem. And let's stay down here a while longer."

"As long as you want. You know," she lay back down and spoke to the sky, "I'm going to remember this night for the rest of my life. Tell my grandchildren about it when I'm old and decrepit. Of course, they won't believe a word. You're the only one I'll ever be able to share this memory with."

"That's how all memories are. You can't wrap 'em up and give them to someone else, like a present. They have to have been there with you. That's why people get married, promise each other to stick around. Like my mamma always said, 'We all want a witness to our life.' And you damn right 'bout your grandchildren not believing you. *I* don't believe it, and I was there."

"I hate it that I'll never see you again. I mean, after America."

"Don't go spoiling the good times you havin' now by worrying 'bout the ones you ain't gonna have."

"That something else your mamma said?"

"My Grandma Julie."

211

The next morning Gavrielle was wakened by men's voices outside. The workers were often subdued before work, dealing with their hangovers from the night before, but this morning they seemed to be having energetic discussions. She pulled on her cut-off jeans and T-shirt and opened the door a crack to peek out. They were standing around in small groups. Finally she saw Aviram and ventured out.

"What's going on?" she asked him.

He nodded for her to step aside. "Nothing that matters to you."

"So why does everyone look all freaked out?"

He puckered his lips into a funny expression. "I guess there's no reason not to tell you. The thing is ... it's like this. The extra work we do at night, like last night – it's all for private contracts."

"So? What's wrong with that? The army doesn't want Hakama to build for anyone else?"

He grinned and shook his head. "The army isn't the problem. The contracts are with the army. They're just not with Hakama. See, Heller signed some small contracts – between him and the army. Private contracts, meaning they're *his* private contracts. Contracts between him, personally, and the army."

"Oh. So Hakama doesn't allow him to do work for anyone else?"

"Not when he's using their cement, wood, and iron." He waited a moment for that to sink in. "And logging our hours on the Hakama payroll. Makes it pretty easy for him to underbid the company."

"I see," she said, feeling disappointed in Mike Heller. "So he's a crook. And he got caught ripping them off."

"Hey, stealing from a thief ain't really stealing, and most of the construction companies are a bunch of crooks. You got any idea how much they rip the army off for? Millions. Heller's just getting some of that taxpayer money back, spreading it around to us."

"Robin Hood."

"Yeah, right. He did pay for some of it out of his own pocket."

"Out of the money he stole, you mean."

"You know, there's no law says you always gotta be such a tight-ass. Foremen do it all the time. Companies expect it. Like offices expect secretaries to steal pens and make personal phone calls. It's no big deal."

"Was that why Heller showed up all of a sudden last night?"

"Yeah, to tell us we had to finish the job. Few guys went back this morning, to do some things that had to wait for the concrete to dry."

"So what will happen now?"

"Some time today a guy in a suit will show up and kick our butts a little."

"Won't you all get fired?"

"Nah. If they fired everyone who two-timed them, they'd never get anything built."

She stared at Aviram for a moment, finding it difficult to grasp how unconcerned he was. How fundamentally different his world was from hers. There would always be another welding job. It made no difference to him where. He could lose his temper and walk off a job, just like that. Men like him, who chose to be transients, did it all the time. What did they have to lose? That's how they go through life. She hated looking at Aviram's future through that perspective. The drinking, dope, and cigarettes would all take their toll, give him that grayish, used-up look. He would always have his beautiful eyes and smile, but ... It saddened her to think of him a decade from now, beginning to feel tired and used up, aging badly. But at least he had his family. While they were still speaking, a car pulled up. A man in a suit got out and went straight to the office.

"Look at that. Bastard must have driven all night. You better go fill the urn with water for coffee."

She did, and soon Heller and the suit entered the dining room, followed by the men who had worked overtime for Heller – not just last night, but on any of the nights that overtime had been logged. There were fifteen or twenty of them. Gavrielle retreated to the kitchen, but hovered near the door to eavesdrop.

The workers took a stab at looking contrite, but quickly slumped into an expression of collective boredom. The suit stood and barked a short lecture, telling them they had a choice: be terminated as of this minute, or stay on and be docked two days' pay. Only one man rose, choosing to leave. Standing behind the suit, Mike slipped him an envelope and touched his shoulder on his way out. Those who remained received another short lecture. Then the suit got back in his car and drove off.

Gavrielle returned to the dining room and said to Aviram, "You don't look very upset about losing pay."

He smiled. "Don't worry. Heller will make it up to us. Partly out of his pocket, partly by approving overtime we won't actually work."

"I don't get it. Why do you guys get any of your pay docked? Heller's the one who did everything – signed the contracts and pocketed the money. How come he doesn't get fired?"

"They'll work something out between them. I told you. They steal from the government, he steals from them. That's how it works. They're not going to fire the best foreman they've ever had, over a few bags of cement. Besides, he's probably got some pile of dirt on them. Docking our pay makes it look like they did something. It's all a show."

"So now I set the tables for breakfast and everything

214

goes back to usual?"

"Pretty much."

Charlie helped her clear away the breakfast mess. "I might not be around today and tomorrow," he said. "Or more. So don't fret none. I'm going to go check out that dive club, see if they got some kind of excursion I might want to go on."

"Okay. But first have a cup of coffee with me. You've gotta hear what happened last night." She was in the middle of the story about Heller being a big crook, when she suddenly stopped, frowned for a second, and then smiled. "Ah, I know! That's it! World War II."

"What about World War II?"

"It's been driving me nuts – that railroad car the dive club uses. I keep trying to imagine it falling off a ship and floating ashore, instead of sinking. But I just now remembered – Romel – you know who that was?"

He rolled his eyes. "Yeah, yeah, the Desert Fox, came charging across North Africa, heading straight for you guys."

"Right. So the British started building railroad tracks across Sinai to Alexandria. I guess that still doesn't explain how that car ended up way the heck down here in the south, but it's better than trying to imagine it swimming ashore."

"Well, good for you. And they say we never have any use for the things we learn in school. But, come on, tell me the rest of the story. I surely hope it ain't gonna end with them canning Heller's ass, and there goes my free B&B."

She obliged and finished the story. Then he asked, "You do that a lot? Remember something, right in the middle of a whole different sentence?"

"When it's been making me crazy, trying to think of something, yeah. Sometimes I wake up in the middle of the night like that."

215

"Eureka?"

She shrugged. "It can happen at work too. Sometimes in the middle of a meeting. Jesse never minded." She listened to herself speak his name, aware that it was the first time she'd mentioned him in casual conversation. "He said lots of geniuses are like that."

She stuck her tongue out at Charlie, who'd put a finger in his mouth, in a "don't make me barf" gesture. Then he stood and waved a goodbye.

After lunch she took Azit for a walk down to Sharm and stopped in at the ice cream shop.

"Look who's here," Lazar said. "You want a cup of coffee?"

"Sure. You got ice?"

"Yeah, I got ice."

"So make mine ice coffee. How are you and Mazal doing?"

"She's gone." He batted at a fly. "Quit yesterday."

"So who's working for you now?"

"Me. Haven't found anyone else yet."

"Gee, that's tough. Tell you what – put a scoop of vanilla ice cream in that ice coffee and I'll help you out tonight," she offered. "I can't get here till after eight. Probably more like eight thirty."

He perked up. "Yeah?"

"Yeah. My penitence for running out on you ten minutes after you gave me a job."

"What do you want an hour?"

"No money. I owe you. I'll settle for the ice coffee, and an ice cream soda tonight."

She was tired when she finished cleaning up after dinner, but Charlie hadn't come back so she didn't mind going to help Lazar out for a few hours. In any case, she didn't feel like reading or going to Simona's.

216

Lazar stayed behind the counter, making the coffee and ice cream sundaes. Gavrielle waited tables and cleared them. It was a slow evening and she took her time scrubbing the Formica surfaces.

"Planning to run out on me?" A familiar voice came from behind her.

She turned to encounter Mike Heller, standing a little too close. "I'm just helping out," she said. "Mazal quit, so Lazar's on his own." She took a step back, mortified to hear herself stammering.

"I could use a cup of coffee," Heller said.

"Anything else?"

"No. And I'll get the coffee. You take a load off." He glanced at the three tables of soldiers. "All your customers look pretty happy."

She was wondering if she should protest about Heller going behind the counter, but Lazar came out of the back room and didn't seem surprised to see him there. So she went to a table and sat.

"What's up, Mike?" the old man asked.

"Just checking up on you. Making sure you're not working my girl to death," Mike said, causing Gavrielle to flush. *His girl? Never mind. That's just him messing with Lazar. Doesn't mean anything.*

"She volunteered." Lazar turned on the faucet to fill the dishpan. "Must be sick of your mug."

Heller returned with two cups of coffee. Her heart was pounding, wondering what he wanted. He sat down, looking awkward and embarrassed, the way he had when he came in to offer her a job.

"Where's your pal?" he asked.

"Charlie? I don't know. This morning he said he was going to go check out the dive club. Maybe go on one of their trips."

"How long do the two of you plan to stay in Sharm?"

"I don't know that, either." So that's why he came in. Okay, fair enough.

217

"You'll give me some kind of notice?"

She relaxed and grinned. "How about the same amount I gave Lazar?"

He allowed a smile to briefly pass over his face. Then he gave her a mock salute, rapped his knuckles on the tabletop, and stood. "Have a good evening, Miss Rozmann." He walked out without touching his coffee.

The next morning the men had finished breakfast and were filing outside with their coffee when Charlie appeared in the kitchen. He startled her from behind, saying, "Girl, you need to come to Tel Aviv with me."

"Nice to see you too. So how was your big excursion?"

"One-man excursion."

"What's that mean?"

"I did a little diving on my own."

"What? Where?"

They heard Aviram's voice outside, shouting, "Heller! You ready to go?"

Soft footsteps moved away from the back door before they heard Heller respond.

He was eavesdropping, Gavrielle thought. Why? And why did he really come into Lazar's last night. Something weird is going on.

"I'll get to where I been at, but first things first." Charlie leaned back to look into the dining room, making sure no one was there. Then he reached into his shirt pocket and removed a length of rolled up toilet paper. He carefully opened it up to reveal a small piece of glass. His eyes lit up as he held it between his thumb and forefinger. "They ain't smuggling drugs," he said.

"Diamonds?" She kept her voice low, eyes wide.

He wrapped it back up and returned it to his pocket. "Either that or bottles smashed into a whole mess of little pieces."

"Where did you get that?" she asked in a whisper.

"I went diving last night. By myself. See, yesterday morning I'm standing there at the dive club, reading through the descriptions of the different places they take people to dive, and I look up and guess what? Them boats are back. You'd got me all curious too, so I decided to take my own little excursion, out to that fishing boat. And man, I couldn't hardly believe it – like something right out of the movies. It's got this little motor on the back and all you got to do is tilt it up, and there it is, right there, this little compartment. Not even a secret door on it or anything. And there's this rubber bag in there, got a metal ring on it, hooked onto another metal ring that's bolted to the boat. But there's no lock or anything. You press this clip thingee and it comes right off. That bag turned out to be full of these things." He patted his pocket.

"So you stole one!"

"One? I took the whole bag."

She couldn't help raising her voice. "Are you out of your mind? How could you do such a stupid thing?" She regained control of herself and whispered when she asked, "What kind of people do you think smuggle diamonds?"

"Crooks. You're the one told me about Amos's cousin, the one who's into diamonds. You said diamond guys like him are all a bunch of crooks, but gentlemen crooks."

"*The brokers.* He's a broker. You think smuggler creeps are gentlemen? What's the matter with you?" She was again having trouble keeping her voice down and frowned, shaking her head. "This has got to be a joke. I can't believe you did that. A boat with a bag of diamonds on it. You know someone's keeping an eye on it. I mean, someone else, someone who lives here, who was *supposed* to get those diamonds. You must have just beat him to it. God, he probably saw you."

219

"Nope. No way. I was careful to keep my head down. I didn't even tilt the motor all the way up. Stayed underwater and lifted it just enough to get my hand behind it, feel around in there and grab the rubber bag. I didn't even know what was in it till I got back ashore, where I could open it."

"I'm sorry, but that's hard to believe. You didn't have a clue what you were looking for. You can't tell me you didn't look inside the boat first – and you couldn't have done that without grabbing the side and tipping it."

"Nope." He shook his head. "I might a done that next, but around the motor seemed the most logical place to look."

"So then you came back here to sleep?"

"Nope. Stayed put, right where I came out of the water."

"All night? You sat on the beach all night?"

"Slept on the beach. I had dry clothes and a blanket waiting for me."

"Who saw you there?"

"No one."

"Come on. And don't think Bedouins don't count. Smuggling is their thing."

"No one saw me. Why you giving me such a hard time? Like I'm some big liar?"

"I'm not calling you a liar, but I don't think you turned into James Bond over night. You just happened to have a blanket on the beach?" She took his arm. "Come on, let's go sit down. I need to think about this. Need you to tell me exactly what you did and who could have seen you. From the beginning."

She made two cups of coffee and they sat across from one another at the end of one of the tables. Gavrielle jerked her head around, startled, when she heard footsteps and turned to see Heller coming

220

through the kitchen door, carrying a small gym bag.

He stood beside Charlie and said, "Gavrielle, I have to put in an order for supplies and need you to go check – see if we're getting low on any of the things on Mordecai's list."

"Okay." As she pushed her chair back she gave what she considered a meaningful look to Charlie. *Do not say anything about where you have been to this man.*

Heller took a seat – leaving an empty chair between him and Charlie – and bent to rifle through the gym bag. "I know it's in here somewhere," he said impatiently, finally straightening up and handing a folded piece of paper to Gavrielle.

When she returned from the kitchen, Charlie was telling jokes. Heller took the list from Gavrielle, thanked her, and left. Gavrielle waited a moment before going to the back door to slide the bolt shut.

Then she sat back down and took a sip of her lukewarm coffee. "Did he ask you any questions?"

"Nope. Only if I've got any other good jokes. He was mostly all bent over, doing something with his shoes. Said he had the laces in wrong."

"Okay. So now tell me the whole thing. You went to the dive club, noticed the boats there and then what?"

He rolled his eyes, but complied. "Well, like I said, I decided to rent equipment and wait until after dark to go check out that boat. But I figured that first I had to find a safe place to go into the water. Not too far away, but where there's sand hills and palm trees and a lot of that reedy crap. Some place no one would see me from the road. See, I'm not an idiot. I knew I had to be careful not to let anyone see me go in. And I knew that if I found anything on the fishing boat, I ought to lay low for the night. Keep my diving equipment for another day."

She nodded approvingly, but asked, "Why?"

"You do think I'm some kind of moron. Like, I'm

gonna rent dive gear the day whatever is on that boat grows legs and then bring that gear back the next morning? Anyway, I told the guy at the club that I hadda go talk to a friend of mine, see what he wants to do. I stroll up the promenade a ways, have a beer, and then take a nice walk along the shore. I figure north of Naama is gonna be better than south, so I go that way. Find the most perfect hiding place and then go out to the road and hitch a ride here, to camp. Stuff my backpack with jeans and a sweatshirt and one of them yucky gray army blankets. And water. And something to eat. Then I hitch another ride and have them let me out by the turn-off to Naama. I wait for that car to be out of sight before I start walking north. Real easy to spot my place from the road, 'cause of these three palm trees. Anyway, I buried my pack in the sand and walked back to the club to rent the gear. That's when my plan almost failed."

"Forgot how heavy it is?" She'd been wondering about this part. How he'd moved the tank all that way.

"No kidding. Like lugging a shit load of bricks."

"So what'd you do?"

"Guy from the club helped me out to the road. Told him my friend was going to come by and pick me up. Then I hitched a lift to my spot. You know, where I could see my three palm trees. It was still a bitch getting everything from the road down to the water."

"And you don't think anyone noticed that – some guy in the middle of nowhere with a tank of oxygen?"

"Are you listening to me at all? Do you get how careful I was?" He sounded angry.

She put a hand on his. "I'm just asking questions that I think need to be asked. Risk assessment."

"So guess what, you ain't the only one spent a lot of years assessing risks. You think you live in a dangerous part of the world? Try Twelfth Street in Detroit. Spent my youth watching dealers switching stash houses, other gangs watching them switch stash houses. Trying to guess where I don't want to be at. Where they likely to come after each other. You did it in a nice office – I been out on the street. I know about people bein' seen when they think they ain't."

"Don't be so mad. I'm just worried about you, is all."

"Yeah, yeah. Okay, let's get your big assessment over with. First of all, in the middle of the day, you got five to ten minutes between cars on that road. And about five meters from the road there was a little bitty sand dune. So as soon as the car that left me off disappeared, I moved everything behind that little hill. Lay down there till the coast was clear again."

She was shaking her head. "It's still hard for me to believe that no one saw you. Someone in the water that you weren't paying any attention to, someone on a boat – maybe even on that yacht. The Bedouin are everywhere and you never hear them coming. But okay, let's say I buy it. No one saw you. Then what? You sat there waiting for it to get dark?"

"Yep. I mean first I had to move everything down to the beach. But after that, yeah, I sat there waiting for it to get dark."

She stared at him. "Never would have figured you to have that much patience."

"It's a good place to think. Staring out at all that water gives you perspective."

"Still that's a lot of hours. I couldn't do it. And all this because what ... I made you curious?"

"What's that supposed to mean? Why else?"

"You sure you didn't maybe meet some guy in Tel Aviv or Eilat, maybe offered you a cut if you'd pick up a package for him?"

"You know what? Screw you." His chair screeched loudly as he stood up.

She raised her voice slightly, but remained calm.

"I'm only asking what anyone who catches you with those diamonds is going to ask. Unless the guy catching you is the one you stole them from. In that case, I doubt anyone will bother asking any questions. Come on, sit back down. I'm on your side. You have to understand that even if your story is true, it's kind of hard to believe."

"Well, you better start believing it."

"Okay. Let's go back to where we were. It gets dark. You get in the water, stay beneath the surface all the way to the boat, find your secret treasure, and swim back. Then you freeze your ass off all night."

"The beach is beautiful after dark. Cold, but beautiful."

"Where's all your stuff now?"

"Left it there by the palm trees. Buried everything. The tank too."

"Well, I guess we'd better go get it. But first I need a few minutes of peace and quiet. To think. So do you. You need to have a story about where you've been, and you have to know what you're talking about when people ask you questions."

"You okay? You look sort of sick."

"God, Charlie, you don't get the mess you might have gotten yourself into, do you?" she said. "There's no way you can even give them back. No way. If those boats show up again and you try to sneak out there – put the bag back where you found it – and you get caught, those guys will never believe you weren't out there looking for more. Not that it would matter if they did believe you. Not if you'd seen their faces. Heard their voices."

"You're making too big a deal. In the first place, if anyone had seen me, I wouldn't be sitting here now, would I?"

"Shush. Let me think."

"Think about what?"

"I'm a smuggler – trying to figure out what kind of fool was stupid enough to rob me." She was quiet, rapping her fingertips on the table, like Jesse used to. "Well, I know the first thing I'd do. Go to the dive club and get a look at their log, make a list of everyone who was there recently – either having their own tank filled or renting equipment from them. That wouldn't be very hard, you know. They leave it lying right there on the table. And remember where you are. That list wouldn't be very long. This isn't Detroit with a few million suspects."

"Come on. It could have been anyone. Soldier, construction worker."

"And the guy who was *supposed* to pick up that bag could be anyone. Soldier, construction worker. Or someone who works at the dive club. Maybe the guy you rented the equipment from. You think you got away scot-free just because no one saw you get in and out of the water? You think the pick-up guy told them, 'Gee whiz, there wasn't anything to pick up this time,' and whoever put that bag in the boat said, 'Oh well, better luck next time'?"

For the first time Charlie looked worried. "Okay, so that's why you got to come to Tel Aviv with me. So I can sell it all to Amos's cousin. Once we get rid of it, no one can prove anything."

"Prove? You think the guys looking for you are going to take you to court? And forget about '*we* get rid of it.' I don't want any part of this."

"I'll split even with you."

"No. No way."

"Come on, I bet it'll more than pay for your ticket to America. Suppose we find out where your father is, but it's far away. You might have to fly there, pay motel bills, rent a car. And it will help me with my tuition. Better we should have it than the bad guys."

"No. You do what you want, but leave me out of it."

"We could just disappear today. Get on the bus. You're the only one down here that even knows my last name."

"The heck I am. What about that form you filled in for Heller?"

"Oh. Yeah. I forgot about that."

She looked at her watch. "Okay, here's what we're going to do. We'll go get your stuff now, but you can't return the dive gear yet."

"Why not?"

"Because you don't have a story. The guy at the dive club will probably get all chatty with you. Ask where you went, expect you to ooh and aah over how beautiful everything was. That's if he's just a regular person. If he's a crook who's suspicious of you, then he's going to be really chatty. So you have to actually dive first. In daylight. I'll drop you off at the beach here. There are corals out in the bay of Sharm el Sheikh too. But you stay in the water. Don't get out until I come back to pick you up. Don't talk to anyone."

"Why?"

"Because you haven't been to Ras Muhammed yet. That's where you were all day yesterday. Where you slept on the beach. When you do talk to someone, you'd better be able to say something intelligent about it. I don't think any of the guys who work here are big divers, but I'm sure most of them have at least been there. So after lunch I'll pick you up at the beach and drive you to Ras Muhammed. It's about forty minutes each way, so you won't have too much time to dive. After that we'll return the gear to the dive club and you can chat all you want.

"From there we'll go to the airport. I'm pretty sure the pay phone there works. I'll call Tonia and ask her to call the office tomorrow, say she needs to speak with me. I'll think of some excuse – why she needs me to come home. We do need to get out of here, but it can't look like we're running away. We have to act completely normal. No more talk of disappearing."

"How come I gotta dive here too?"

"Because if you weren't going to dive anywhere today, why didn't you return your equipment first thing this morning, when you got back from Ras Muhammed? Why would you keep schlepping it around with you?"

"Geez. You sure you ain't some kind of criminal mastermind?"

"I'm sure I'm definitely not, because that whole story falls apart the minute someone from the dive club compares notes about you with someone here – someone who sees us driving off toward Ras Muhammed today. But I don't have a better idea."

"Come on, you think these guys are KGB – going to interrogate me about all these details?"

"I promise you, someone is thinking very hard about nothing but these little details." Her voice grew angry. "You realize, don't you, that I still have the option of continuing a very promising career in the IDF? Where do you think that goes, if I'm caught helping a smuggler get away with it?"

"Oh." He looked contrite. "I didn't think about that. Sorry. But you aren't really helping a smuggler get away with it. You're helping a guy who ripped off a smuggler get away with it."

"You plan to take that bag from here to Tel Aviv, don't you? You think that isn't smuggling? So please take this seriously. You need credible answers to questions. No clueless stuttering." She stopped to drink some cold coffee. "I have a horrible headache. You're going to have to come up with the rest of the story. You'll have plenty of time to think about it while you're diving in the bay at Sharm."

"What rest?"

"Who gave you a ride to Ras Muhammed? I think a couple would be most typical. What are their names, where are they from, where did you meet them? You figure all that out by yourself. My head really is exploding."

The next afternoon it was Heller who answered Tonia's call and came to knock on Gavrielle's door. He remained outside, talking to some of the men, giving Gavrielle her privacy while she called Tonia back. After Gavrielle hung up she stepped out of the office, letting him know she was off the phone. She waited for him to come up the steps.

"I'm really sorry," she said. "Really. But I have to go home. I'll stay and work this weekend, like I said I would, but my grandmother's going into the hospital for surgery on Tuesday, so I'll have to leave on Sunday or Monday."

He stared at her for a moment, his expression inscrutable to her. "Nothing serious, I hope."

"I don't think so. Something about her leg. She has a prosthesis."

"Will you be coming back?"

"No." She hung her head, staring at the floor. "I really am sorry."

He shrugged. "Can't say I expected you to last this long."

"Well, I'd better go set up for dinner."

"Wait." He bit his bottom lip, thinking. "There are only four men staying down here this Shabbat. The food will be ready as usual. They'll manage." He stepped into the office and returned with two airline tickets. "Here. You might as well go home tomorrow, be with your grandmother. We'll mail you your check."

"Oh never mind about that," she stammered. "This

ticket for Charlie and letting him stay here — that's more than enough."

"Nonsense. You work, you get paid. Anyway, I already reported your hours. I have to pay you." He clomped down the steps.

Gavrielle couldn't wait to be out of Sharm and insisted that neither of them leave camp. They sat in the dining room, reading and playing gin rummy. Then she used up some of her nervous energy scrubbing. The camp kitchen had never been so clean.

At the airport on Friday Heller kept himself busy. Gavrielle wondered if he might be angry and purposely ignoring her, but was just as glad not to have to say goodbye to him and/or apologize again.

She did say to Charlie, "Listen, I'd like a few minutes in private to say goodbye to Aviram. He's been a good friend to me."

"Indeed. I seen the way his eyes are always glued to you."

"Cut it out."

"Okay, okay. I shouldn't be razzin' you about him. I know he looked out for you. He's a good guy."

Aviram saw her looking his way, waved, and came over.

"I hear you're not coming back."

"No." She held out her hand. "Thanks for everything. It was great getting to know you."

He ignored her hand and gazed at her with a sigh. "Too bad you're such a prude." He put his hands on either side of her face, pulled her closer, and lightly brushed her lips with his. More a warm breath than a kiss. "We could have had a nice time."

She blushed and shrugged. "I've never seen the point of that kind of thing."

He sighed again and shook his head. "You intellectuals can be awfully dumb. Point? The point is

229

that what you mostly get in life is load after load of big fat turds shoveled your way. So when something good finally comes along, you're going to whine because it won't last forever? What's forever? You ..." He kissed her forehead and then raised a hand to make a quick motion overhead. "You would have been like a falling star that I caught for just a moment. A man has to be a fool to say no to a falling star."

Part 5

Jerusalem

Friday, July 12, 1974

Gavrielle and Charlie disembarked in Tel Aviv, where she received a final, less poetic goodbye from Aviram.

"You think that diamond whatchamacallit is open?" Charlie asked, as they exited Ben Gurion airport.

"The Diamond Exchange," she said. "I suppose so. But according to Yechi – Amos's broker cousin – it's harder to get into that place than most countries. And I have no idea if he's even working today."

"Can we try? If we could just sell them to Yucky –"

"Ye-chi, Ye-chi." She corrected him, loudly demonstrating the guttural "ch" sound, like clearing one's throat.

"Like you said."

"And there's no 'we' here."

"Okay, okay. If *I* can sell them to whatshisname, then the whole thing will be over with and we can have a nice weekend. Unless you're looking forward to giving me a bunch more dirty looks."

"I can give you plenty of dirty looks, either way." But she gave in. "We have to go over there." She pointed. "Where all the busses are. Find one to Ramat Gan."

After breathing clouds of exhaust fumes, they were finally seated on a bus.

"How come there's so many Jews in the diamond business anyway?" Charlie asked. "I mean, didn't they all live in Poland and Russia and like that? Never heard of any diamond mines in them countries. Seems like my people ought to be selling all the diamonds."

"Jews don't own the mines. They're polishers and brokers. And if you were a Jew in Europe, you'd much rather buy and sell diamonds than grand pianos."

He gave her a blank look.

"What other business can you wrap in a

handkerchief and put in your pocket? You know, when they come pounding on the door to kick you out of the country," Gavrielle explained.

He looked taken aback and made no response, following her off the bus at a stop a block from the Exchange. She shielded her eyes with one hand and pointed with the other. "That's it, up the street there. That glass tower."

The 22-story building was one of the tallest in the country.

"But let's get coffee first," she said and didn't wait for his response before turning into the coffee shop they were standing next to. Once they were seated and she had a cup of coffee and a plate of gooey pastry in front of her she said, "I'm sorry for being so crabby."

"I'm the one who's sorry. I should never have even told you about the whole thing, so you wouldn't be all worried."

She opened her mouth to say, "How about being sorry for doing it?" but didn't. Instead she said, "I'll get over it."

"You been in there before?" He nodded in the direction of the tower.

"Just once. Amos took me with him. He gets a kick out of going to visit Yechi. Goes on about their security guards – how they outgun several minor world powers. It is true that they don't let anyone in without calling the broker to make sure they really do have an appointment, and then they make you leave your passport or ID with the guards. But Amos – he likes to joke about cavity searches on your way in and out. Don't worry, that's not true."

"Pretty secretive, huh?"

"Oh yeah. They're just barely willing to admit there's such a thing as diamonds. Of course, they need to be paranoid, since they really are a bunch of crooks. Not that any of them admit it. Talk to any dealer and he'll swear he's the only one who's on the up and up. But what can he do? He has to deal with a bunch of *goniffs*."

"How do they get away with it?"

"I guess it's the same in Belgium or any place diamond brokers operate. The governments are all hands-off. Scared that if they hassle them, they'll put their business in their pocket and take it elsewhere, along with the mountains of foreign currency they bring in. So the brokers do pretty much whatever they want, use their imaginations when they write out invoices or file tax returns. They do smuggle stones, but I think just back and forth between here and Europe and New York."

"So if a diamond broker wants to smuggle stones, he doesn't have to swallow them or shove them up his ass?"

"No, they hang them around their wives' necks or wrap up a nice little package and make out a proper invoice – to someone in some other city. I mean, other than the city they're flying to. Then they waltz through the 'Nothing to Declare Line' at the airport and if they get stopped they say, 'Of course I'm not declaring them, they're just passing through, in transit.' If they don't get stopped, they tear up the invoice. 'Silk-glove crime,' they call it."

"Ha. What other kind of stuff they do?"

She tried to remember things she'd heard from Yechi over the years. "I think polished Russian stones get taxed in America, but Israeli ones don't. So they bring Russian diamonds into Israel, mix them up with Israeli ones, and re-export them all as Israeli."

"Your government ever try to do anything about it?"

"Are you kidding? You know how much money the brokers donate – to *all* the political parties. They used to have to turn in a declaration of their net worth,

234

together with their income tax returns. But last year, after the war, when the government was desperately trying to scrounge up money, the diamond guys bought more than twice as many war bonds as they were asked to. Only they wanted one teensy-weensy little favor in return – not to have to file those pesky declarations any more. And now they don't."

"You know all this stuff about how the world works, so how can you act so naïve?"

She shrugged. "Knowing it goes on doesn't make me want any part of it. I think that's one reason I always wanted to be in the army. I used to be *really* naïve about that. Thought people who are responsible for the security of the country, for protecting our lives, who deal with life and death every day – how could any of those guys ever take a bribe or anything like that? But more than one Israeli soldier has been caught selling weapons to Arabs. And the big shots? Who knows how much money changes hands under the table in arms deals. That's mostly what made me stop thinking of the IDF as some kind of substitute family. Sound like a moron, don't I?"

"Nope. Sound like a good person."

They approached the shiny edifice of the Israel Diamond Exchange. Two guards armed with Uzis stood inside the glass doors and Gavrielle spoke to them through an intercom.

"Yechi isn't here," she said to Charlie. "And they have no idea if he might come later. They said if we have ID to give them, we can wait in the library."

"They got a library in there about diamonds?"

She nodded.

"Okay, yeah, let's do that. Give him a couple of hours to show up."

Charlie spent his time in the library going through the indexes of books, looking for information about the price of uncut diamonds. Gavrielle browsed more generally.

They both read in silence. After about half an hour, Gavrielle said, "Well, here's a possibility. It says here that India polishes the same kind of stones that Israel specializes in. Except Israel has a better reputation for quality workmanship, so Israeli polished stones cost more and Israeli dealers have been known to import Indian goods, mix them in with their own, and resell them at a profit. I suppose that profit would be even bigger if you smuggled them in."

"Yeah, hey, that could be it. So say, like a ship from India is going past Sharm anyway. All that yacht has to do is get close to it. Then someone tosses that rubber bag overboard, attached to some kind of life preserver type thing."

"Yes." Gavrielle nodded. "That could explain why the yacht shows up to so often. It doesn't go back and forth between here and India or here and Sierra Leone. It just hangs around out by the shipping channels, waiting for the next ship that has a smuggler from their gang on it." She frowned and drummed her fingers on the table. "But I'm not sure it makes sense. I mean, how far out are the shipping channels? I have no idea. And that's a big ocean to go throwing a dinky bag of diamonds in."

Charlie sat watching her, a wide grin on his face. "There you go again. Having to know everything. What do you care where they're smuggling the diamonds from or why? You're fretting on all that and don't even care what they're worth."

"I thought *you* were getting that all figured out."

"Nah. Too complicated. You have to know where they're from, how much they weigh, all about color and brilliance. I got no clue."

"Maybe," she said, mostly to herself, "they use a really big flotation device. With a transmitter on it, broadcasting a signal. All the yacht would need is an ADF tuned in to that frequency ..."

Finally she closed the book, resigned to never knowing. *The only way I'll ever know is if the bad guys catch us, so I guess I have to be grateful for blissful ignorance.* She looked at her watch, went to speak to the guards again, and came back shaking her head. "Nope. Look, it's Friday. If he was coming, he'd be here by now. You ready to go to Jerusalem?"

"Yeah. You told Tonia and Amos about me?"

"Of course. When I called her back yesterday. She was happy to hear you're coming. They're always complaining about me never bringing any of my friends home, in complete denial of the fact that I have no friends. Come on, let's go." She stood up and carefully returned all the books to the shelves, before shrugging into her pack.

Back on Jabotinsky Street, Charlie shook his head as he looked around. "Once you get used to the cars being so dinky, it's a lot more ... I don't know, modern here than I thought it would be."

"You didn't expect paved roads and street lights?"

"I didn't think you rode around on camels and donkeys, but I guess I didn't really give much thought to what it would be like."

During their bus ride to Jerusalem Gavrielle pointed out various landmarks, most of them sadly having to do with one war or another. When they got off at the central bus station Charlie gaped at a group of Orthodox Jews. "Man, how can they go around in them long coats in this heat? That guy's even got a fur hat on! Does Amos dress like that?"

"No, he's modern Orthodox. You'll see. You'll like him. He's like you – everybody likes Amos."

"And Tonia?"

Gavrielle thought for a moment. "She isn't always as

237

likeable as Amos, but you end up loving her." Then she smiled, poked him, and said, "You know what? We're going to get a taxi – give you a quick tour of the city instead of going straight home."

She asked if he was hungry, thinking they could stop at Richie's, on King George Street. It had recently opened – Jerusalem's first pizza place – and she wanted to show it off. But Charlie said no, he wasn't hungry. *Yeah, like he was going to be impressed anyway*, she realized what a dumb idea that was. *He's American.*

She asked the cab driver to stop so they could walk along the trenches of Ammunition Hill – where Amos had been wounded in the Six Day War – and then drove up to Mount Scopus for a look at Hebrew University and a view of the Judean Desert. Their last stop was on the Mount of Olives, with its stunning view of the city.

"That's something Christian," Gavrielle pointed down at a structure in the garden below. "I don't remember what it's called in English. In Hebrew it's *Gat Shmanim*. I don't remember what happened there, but something important."

Charlie murmured, "*Gat Shmanim, Gat Shmanim,*" trying to think what that might be in English. "Could it be the Garden of the Gethsemane?"

She shrugged. "Sounds sort of right, but I can't say for sure. Why don't you ask the driver? I bet they know all the names in English."

Charlie did and was told that he was indeed looking down over the Garden of the Gethsemane. He stood there for a long while. "I can't believe it. This is so cool. I mean I knew I was coming to the Holy Land and all, but I never stopped to think about what places from the Bible might still exist. The Garden of the Gethsemane! You know what happened there? That's where Jesus was praying when Judas betrayed him. Right there. Right down there."

"I don't know what that building down there is. I do know it's real pretty and you can go inside. The entrance is from that road down there. But we don't have time today. I don't want to show up at Tonia and Amos's at the last minute before the Sabbath starts."

They returned to the cab and as they drove past the Old City walls and into West Jerusalem, Gavrielle pointed out where the City Line had been – marking the border between Jordan and Israel. When the cab stopped on Tonia and Amos's street, Gavrielle paled.

"Oh my God." She grabbed Charlie's arm. "Look! Heller! That's Heller up there with Amos."

Charlie squinted at the two men getting into Amos's pick-up. "You sure? What'd he be doing here? What'd he be doing with Amos?"

"I don't know. But that was him."

After the pick-up drove off Charlie paid the driver and Gavrielle got out, looking around as if expecting someone else to jump out of the bushes. She tried to convince herself that the panic she felt was ridiculous. Mike Heller was not some diamond smuggler who was going to pull a gun on them. But he *had* been acting weird the last few days.

"We gonna stand here all day?" Charlie asked.

"I'm trying to think, but my brain isn't functioning. I can't think of a single reason, good or bad, for him to be here. Can you?"

"Nope. Don't wanna bother trying. We gonna find out, sooner or later. Let's go in. I'm pooped."

She began walking, as if through a sea of molasses, as she led Charlie into the house. They found Tonia alone in the kitchen, cleaning the *plata* – the large hot plate that would keep the food warm during the Sabbath.

Tonia turned to them with a wide smile. "Finally."

239

She gave Gavrielle a big hug. "And you must be Charlie." He also got an embrace, but one that left daylight between them. "We're so glad you decided to come. Are you guys starving? Did you eat anything? Can I make you coffee? Or do you want a shower first?"

"Coffee sounds good to me," Gavrielle said.

"I think I'll take you up on the shower," Charlie said. "Give you two a chance to get some gossiping about me out of the way."

Tonia laughed and declared that she liked him already. Then she called Sarit to take him up to his room and show him where the bathroom was. "There's a towel on your bed," she called after them.

She made two cups of instant coffee and sat at the table with Gavrielle. "You are never going to guess who else is here."

"My boss? Was that really him I saw with Amos?"

"Yes. Mike actually got here a while ago. Said there's something he has to talk to you about. He and Amos were in the living room, yakking about construction stuff, and all of a sudden Amos decided he needs Mike's advice on something, so he took him over to the house he's remodeling."

Mike? That's so weird to hear her call him that. "Didn't he say what he wants?"

"Nope. Did the two of you … did he, you know, show any interest?"

"God, no. He was a nice enough boss, but that's it."

"Well, maybe he didn't think it was appropriate, you know, as long as he was your boss. But now that you've quit working there, he decided not to waste any time … Okay, okay. Don't give me that face. I know I'm sticking my nose in. So then, what was with you asking me to call his office down there? Are you going to tell me what that little drama was all about, or is that out of bounds?"

240

"That's a long story. I'll tell you about it, but not now. Not when Heller could come through the door any minute. Why don't you get on with all your questions about Charlie – or I can save you the trouble," Gavrielle said with a smile. "Yes, he's a few years younger than me, but that doesn't matter because we're just friends. Really good friends, but that's all. He's American. And guess where he lives? In Michigan. Even has family in Grand Rapids."

"Oh, well that's a coincidence for you. Out of all the cities ... It's such a pretty town."

"He wants to do some sightseeing in Jerusalem, and after that I'm going to go back there with him. To Michigan. He volunteered to help me look for my father." Gavrielle spoke quickly and then changed the subject. "Is Nanna Nella sleeping?"

"Yes. She's begun taking longer naps. But she's fine. How did you and Charlie get to be such good friends, so fast?"

Gavrielle shrugged. "I don't know. But we have a lot more in common than you'd think."

"Well, if you're set on going to America, I'm awfully glad you've got a friend who can look out for you. I would have worried to death if you went to the States all by yourself."

"Do you hear how funny that is? I'm twenty-seven, a college grad, and an officer in the IDF. When you went there – all alone – you were a lot younger and a high school dropout."

"This is true. Still, I would have worried. What did Charlie study?"

"Art and architecture. He's real smart. And, an orphan like me. This young white couple, who aren't that much older than him, took him in."

"Ah. So you do share a lot in common."

Car doors slammed outside and Amos and Heller came through the back door.

241

"Hey, Gav." Amos gave her a hug. "Almost forgot what you look like."

"Hello." Heller nodded.

"Hello." Am I supposed to call him Mike? That would feel too weird. But so would Heller.

Tonia offered him coffee, but he said he had to get going. "Can I talk to you for a minute, Gavrielle? Bureaucratic issues."

"Sure." Gavrielle began to gather some courage, thanks to how nervous Heller looked. "Why don't I walk you to your car?"

Heller led her to a dark sedan and suggested they get in. Then he turned toward her, his left arm draped over the steering wheel.

"Don't be afraid," he said. "But we need to have a conversation. I think you can guess what it's about." His solemn expression brought her panic back.

"Did I do something wrong? Forget to fill in some form?"

He sighed. "It's about the package. The package Charlie took off that boat."

She paled, and tried to imagine turning into a bird and flying out the window. He waited a moment before going on.

"Aviram asked me to talk to you. *He* was supposed to pick up that package. He's been in a bad way, ever since he saw it was gone."

In a bad way? Aviram? Seemed in a perfectly good mood to me.

"Then someone told him they saw Charlie take it. Listen ..." He looked her in the face. "You guys aren't in any trouble. Not yet anyway. Just give me the package, I'll take it back to him, and the problem goes away. And Aviram has learned his lesson. After this he wants out. He knows it was stupid to get involved with those people. But right now he's into them for a lot of money

242

and you don't mess with these guys. So he asked me to come beg you to give it back. He'll give you some kind of reward."

"I have no idea what you're talking about. And I had a long talk with Aviram at the airport. He didn't say anything to me."

"He didn't find out it was Charlie until after we got off the plane. Then one of the other guys mentioned seeing Charlie in diving gear, nosing around that fishing boat."

"I told you, I have no idea what you're talking about." She met his gaze with her chin raised, certain he was lying about something.

He sighed again and turned in his seat to face forward. "Okay, listen, let's stop wasting time. The other day – when I came into the dining room – when you and Charlie were in there talking – I left a small tape recorder under the table. So I heard everything you said, about the package, taking Charlie to Ras Muhammed, everything. It was quite impressive."

She stared at him for a long moment, keeping her face blank. *So he hadn't been fixing his shoelaces when he bent down under the table.* She was strangely calm, thinking.

"You're a terrible liar," she finally said. He failed to respond and she went on. "Sorry, but that doesn't make any sense. Why the heck would you be spying on me and Charlie two days ago, if Aviram didn't find out about whatever Charlie supposedly did on some boat until after we got off the plane this morning?"

He didn't seem to have an answer.

Her eyes narrowed. "Aviram isn't in any trouble. *You* are! *You* were supposed to pick up the diamonds."

"Diamonds?" He didn't hide his surprise.

"What? I'm supposed to believe you didn't know what you were smuggling?"

Obviously flustered, he said, "Shit. Okay, I've made

243

a mess of this. You're right. I am a terrible liar. I just thought that telling you Aviram was in trouble would be the easiest way to get you to give whatever it was back. I mean, you wouldn't want anyone killing him."

"But you assumed I wouldn't consider your life worth saving?" She leaned back, relaxed, almost enjoying herself. At least she no longer felt afraid of him. *If he was going to threaten me, he would have done it by now.* Her brain was spinning, trying to work out what was really going on.

Heller emitted a loud and vocal sigh. "All right, I'll tell you the truth. Doron noticed those boats too and he —"

"Who's Doron?"

"The cop. The one and only cop in Sharm. Anyway, he knows I've got a good friend in the Border Police and asked me to call him, see if he'd heard anything about some kind of small-scale trafficking gang. My friend said no, he hadn't, but asked me to keep an eye on those boats – keep track of when they come and go. There are always new gangs popping up. So he told me to pay attention to strangers."

"Like Charlie."

"Yes. Like Charlie."

"That's why you were so nice to him – let him stay in camp for free. Keep your friends close and the people you have to spy on closer." There was no animosity in her voice.

"I would have let him stay anyway. I think I'm a pretty nice guy. But, yes, that was another reason to have him in camp."

"And you called your Border Police guy and had him check him out. That's why you asked Charlie what flights he'd taken."

"Yes. He came back clean. Was on the flights he said he was and no other traveling outside of the U.S. He

244

never even had a passport before going to Rome. No known contacts with any bad guys. Well, a few criminal types in Detroit, like local drug dealers, but no foreigners or anything."

Her eyes narrowed again. "So I still don't see why you were spying on us."

He drummed his fingers on the steering wheel. "Look, I had a foreign national in my camp – on our most strategic naval base – and the local cop thinks there's something fishy going on. Then that foreign national disappears, is gone all night, no one from the Dive Club took him anywhere ... so when Charlie came back and went slinking into the kitchen, I followed him. Listened by the door. I couldn't hear much. Just enough to know he'd gotten something off that boat and you were scared."

She considered his new story before saying, "Okay, I'll buy that. But why didn't you just tell me that in the first place? Why make up all that other crap?"

"I don't know. Trying to keep all options open. I had no idea what it was that Charlie had found. I might need you thinking I have some kind of contact with the bad guys, in case you need to be scared into giving it back. You are going to give it back, aren't you?"

She ignored his question and asked, "What did you think it was?"

He shrugged. "Money. Drugs. Arrangements for bringing people would be the worst. The wrong kind of people, disappearing into the mountains where they can pretty much do whatever they want. Set up training camps, give bomb-making classes. When I heard you two talking about a package, I thought perhaps detonators, small amounts of explosives. Maybe information. Records. A list of targets. How do I know?"

"You thought Charlie might be involved with something like that?"

245

He shrugged again. "What do I know? Anything's possible with a young guy who thinks he's in Adventure Land. Maybe he's a Black Panther."

"So why did you give us tickets for today?" she asked. "Why not keep us down there where you could spy on us for a few more days."

"I wanted you out of Sharm."

"Why?"

"Why? For your safety. Why else?"

"Oh." That was the only reason she hadn't considered.

"So no bad guys are after Aviram? Or you?"

"No." He shook his head.

"What are you going to do now? Rat Charlie out to your Border Police guy?"

"No. I don't give a rip about diamond smugglers. But you two have to get rid of them."

"I know …" Gavrielle was thinking again. "So maybe you could help with that. Turn them into the Border Police." She turned to him, eyes pleading.

"Thank God. That's what I was about to suggest. I'm pretty sure there's some kind of reward for contraband. Some percentage of whatever it's worth."

"Could you …" Gavrielle stopped and smiled. "I don't know if I should even bother asking you to do this, you're such a bad liar … But could you maybe tell the police guy that you asked Charlie to keep an eye on the boat – I mean seeing as he was hanging out at Naama Bay everyday – and he went beyond the call of duty, went to check it out, with no concern for the danger he was putting himself in."

"Yes, I think I can manage that. And when I get back to Sharm on Sunday I'll start a rumor – the Border Police had an undercover guy down there who found a stash of diamonds on a boat."

"Thank you. Thank you. This is all such a relief.

Now all I have to do is convince Charlie. But I doubt that will be very hard. I'll go get him."

She opened the door but before she got out Heller handed her a business card. "If you don't receive your paycheck from Hakama in the next few weeks, you can reach me at that number."

"Okay. Thanks. I'll be right back."

Charlie required no convincing. He listened to what Heller had to say and shrugged, looking as relieved as Gavrielle felt. "Okay. Sounds good. I didn't know how to get rid of the damn things anyway."

He leaned forward and took the rubber bag from where he'd tucked it, in the small of his back. "Just one thing," he said as he opened it. "I'm keeping three of these babies, but I promise I won't try to sell them. They'll be my souvenir-of-Sinai engagement ring for the lucky girl I ask to marry me someday. You guys have any brains, you'll do the same. Here, I brought paper towels for all of us."

Heller and Gavrielle looked at one another and both shrugged.

"Who's going to know the difference?" Heller said, and Charlie counted out one-two-three diamonds for each of them. Then he closed the bag and handed it to Heller.

Gavrielle couldn't resist asking, "How do we know you're really going to turn them in?"

"I guess you're just going to have to trust me."

Charlie got out of the car and stood by Heller's window. "Thanks, man. Really. Coming all the way here and saving my butt. I sure appreciate it. You'll be the co-star of all the stories I tell my grandkids about this place."

"The Border Police should call someday next week. If they don't, you call me. Gavrielle has my card. Enjoy our beautiful little country. And take good care of this one in America." He nodded at Gavrielle.

247

"I will do that. I will indeed."

Gavrielle added words of gratitude of her own and then Charlie slapped the top of the car and Heller drove off.

Part 6

West Bloomfield Township

Tuesday, July 23, 1974

"This rinky-dink plane's got way better seats than the Jumbo Jet did." Charlie turned his head and bent forward, making sure Gavrielle was awake. "Don't you think?"

She was slumped against the side of the plane, staring out the tiny window, and did not respond.

"Don't you think?"

"What?" She turned her head slightly toward him.

"What you thinking so hard on?"

"Nothing. Just tired."

He leaned closer to the window, but their seats were over the wing and there wasn't much to see. He glanced at his watch. "'Bout forty minutes we land at Metro."

"I know."

"Geez, try to cool it, why don't you? Ain't healthy to get so over-excited." He rolled his eyes, but then his expression changed to one of concern. "You feeling sorry you came?"

"No." She finally turned to look at him. "Not sorry. Scared. Not just about my father. Right now the scary thing is the immediate one – arriving as an uninvited guest at the home of people I've never met."

"What, I don't count? Maybe my name ain't on the mortgage, but I got full invitational rights."

She smiled.

"You trust me?" he asked.

She nodded.

"So knock off the worrying. Everything's gonna be all right. I got you. And Charlene and Reeves are good people – their house has a great vibe. You'll see. First thing tomorrow we'll call that guy in Florida, see what's with him. You gotta put your head in a different place. You're on vacation. Seeing the U. S. of A. for the first time."

Reeves was waiting for them at the gate. Charlie greeted him with a wide smile and a clap on the back, saying, "Hey man, what's up? Where's Charlene? What's wrong?"

"Nothing's wrong. She doesn't feel so hot, is all. Coming down with a cold or something."

Charlie turned around and unceremoniously said, "Reeves, this is Gavrielle. Gavrielle, this is Reeves."

"It's nice to meet you." Gavrielle shyly offered her hand. It was hard not to laugh out loud at the idea of Reeves as Charlie's foster father. Charlie was taller and Reeves didn't look much older.

Reeves took her hand and said, "Very nice to meet you. We're glad you could come." Then he turned around, saying, "Come on, let's go get your bags. I think I'm okay where I parked, but this airport drives me nuts."

Down at baggage claim Reeves stood aside, while Charlie snatched their suitcases from the carousel. Then Reeves led them outside and showed them where to wait while he brought the car around. A few minutes later he pulled up to the curb in the Valenti's green Ford Ranch Wagon.

"Shit, what'd he bring the dragon wagon for?" Charlie complained.

Charlie put their luggage in the back and insisted that Gavrielle sit up front. He took the seat behind her, where he could lean forward to talk to Reeves.

"So how sick is Charlene?" he asked.

"Just a cold," Reeves answered as he pulled onto M-39. "So, how was Rome?"

"I better wait to tell you all that. So I don't have to repeat it all to Charlene." Charlie leaned back and stared out the window, obviously glad to be home.

"So, I guess you're from Israel?" Reeves glanced at Gavrielle.

"Yes."

251

"First time in America?"

"Yes."

"You guys must be beat."

"Not so bad," Gavrielle said. "We both managed to sleep a few hours between Tel Aviv and New York."

"Are you hungry?"

"Not starving," Charlie said. "We can wait till we get home. 'Less you'd rather stop."

"Do they have shopping malls in Israel?" Reeves asked Gavrielle.

"I don't know what that is."

"A mall? It's a whole bunch of stores in one place. All enclosed, you know, under one roof."

"No." Gavrielle shook her head. "We have a department store in Jerusalem, but nothing like that."

When they were approaching Northland, Reeves said, "I think I will stop. We can get something at the Big Boy and Gavrielle can see what a mall is."

Gavrielle did stare open-eyed at the endless rows of stores in the enormous mall, but expressed no interest in shopping. Reeves led them to a booth in the Big Boy.

"After this you'll be on your own until dinner," he said, "so have a real meal, even if you don't feel like you're starving now."

While they were eating, Reeves and Charlie talked mostly about the work Reeves had finished on the apartment over the garage, which they were planning to rent out to a young couple.

"Is Charlene working a lot, driving that bookmobile?" Charlie asked and then turned to explain to Gavrielle what a bookmobile was.

"One morning a week to a bunch of old folks homes, and three afternoons to different neighborhoods, for the kids."

"And she's working at Rick's gym?" He referred to Reeves' best friend from high school.

252

"Don't let him hear you call it that. It's a Fitness Center and Spa. And she pretty much goes over there whenever she feels like it. Gets the mail, checks the receipts and books. Rick likes for her visits to be unexpected. Thinks it keeps the staff on their toes. He was right about the whole exercise thing becoming a big deal. He already opened another place in Dearborn, and the other day he told me he's looking for locations for two more."

"Becoming a big tycoon?"

"He's doing all right for himself. Sort of kills Charlene that he was right and she was wrong – predicted he'd lose his shirt. And now she's ended up working for him. But they get along all right. Rick and Kim are coming over for dinner some night this week, assuming Char's feeling better."

When they drove around the house and down the driveway, Charlene skipped down the porch steps in her ratty blue bathrobe, clutching a wadded up tissue. She hurried toward them, but stopped short, keeping her distance.

"Geez Louise, Charlie Freeman, I forgot how tall you are. Pretty soon I'm gonna need a ladder to give you a hug. But I can't give you one today, anyway. You don't want whatever I've got. Besides, what I really ought to do is hit you over the head. I was so worried about you." She socked his arm. "It was awful, not knowing where you were – having to wait for a stupid telegram. I even called that school. They let me talk to your teacher."

"Francesca? You talked to Francesca?"

"Yep. She told me the only person she'd seen you being friendly with was another student. A girl from Israel. So I guess that would be you." She turned to Gavrielle.

"Yes, that's me. I'm Gavrielle. I really apologize for

imposing like this."

"Apologize? Are you kidding? We sing Hallelujah on every very rare occasion that Mr. Free brings a human being home with him. We've begun to think he's ashamed to admit to anyone except stray dogs that he knows us. Anyway, you're here, safe and sound. That's what counts." She stopped to blow her nose. "All Charlie's first telegram said was that he was taking a trip. Please don't tell me that was to Israel."

"Sorry, but it was."

Charlene shook her head. "No offense, but that had me sick with worry. I mean, I'm sure it's a lovely country, but ..."

"I know. We do have a lot of problems," Gavrielle said. "But I promise you, they look a lot worse from far away." She stopped to look around. "All this land – it's yours?"

"Yeah, all ours to mow and weed," Charlene said, but couldn't hide how much she loved it.

"It's so beautiful. Oh my, look at that. You have your own baseball park."

"Diamond." Charlie corrected her. "It's a softball diamond."

"And that over there – that's a cornfield?"

"I don't know if twenty short rows count as a cornfield, but yeah, that's corn," Charlene said. "And that little building to the right is the cook house. Has a big grill in it. Charlie will have to fix some of his famous barbecue for you. Now come on in and meet Charlie's Grandma Julie. I think she's still having a lie down, but she'll want to get up for Charlie." Charlene turned back toward the house. "She's going to make her famous fried chicken for dinner. Said to tell you she bought the kosher chicken, and got a brand new pan to fry it in. Because she didn't know, if you were, you know, kosher."

"That was so thoughtful of her," Gavrielle said. "I'm not. Kosher, I mean. Except, um, I don't eat pork or seafood."

Charlene pulled the screen door open and went inside, calling over her shoulder, "I've got iced tea, lemonade, and brownies. Not a smidgeon of seafood in any of it."

In the kitchen Charlene set glasses on the table next to the pan of brownies, and took the pitchers of lemonade and tea from the refrigerator. "You guys help yourselves. And go wake your grandma up, Charlie. I'm going to go lie down for a while. Gavrielle's got clean sheets in the blue guestroom."

Half an hour later Charlene climbed the stairs, glad to find the door to Charlie's room open and him alone in it. She closed the door behind her and sat on the bed. Charlie moved his open suitcase to the floor with a loud thud, and looked at her warily as he sat next to her.

"Thought you were gonna take a nap," he said.

"I am. I just wanted to tell you – unless Reeves already did."

"Tell me what?"

She smiled like a little girl. "Get that look off your face. It's good news. I'm going to have a baby."

It took a moment for a smile to spread across Charlie's face. "A baby. Wow." He almost said, "After all this time," but bit it back. "That is great news. How are you feeling?"

"Just fine. Or I was, until I got this stupid cold. I only found out two weeks ago."

"I'm really glad for you guys. Wow. I don't care about your cold, I gotta give you a hug." He did so, and pulled back to go on. "That'll be something – a little baby in the house." He was genuinely happy, though he couldn't help wondering how this would change things. There was, however, one definite bright side to it. *If*

255

she's looking at having a real kid, she ain't gonna care much about trying to run my life. "So, you're only, like two weeks?"

"More like a month and a half. Took me a while to figure out that I'd better go to the doctor."

"So, like April?"

"Yeah. But he didn't give me an exact date yet."

"You got boy names and girl names picked out?"

"We've had those for years. Just not the same ones. We'll have to fight that out after we know what it is."

"What're you hoping for?"

She shook her head. "I really don't care. Ten fingers and toes. I've always wanted to have a couple of both, so ..." She shrugged.

Charlie hugged her again. "You got any a that morning sickness stuff?"

"No. So far I feel great. Gavrielle seems real nice."

"She is. You go get your lie down. Gav and me can take care of ourselves. I'll help Grandma Julie get dinner." He paused, saying to her back. "I'm really, really happy for you guys. For me, too. Lucky kid, to have you guys for parents. Really lucky."

During dinner, Charlie told them all about Rome and their time in Sharm el Sheikh – minus the diamond smugglers. Then Reeves turned to Gavrielle and changed the subject. "What happened to you guys, almost losing a war? After '67, you were supposed to be like some kind of superheroes."

She sighed. "Yeah. That was our problem – we thought so too." She paused to lick her fingers. "Grandma Julie, this is the most delicious chicken I've ever tasted."

"Eat up." Grandma Julie pushed the serving platter towards Gavrielle. "They's lots more."

Gavrielle was happy to oblige, and helped herself to

another drumstick. Then she looked back at Reeves. "People in Israel who think they are clever say that between '67 and Yom Kippur the Arabs and the Jews both changed – got to be a whole lot more like each other – the Arabs learned how to fight and we learned how to deceive ourselves."

"But how the heck did they make it across the Suez Canal? Back before the war happened, I saw a thing on the news – this great line of defense you built, like impossible to get through."

"Yeah, our famous Bar Lev Line." She sighed again. "Concrete banks all along the canal and hard-packed sand behind them – mountains of sand, sixty feet high, like a three-story building. How's a tank ever going to get over that? And behind that was a string of forts, with tanks backing them up. We kept the tanks farther east, out of missile range, but they were supposed to be able to get to the canal in 15 minutes, half an hour tops. And just to be on the safe side, we also had a last-resort secret weapon. If anyone in the forts saw Egyptians crossing in boats or building a bridge for tanks, all they had to do was turn a valve that would release some kind of flammable oil."

"Yeah, I remember that. You toss a bomb out there and get this huge wall of flames. No one could make it through alive. So how did they get through all that and kick your butts?"

"They had their own secret weapon," she said sarcastically. "Pumps. My country was almost wiped out because British manufacturers started making really good turbine pumps that can blast out a thousand gallons of water a minute."

"To put out the fire?"

"No. The fire never happened. But the Egyptians hooked those pumps up to fire hoses and turned them on our mountains of sand. It's not like we never thought they might try something like that, but the best

257

pumps we knew about would have taken twelve hours to breach the sand. Those new British pumps – in less than half an hour they blasted a series of passes through our man-made mountain range. Explosives finished the job and their tanks drove right through."

"The Arab tanks just swam across the water?"

"No, that was secret weapon number two – this one from the Russians. Back when the Soviets were thinking about invading Western Europe – and having to cross rivers – they developed a new kind of portable bridge. The old kind would have taken over two hours to assemble. The new Russian one was like big pontoon-shaped pieces of Lego. Shove them in the water, connect them all together – right there by your shoreline where it's easy to work – and drag them across. Whole thing took them less than half an hour."

She stopped and stared out the window. "But mostly we screwed up because we were complacent. Didn't feel threatened. Everyone remembered the pictures of sand dunes littered with Egyptian army boots."

By now Gavrielle seemed to be speaking to herself. Then she gave her head a quick shake. "Sorry, I must be putting you all to sleep."

"No," Reeves said. "Go on. What's with the boots?"

She looked uncertainly around the table, but Reeves asked again, so she answered. "In '67, thousands of the Egyptian soldiers who were sent into the Sinai turned around and ran. They threw their boots away because it's easier to run on sand in bare feet. But after the Yom Kippur War there weren't any boots. That war left the desert covered with long electrical control wires. The ones the Egyptian soldiers used to guide their Sagger missiles. To incinerate the boys in our tanks."

"I think that's enough war talk," Grandma Julie said. "You haven't told us about Jerusalem yet." She looked at Charlie.

258

"Wait," Reeves said. "Just one more question. What about your great wall of fire? Why didn't it happen?"

Gavrielle shrugged. "Depends on who you ask. If you ask us, it was out of order. Hadn't been working since July. A team was scheduled to go down there and start repairing it. Guess when – the day after Yom Kippur. If you ask the Egyptians, they say teams of their navy commandos crossed the canal underwater and plugged up the pipes that the oil was supposed to come out of."

"Who do you believe?"

She shrugged. "Both, I guess. No reason both things can't be true."

Gavrielle insisted on doing the dishes, and Charlene stood next to her, drying.

"So tomorrow you're going to call that guy in Florida?" Charlene asked.

Gavrielle nodded. "Just so you know – in case you're in the room when I talk to him – I'm going to lie about who I am. Tonia told me I shouldn't say I'm trying to find my long-lost father."

"Smart lady."

"I'll pay for the call, of course."

Charlene made a loud noise of dismissal through pursed lips.

The next morning Gavrielle came downstairs carrying the page with Jesse's pedantic block printing on it: DAVID SHAYNE 863-337-6938. She put it next to the phone and made a cup of instant coffee. It wasn't long before Charlie appeared. He picked up the paper and set it back down.

"So, today's the day?"

She nodded.

He glanced at the clock. 8 am. "Better wait a couple of hours."

"I know," she said.

259

"It's Wednesday, ain't it?"

"Yes."

"If this Shayne guy was, say, twenty-three when he got discharged from the army in 1945 – so that makes him, what, fifty-seven? Must still work a job, so he probably won't be home."

"I know. But maybe he has a wife who doesn't work – can tell me when would be a good time to call."

Reeves came into the kitchen, in paint-spattered shorts and T-shirt. "Morning."

"You forget it's summer vacation?" Charlie said. "What you up so early for?"

"Wanna get some work done on the yard, before it's too hot. You set the table, Charlie. I can manage scrambled eggs."

They stared at different sections of the newspaper while they ate. Then Reeves went outside and Gavrielle stood at the sink, washing the dishes and silently rehearsing what she would say to David Shayne.

"Good morning." Charlene came in, uncombed and in her robe. She stood at the window for a long moment, watching Reeves on the riding lawn mower. Then she put a hand on Gavrielle's shoulder. "You don't have to do that."

"At home I'm the designated dishwasher. Because I'm not much of a cook. But Tonia taught me how to bake, if you'd like some strudel or popovers."

"Why don't you relax and get your phone call over with, before you get all busy?" Then Charlene turned to Charlie, who was still at the table pretending to read the newspaper. "And you, Mr. Freeman, what are you planning to do with yourself until school starts?"

Gavrielle turned her head to watch his reaction.

Before Charlie could respond, Charlene said, "Hey, I forgot to tell you. You had company while you were gone. Two guys – friends from your old neighborhood."

260

Charlie froze. "What guys?"

"Eddie and his cousin Marvin. Carvin' Marvin." Charlene grinned.

Charlie's face grew worried, causing Charlene to frown. "They are friends of yours, aren't they? Grandma Julie sure was glad to see them."

"Eddie was my best friend, but that been way back. Ain't seen neither of them in a long time. Not since way before the riots. How'd they know I was out here?"

"Eddie saw that article about you in the Free Press. It told how you went to live with some hot shot who used to play basketball for State. Carv guessed it must be Reeves Valenti."

"So." Charlie looked wary. "What they say? Just asked if I live here and you told them I'd be back in a few weeks?"

"Actually, they stayed for a nice long visit. Had dinner with us. But we didn't talk much about you."

"You do know, don't you, that Carv ain't no tax-paying citizen?"

"Well, he must be now. He said he owns a club downtown. The Black Cat. He must pay taxes on that."

Charlie couldn't help grinning. "I meant that he's a criminal. Pushes dope for the Italians."

"Not any more." Charlene seemed to be enjoying this conversation. "He *was* one of their lieutenants, but then he went to work for some old friend of his – black guy who became one of the biggest dealers in the city. But he got out of that too. Now he just has his club. Said he's completely legit. He gave me his card, so you can call him." She found it in the drawer by the phone and handed it to Charlie. "Maybe we can all go down to his club some night."

"Imagine that. Little miss suburban housewife was all fine with lettin' a De-troit gangster into her house. Eddie say anything 'bout me havin' something belongs to him?"

261

"No. Like what?"

"Nothin' important. Just that Willy Horton jersey I used to wear for softball games. I always thought it might a been Eddie's. Thought maybe he wanted it back."

"He didn't say anything like that. But I'm sure you'll be seeing him again – have a chance to ask about it." Charlene walked behind him and patted his shoulder. "I think I'll go back to bed. Read my book."

After saluting her, Charlie went through the kitchen and screened-in porch, outside to collapse on the canopy swing. Gavrielle finished rinsing the dishes and joined him there.

"How come you looked so freaked out when she mentioned that Carv guy?" she asked.

Charlie stared at the ground for a long while. "Eddie – he was my best friend. Only real friend I ever had. See, you ain't the only one, Gavrielle. I just don't go 'round broadcasting it. But after me and my mom moved to a different neighborhood, me and Eddie didn't see each other so much. Pretty soon we didn't see each other at all. I guess I didn't really mind not seein' him, 'ccount of not wanting everyone to think I was friends with Carv."

"Why's he called Carvin' Marvin?"

"He's had some issues with knives. After he started dealing for the Italians, I was glad to keep my distance. Then one day, after I ain't seen Eddie for at least a year, he knocks on my door holding this package. It's about yay big." He held his palms apart, about the width and then the length of a shoebox. "All wrapped in brown paper and taped up. Asks me to hold on to it for him. I didn't want to, but he kept asking over and over and promised he'd come to get it in a week. So I took it."

He paused, touching a foot to the ground to make the swing move. "Then the riots broke out, and I took it with me to Charlene's house in Dearborn. Kept it in the back of my closet. When we moved out here, it came along with us."

"What's in it?"

"Got no idea. Never opened it. Didn't want to know what's in there."

"It's a wonder Charlene didn't find it. You know, cleaning your room while you were at school, or now, while you were away."

"When we moved out here, I didn't hide it in my room."

"So where?"

He stood and took a few steps, followed by Gavrielle, to where they could see Reeves on the lawn mower, finishing up the softball diamond.

"Out there." He nodded towards Reeves. "Buried it under second base."

Gavrielle looked horrified and grasped his arm. "What if it's a bomb? Reeves could drive right over it."

"A bomb? Guess we know where you grew up at. It ain't no bomb."

"What do you think it is?"

"Maybe money. Maybe drugs. Could be some kind of record book. You know, like where they got their money stashed. Or it could be nothing – some stupid thing of Eddie's. Like the youth group at his church was having a treasure hunt and he found the thing you need to win the treasure."

"You never told Charlene and Reeves about it?"

"Why would I put that on 'em? Suppose it was full of drugs, what they gonna do? Flush 'em? And then when some real gangster comes after Eddie, wanting their product back – what they gonna do then? They're better off not knowing nothing. 'Sides ..." He looked slightly ashamed. "I didn't want them thinking of me that way – you know, 'You can take the boy out of the hood ...'"

Her face was blank.

"It's a saying," he explained. "Hood means neighborhood."

She frowned for a moment. "Oh, I get it – but you can't take the neighborhood out of the boy."

"Yeah."

"So what are you going to do now?"

"Wait until the middle of the night and dig it up. Call Carv and tell him to come get it – meet me at Northland." He turned and put thumb and forefinger on her elbow. "Come on, let's you make your phone call."

Instead of starting toward the house, she turned to face him. "Haven't you ever been back to Detroit?"

"Nope."

"Not even once? You walked out of your apartment with a couple of duffel bags and never went back?"

"Nothin' to go back for. Only so-called family I got left is my shit head stepfather and I'm perfectly happy for him to think I'm dead. For all I know, he's dead."

"So that's like a whole different life. And it's over."

"Indeed."

She thought for a moment. "But Carv and Eddie are your friends."

"Maybe. Maybe not. Depends what's in that box and what they been thinkin' all these years – 'bout me disappearing with it. Tell you one thing – when I get Carv on the phone, first words out a my mouth gonna be, 'Hey, come get the box Eddie gave me. I'm gonna be the one brings it up, not him.'"

"Hello, is this the Shayne residence?" Gavrielle inquired.

"Yes, it is. Mrs. Shayne speaking."

"My name is Gavrielle Rozmann. I'm here visiting from Israel. If possible, I'd like to speak with your

264

husband – about the time he spent in Palestine, after World War II. I'm writing an article about all the foreign volunteers who came to help us."

"Oh, hon, my Davey would have loved that. But he passed, going on two years ago."

"I'm so sorry to hear that." Feeling as if she might faint from unbearable disappointment, Gavrielle squeezed her eyes shut and forced herself to concentrate.

"Thank you. He would have loved to meet you. He was mighty proud of what they did."

"Is it true that he was making a list of names? Of all the volunteers?"

"Yes, that he was."

"Do you have that list?" She squeezed her eyes even tighter.

"Can't say I've seen it, but then I haven't been looking for it, have I? I haven't had the heart to clear out his desk – left it pretty much the way it was. You hold on, hon, let me go have a look-see."

After what seemed forever, she came back on the line. "Yes, I found it. Have it right here in my hand."

"That's wonderful." Gavrielle could hear the rustling of papers.

"There's about a hundred, hundred twenty names on it. I see he got addresses and phone numbers for most of them. Typed it out and made a carbon. I could mail the copy to you, if you'd like."

"Oh could you? That would be wonderful. And so kind of you. I'd really appreciate it." She put Charlie on the phone – to give her the Valentis' address – and then reclaimed the receiver. "Mrs. Shayne, I hate to further impose on you, but could I ask you to look through the list now, see if you can find a particular name?"

"Surely. My Davey would want me to help you all I can. Who is it you're looking for, hon?"

"His name is Lou. L-o-u. I don't know the last name,

but he's half Irish and half Italian so it might be one of those kinds of names. Not a Jewish name, anyway. He's from a Catholic family. And, back then, he lived in Chicago."

Mrs. Shayne mumbled to herself as she turned the pages back and forth. "I got three addresses in Chicago, but they're all Jewish – Goldshmidt, Katz, and Mandel." She rustled the pages some more. "I'm sorry but I don't see any Lou."

"Oh."

Then Mrs. Shayne spoke again. "Now wait just a second. Here's one just caught my eye. Brody's Irish, ain't it? I think so. I see a Luciano Fergus Brody. Could be L-o-u was a nickname, couldn't it?"

Gavrielle's eyes opened wide. "Yes, yes, of course it could. That must be him. Is there an address and phone number?"

"Sure is, hon."

Mrs. Shayne read the phone number and street address on Magnolia Road in Ladue, Missouri. "It even says where this one works at," she added. "McDonnell Douglas, at the Lambert-St. Louis International Airport."

Now Gavrielle feared she might faint from this unexpected success. She thanked Mrs. Shayne profusely, over and over. Then she hung up and threw her arms around Charlie. "It's him. It's got to be him – working on the engines of the biggest airplanes he could find."

Charlie grasped both her hands and danced around the kitchen with her. "You found him. You really found him. And St. Louis ain't so far. I can take you there."

Gavrielle looked like she might cry. "Luciano – that's from his Italian-Catholic mother. Fergus Brody – that's from his Irish-Catholic father. It's him. It's got to be him." *Please God, let him still be alive.*

266

Grandma Julie came in. "What's all the commotion about?"

"Gavrielle just made the call to Florida. Her father lives in St. Louis. I'm going to take her to meet him."

Gavrielle had slumped down in a chair.

"What's the matter?" Charlie asked.

"I don't know why I suddenly feel so exhausted." She was pale, her voice weak. "I can't believe it was so easy. All these years, and all it took was one phone call. One lousy phone call."

"Listen, Angel girl," Grandma Julie said, taking the chair next to Gavrielle and patting her leg. "I know that be good news for you, but you don't need to be getting all worked up. A man what's only a father on the say-so of some laboratory test ain't no father. A child's parents are them what raised him up. For you, that be your grandma, so she's your mamma and your pappa. I know you got to go see this man, satisfy your curiosity, but don't go making more of it than it is. You still you, no matter who he turn out to be."

"What's the matter with you, Grandma?" Charlie said, obviously annoyed. "Course she's gonna get all excited. Anyone would want to know who their father is. So would you. And she could have half-brothers and sisters."

"You think you can become the child of someone after you're all growed up? Just like that?" Grandma Julie snapped her fingers. "Anyway, ain't no matter where you come from, no how. 'Portant thing is where you going to. God gave your life to you, not to your parents. Up to you to do somethin' good with it. Some children come from good families and turn out rotten no-goodniks. And the opposite. 'Portant thing is how you gonna raise up your children. That's the family that matters. That's the future. No point in gettin' all worked up 'bout the past."

"Just hush, would you, Grandma? Please."

"That's okay," Gavrielle said, surprised that Charlie's grandmother held such strong opinions on the subject, but not at all annoyed by those opinions. "Those things she's saying – I think them all the time."

"Well, you shouldn't. Course you ain't gonna go live with him or nothin' like that, but you'll know what kind a man you got half your genes from. I don't hardly remember my dad, but havin' a solid feelin' 'bout what kind of man he was means a lot to me."

"All right, all right, this old woman done talkin'." Grandma Julie pushed herself up from the chair with her usual groan.

"What's going on?" Charlene emerged from her room. They told her, and her face lit up. "That's wonderful, Gavrielle. I'm so happy for you."

"I want to take the Mustang, drive her to St. Louis," Charlie said.

"Sure. That's not a problem." Charlene went to the porch and returned with the Triple A Road Atlas.

Gavrielle and Charlie discussed what she should say when she called Lou Brody, while Charlene studied the maps of the Midwest.

"Looks like an eight or nine hour drive," Charlene said. "Not counting stops."

At 8:00 that evening Gavrielle drained a bottle of beer before sitting down to dial the number of Luciano Fergus Brody.

"I don't know if you know," Charlie said, "but west of Chicago is a different time zone. An hour earlier."

She shook her head. "No, I didn't know. No wonder American cars are the size of buses. Israel is probably smaller than one of your zip codes." She closed her eyes and dialed the last digit.

Ring. Ring. Ring. A woman's voice answered. "Hello. Brody residence."

"Hello. May I please speak to Mr. Brody?" Gavrielle pressed her palm to her chest, trying to calm the pounding of her heart.

"May I tell him who's calling?"

"Certainly. My name is Gavrielle Amrani. I'm a journalist from Israel, and I'm writing an article about the soldiers from all over the world who volunteered to help our military during our War of Independence. So I'm trying to contact as many of those men as I can." Gavrielle was reading a prepared speech and knew that's how she sounded, but plowed on. "From the widow of one of those volunteers, a Mr. David Shayne in Florida, I've learned that Luciano Fergus Brody was one of them. If that's correct, I would love to interview him."

"Yeah, that's right. He was over there. Hold on a sec." Gavrielle could hear her calling, "Lou, it's for you. Some reporter from over there in Israel."

Gavrielle put her hand over the mouthpiece and whispered to Charlie, "She's getting him." He moved closer and pressed his ear to the receiver to listen in.

"Hello, this is Lou Brody."

Gavrielle froze. She had the impression that he had hurried eagerly to the phone and his voice was friendly, encouraging. Yet her vocal cords seemed to have ceased functioning. Charlie poked her, hard, and she continued reading from the paper, but hesitantly, almost stuttering. She ended with, "I would really love to come to Missouri and interview you."

"Where are you now?"

"In Michigan."

"Well, I'm more than happy to co-operate, but there's no need for you to come all that way. I can tell you whatever it is you need to know over the phone."

"Oh, it's no trouble. Our editors insist that we conduct interviews in person, whenever possible. Anyway, I also have some people in Iowa to speak with.

And the paper wants me to get photographs of anyone who agrees."

"Well, come on then. You can pretty much choose a day. We don't have any plans to go anywhere for the next few weeks."

"Would it be better for you on a weekend?"

"Doesn't really matter. I could take a long lunch with you whenever, long as you let me know a day in advance. I normally go to lunch about one, but that's not carved in stone."

"How about the day after tomorrow?"

"Sure, no problem. You have something to write with? I'll give you my number at the office and directions how to get there." He began with the directions, but she interrupted him.

"Excuse me, Mr. Brody, but the paper has arranged an American assistant for me. I'm going to put him on the phone, since he'll be the one driving."

Charlie wrote down the directions, occasionally saying, mmm, or uh-huh, and ended with, "Thanks a lot. We're looking forward to meeting you. We'll plan for one o'clock, but we'll give you a call when we're about an hour out."

Charlie hung the phone up and turned to pick Gavrielle up and whirl her around, but there were no giddy laughs from her. When he put her down, she said that she was tired and went up to her room.

Charlie and Gavrielle spent most of the next day getting ready for the trip – plotting it out on the Triple A map, washing the Mustang and gassing it up, and packing. Later in the afternoon Charlie took her on a tour of the local sites, including the observatory at Cranbrook and a leisurely tour of the campus of Cranbrook schools. Most of the people they encountered on its walkways knew Charlie and greeted him with wide smiles and high fives.

"It's easy to see why you love this place. These gardens are incredible. And a lake, no less. It's not like any school I've ever seen." Gavrielle sighed, looking around. "Have you said anything to Charlene?"

"Not yet. The Cranbrook grad program sent me some stuff in the mail, but I got to it before she did."

"You want me to talk to her?"

"What, like I'm some kind of baby, can't speak his mind?"

"Well?" She shook her head, smiling. "Look, it's easy for me. And if I speak with her tonight, after you've already gone to bed, then she'll have a couple of days to think it over while we're gone. Soon as we get back, you can have your talk."

"You know what? Okay. Yeah, okay."

Late that evening Gavrielle was glad to find Charlene out on the canopy swing, alone.

"Can I talk to you about something? About Charlie?"

"Sure."

Gavrielle settled herself and took in a deep breath. *God, just look that expression on her face. She's getting ready to hate me.* "I love the weather here. The air feels so fresh." She leaned back, appreciating the stars. *So she'll be pissed at me. So what? We aren't part of each other's lives, and Charlie needs her to hear this.* She straightened a little. "So what I wanted to talk to you about is ...When Charlie and I met in Rome ... there was something we had in common. We'd both gone there as a temporary escape from some problem."

"Charlie had a problem he couldn't talk to me about?"

"Actually ... you sort of *are* the problem." Gavrielle gave her an apologetic smile. "I mean, you being so set on him going back to the University of Michigan for grad school. But the thing is – he isn't. He didn't even register there. I guess he sort of lied to you about that. He's going back to Cranbrook."

Charlene stared at her, blinking. Gavrielle couldn't tell if her expression said, "What are you talking about?" She was simply unable to fathom that Charlie had lied to her. Or did it, in fact, seem more like a "Who the hell cares about that?" look.

Charlene remained silent, so Gavrielle plunged on with the speech she had practiced.

"He couldn't bring himself to tell you and perhaps get into an argument with you. Mostly because he's so grateful to you, and dreads the thought of letting you down. But besides that – and this is just me talking, Charlie never said anything like this – but I think there are probably some other emotions involved that might pop out during an argument. Feelings you might misinterpret."

"What are you talking about? What feelings?"

"Anger. Resentment. Not at you. Not at all at you. It could sound that way to you, but it wouldn't be. You see, people like me and Charlie are always getting told how lucky we are. Such good, kind-hearted people came along and rescued us. Even when people don't say it out loud, we know they're thinking it."

"So who would he be mad at? The people who call him lucky?"

Gavrielle frowned and shook her head. "No. We don't get mad at anyone in particular – just at the way things are. I don't really know how ... let me think a minute." She stared at the sky. "Okay, look, it's not at all the same, not at all, but the best example I can think of is Holocaust survivors. They always get called 'the lucky ones.' Think of someone who lost all his civil rights, got deported in a cattle car to a horrible ghetto where there was no food or medicine, and then got shipped off to a concentration camp where he was

272

worked almost to death while his whole family was murdered. But he survived. How lucky can a guy get? It's like the more he suffered, the luckier he is not to be rotting in a mass grave with his children. And the person standing there telling him how lucky he is had a normal life, never suffered a millionth of anything like that. They're also alive, but apparently there's nothing lucky about that.

"And even though Charlie and I aren't anything like Holocaust survivors, it's sort of the same idea. The worse our lives were before our saviors showed up, the luckier we are. Lucky, lucky us." Gavrielle paused for a moment. "I never call anyone lucky."

Charlene blinked again and emitted a long sigh. "Reeves and I pretty much always understood what you're saying, though we thought of it differently – that he'll probably never feel like he can take his place in this family for granted. I think we even said to him once – the happiest day of our lives will be the one when he shouts that he hates us, stomps up to his room, and slams the door." She shrugged. "He's never done that. But honestly, I don't see anything I can do about it."

"There isn't anything – except to understand how fed up person can get with having to feel grateful all the time. Once in a while, we'd like to feel entitled." Gavrielle paused for a moment. "Charlie wants to spend the next two years at Cranbrook, becoming a world class architect. Then he wants to be a successful professional and make some money. To him that isn't copping out. That's normal life. The way it is for everyone else."

"That would be such a waste. He's so special. He could do so much good." Charlene sighed again.

"I don't think it will make that much difference how he makes his living. The people he does anything with will benefit from having him around. He is special."

"But he won't be happy unless he thinks we're dying

273

for him to become a rich architect?"

"Something like that." Gavrielle grinned. "But you know what? People get bored. They don't go on wanting the same things forever. Maybe at first Dr. King was perfectly happy being a great minister. And what's wrong with having successful black professionals as role models? And if Charlie opens his own business, who says it won't be in Detroit? Who says he won't hire a lot of young blacks and be their, you know, mentor, I think is how you say."

"Yes, that's how we say."

They sat in silence for a long while before Gavrielle spoke again, staring into the distance. "You know, part of officers training for the IDF is learning how to navigate. The guys get dropped off in the middle of nowhere and have to find their way to a specific location. They've had time to study a topographical map of the area, and they have that map with them, but it's all sealed up. If they can't find their way without opening the map, they fail.

"The trainers always tell the guys the same two things about getting lost. Number one – the most important thing – is to admit you're lost. The minute you're no longer sure where you are – you think you should have found the next landmark by now, but you haven't – stop. Don't think, 'If I go just a little bit farther, and then a little bit farther, I'll find that palm tree or *wadi*.' That's the worst thing you can do. Compounding your mistake is the way to lose yourself beyond salvation. The second thing is to turn around. Retrace your steps to the last point where you knew for sure where you were. Before you got lost. That's your safe place."

Charlene waited for her to get to the point.

"Life is like that for most people. When they feel lost in their lives, they have a safe place they can go back to

274

– where they were before they made a bad decision. But people like Charlie and me, it's ... we don't have a safe place." Her voice began to trail off. "We were born lost. I mean, the process of becoming us was disrupted. That's how it feels for me, anyway. There's no place I can look back on and say, there, that was the real me, the girl I was meant to be, that I want to be. I still remember what that felt like. So we stay lost and confused longer than other people do. Because we were never given our map to study – we have to make up the way for ourselves."

Charlene reached for Gavrielle's hand and squeezed it.

Gavrielle sat up straight. "Gosh, I'm sorry for blathering on like that," she said. "I only meant to tell you about Cranbrook. The rest ... that's just me trying to figure out my own life."

Charlene shook her head and squeezed Gavrielle's hand again. "It wasn't blather and I see how lucky Charlie is to have you for a friend." Then her expression turned to one of sadness. "He's going to need one." She turned to look Gavrielle in the face. "I'm going to tell you something that you can't tell him. Not now, and maybe not ever. It's the reason I was sitting out here worrying. Funny, I was about to come looking for you, try to get you alone so I could ask what you think I should do ... Anyway, where he's going to school should be his biggest problem."

"Why? What's wrong?"

"Grandma Julie ... she hasn't been doing too well, and I took her to have some tests done. So far they can't say what's wrong with her, but don't seem to think it's anything life threatening. So it's not her health I'm sitting out here worrying about. The thing is, she called me into her room last night, started going on about how she can't take that secret to her grave."

"Oh no. What secret?"

"Apparently, Samuel Freeman was not Charlie's father."

Gavrielle's mouth hung open, her first thought not of concern for Charlie. "Our lives are like some kind of freaky fun-house mirror," she said, her voice barely audible. Charlene gave her a blank look, and when Gavrielle spoke again it was in a normal voice. "So who is his father? Does Grandma Julie know?"

"Seems she's known for a long time. Never planned on telling him." Charlene tilted her head and looked at Gavrielle. "Oh, wow ... sort of like with your grandmother. I hadn't thought of that. Wow, you and Charlie ... that is sort of creepy."

"And me caring so much about finding out who my father is – that made Grandma Julie change her mind about keeping the secret?"

Charlene nodded. "But not entirely. She still doesn't want to tell him. She just asked me to be the keeper of the secret. Those are her words. She wants me to be the one who has to decide whether or not to tell him. But if I decide to tell him, she wants me to wait until after she's gone."

"Dead, you mean?"

"Yeah. Dead."

"So what are you going to do?"

"I don't know. The only thing I'm sure of is that if I am going to tell him, it's going to be now. I won't keep it from him for years, waiting for her to die. He'd never forgive me. I think he should know. Don't you?" Her voice was small, hesitant.

"Who is his father? Is it anyone he knows?"

"Yes. He's from back in Marshall, where Charlie grew up. I guess he was good friends with both Cairo and Samuel."

"Cairo is Charlie's mother's name?"

"Yes. It's what Samuel called her. Short for Caroline.

Charlie's real father is a lawyer. Helped us with a few legal things, about custody and making sure Charlie will inherit Grandma Julie's house."

"You mean Billy Bates," Gavrielle said. "Charlie talked about him. Likes him."

Charlene nodded.

"Did Samuel know?"

"Grandma Julie doesn't think so."

"What about Billy Bates? Does he know?"

"He suspected. Asked Cairo when he heard she was pregnant, but she lied to him. So what do you think I should do?"

"Tell him. Of course you have to tell him. But you should tell Billy Bates first."

"What? Really? Why?"

"Because the best thing for Charlie would be to hear it from Billy Bates. For Billy Bates to come see him. That would be the best way to show he accepts him. Wants to be in his life. You can't imagine how thrilled I would have been, if my father had come looking for me. Of course, it's different for Charlie, since he thinks he knows who his father was. That will be a big shock to get over. And Billy Bates might not want anything to do with him, and then you'll be stuck telling Charlie that Samuel wasn't his biological father *and* that his real father is a complete jerk. But you do have to tell him."

"I never would have thought of it, but it does sound like a good idea to tell Billy Bates first and see how he reacts. But if he is a jerk, why bother telling Charlie anything at all? Why break his heart twice?"

Gavrielle thought for a moment. "The truth is always the best. Even if it's difficult to hear. If I go to St. Louis and find out my father's a huge creep, I won't be sorry I made the trip. And Billy Bates has kids, doesn't he? They don't have to be jerks, just because their father is. They're Charlie's relatives, too."

"You think about things I never would." Charlene

277

sighed.

"Was Billy Bates married when he had the affair with Cairo?"

"No."

"So there's some chance his wife won't totally hate Charlie." Gavrielle thought again. "There is one thing I *would* lie to him about. Tell him Samuel knew. After all, for all you know, that may be the truth. Tell him Samuel knew and loved him so much he didn't care. Just make sure Grandma Julie will stick with that."

Charlene gave her a curious look. "I thought you'd be more upset for him."

Gavrielle raised her arms and stretched. "First let's see what Mr. Bates says. I mean, it could turn out to be a good thing. Charlie could end up keeping all his good memories of Samuel and getting some new people in his life." Gavrielle suddenly realized that part of her was jealous of Charlie. Then she thought of something else and turned to Charlene. "Does it worry you? Like you might lose Charlie?"

"No." Charlene stretched out the word, shaking her head. "That never entered my mind. I've never felt like a parent to him. How could I? More like a big sister. I have thought a lot about Cairo, all these years – wondering if she approves of what we've tried to do for him. Or does she see us as some kind of interlopers, who hijacked him to a different world. A world he doesn't belong in. I tried asking myself what she would have done about this whole Billy Bates thing. Of course, the answer to that is pretty obvious – I mean, she didn't tell him, did she? Of course, he was a little kid and Samuel was still alive and then eventually the lie was so old ..."

"She would never have told him," Gavrielle said. "She'd have been too afraid it would make him think badly of her. Knock her down from perfect wife and

278

mother to whore who had an affair."

"Yeah, there's that," Charlene said. "I'm having a bit of trouble with that. I always thought of her as some kind of saint. The perfect woman. Strong, courageous. Very involved with the civil rights movement." She sighed. "Did he get a scholarship or something?"

"What? Who? Billy Bates?"

"No. Charlie. Did he get some kind of scholarship to Cranbrook?"

"Partial one. He'll have to take out a loan for the rest."

"Mmm. Yeah. Figures. That place costs a bomb." Charlene shifted her weight, as if about to get up.

"Can I ask you something?"

"Sure." Charlene leaned back.

"You and Reeves. Charlie told me about, you know, when you were young, how you broke up with him after high school, and you didn't get back together until after college. So how did you get back together? I mean, what made you suddenly think he was the one? That you could spend your whole life with him?"

Charlene bit her top lip for a while. "In high school, well, you know, Reeves was my first love. Only love as it turned out – I never wanted anyone else to touch me. Not like with Reeves, anyway. But when I was sixteen I thought there were lots of Reeves out there, just waiting for me. I knew I was lucky to have him for a boyfriend, but I never thought there was anything special about us. It was like, okay, Reeves is my high school boyfriend, but we'll grow up and go out with lots of other people. I assumed that anyone who wanted to go out with me would treat me the way Reeves did. Look at me the way he did. And I would lust after a few of them. I'd go through a bunch of guys like that, until I finally found the one that was right for me. I never imagined myself married to Reeves."

"Why not?"

279

"Reeves ... he's a wonderful guy. You've been around him. He's so easygoing. Takes things like they come. Doesn't over think everything to death, the way I do. I guess that's one of the things that makes us good together. But when I was a teenager, I seemed to spend most of my time looking around and mostly disapproving. Of my parents, who didn't have what I would call a good marriage, of everyone else in our suburban neighborhood with its Clean-up, Paint-up, Fix-up week. I was the judge of the world, and none of those other people cared about anything but paying the mortgage and mowing the lawn. I wanted something else. Better. Something that counted. I had no idea what, but there had to be something more. Something that matters. So I dumped him and went out in the world looking."

"And then you saw Reeves again – and what had changed? What happened?"

Charlene thought for a long time before answering. "Charlie happened. Reeves is so good with him. He never has to sit around trying to figure out what might be a good thing to do for Charlie. He just does whatever he feels like, and it always turns out to be the right thing. Always says the right thing. Nothing earthshaking. Simple stuff. Guy stuff.

"I know everyone sort of thinks of Charlie as 'mine,' but the truth is, Reeves is the one who makes him feel at home. In his easygoing, seemingly clueless way, he's much better for Charlie than I am. So when Charlie came into my life, he made me see Reeves in a whole different light. I love Charlie, and I wish to God he had never needed help from anyone, but since he did, I love that we were able to offer him a home. That I was able to do this thing – this really worthwhile thing. But I could never have done it without Reeves."

Charlene sighed, but with a content smile. "Once we

have a couple of kids of our own, we're going to take in some foster kids. Fill this big old house up." She stood up and grinned. "And, in case you're wondering, the reason I took the time to rediscover Reeves in all his wonderfulness was that no other guy ever looked at me quite the way he does."

Gavrielle and Charlie got up early the next morning. Charlie put the sandwiches Grandma Julie had fixed for them in the cooler and made a thermos of coffee. Reeves and Charlene, both in their bathrobes, walked them out to the car to say goodbye. As Charlie pulled up the curved drive toward the road, Gavrielle watched them in the rearview mirror, each waving a hand. *They must be dreading talking to Billy Bates. Or maybe not. They seem to know him pretty well.* Then Charlie turned onto West Maple Road, and Billy Bates and the Valentis were banished from Gavrielle's thoughts.

She was on her way to meet Chicago Lou. *Now he's St. Louis Lou. Ha ha. Does anyone ever call him Luciano? Did he ever tell his wife about a girl in Palestine? Stop obsessing. You're going to see him tomorrow, ask him anything you want. Why don't you try to enjoy this trip? When are you ever going to be driving across America again?*

"Are we stopping at Northland?" she asked.

"Yeah, I talked to Carv. He'll be there."

"Where's the notorious package?"

"In the trunk. I dug it up last night. Saw you sittin' on the swing with Charlene."

"Mmmm."

"So what'd she say?"

Gavrielle looked startled, almost afraid, but then remembered what he was asking about. "Oh, I forgot – I haven't spoken to you. Sorry. She's fine with you going to Cranbrook. Agrees that you have to find your own way."

"Charlene? Charlene Valenti? That little blonde woman back there? She said that?"

"Yes. It'll be all right, Charlie. You'll see when we get home. I promise."

"You promise?" He turned his head, giving her a strange look. "What the heck you got to promise?"

"Nothing. I have no idea why I said that."

She switched on the radio, and soon Charlie turned into the huge deserted parking lot of the Northland shopping mall.

"Stores ain't open yet," he said. "But there's a coffee place where Carv's going to meet us."

He pulled into a space and retrieved a brown paper shopping bag from the trunk. Holding the door to the mall open for Gavrielle, he said to her back, "Just so you know, you might think Carv looks sort of scary. Got this big scar on his face. But he's okay. He's a good guy."

"Dope dealer with a heart of gold?"

"He's a good guy. Believe me."

Carv was waiting for them, in jeans, black T-shirt, and sneakers. Charlie was surprised to see him without his boots and the fedora he always used to wear, with a red feather in its brim. He rose to slap Charlie on the back and pull out a chair for Gavrielle.

"So the prodigal foster son finally comes home. What can I get for you?" he asked as he seated himself. Both Charlie and Gavrielle said, "Just coffee."

"You sure?" He grinned at Charlie. "They got them Boston Cream donuts you like."

Charlie raised a hand, palm out, and shook his head.

"How about our tourist?" He turned to Gavrielle. "You ain't been to America, you ain't had a Boston Cream donut."

"I thought a hot fudge sundae is the thing I just have to have."

282

"Indeed. That too. But this joint ain't got them. Make sure the big world traveler here stops on the way home to get you one."

"You know what," Gavrielle said brightly, not at all frightened of this surprisingly pleasant young man. "I've never had any kind of donut. Maybe I will try one."

Carv raised a hand for the waitress. She was passing with a full pot of coffee and he pointed to his half-full cup and turned over the cups in front of Charlie and Gavrielle for her to fill. "And can you please bring the lady one of your delicious Boston Creams?"

"Look who learned manners," Charlie said, after the waitress was gone.

"I'm the host at my nightclub, ain't I?" Carv smiled widely, showing straight, white teeth. "Down at The Cat we get some Emily Post-style white folk."

"What's your club like?" Gavrielle asked.

"The younguns want mostly funk. You know, Sly, the Isley Brothers, the Bar-Kays, Stevie Wonder – that kind. But we play plenty of R & B, and it's Detroit, ain't it? So there's gonna be Motown. Once in a while we open on a Wednesday for an old-timers' night. Duke Ellington, Billie Holiday, Eartha Kitt."

"So you're not open every night?"

"Nah. Just weekends. 'Cept, like I said, sometimes we open on a Wednesday – either for a big band evening or a live night – for local bands, ain't made their name yet, willing to play for next to nothin'. We take a dollar at the door on those nights and all the bands got to split that take."

"The rest of the nights, the music isn't live?"

"Nah. It's all DJs these days."

"How come?"

Carv rubbed his thumb against his first two fingers. "You get a DJ for fifty bucks. Live band with any kind of name gonna run you five hundred. Anyway, the kids

283

prefer a DJ. They wanna come one night, hear all their favorites. They got no interest in sittin' 'round tables, watchin' someone they paid a bundle to see. They wanna get in cheap and dance all night."

Gavrielle smiled and shook her head. "I was imagining like in the movies. Old movies I guess. With an enormous stage and a guy in a white suit comes tap-dancing down the stairs."

Carv grinned. "Good old Cab Calloway. Detroit used to have clubs like that. Lots of 'em. Over in what they called Paradise Valley. Black neighborhood – but more than that. It was a real community, with black everything. Hotels, restaurants, hospital, you name it. That's all gone now."

"Why? What happened to it?"

"Urban renewal happened to it. The geniuses on that commission renewed Detroit right into the ground – demolished its best neighborhood. Paradise Valley disappeared – over a thousand homes, hundreds of businesses. Lot a great bars and clubs." He made a rude noise with his lips. "All for half a mile of the Chrysler Freeway."

"Sounds like it's too bad there weren't any black people on that commission." Gavrielle looked sideways at Charlie, but he ignored her.

The waitress returned, set the donut in front of Charlene, and walked away.

"She don't approve of a nice white girl like you sittin' with two black dudes. But guess what! She can't refuse us service. No one in the whole damn country can. Not even in Dearborn, Michigan. We got our civil rights."

"Lay off, Carv."

"Just sayin'. So, Charlie, Rome ain't been enough? Had to go on to Is-re-al?"

"If you've got your own personal guide, why not?"

"What places you been at?"

"The Vatican, the Forum –"

"Not in Rome. The Holy Land, man, where you been at in the Holy Land?"

"All the Christian places in Jerusalem – the Holy Sepulcher, Garden of Gethsemane, Via Dolorosa, everywhere. And up by the Sea of Galilee. We even went to the place where Jesus gave the Sermon on the Mount. It was beautiful. You woulda loved –"

"This is so delicious!" Gavrielle broke in, too loudly. She had bitten into the donut and was struggling to keep the cream filling from gushing all over the table. "Sorry. I didn't mean to interrupt – but this is so delicious!"

Carv grinned. "We better get the girl another one."

"No, no thanks. This *is* the most delicious thing I've ever tasted, but it's like an infusion of pure sugar." She set the donut on the plate and wiped her mouth with her napkin. "In way of thanks for this gourmet delight, I will be happy to show you around Jerusalem, any time you come."

"You best watch what you be sayin'. Person might take you up on that."

"You ain't scarin' me," Gavrielle said. "I be meanin' what I be sayin'."

"You mockin' me, girl?" Carv leaned in toward her.

Gavrielle leaned in farther. "Man, when I be mockin' you, you be knowin' it."

Carv smiled. "The Israelean chick don't scare easy," he said to Charlie. "I's just fooling with you." He winked at Gavrielle.

"I know," she said and returned her attention to the donut. "And I meant the invitation to visit. Israelis don't say things like that just to be polite, the way Americans do."

Under the table, Charlie nudged the paper bag toward Carv. "Box Eddie gave me is in there."

Carv picked it up and looked inside. "You really didn't open it? Seriously?"

"No."

"Want to know what's in it?"

"No."

"I gotta tell you one thing." Carv lightly tapped his forefinger on the tabletop. "I dint know nothin' 'bout it. It all been Eddie. He done it thinkin' he's helpin' me, but he never told me nothin' 'bout what he done. Not till we been on the way home from lookin' for your skinny ass in West Bloomfield. Till then, he never said nothin'."

"I thought that was the reason you guys went out there. Looking to get the box back."

"Hell no, man. What's the matter with you? Maybe Eddie been worried about it, but I dint know nothin'. I just wanted to see good old Charlie. See you doin' so good in school and all. You got it comin'. How come you never come back to check in with us?"

Charlie looked away. "Detroit ... those weren't the happiest years of my life."

"I read that, man, losin' both your folks and all – and then that shit-ass of a stepfather. But it still be where you from. You still got people."

"What people? I ain't got no people."

"You got me. You got Eddie. And Eddie's mom. That woman been all over herself happy when she heard we found you."

"Yeah?" Charlie smiled shyly.

"Yeah. What you think? Dint she always treat you like you was Eddie's brother? Thought you was a good influence. Not like me." He grinned.

"So you're doing all right. Your club?"

"Indeed. You gotta bring your lady downtown. She know how to move?"

Charlie turned to wink at Gavrielle, and they both

286

grinned. "Not so much. But I gave her one lesson. Listen, we gotta get back on the road. Long drive to St. Louis."

"I know. You go on. I got this." Carv nodded at the table.

Charlie pushed his chair back to stand, but then sat back down. "Okay, what's in the box?"

Carv shook his head. "You gonna be real pissed off, but I swear I dint known nothin' about it."

"So what – drugs?"

"Nah. What Eddie want drugs for?" Carv leaned back and lit a cigarette. "You remember Big G?"

"Old man Ballerini's asshole kid? Yeah, I remember him."

"The punk shot someone. Shot him dead. His father told him to take the gun he used down to the basement of the funeral home, pack it up in a box full a rocks, and give it to me to dump in Lake St. Clair. I wasn't supposed to know what's in it. Wouldna known, but Eddie, he been workin' for old man Ballerini and was just finishin' sweepin' up the basement. He always been afeared of them Italians, so when Big G came down to box up that gun, Eddie hid. But he watched Big G put it in the box, without wiping his prints or nothin'. So Eddie, he waited for Big G to go upstairs, took another box, filled it with rocks, and switched it out. Clueless me come down and fetch that box of rocks, send it to the bottom of the lake. Eddie shoved the box with the gun in his backpack."

"Why'd he do that?" Gavrielle asked.

"Thought he was helpin' me. Back then I been working for the Ballerinis and wantin' out. Eddie knew that a gun with Big G's prints and a murder on it – can't get more leverage than that. But I ain't never been in need of that kind of assistance, so Eddie never told me 'bout it."

"Is it loaded?" Charlie asked.

287

"Got no clue. For all I know, could be one in the chamber and the safety off."

"Shit, Carv, you're lucky I never opened that box. Woulda come downtown and used it on you."

Carv grinned. "That be a shame – mess up Big G's prints. Listen, man, I am sorry. Eddie shouldna done that. But how he spose to know all Detroit gonna be on fire, and you gonna disappear?"

"What you gonna do with it?"

"Don't know. Big G came in The Cat while back, wantin' to send in some guys to push product. But I don't 'llow that. I 'spect he'll be back sooner or later, give me a hard time. Little leverage might come in handy after all."

"Wow, that was some story," Gavrielle said as she climbed back into the car. "I think it'd be really cool to go to his club. Will you take me?"

"I was thinkin' Greenfield Village be more your speed. Last thing I 'magined was you wantin' to get all chummy with a dude like Carv."

"Only if you give me some dance lessons first."

He laughed and shook his head. "Now you 'mindin' me of Charlene."

"You taught her to dance?"

"That girl already had her moves. Had a hard time with rock 'n roll is all."

"So that's great. The four of us can go to The Cat together."

"Could be."

Once they were on the expressway, Gavrielle seemed to turn inward, putting her bare feet on the seat and hugging her knees. Charlie switched on the radio and neither of them spoke for a long while. Then Gavrielle switched it off.

"How about telling me some stories? You know,

288

about Detroit and your childhood and all?"

"Okay." He thought. "But I got a better story than that for you. I never told you about Olivia Killion and Mourning Free. Those two are the reason Charlene thinks we're some kind of family."

Charlie took his time, and the tale of the white girl and her black friend – who in 1841 boarded a steamship together, heading to Detroit – got them almost all the way to Missouri.

"Few minutes we gonna be drivin' over the Mississippi."

"River? The Mississippi River?"

"Yep."

"We have to drive over it?"

"Yeah, but don't worry. There's this thing called, you know, a bridge."

"Ha ha. How wide is it?"

"I don't know. Maybe half a mile? Nah, lot less than that."

They were soon on Eads Bridge and Gavrielle sat up straight, mesmerized by the sight of all that water flowing beneath them.

"What's the big deal? Ain't you got no bridges in Israel?"

"Sure. You were on one – over the Jordan River. Which, you'll remember, is about as wide as your driveway. This is Huckleberry Finn's river, isn't it?"

"Yep."

On the other side of the bridge Charlie pulled into a gas station to fill up. He also bought a map of the city, which he spread over the steering wheel and studied for a few minutes, marking both the route to the airport and places of architectural interest that he planned to see while they were in St. Louis.

Gavrielle began to feel anxious. Tomorrow. How am I going to get any sleep tonight?

Charlie glanced over at her. "Getting excited?"

She didn't feel like talking about it and said, "Yeah, I can hardly wait to do some sightseeing, hear your scintillating lectures on bargeboards and cupolas."

Though it was still early in the evening, they were both exhausted when they pulled into the parking lot of a Holiday Inn on the outskirts of St. Louis. They briefly considered the option of sharing one room with two beds, but simultaneously shook their heads, saying, "Nah."

"I ain't setting no alarm," Charlie said at Gavrielle's door. "We don't have to be there till one o'clock and it ain't that far. Put that No Disturb thingee on your door, but take it off in the morning, so I'll know you're. I'll do the same. You up in time for their breakfast and I'm still sleeping, you go on down without me. Probably just gonna be some kind of fruit and a muffin, but at least they'll have coffee."

Gavrielle washed her face and brushed her teeth and then stepped out onto the tiny balcony. She was surprised to see two people in the pool, and glad she had stuck her bathing suit into her suitcase at the last minute. She changed into it, put on the thin terry cloth robe she found hanging in the bathroom, and went down for a swim. The mindless motion was relaxing and she was surprised to look up at the clock and see that she had been doing laps for close to an hour. *I didn't know I was capable of swimming for that long.* She climbed out and twisted her hair to wring it out. Then she noticed Charlie, lounging on a green and white lawn chair, watching her.

"How come you didn't come in?" she asked.

"Too beat."

"Oh, look over there, is that one of those spa thingees?"

Charlie stretched forward. "Yeah one of the modern kind. Fiber glass. Go on, get in."

She climbed up the steps and slid in, then looked up at Charlie and said, "This is absolute heaven. If they'd only let me have a Boston Cream donut in here, I could die happy."

"Wait. I give you something better than a donut." He found the switch for the jets and turned them on.

She jumped at first but soon groaned. "Oh my God, this is the best invention ever. I'm going to have one of these at my house."

"Cost you as much as a kitchen."

"Who needs a kitchen?"

He sat on the edge, the water up to his knees. Gavrielle took hold of one of his feet and said, "Thank you, Charlie Freeman. Thank you for talking me into coming to America, and for bringing me to St. Louis."

"You nervous 'bout tomorrow?"

"Not really. I was, sort of, when we crossed the river. It was, like, we're officially here. In his state. I came down here thinking that swimming would help me organize my thoughts about what to say to him, but my mind is pretty blank. Refuses to co-operate. *Que será, será*, I guess."

"They allow plastic glasses in there. Want me to bring you some lemonade or something?"

"No thanks." She enjoyed the warmth in silence, then said, "There's another thing I really need to thank you for. For not seducing me. You certainly could have."

"I know."

"But it's so much better for both of us that you chose not to do that."

"I know."

At noon the next day Charlie called to tell Mr. Brody they would be at his office in an hour. Gavrielle remained strangely calm, until they pulled into the parking lot of his building. Then she suddenly looked

291

like she would either faint or throw up.

"You okay?"

"Yes, fine." She took a few deep breaths and opened the car door, murmuring in Hebrew, "*Tamut nafshi im plishtim.*"

"What was that?"

"What?"

"What you just said."

"Nothing important."

"So tell me."

She sighed. "Let me die with the Philistines."

"Like, Samson?"

"Yeah. I forgot you know your Bible."

"So the dead that he slew at his death were more than they that he slew in his life," Charlie quoted from the book of Judges as he held the door of the building open for her. "You planning on killing a bunch of folks in there?"

"No. It's become like a saying. Doesn't usually have anything to with Samson or sacrifice on the battlefield. People say it more like the Israeli version of 'It's now or never,' or 'Here goes nothing.' Something like that."

"There's some chairs over there," Charlie said. "I'll wait down here in the lobby. Chicago Lou can probably call that lady at the desk there, if you need me to come up for anything. You could probably have her tell him you're on the way up."

"Okay, yeah, that's a good idea." She felt basically dysfunctional, incapable of orderly thought. "I don't know how to do this." She turned to him helplessly.

"Told you, you dint practice hard enough last time you found a missing father." He smiled and put his hands around her upper arms. "Course you don't know how to do this. Neither does he. But you're just two nice people gonna have a talk with each other, that's all."

"You're the only person in the world who could have

292

made me smile right now."

"I know. Now you go get 'em, girl." He put his hand on her shoulder. "It's gonna be all right. I'll be here waiting."

"Thank God for that. Thank God for you. Really, Charlie."

"Yeah, yeah. Get on with it. Stop talking to me and go talk to that guy up there."

Gavrielle went to speak with the lady at the desk, who told her Mr. Brody was expecting her and pointed toward the elevator.

The door to Mr. Brody's office was open, but Gavrielle lightly rapped her knuckles on it.

"Ms. Amrani?"

"Yes."

She hesitantly stepped across the threshold. Luciano Fergus Brody was on his way around his desk to meet her, but abruptly halted. He fleetingly wore a strange expression, but it managed to morph into a smile as he shook her hand.

He was not at all as she had imagined him. He was tall and thin – almost gaunt, with sunken cheeks. His blonde curls were gone, his head entirely bald. He was neither attractive nor unattractive. A middle-aged man no one would notice on the street.

He ushered her not to one of the hardback chairs that faced his desk, but to one of two comfortable armchairs that had a small round coffee table between them. Gavrielle was carrying a large cloth bag that Charlene had lent her. She set it down and leaned over to take out her pen and notebook, planning to go on pretending to be a journalist, grilling him about his early life and the time he spent in Israel. Before seating himself across from her, he picked up the phone and politely asked someone to bring coffee and cold drinks.

What made my mother fall in love with him? What did she see? What on earth did she think was so special about this ordinary man? He must be successful, to have such a huge office. Intelligent. Hardworking. One of thousands of boring men, climbing the ladder. Does he have three martini lunches? Smoke cigars? Is he home on time for dinner every night? Fool around with his secretary at the office Christmas party?

Gavrielle had expected him to have more of a presence – to radiate energy. Charisma. Had his generous help to those Jewish refugees been the only notable thing he'd done in his life? One grand gesture, before settling in to pay the mortgage and mow the lawn? Then she scolded herself. *Who are you to disparage a good, decent man like him? What grand gesture have you ever made?*

"I hope you didn't have any trouble finding the place?"

"No. No trouble."

A woman came in and set a tray of coffee, cokes, and pecan sandies on the table.

Mr. Brody poured two cups of coffee, added two packets of sugar to his, and sat back, an expectant smile on his face.

No, I can't do this. He doesn't deserve to have me sit here and lie to him any longer. She silently reached into Charlene's bag and pulled out the teddy bear Lou Brody had given to Ilana Rozmann two and a half decades ago. She also retrieved the letter he had written and silently placed both on the table.

"Ilana," he said softly. He picked up the toy bear and stared at it. Then he put it down and looked at Gavrielle. "The minute you came through the door ... for a moment I thought you were her. You're her daughter."

Gavrielle nodded.

"Is she well?"

"No. She died. A long time ago."

He picked up the envelope, removed the letter, read it, and put it back. "So she received it?"

"No. She never saw your letter. Neither did I, until a few years ago."

"And?" he asked.

Gavrielle could see that he hadn't yet made the connection. She leaned back into the chair and waited. He stared at her, his face blank. *He's seeing in my face the same things I'm seeing in his. The way my eyes are a tiny bit too close together. Like his. My face is a bit too long. Like his. I have the hair he used to.*

"You're my daughter?"

Gavrielle nodded, determined not to cry.

"Ilana was pregnant?" His voice was almost a whisper. He stood up and slowly paced. "Why didn't she answer my letter?"

"She never got it. My grandmother collected the mail that day. Opened your letter and read it. You were trying to steal her daughter away to America and she wouldn't allow that. So she made your address illegible and hid the letter. I don't know why she didn't just burn it. A few years ago, when we were moving, I found it hidden in her closet."

He sat back down, obviously shaken. "Ilana ... what happened to her?"

"She died giving birth to me. One day in February 1948, she was with her parents at the street market on Ben Yehuda Street. In Jerusalem. There was a huge explosion. It killed my grandfather, took one of my grandmother's legs, and injured my mother very badly. The doctors didn't think she would survive a day, but she held on long enough to have me."

He sat in stunned silence.

"Don't worry," she said. "All my life I've dreamed of meeting you. Knowing who my father is. But I didn't come to ask for money or anything. And if you don't want your wife to know about me, I'll keep the secret."

"Secret? You were never a secret. I never knew you existed. You've read that letter – you know I wouldn't have abandoned her. I thought she chose not to answer it. She more than once said it would be too complicated, us trying to be together." He stopped talking and sat back down, with tears in his eyes.

Gavrielle watched him, her expression blank, disturbed that she felt no emotion. She felt nothing at all.

"So you had neither mother nor father."

"No. Just my grandmother. She was the only blood relation I had on earth. That's why I always wanted to find you. Do you have children?"

"Two sons."

"My half-brothers," she said, still feeling nothing.

"Oh, yes. You're right. I hadn't thought of that."

"So you believe me?"

"Of course I believe you."

"I would be happy to meet your sons some day. They wouldn't have to know who I am. You could introduce me as the daughter of someone you worked with in Palestine."

He didn't respond for a while. Then he pressed his glasses to the bridge of his nose and sat up straighter. "My sons are not close by. David teaches mathematics at Iowa State, but he's spending the summer in Vancouver, working for the father of a young man he met in college. Daniel is working on a ranch in Colorado."

"A ranch? Like a cowboy?" She smiled with delight. "That sounds like fun."

"Not to me. It's dirty, sweaty, mindless work. And extremely underpaid."

There was a double picture frame on his desk and he rose to hand it to her. "There they are. That's David." He pointed at the one wearing glasses. "And that's

296

Daniel. He's the younger."

Gavrielle studied the photos. They were both handsome boys. Both dark-haired. "They're good-looking guys," she said. "They must take after their mother." Then she realized what she'd said and put her hand over her mouth. "I didn't mean ... I meant because of the dark hair and eyes."

Lou Brody removed his glasses and pressed his fingers to his eyes for a moment. "Yes, only you seem to have gotten my coloring. Of course, your mother's was the same. What do you do for a living?"

"I'm an intelligence officer in the IDF. Technical branch. I like to take things apart. I guess I must have gotten more from you than my hair color."

He took the photos back and handed her the second picture frame that stood on his desk. "Our wedding picture," he said. His hair was longish, blonde curls pushed behind his ears. He wore an ill-fitting tuxedo with what Gavrielle thought was a hideous brocade vest. His wife reminded Gavrielle of Tonia, only not as pretty, her features less delicate. It was as if a sculptor creating Tonia had stopped before chiseling off the final layer of marble.

"Your wife is very pretty." She handed the photo back.

"Sophie. She knows about Ilana. Well, if she remembers. I did tell her when we first met. And I *will* tell her about you this evening. We have no secrets from one another. I have no idea how she will react. As to arranging for you to meet the boys, about that I will yield to Sophie's wishes. I won't let you leave, however, without giving you their addresses and phone numbers. And I will make sure they receive yours. You are all adults and have every right to contact one another or not, as you wish. That's the business of the three of you, not mine and Sophie's. Why don't we get that out of the way now?"

He handed Gavrielle a notepad and pen. "Please write down the numbers where I can reach you. Your hotel here and also where you can be reached in Michigan. And your address and telephone in Israel."

While she followed his instructions, he wrote down the information about his sons. While Gavrielle knew this exchange of information was important, she couldn't help finding his business-like manner annoying, if not offensive.

He looked over at her. "So your name isn't Gavrielle Amrani?"

"Gavrielle, yes. Amrani is the name of the family my grandmother and I have been living with."

"You thought I might recognize Rozmann?"

"Yes."

"So if you're not a journalist, why do you have an 'assistant' with you?" Lou asked as he handed her the paper. "Is he your husband? Or boyfriend?"

"No. I don't have either of those. He's a good friend."

"Did he drive you here?"

"Yes."

"Where is he now?"

"Downstairs. In the lobby."

He squinted at the page of contact information Gavrielle had given him and slid it into a desk drawer. "I would like to invite you – and your friend – to the house tomorrow. But obviously I can't do that without speaking to Sophie. So I'll call you at the Holiday Inn this evening, if that's all right?"

"That's fine," Gavrielle stood, resenting the sense of dismissal. *A job interview lasts longer than this.* "So maybe I'll see you tomorrow." She reached for her bag and returned the teddy bear and letter to it.

"No, no, please, I didn't mean for you to leave. Not without me, anyway. I made reservations for lunch at a very nice place. I want to hear a lot more about Ilana. And about your life."

He picked up the phone and spoke to the lady in the lobby. "Has a nice young man been sitting there for the last half hour? So please inform him that I will be down shortly, together with his lady friend, and we count on him joining us for lunch." He rearranged some papers on his desk and then made an "after you" gesture. "Oh, wait." He halted. "I just remembered something. I think it must still be here."

He went to the bookcase, removed a large black Holy Bible, and retrieved a photograph from between its pages. "It's the only one I have of her." He handed it to Gavrielle.

The photograph was old, black and white, and indistinct. Young Lou had an unruly head of curls and wore some kind of makeshift uniform. Ilana was in jeans and a white cotton shirt. He was staring into the camera; she was staring up at him. Gavrielle studied it for a long time before handing it back. Lou Brody took another long look at the photo and then at Gavrielle. "The likeness is truly amazing," he said. He sighed and stared at the picture again, before holding it out to Gavrielle. "You should have it." She didn't argue, though she could see that he was not eager to part with it.

The restaurant was the fanciest Gavrielle had ever been to. Waiters in tuxes, linen tablecloths and napkins, gold-colored rims around the white plates, fresh flowers, and miniscule portions. They spent two hours at the table, lingering over the meal, then coffee and dessert, then more coffee.

"Long lunches," Lou said. "One of the prerogatives of working at the same place forever."

Lou told her everything he could remember about Ilana, but that was surprisingly little. He had never met, nor even seen, Gavrielle's grandparents, had never

299

seen the inside of their home, had never met any of Ilana's friends. So Gavrielle learned only the following: Ilana hated to wear dresses, didn't use make-up, loved licorice and ice cream, her favorite meal was schnitzel and chips (what Israelis call French fries), and she loved the movies and American music.

You could say those things about almost any Israeli teenager. Why does he have nothing to say about the way they felt about each other? Oh, Lord, why can't I give this nice man a break? I read his letter. What more could he say?

But Gavrielle couldn't shake the feeling that this was all too civilized and polite. Several times Lou wore a strained expression, almost as if he realized what a big let-down he was, but Gavrielle managed to keep a smile on her face. He did seem intrigued by the details of her life and would have been happy to debrief her about the Intelligence Branch, but of course she couldn't talk about any of that. He also seemed genuinely interested when she told him about the Amranis and Tonia's family, including the historical facts of what had taken place at Kfar Etzion.

When Lou finally consulted his watch and said he'd better get back to the office, Gavrielle felt mostly relieved. She was exhausted. Back at his office building, they stood in the parking lot by the Mustang, saying their goodbyes. Then Lou stepped forward and gave Gavrielle an awkward hug.

"So?" Charlie said as they drove off.

"I don't want to talk about it."

"Feel like seeing any sights?"

"The only sight I want to see is that spa. And today I'll ask you to bring me one of those plastic cups – full of alcohol."

"Yes, ma'am. But you thought he was a good guy, right?"

300

"He was okay. But it's all so weird. I don't even know what to call him. Dad? That's a joke. Mr. Brody? Lou? 'Hey you' sounds better than any of those." *Geez Louise, keep your big trap shut. Charlie may be struggling with that same problem as soon as we get home.* "Let's not talk about it now."

The Holiday Inn looked like heaven to her. A room with a door she could close. No need to talk to anyone. She went there and collapsed on the bed for a while, but soon put her still damp suit on and went down to the pool. Charlie was already there, in his suit and terrycloth robe.

"What does the lady want from the bar?"

"Surprise me. Some kind of fancy drink."

"Sweet?"

"Yes."

"Fruity?"

"No."

She was already in the spa when he returned, carrying a plastic glass filled with dark liquid and a layer of something creamy on top. In his other hand was a paper bag containing two small bottles of water, a bottle of beer, and a second plastic glass.

"What is it?" She reached for the drink.

"Kahlua and vodka together is called a Black Russian. Topped off with cream like this, makes it a White Russian. Girls usually like them. Stick your finger in and stir it all up. Bar tender usually mixes it, but I told him to leave it like that. Thought you might like the way it looks. But take it easy. There's a lot of alcohol in there."

"Good. Can you turn on those squirty things?"

"Jets. They're called jets."

He turned them on and then set the paper bag on a table, poured his beer into the plastic glass, and climbed in to join her.

"This is perfect," she said. "I'm never getting

out."

At 7 pm, a showered and shampooed Gavrielle knocked on Charlie's door. There had been no message from Lou Brody. Charlie rang down to the desk to make sure, but they hadn't missed any calls.

"I don't know about you," he said, "but I'm starved. Been starved since before that fancy-schmancy non-lunch. I seen a Howard Johnson's not far from here we could go to. 'Less you're too scared of missing his call. Maybe they got some kind of room service here. Or we could order a pizza."

"No. He can leave a message. Or really strain himself and call back. Let's go out."

In the car Charlie said, "You know you're giving him a raw deal. Far as I can see, he's behaved about as perfectly as anyone could. Given, you know, the circumstances."

"He's just so ... I don't know. Cold."

"I didn't notice you throwin' your arms around him. Look, it's a tough situation for both you guys. You had twenty-seven years to think about him. And then a few days to prepare yourself to actually meet him. He had nothing. Just got the biggest surprise of his life. I'd say he rose to the occasion extremely well."

"Why do you suddenly sound like some college professor?" She kicked her sandals off and put her bare feet on the dashboard, though she knew that annoyed Charlie.

Charlie ignored the grumpy gesture and said, "You just wanted him to be some kind of Superman or something."

"I did not. I'm not an idiot."

"You been waiting to meet this man all your life. Ain't many folks worth waiting twenty-seven years for. Know what I mean?"

When they got back to the Holiday Inn, the red button on the phone in Gavrielle's room was blinking.

"You want me to go, so you can listen to it by yourself?" Charlie asked.

"No." She put the phone on speaker and pressed the button. A nervous woman's voice said, "Hello, Gavrielle. This is Sophie Brody. Lou Brody's wife. Lou and I would love to have you and Charlie for lunch at our house tomorrow. We usually eat around one, but any time would be fine with us. Or it could be dinner, if that's better for you. Just let us know. I know Lou already gave you the address, but just in case." She read their phone number and address into the machine, followed by directions on how to get there from the Holiday Inn.

"Okay, good," Charlie said. "There ain't gonna be any big drama here. Nice, civilized people, behaving themselves."

Gavrielle collapsed on the bed. "Can you call her back? Tell her we'll come at one?"

"Sure."

After a very brief, very polite conversation with Sophie, Charlie stretched out on the bed, as far from Gavrielle as he could get without falling off. He found the clicker on the nightstand and aimed it at the television. Gavrielle fell asleep halfway through Gunsmoke. Charlie stayed until Columbo was over.

The next day, they turned off the highway onto a busy street, both sides lined with small groups of one and two-story commercial buildings. They all looked new and tidy, with ample parking and well-trimmed strips of grass. A few of the buildings flew the American flag.

Charlie slowed at an intersection and squinted at the street sign. "It oughta be the next one. After them stores up there." He turned right, onto Magnolia Drive, and immediately pulled into the parking lot behind the stores on the corner.

"Feel like sitting here for a minute?"

"Yeah." She gazed at the quiet, shady street ahead of them. You could barely see the houses for the trees. The lawns seemed to be cared for by someone using a slide-rule. *America. As long as nobody gets sick or dies, these people had better not ever complain about anything. Do they have any idea how different their lives are from just about everyone else who ever lived on this planet?*

Tonia subscribed to some American magazines. Gavrielle had often stared at the photographs of this type of neighborhood, feeling a strange nostalgia for something she had never experienced. The homes were so open – no walls, fences, or tall hedges. At least not out front. Many of the front yards and sidewalks bore evidence of children – jump ropes, scooters, Hot Wheels, bicycles, roller skates. She could see the hopscotch board kids had drawn in the nearest driveway. More garages than not had a basketball hoop above the door. Several more American flags waved in the pleasant breeze.

Charlie started the car again and soon pulled into the Brody's driveway. Gavrielle sat perfectly still, making no motion to reach for the door handle.

"St. Louis spose to have a nice zoo," he informed her, for lack of anything better to say. "I'm pretty sure we passed it on the way here. Think you might feel like going there after lunch?"

"Yeah, okay." She stared at the door to the two-car garage, wondering if the Brody family had one of those clicker things that opened it, just by pressing a button.

"Before we leave, I do want to see the Cathedral Basilica and the Jefferson Memorial by the museum. But don't worry, I ain't gonna spend hours walking around the museum. I care about seeing the buildings, not what's inside them."

"Mmmm. My friend, the architect." Poor Charlie. Trying so hard. Does he think chitchat is going to make this any easier?

She still made no move to get out of the car, continuing to stare at the house – pale yellow with white trim. Its three sections reminded her of something built of large blocks of Lego. First, the garage jutted out front, a sash window with dark gray shutters in the center of the high peak of its roof. Even its door was decorative in a tasteful way, a row of tiny-paned windows running across it. Then, farther back, a portico sheltered a small porch and the front door to the house. Still farther back, the wall of what she guessed was the living room consisted of two gray-shuttered floor-to-ceiling windows, each a matrix of square panes. The landscaping was minimal – a stretch of perfect grass, and beds of flowers on either side of the porch steps. Boxes of geraniums embellished the windows.

The front door opened and a pleasant-looking woman began walking toward the car. Sophie Brody was slim and all in white – short-sleeved blouse, skirt, and sneakers. Soft curls of dark hair escaped the clip at the back of her head.

Charlie hurriedly rolled down the window.

"You're Charlie?" Sophie leaned down, her eyes flitting to Gavrielle.

"Yes, ma'am."

"Well, what are you all doing, sitting out here in this heat? Come on in." She pulled his door open and offered her hand when he got out, saying. "I guess you've figured out that I'm Sophie." Then she skirted the car to hold Gavrielle's hand.

"So this is Gavrielle." She put her hands on Gavrielle's shoulders and held her at arm's length.

"Lordy me, you're a pretty thing, aren't you?" She released her grip on Gavrielle and then turned to link arms with her, leading her toward the front door. "I can't say this isn't a big surprise. A huge surprise. Funny how life turns out. Lou always had his poor heart set on a daughter. He wanted to keep trying for a girl, but the boys had me all worn out. I said we could have a whole yard full of boys trying to have a girl. Come on, Charlie. My, my, you're almost as pretty as she is."

Charlie quickened his step, to hold the screen door open for them.

"Lou will be back in a jiffy. He went out to light the grill for the steaks and Lord, didn't he realize that he was clean out of charcoal lighter. I hope you're hungry. Besides the steaks we've got baked potatoes with sour cream and chives, corn on the cob, and creamed peas. And for dessert, my world-famous lemon meringue pie. Lou always complains it gives him a stomach ache, but you wait and see – he'd eat the whole thing if I let him. We spend all summer in here." She led them to a spacious screened-in porch, where a table was set. "What can I get you all to drink?"

Charlie and Gavrielle exchanged nervous glances. "Coke?" he said hesitantly.

They sat on wicker chairs around a small table laden with bowls of peanuts, grapes, and pretzels. Sophie quickly returned with the soft drinks. "You get too hot, just say the word and I can turn the fan on."

"Is our car going to be in Mr. Brody's way?" Charlie asked.

"No, no. You chose just the right place. That's a cute old Mustang you've got. Lou's thinking of learning to restore old cars. Wants to make sure he'll have something to keep him busy when he retires. He used to do that with his dad, you know, when he was a teenager. Fix up old junkers and sell them to the kids at school. He loved making things go. Even tried to put a motor on his mom's old washboard ringer. Then him and his brother Jerry – poor Jerry, he was one of those thousands of sweet boys that died on the beaches at Normandy – but when they were kids the two of them used to build go-carts together. Thought they could make a business of it, and I bet they could have, if Pearl Harbor hadn't happened. That was two days before Lou's eighteenth birthday. He was a senior in high school. Coulda finished, but he quit to enlist. Never did get his diploma. Imagine that – getting as far as he did with no formal education."

They heard the garage door opening.

"Here he is. He never did see any real combat, you know. Got plenty of shells rained down on him but, God bless, he never had to fire his gun. We're out here, love," she called to Lou.

Lou came in and set a small brown paper bag on an end table. "Good to see you again, Charlie." Charlie stood and they shook hands. "Good to see you, Mr. Brody."

Gavrielle also got to her feet, though she was uncertain of the protocol for women.

"And Gavrielle." Lou smiled broadly. "I'm so glad you could come. I'm just going to get the charcoal charged up. You any good with the grill, Charlie?"

"He's a professional," Gavrielle said. "They have a whole cookhouse in their backyard, with a huge grill. He even makes his own barbeque sauce."

"Well, then maybe I'll let you take over. I'm pretty useless. Tend to get everything too well done."

The two of them went outside, leaving Gavrielle with Sophie.

"Would you like to see some pictures?" Sophie asked. "Of Lou and the boys?"

"Sure."

Family albums proved to be a safe way to pass the time, though there was never any danger of an awkward silence when Sophie Brody was in the room. So Gavrielle had a brief glimpse into her half-brothers' childhoods. Family vacations at the Lake of the Ozarks. Camping. Fishing. A trip to the Grand Canyon. Daniel playing the lead in *The Music Man*.

Lou came in to get the steaks and Sophie rose, saying she needed to finish up in the kitchen. Gavrielle followed her, asking, "What can I do to help?" and then standing there idle until Sophie began handing her things to put on the table.

When they were seated Lou said, "We always join hands and say Grace. But if you're uncomfortable with that, Gavrielle –"

"That's fine," she said, and held her hands out to Sophie and Charlie. She again felt an indefensible resentment. *Why does he have to be so polite? So unfailingly kind and considerate?* She realized that she seemed to be desperately seeking an excuse to be angry with him. Something to complain about. *What's wrong with me? No, what's wrong with him? A thing like this can't happen without strong emotions. He should be thrilled, appalled, afraid, worried. Something. It's like we're unexpected dinner guests and they're being perfect hosts.*

The next two hours were no different. Lou spoke about his experiences during the war – especially having been with General Eisenhower when he made the German townspeople walk through the concentration camp at Ohrdurf. "That's how I ended up on a train to Marseille, thinking I had to find some way to help those people. They had absolutely nowhere else to go."

"How did you meet my mother?"

He smiled sadly. "She came along while I was

308

standing next to a kiosk in Tel Aviv, trying to get directions to the port. Her English was perfect. Like yours."

"How did she get along with her parents?"

He pursed his lips and thought. "I couldn't really say. I can't remember her talking about her father at all. I guess she had her frictions with her mother, like all young girls. Her mother was never happy with the way she dressed, that sort of thing."

"What did she like to talk about?"

"She was very patriotic. Hated the British. Oh, and I do remember her talking about not wanting to live in a city. Told me about the time she'd volunteered to help pick oranges. And she wanted a lot of children. At least four. I remember that." Then he looked helpless. "I'm sorry I can't tell you more. It was so long ago and we didn't spend all that much time together. I'd be able to get to Jerusalem for a day and then it might be a month before I saw her again."

"You know, as time goes on, things might jog your memory," Sophie said. "If he does remember anything else," she went on, turning to Gavrielle, "he can write it to you. In a letter."

Gavrielle nodded and Sophie rose to get the pie and coffee. Gavrielle didn't much care for the pie – thought it was going to give *her* a stomach ache – but said several times how delicious it was. Gavrielle helped Sophie clear the table and then Lou showed her some more photo albums. When she looked up and said that she and Charlie should be going, no one argued. But before they made it to the front door, Lou took Gavrielle aside.

"Davy didn't say much when I told him about you. I'm sure that was because it came as such a shock. Daniel's another story. He takes just about anything in stride and said he will probably be contacting you. 'One of these years,' is how he put it. He said he might be going to Spain next year, to hike the *Camino de Santiago*. The Way of Saint James, we call it. Thought the two of you might work out a meeting."

"That would be good." She nodded, though she hadn't the slightest idea what the Way of Saint James was.

Then Lou picked up the thick envelope that lay on the boot box by the door. "I want you to have this." He put it in her hand. "It's only a tiny fraction of what I owe you – all those years of child support –"

"I told you, I didn't come here looking for money." She tried to withdraw her hand, but Lou refused to let go.

"I know you didn't. And don't think Sophie doesn't know about this. She completely agrees. It would be more, but it's all we have on hand right now. At least it should help with what it cost you to come over here. And I want you to promise me." He looked into her eyes. "Promise me that if you're ever in trouble – anything I can help you with – if you ever need money – promise me you'll ask."

He pressed her hands again and she clasped the envelope. "Thank you."

"No thanks necessary. So you're going back to Michigan tomorrow?"

"Yes."

"Then how much longer before you go home to Israel?"

"Another ten days or so."

He nodded. "Well, have a safe trip. I'm grateful you came. I'm sure we'll see other again. I know we all need some time to digest this situation. It's difficult, isn't it, with us being complete strangers? But we'll get used to it, find some way to be in each other's lives."

He walked her to the car and bent to say goodbye to Charlie again. "If you guys feel like a hamburger later, the Charcoal House has the best in town." He stood there looking sort of pathetic, so eager to be helpful.

Charlie started the engine and backed out of the driveway. They both turned to wave and then Gavrielle held her breath until the Brodys were out of sight.

Charlie switched on the radio and let her brood for a while. Then she took out the envelope, removed the stack of bills, and counted them. "Two thousand dollars," she said. "I got bought off cheap."

Charlie put on the signal and turned sharply into the parking lot of a strip mall. "Ain't you gettin' tired of being a bitch? What you want the poor man to do? I bet if he didn't give you nothin', you be whinin' 'bout that. He can't give you back your childhood. He can't change the past. I think that right now I oughta be sittin' next to a real happy young woman, not one what still can't stop feeling sorry for herself."

She gave him her dirtiest look for a long moment and then got out of the car and slammed the door. She stomped toward the little store, then came back, opened the door, and slammed it again. Harder. Then she got back in.

"Should I go buy you a hammer, so you can really break somethin'?"

"No. I'm finished. You're right. I know you're right. There's no better way he could have behaved. His wife, too. I would never manage to be that nice, in her situation."

"Damn right I'm right. What we gonna do now?"

"Go look at your buildings. Then if the zoo's still open, let's go there too. I like zoos."

"So do I. So that's where we're going. First place Charlene ever took me was the Detroit Zoo. I was fifteen, but never been there before. And the zoo's in between us and the Holiday Inn. Those buildings I want to look at are way over on the other side of the city. By the river. I can see them tomorrow, on our way

311

home. Might as well take a look at the old courthouse too. It's pretty famous for its architecture."

"Okay." She smiled an actual smile. "Damn, I never knew slamming a car door could feel so good. But thanks for yelling at me. And sorry about your door."

"Long as you ain't slammin' it on me. You know, they used to sell slaves there. Right on the steps. I mean, of that courthouse we're going to see tomorrow."

It was ten o'clock the next morning by the time Charlie got his sightseeing done and they were ready to get on the road. Gavrielle sat staring at the Mississippi River while he looked for a pay phone. He wanted to tell Charlene and Reeves that they wouldn't be home before ten o'clock that night. Maybe later. No way would they be there for dinner.

"It's really something," Gavrielle said when Charlie came back, never taking her eyes off the river.

"Wait'll you see the Detroit River. Now that's a beautiful river. All green and blue. Not like this mud hole."

Once they had crossed the river, he asked, "You know any car games?"

"What's a car game?"

"You know, like a game kids play on a trip, so they don't get bored. Like you got to spot something starts with a certain letter of the alphabet. Or find some combination on a license plate."

"No." She looked at him as if he had gone crazy.

He chuckled. "That's right, I forgot. You live in that teeny, weeny little country. Ain't got no time to get bored. By the time you make it into third gear, you already arrived at where you're going."

"Ha-ha."

Charlie reached over and squeezed her hand for a moment. "Glad to see you feeling good."

"I do. I feel good." If I'm ever going to see Lou Brody again, he's going to be the one who makes it happen. I don't have to think about it any more. If he does, he does and if he doesn't, he doesn't. It's no longer my problem.

"What kind of stuff do you want to do, the last ten days you're here? Besides learn how to dance and go hang out with your new gangster friend?"

"How does it work with Reeves' parents' cottage? Can you ask to go there?"

"Yeah, I can ask, and they'll say yes. Might get roped into helping them do some work on it. Those folks are always painting something or other."

"That sounds like fun. I like doing physical work. I mean, I wouldn't want to do it all day, every day, but it is a good feeling."

"Don't go tellin' Charlene that. She got a mile-long list of stuff needs doing around that old place."

"So why don't we help her out with some of it? Spend one day at the cottage, one day driving around Detroit and the notorious Dearborn, one evening at Carv's club, and the rest of the time doing some of the things on Charlene's list."

"Okay. You one crappy tourist, but it don't sound like a bad plan to me."

They pulled off West Maple Road into the driveway at 11:30 that night. Charlene came out to see how they were and went back to bed. Neither Charlie nor Gavrielle got up before eleven the next day. When Charlie came down, the empty house was explained by a note on the kitchen table. It was Charlene's morning to drive the Bookmobile around and Reeves had gone into the high school for a staff meeting. Grandma Julie was outside, watering her patch of greens. Charlie came up behind her and kissed her cheek.

"How's it goin' Old Lady?"

She started singing R-E-S-P-E-C-T.

Charlie laughed. "You got more respect than you know what to do with."

"What fool thing you plannin' to do today?"

"We're going to spend the day helping out around here."

She laughed. "Day half gone, child."

"We can still get something done. What you think we oughta start with?"

"Get up on the roof, clean out them eaves. Wash the storm windows, get 'em ready to go on. Clean out the garage. Cookhouse too – gotta scrub that grill in there and clean the refrigerator. Pull the weeds from the flower beds. Wash the Mustang and the wagon when Reeves gets back."

"Whoa ... all right, all right. We'll find somethin' to do."

When Gavrielle came down for breakfast she declined the offer to climb up on the roof. "You can have that one. But I know how to wash windows."

"You really want to do this?"

"Yes, I do. But first you have to feed me."

When Charlene came home she found Gavrielle outside the garage, shining up the last of the storm windows with a wrinkled wad of newspaper.

"What are you doing?"

"Why, am I doing it wrong?"

"No." Charlene eyed the display of storm windows leaning against the garage, trees, and Adirondack chairs. "No. You're doing it very right. They've never been so sparkly. But why on earth are *you* doing it?"

"Feels good to be useful."

"So how was it? With your father?"

"Good. It was good. You go on in. Soon as I finish this last one, I'll be ready for a cup of coffee."

They were soon at the kitchen table and Gavrielle briefly told her about their trip to St. Louis. Then she nodded at Charlene's belly and asked how she was feeling.

"All better. With the sniffles gone, I feel the same as I always do."

Gavrielle looked over her shoulder and lowered her voice. "Did you talk to him?"

"Yes." Charlene smiled. "Everything's going to be all right. It's a good thing we took your advice."

"So." Gavrielle raised her voice back to its normal level. "What do you want me to do next – pull weeds or clean the cookhouse?"

"When did you say you're moving in, Cinderella?"

Gavrielle smiled. "I do enjoy helping out. Really."

"It's nothing to do with earning your keep?"

"No. Not at all. It was nice, doing those windows. Outside, in the sun. You have such a wonderful place to live."

"I know. I sometimes feel guilty, for having this perfect life – without having done anything to deserve it." Charlene rose. "I have to go to the grocery store. If you really want to help out, I guess the best thing would be for you to clean the cookhouse. I've been thinking of having a party for you. Like the day before you leave. Not a big one. Have my father over, and Reeves' folks. Anyone Charlie wants to invite. Of course, we'll have to wait and see if he feels like a party at all. But, anyway, start with the cookhouse. Come, I'll show you where everything is."

"Okay. And tomorrow – Charlie said the big garage needs to be cleaned out."

"Oh, that's not one for you. That's a really big job. Gotta move everything."

"Well, if you guys are going to be around tomorrow ... I mean, maybe that's something the four of us could do together."

"Yeah, we could." Charlene paused. "We could take the record player out there. With all four of us together, it might even be fun, instead of torture."

That evening they sat down to dinner together – all but Grandma Julie. She'd fled to one of her friends. When they were nearly finished, Charlene said, "By the way, Charlie, Billy Bates is coming over later. There's something he wants to talk to you about."

"Like what?"

"I don't know. You'll have to wait and see what he has to say." She avoided Charlie's eyes and stood to clear the table. Reeves quickly got to his feet to help.

Charlie started to get up, but Charlene waved him back down. "You two aren't going anywhere. Not after I made dessert – double devil chocolate cake with butter cream frosting."

"Reeves' favorite," Charlie said.

"I don't recall having to force-feed it to you either."

At 8 pm Billy Bates' red Firebird came slowly down the drive. Charlie had been waiting on the porch and went out to meet him. Charlene, Reeves, and Gavrielle all stood transfixed at the kitchen window. Billy Bates took Charlie's arm and led him for a walk, back towards the softball diamond.

"How did you tell him?" Gavrielle asked.

"I asked him to meet us at a coffee shop in Ecorse," Charlene said. "I had this feeling that he already knew what it was about, before we even came through the door. Then I started hemming and hawing like an idiot, trying to make chitchat. Thank God, Reeves shut me up and just blurted it out. 'Grandma Julie told Charlene that you're Charlie's father.' Billy was quiet for a minute or so, before he said that he'd always thought so. He asked if Charlie knows. Reeves said, 'Not yet. We thought we should ask you if you want to be the one to tell him.' Billy said, 'Yeah, that would probably be best.' So here we are."

"Did he seem happy? Disturbed?"

"He didn't really show any emotion," Charlene said. "Maybe a little embarrassed. Told me to call him when you guys got back, and he'd come over the next evening."

Billy and Charlie seemed to be chatting, perhaps teasing one another. Charlie punched Billy Bates' arm. Then Billy stopped and turned to face Charlie. He spoke for a few minutes before Charlie backed away, arms raised, shaking his head. Gavrielle looked away first and all three of them went to sit at the table. Gavrielle poured more coffee. It was another twenty minutes before Charlie came in.

"You couldn't have told me?" he shouted at the room in general and stomped up the stairs, slamming the door to his bedroom.

Gavrielle almost said, "Well, he finally thinks he hates you," but managed to keep her mouth shut. Charlene rose to go outside, hoping to catch Billy Bates, but his car was already disappearing around the curve of the drive.

"Do you think he already told his wife?" Gavrielle asked in a whisper.

"Yes. At least he said he was going to." Charlene spoke at a normal volume.

"So that's good. She knows and he still came."

"He didn't expect her to be angry or anything. A long time ago he'd told her that he suspected it. And I guess she's real religious. Baptist, like Charlie. He said she's always liked Charlie, but even if she didn't, she'd do her best to do the right thing."

Gavrielle let out a huge sigh of relief and smiled. "Is there any more of that cake?"

"Sure," Reeves said and rose to get the cake and three plates.

317

"Who's going to take some up to Charlie?" Reeves asked, looking from Gavrielle to Charlene.

Charlene winked at Gavrielle and stared at Reeves for a long moment. "You are."

"Me? Come on, Char. You know I don't know how to talk about this kind of stuff."

"That's why it's you. Double devil chocolate cake will be a lot more comforting than one of us yakking at him. Isn't there some sport thing on TV you guys could watch together?"

Reeves squared his shoulders and picked up two plates of cake. "Just don't finish all the cake," he said. "We're gonna want more. And ice cream."

About fifteen minutes later Reeves and Charlie came down to watch television. Charlene made popcorn. They heard the back door close behind Grandma Julie, but she slipped into her bedroom without showing her face.

The next day the four of them went to work on the garage. Charlene and Reeves kept turning down the radio to accommodate a series of loud arguments – she wanted to throw out most of what they were moving around. He wanted to keep all of it. He won most of those battles, because what was the point of having a big garage if you couldn't fill it with junk you might possibly need some day?

"You regretting this yet?" Charlie asked Gavrielle, as they lugged a huge old desk back to its corner.

"To tell you the truth – it's the nicest time I've had in America. For me, working together is the best way to spend time with people. I think I'm learning to be a little bit more sociable, but I know I'll never understand the point of small talk."

When they finished, they all flopped down on the grass for a beer. Then Charlene and Reeves went inside to shower.

"You knew?" Charlie asked Gavrielle, as soon as they were alone. "The whole way to St. Louis and back, you knew?"

She nodded. "You're mad at me."

"I was. Real mad. But then Charlene told me what you said – how much you would've liked for your father to be the one that came to you. And you were right, I guess. It was probably easier hearing it from him than it woulda been from Charlene, with no one knowing how Billy might react. And if I have to have a mystery father, best it be Billy."

"Now you've got my problem. What to call him."

"Nope. He ain't never gonna be 'Dad' any more than Reeves will. It's a couple a years already I stopped callin' him Mr. Bates. He's Billy, and he's still gonna stay Billy. What you starin' at?"

"It's just ... when I look at you – it's so clear, so simple – you're Charlie. Funny, smart, good-hearted, smartass Charlie. You always will be. It wouldn't matter a bit who your father turned out to be. That could never change the tiniest thing about who you are. It's so easy for me to see that about you."

"Makes it easier to see the same thing about yourself, don't it? I was thinkin' the same 'bout you last night."

She nodded. "I guess you just have to keep your mind on what really matters – what kind of life you're going to make for myself. The choices you're going to make. I've made one. I don't know if I'll be that lucky, but at least I finally know what I want – a family of my own. Like Charlene and Reeves. Like Tonia and Amos. Even like Sophie and Chicago Lou."

He reached for her hand.

"You sure spent a lot of time staring at Charlene and Reeves today," Charlie said. "What was that about?"

"Did you ever notice, even when they're having a

319

fight, they always look each other right in the face?"

"What're they supposed to look at when they're talking to each other?"

"People avoid each other's eyes all the time. But not those two. It's like they have these laser eyes that automatically lock onto each other's."

"So?"

"So nothing. I was just wondering if they do that because they love each other so much, or if doing that – paying real attention to one another – is what keeps them loving each other."

Charlie groaned. "You better go ask the chicken about the egg."

"You asked." She shrugged, grinning. Then she grew pensive again. "It's funny," she said. "Since meeting my 'real' father, this is the first time – through all the years I've been living with Tonia and Amos – that I realize how much I love them. Share with them. How they are my real family."

He put his arms around her and she rested her head on his shoulder. "It does feel like fate – you and me. Like there was a reason for us coming into each other's lives. The flaky people have it right." She sat up and quoted from a book she had read. "The right person comes into your life just when you need them. And their job is to make sure you don't need them any more."

Nine days later Charlie drove Gavrielle to Detroit Metro. They'd arrived early and sat in the car.

"So, how come you didn't?" she asked.

"Didn't what?"

"Seduce me."

"We still got time." He raised his eyebrows and turned to look at the back seat.

"Seriously."

"You didn't want me to. Oh yeah, I know you did sometimes – real bad – but not for real."

"I guess that's true. And what about you? You didn't want to?"

"What do you think, dumbbell? You're gorgeous and I'm a guy. But you are one serious person. Guy can't just mess around with a girl like you. And don't go takin' offense, but I ain't never gonna get serious with no white girl."

"You're kidding. I never would have guessed you'd say something like that."

"Think I'm colorblind? Hell no. This country's still way too messed up for that. It's getting better all the time, but still messed up. Once I'm educated and got some kind of professional reputation, I'll go back to the good old Motor City, find a nice black girl and have my family."

She smiled. "I have no idea how one goes about looking for someone to marry. I'll have to start trying to figure it out after I get home."

"Well, hallelujah, amen to that. Everyone, everywhere needs a family. But people in a crazy ass country like Israel? Don't see how anyone could get along without one." He looked at his watch, but relaxed again. "Hey, you never told me what you're gonna do 'bout the army. You going back?"

"I don't know. Probably for a while, see how it feels. For one thing, an army is a pretty good place to look for men." She smiled. "But I'd be surprised if I couldn't get a job with any of the private companies the IDF works with. I already know people at all of them. They know me. Know I'm good at what I do. And there are lots of men working at all of those places, too."

"So you got it all figured out." Charlie slapped her thigh. "That's good. Just don't go thinking you don't need me any more, 'cause that is absolutely not true. False and erroneous. Even if it's just knowin' I'm out

321

there in the world somewhere, you gonna be glad Charlie exists. And maybe a miracle will happen and the telephones in Israel will suddenly start to work right. And someday some guy's gonna invent a way to beam messages around, like on Star Trek. I heard some guys in the military already got something like that. So don't you go losing contact with me. For one thing, you're not allowed to get yourself married without my approval. You got anyone in mind? Some guy you worked with maybe?"

She flushed and couldn't help smiling.

"Wow. You do got someone in mind."

She shook her head and flushed more deeply.

"What, some guy you knew in the army?"

"No."

"Does Amos Amrani have a younger brother?"

"It's no one from his family. But I do want someone like Amos."

"All nice and swarthy?"

"No, not the way he looks. I mean, I do like the way he looks, but what I meant is the way he loves Tonia. He'd kill anyone who hurt her. Like, for real."

"Geez. I think Reeves really loves Charlene, but I don't see him killing no one. Is it someone I could guess?"

"I don't know. Maybe."

He screwed his face into an exaggerated frown, trying to think who else he'd met in Israel or had even heard her talk about. "Lordy me, not Aviram!"

She shook her head, making a loud tsk-tsk sound. "He's married and even if he wasn't – I mean, come on. No."

Charlie thought some more and then said, "You gotta be kidding. Heller? Aha. I knew you had a thing for him. Even when you thought he was crooked." He heard no denial. "Ha. First Carv and now him. I guess you got a soft spot for the criminal element."

"I like you, don't I? Mr. Diamond Thief."

He shook his head. "So, you gonna call him?"

"I don't know. Maybe. He may not be crooked, but I'm not totally convinced he's one of the good guys. But what can I say – I think he's worth checking out. I'll see how I feel when I get home."

"You gotta write me letters," Charlie said. "I gotta hear about this."

"I've never written a letter to anyone," she said.

"You ain't never had no one to write one to. Now you do."

"I know. I was just being ornery. Of course I'll write to you. Even if you hadn't asked me to. Now get my suitcase out of the car. I'm going to miss my flight."

They stood facing one another and he said, "There's no way I ain't doing this." He bent to give her one long kiss. When she stepped back she felt faint and flushed. After a moment, she put her palm to his cheek. "I'm going to miss you Charlie Freeman. The guy who changed my life. Now get in the car and go. And don't stand here watching me walk away."

Friday, August 9

It was still dark when they landed in Tel Aviv. Gavrielle would have to wait for a bus to Jerusalem. Or shell out for a cab. She looked longingly in the direction of the Mediterranean. *In less than an hour the sun will come up. I feel like watching that. No, no way. What would I do with this stupid suitcase, drag it along the beach?* Then she looked in her handbag for her hairbrush and felt the thick envelope Lou Brody had given her. *Okay, Rozmann you've spent twenty-seven years pinching pennies. It's time to spend some money. But not on a cab.* She dragged her suitcase over to the car rental counter and, forty minutes later, parked a green Subaru Justy in the lot at Gordon Beach.

She shoved her purse under the driver's seat and walked through the sand, carrying her sandals, the car keys, and a bottle of soda water. She was wearing a simple striped summer dress and, for the first time in her life, felt completely unencumbered. The waves were gentle and she ran into them, playing and splashing as she never had as a child. Then she sat and watched the sun come up, toasting it with her soda water.

Joggers and dog walkers began to appear. She smiled and said, "Good morning," to each of them. Then she walked up Hayarkon Street and found a place to have a simple breakfast. When she finished, she looked at her watch. Eight-thirty. *Is that still too early to see what it would feel like to call Mike Heller?*

The End

324

I hope you enjoyed *The Summer of 1974*. If so, even a brief review on Amazon would be greatly appreciated.

The story of Tonia and Amos Amrani (and Gavrielle's mother Ilana and grandmother Nella) began in **The Lonely Tree**, available on Amazon.

Charlie Freeman's story began in **Whatever Happened to Mourning Free?** Book 3 of the Olivia series, also available on Amazon.

Books 1-4 of the Olivia series are available on Amazon, in eBook and paperback.

- Olivia, Mourning

- The Way the World Is

- Whatever Happened to Mourning Free?

- The Summer of 1848

Book 5 of the Olivia series, *Money and Good Things*, will be released in the fall of 2019.

More about me and my books can be found on:

- Books by Yael Politis on Facebook

- My website yaelpolitis.com.

Contact me at **yael@yaelpolitis.com**

Made in the USA
Coppell, TX
28 March 2022